CW00550888

hidden talent rediscovered

Bello is a digital-only imprint of Pan Macmillan,
established to breathe new life into previously published,
classic books.

At Bello we believe in the timeless power of the imagination,
of a good story, narrative and entertainment, and we want to
use digital technology to ensure that many more readers
can enjoy these books into the future.

We publish in ebook and print-on-demand formats
to bring these wonderful books to new audiences.

www.panmacmillan.com/imprint-publishers/bello

Richmal Crompton

Richmal Crompton (1890–1969) is best known for her thirty-eight books featuring William Brown, which were published between 1922 and 1970. Born in Lancashire, Crompton won a scholarship to Royal Holloway in London, where she trained as a schoolteacher, graduating in 1914, before turning to writing full-time. Alongside the William novels, Crompton wrote forty-one novels for adults, as well as nine collections of short stories.

Richmal Crompton

LINDEN RISE

BELL

First published in 1952 by Hutchinson & Co.

This edition published 2017 by Bello
an imprint of Pan Macmillan
20 New Wharf Road, London N1 9RR
Associated companies throughout the world

www.panmacmillan.com/imprint-publishers/bello

ISBN 978-1-5098-5958-0 EPUB
ISBN 978-1-5098-5956-6 HB
ISBN 978-1-5098-5957-3 PB

Typeset by Ellipsis Digital Limited, Glasgow

Visit **www.panmacmillan.com** to read more about all our books
and to buy them. You will also find features, author interviews and
news of any author events, and you can sign up for e-newsletters
so that you're always first to hear about our new releases.

LINDEN RISE

Chapter One

A solitary figure was making its way along the winding country lane. It was a short, stocky figure, carrying a baggy umbrella in one hand and a rush hold-all, secured by leather straps, in the other.

Matilda Pound was going out to service for the first time. She was fifteen years old, solidly and somewhat clumsily built, with a smooth, round face on which the features seemed to have been fashioned by a hasty and inexpert hand. Her cheeks were crudely red, her nose shapeless, her mouth too large, her eyes black and bright and staring. Plodding along in the dark sack-like coat that reached her ankles and the uncompromising black straw hat that rested on her ears, she looked from the distance like a mechanical toy.

She had come by horse bus from her home in a neighbouring village, and was now walking from the bus stop to her new "place." Her trunk had been sent by carrier's cart, and the hold-all contained her night things and a print dress and apron in case the trunk did not arrive till next morning.

The lane had originally been a path through the wood, and on either side a sea of bracken seemed to be trying to burst its barriers, thrusting tawny-green fronds through the low railings. At one point it spanned a stream that rippled over its bed of pebbles between silver birches and oak saplings, vanishing like a slender shaft of light in the green distance. A keeper's cottage stood by the roadside, so weathered and mellow that it might have grown up with the wood. A couple of beehives and a yew tree, trimmed to the shape of a bird, almost filled the tiny garden.

Then the wood came to a sudden end, and in its place stretched on one side a field of wheat, changing from gold to deeper gold as the breeze passed over it, and, on the other, a meadow with fresh blades of grass springing up on the lately mown surface. Instead of the railings were hedges, bright with convolvulus, vetch and flowering blackberry.

Tilly noticed none of these things. She had lived in the country ever since she could remember and took fields, woods and hedges as part of the normal background of life. Her eyes were fixed on a point ahead of her where the lane dipped through the trees into a village in the valley. She could see rooftops, a church tower, the long spreading buildings of a farm, the gleam of a river . . . It was the village of Priors Green, and one of the cottages clustered at the foot of the hill must be Linden Rise, her new "place."

Though her home was in a nearby village, she had never been to Priors Green before, nor had she met her employer, Mrs. Culverton, who had rented Linden Rise for the summer holidays. Her aunt had made all the arrangements through the Vicar's wife, and Tilly herself had not been consulted. She was to go to Linden Rise for the six weeks of the summer holidays and do the work of the cottage under the direction of Mrs. Horseferry, the cook-housekeeper.

A chiff-chaff's note throbbed suddenly through the silence, a dog barked from a farm on the hillside and, as if encouraged to join the symphony, the clock in the church tower slowly struck five.

Tilly considered . . . Her aunt had arranged with Mrs. Horseferry that she should be at Linden Rise by half past five, but, so anxious was she for Tilly to make a good impression, she had turned her out of the house soon after four. Perhaps she'd better wait a few minutes, thought Tilly. She had been trained by her aunt in habits of obedience and punctuality. "Half past five's half past five," she seemed to hear her aunt saying. "Not five o'clock nor six."

She went to the stile that led into the meadow and, setting the rush hold-all on the grass by the roadside, sat down, stiffly upright, on the lowest step, her umbrella across her knees, gazing in front of her.

She was curious about the new "place", but neither elated nor apprehensive. She had always been a docile, biddable child, accepting philosophically the ups and down of life. Her mind went back to the home she had left and she felt a faint stirring of relief at the thought that she would not be returning to it. Even here, through the peace of the countryside, her aunt's shrill voice seemed to follow her, upbraiding, reproaching, admonishing.

Her mother had died at her birth and her aunt had brought her up in the straight path of "respectability," grudging the money and trouble the child cost her, exacting penalty for the slightest misdemeanour with a hard and heavy hand. But something sound at the core of Tilly had saved her from bitterness or even resentment. She enjoyed the small precarious pleasures that came her way—games with other children, Sunday School treats, occasional shopping expeditions into Bellminster, the neighbouring town—and endured with good-natured stoicism the rigours of her aunt's "rearing".

Sitting there on the stile in the sunshine, she thought of the cottage kitchen—scoured to so forbidding a cleanliness that her aunt's eye seemed to glare at her from every polished surface—and the little room that opened off from it, used by her uncle as a work-room. He was a shrivelled monkey-like old man, paralysed from the waist down, who spent his days in an invalid chair, muttering to himself, making model ships that his wife took into Bellminster for sale at regular intervals. Tilly was sometimes sent in to the work-room to help him, but he seldom spoke to her, and his rheumy, red-rimmed eyes and fierce, spasmodic mutterings frightened her so much that she was glad to escape to her aunt's brisk scolding.

And now all that was over. She was grown-up, fifteen years old, and starting out into the world with a trunk full of sensible clothes and a head full of sensible advice.

"Mind your manners and keep a still tongue in your head," her aunt had said. "You're lucky to get your feet under a gentleman's table, and, if you don't suit, don't come running back to me. I've done my duty by you and from now on you can shift for yourself."

And that, in Tilly's eyes, was only right and proper. There was in her a vein of sturdy self-reliance that made her well satisfied to be independent.

She looked down with pride at her new boots of heavy black leather, her thick black woollen stockings and her new coat. Her aunt had kept an account of what they cost and Tilly was to pay her back from her salary of five shillings a week. In her matter-of-fact, unemotional fashion she was feeling pleased with life. It was good to be sitting here in her new outfit, her nightdress and print dress and apron in the hold-all at her feet, her umbrella on her knee, her "place" waiting for her down in the valley.

After about quarter of an hour she roused herself, picked up her hold-all, grasped her umbrella and began to walk down the road towards the village in the valley. The lane wound behind a clump of trees, then joined a main road at a point where a half-obliterated signpost gave the direction "Priors Green". She passed a post-office, a general shop, a church and vicarage, separated from each other by a sleepy overgrown churchyard, a village green and a blacksmith's forge, the furnace looking small and angry through the open door in the sunlight.

"Turn to the left after the forge," her aunt had said.

Tilly turned to the left into another lane and crossed a humpback bridge beneath which the river flowed drowsily over smooth flat boulders. Beyond the bridge the lane rose sharply, then descended . . . and there at the crest of the little hillock, behind a row of pollarded lime trees, stood Linden Rise—a long, low white-washed cottage with a green painted door and a green latticed porch. Tall narrow windows opened on to a verandah with a sloping green roof that ran the length of the house. Above were smaller windows with rounded tops. A row of potted geraniums on a shelf in the porch struck a bright note of colour. The whole had an air of gaiety and elegance and charm.

Tilly stood for a moment, looking at it, then remembered her

4

aunt's injunction: "Don't you dare to go to the front door. It's Tradesmen's Entrance for the likes of you."

There wasn't a Tradesmen's Entrance, but the small path, bordered by lavender bushes and snapdragons, took a sharp turn to the right after reaching the porch and disappeared round the side of the house. Tilly hesitated a few moments, then opened the gate and followed it. Behind the house an untidy garden stretched down to an orchard of gnarled apple trees, and beyond it hills with wooded slopes rose sharply to the sky-line.

The back door stood open. Tilly put down her hold-all and knocked. For the first time she was conscious of a slight feeling of apprehension. Her heart began to beat more quickly as she waited.

Suddenly a woman appeared in the open doorway. She was a large woman, with a massive projecting bosom and massive projecting buttocks, the two joined by a waist of almost fairy-like proportions and supported on a pair of small, dainty feet. She wore a black silk dress with a white tucker and cameo brooch at the neck. Beneath an elaborate erection of grey hair, heavy-lidded eyes gave the sallow face a sleepy, almost torpid, look.

"Matilda Pound?" she said in a deep majestic voice.

Tilly gave a little bob.

"Yes, ma'am," she said.

"Come in, child."

Tilly took up her hold-all and entered the kitchen. It was a pleasant little room, with curtains and table-cloth of blue-and-white check and a row of twinkling pewter pots on the chimney-piece. A fair girl in a dark skirt and frilly blouse sat at the table. She had a small petulant mouth, china blue eyes and tightly frizzed hair.

"I'm Mrs. Horseferry," said the large woman to Tilly.

"Yes, ma'am," said Tilly, setting down the hold-all on the floor.

"Do they call you Matilda or Matty?"

"They call me Tilly, ma'am."

"We'll call you Tilly, then. Take off your hat."

Tilly leant her umbrella carefully against the wall and took off her hat. Her black hair was plastered to her head with perspiration.

5

"And your coat, child."

Tilly took off her coat, revealing a voluminous skirt of navy blue serge and a blouse of the same material, buttoning tightly up to the neck. A petersham belt defined sketchily a waist that would have been thick even without the unwieldy folds of serge that it enclosed. The fair girl gave a shrill scream of laughter, but Mrs. Horseferry's sleepy brown eyes rested on the small ungainly figure with approval.

"Not one of the flighty ones, anyway," she said.

"No, ma'am," said Tilly, with a touch of complacency in her voice.

She had once heard her aunt say to her uncle: "Thank heaven, the girl's homely. They're easier to raise," and ever since then she had vaguely considered her lack of looks as something that reflected credit on herself.

"This is Emmy," said Mrs. Horseferry, with wave of her hand towards the girl at the table.

"Pleased to meet you," said Emmy in a high-pitched, affected voice.

"Emmy's not part of our staff," said Mrs. Horseferry. "She's a housemaid from the family's London establishment. She's only come down to bring the family's plate and linen and help prepare the rooms."

"And how they're going to put up with it beats me," said Emmy, raising her hand to pat her hair. "I may be funny, but it'd drive me melancholy mad in a week. All this so-called nature! What are they going to do all day? That's what I want to know."

"They'll find things," said Mrs. Horseferry indulgently.

"The Quality always finds things to do. After all, when you come to think of it, they're trained to idleness same as the likes of us are trained to work. They can always fill their time with odds and ends. It's born in them."

"Well, I must say, it's a mystery to me what they want to come here for," said Emmy, rearranging the frills of her muslin blouse with a flourish designed to show off a ring set with a large piece of green glass. "Trees and so on are all right in their way, but when

6

you've seen a tree you've *seen* it. You don't want to go on looking at it day after day after day."

"They always like the country, do the Quality," said Mrs. Horseferry. "That and climbing mountains and having cold baths and riding to hounds in all weathers."

"I know," said Emmy with a sigh. "Born in the lap of luxury and always trying to get out of it, that's them . . . Well, thank goodness I goes back tomorrow, and then"—with a slow secret smile—"me for me holiday in Margate."

"Yes," said Mrs. Horseferry wistfully, "there's something *about* Margate. I've always said so and I always will." She turned her sleepy eyes to Tilly, who was standing listening with ingenuous, childlike interest. "Have you had your tea, Tilly?"

"No, ma'am."

"We've not had it either," said Mrs. Horseferry. "It's taken us all day getting things to rights. Put the kettle on, Emmy. There's some eggs and tinned salmon in the larder . . . Your trunk has come, Tilly. I'll take you up to your room."

"Thank you, ma'am," said Tilly.

She took her hat and coat and umbrella in one hand, the hold-all in the other and followed Mrs. Horseferry into the narrow passage-like hall and up the staircase. The round bright boot-button eyes darted about, catching mysterious glimpses through half-open doors . . . a sitting-room with lace curtains and chintz chair covers and a tall standard lamp shaded by frills of pink silk . . . a dining-room with a lace-edged cloth on the table and miniatures on the wall . . . a bedroom with a white crocheted quilt and a chintz-skirted dressing-table . . . then another flight of stairs that was little more than a ladder and that led to two attic rooms immediately beneath the roof.

"This one's yours," said Mrs. Horseferry.

Tilly stood looking around her. The ceiling, of bare unpolished rafters, sloped sharply to the floor. The only window was a skylight just above the small iron bedstead. Against the wall a scarred chest of drawers supported a discoloured mirror. Her tin trunk stood at the foot of her bed. There was no change of expression on the

7

round, plain face, but something behind it seemed to glow and sparkle as the bright eyes moved around. At home she had always slept with her aunt, while her uncle slept on a camp-bed in his work-room, and she had never even considered the possibility of having a room of her own.

"A nice room," commented Mrs. Horseferry a little uncertainly.

"Yes, ma'am," said Tilly.

Mrs. Horseferry opened a door, revealing another room of larger proportions, with a dormer window overlooking the garden, and a dressing-table and wardrobe of deal. A hip bath, with a large sponge in it, stood on the floor.

"My room," said Mrs. Horseferry. "Not princely, but serviceable."

"Yes, ma'am," said Tilly.

"Emmy will sleep with me tonight and go back to London first thing in the morning . . . We share the hip-bath. You must have a bath every Saturday night and carry your water up from the kitchen."

"Yes, ma'am" said Tilly.

"I'll leave you to unpack your trunk, then you can come down and we'll have tea."

Mrs. Horseferry manoeuvred her gigantic bosom and posterior down the ladder with unexpected agility, and Tilly was left alone. She stood for a moment, gazing round the room, then set to work unpacking her things. She had three of everything—"Two to wash each other and the third to fall back on, as her aunt put it— three heavy calico nightdresses, three heavy calico chemises and pairs of drawers, three petticoats of dark blue twill, three calico bodices, made from the material left over when the nightdresses had been cut out, three print dresses, three aprons, three plain *white* caps, three pairs of black ribbed woollen stockings.

"No one shall say," her aunt had said with the familiar note of grievance in her voice, "that I've not done my duty by you."

Tilly herself had made most of the "outfit" under her aunt's direction. Not a seam or hem or buttonhole that had not been the occasion of harsh upbraiding. The more tricky joints of the bodices had drawn the palm of her aunt's hand several times down on

Tilly's black head, but Tilly's head was a hard one and, as dressmaking under her aunt's direction was the only sort of dressmaking she knew, she took for granted that it was the normal procedure. She tidied her hair, hung her brush and comb-bag by its tape from the handle of the chest of drawers, changed from her boots into a strong pair of house shoes, then descended the ladder, hurrying almost guiltily along the carpeted passages till she reached the now familiar kitchen.

The kettle was boiling on the fire and the table was laid with fresh lettuce, bread-and-butter, tinned salmon, egg-cups and a large slab of cake. Mrs. Horseferry was putting tea into the teapot and Emmy was standing in front of a mirror on the wall, holding out a strand of hair that had escaped her curling-tongs, pushing it up one single hair and tucking it in among the tightly frizzed waves. Tilly stood by her, watching absorbedly.

"The convenience, Tilly," said Mrs. Horseferry majestically, "is at the bottom of the garden. There is one in the house, of course, next to the bathroom, but that is reserved for the family."

Emmy turned from the mirror with a swing of her long skirt that gave a fleeting glimpse of a flounced cambric petticoat.

"Reelly!" she said with a shudder. "I may be funny but I reelly couldn't bear it. Not an outside one. Downright rude, I call it."

Tilly washed her hands and face under the tap, lathering them freely with red carbolic soap, dried them on the roller-towel, then made her way to the closet in the garden. The sun beat down on her as she passed the beds of stocks and marigolds and pinks. A hedge of sweet briar enclosed the closet. She drew in the heavy sweetness with a feeling of refreshment. She felt hot and sweaty in her serge blouse and woollen vest. Her aunt always grudged her summer clothes ("Only a month or two's wear and you've grown out of them by next year," she would say), and to Tilly summer had always been associated with the smell of hot serge and the sensation of a thick woollen vest sticking tightly to her skin . . . Her thoughts went to the hip-bath in Mrs. Horseferry's bedroom, and she imagined herself sitting in it, squeezing tepid water from the sponge over her body. At home she had bathed in a wooden tub, using water in which her aunt had already bathed, washing herself with a piece of flannel. The thought of the hip-bath filled her with secret excitement.

The "convenience", too, impressed her by its magnificence. It was not an ordinary earth closet. It had a plug that brought a flush of water and real toilet-paper instead of pieces of the *Bellminster Advertiser*. The flush of water sent a few drops on to the red tiled floor, and Tilly carefully wiped them up with her handkerchief before she left the closet.

When she reached the kitchen the other two were sitting down to tea.

"Draw your chair up, child," said Mrs. Horseferry, pouring out a third cup. "Here's your egg. Help yourself to bread-and-butter."

"Thank you, ma'am," said Tilly, drawing up her chair and taking her place at the table. Her face glowed red with heat and kitchen soap. Her hands were large and ungainly and roughened by work. Emmy threw her a glance of fastidious disdain and continued the interrupted conversation.

"You know madam, I suppose?" she said to Mrs. Horseferry.

"Mrs. Culverton?" said Mrs. Horseferry. "No, I've never met her. It was her cousin I was cook to and it was her cousin that retired me on a pension when she shut up her house and went to live abroad."

"I never met her cousin," said Emmy.

"A nice lady," said Mrs. Horseferry reflectively. "A great one for animals. Dogs and things. Didn't mind what she ate herself, but they'd got to have the best of everything. The Quality's like that about animals, especially on the female side.

"I know," sighed Emmy. "Barmy."

"Well be that as it may," said Mrs. Horseferry, I found lodgings over at Bellminster and I've lived there ever since. Not a princely pension. It's been a squeeze at times to make both ends meet. I remember I thought at the time that, if I'd been a cat or a dog or even a canary, she'd have seen to it that I ended my days in comfort, but, as I was a mere human being, she thought a pound a week sufficient."

"I know," said Emmy again, lifting her egg-spoon to her mouth with little finger elegantly cocked. "Chicken liver for the dog and kippers for the kitchen."

"Anyway," said Mrs. Horseferry, "when Mrs. Culverton took this holiday cottage she remembered that I was in the neighbourhood and wrote to ask me if I'd oblige by coming here as cook-housekeeper for the summer. Quite a civil letter, it was."

"Oh, yes," said Emmy, shrugging her thin shoulders. "Madam's quite civil. High and mighty as you please and all for working you to the bone, but—civil, yes."

"Civil is as civil does, of course," said Mrs. Horseferry. "Have some salmon now, dear? And you too, Tilly."

"I don't mind if I do," said Emmy.

"Thank you, ma'am," said Tilly.

Mrs. Horseferry helped them to tinned salmon, then turned her sleepy eyes to Emmy.

"I'm not one for gossip," she said, "but I'd like to know what the family's like. As a family, I mean. What about a little onion to give it a relish?"

"No, thank you," said Emmy with a shudder. "Not onion. . . Just a little vinegar, if you've no objection, to take the richness off." She sprinkled vinegar freely over her tinned salmon, then began to remove the bones and skin and place them along the edge of her plate. "I may be funny, but anything in the nature of an onion seems to clog my stomach . . . Winkles, now. I can't eat half a dozen without heaving." She paused to remove an infinitesimal piece of skin and place it on the edge of her plate. "Well, as to the family. Genteel, but not the cream of Society. Their house is in Streatham, which speaks for itself to them as knows what's what and what isn't."

Mrs. Horseferry evidently knew. She nodded understandingly.

"What's *he* like?" she said.

"Ever so nice," said Emmy. "A reel gentleman, *he* is. A smile and a kind word for everyone, that's him. Different from *her*."

"She's difficult, is she?" said Mrs. Horseferry. "Tilly, have you never been told to take your spoon out of your cup when you drink your tea?"

"No, ma'am," said Tilly.

"Well, you have now," said Emmy tartly. "Difficult's the word, all right, Mrs. Horseferry. Hard. Cold. Proud. Never a word of thanks. Queen of the Cannibal Isles, that's her."

"I know," said Mrs. Horseferry with a sigh. "I've cooked for many a one like that in my time. There's a knack, you know, in managing them. Easy when you've picked it up. And the children?"

"Oh, just children," said Emmy vaguely. "Master Edmund's the eldest. Fifteen, and old for his years. Proper little gentleman, he is. Good-looking, like his Pa, too. Then there's Master Richard.

"How old is he?"

"Thirteen. A real boy. Clever, too. Beats his brother at brains, but not so good-looking. Miss Althea's the pick of the bunch for looks, of course."

"She comes next to Master Richard?"

"Yes. Eleven, she is, and pretty as a picture. Flower-like, if you know what I mean. And that's the lot . . . Oh, except Miss Vere."

"She's the baby, I take it?"

"Well, she's nine. No beauty and on the sulky side, but not much trouble."

"Who's going to look after them here? Their nurse's on holiday, isn't she?"

"Yes. They're having a Miss Maple for what's called a holiday governess. Swank for nurse, if you ask me."

"Please, ma'am," said Tilly suddenly.

"Yes, Tilly?" said Mrs. Horseferry.

"Can I have a bath in the hip-bath tonight? "

There was a short silence, then:

"I shall want it tonight," said Emmy curtly.

"I'll have it after you, then," said Tilly.

They stared at her in surprise, but neither of them was as surprised as Tilly. She'd never heard herself speak like that before, and she didn't know what had made her do it. Then suddenly she knew. It was because her aunt wasn't there to take her up sharp.

The words were the first independent gesture of her life and she found deep pleasure in them.

"It's not Saturday," said Mrs. Horseferry doubtfully, "but I suppose there's no reason why you shouldn't."

The shadows were lengthening over the garden by the time they had washed up and put away the tea things. Emmy yawned and stretched.

"Bed for me!" she said. "I may be funny, but this place is giving me the willies already. Might as well be on a desert island and have done with it."

"What about supper?" said Mrs. Horseferry.

"No, thanks," said Emmy.

"We had a late tea, of course. Just a cup of something?"

"No, thanks," said Emmy. "Bed for me! I don't think I'll have a bath, after all. I'll wait till I get back to town life. There's a special bath for the staff at Streatham. A shower, too, if you care to use it. I'm not one for showers, myself. They're a shock to the system and my system's always been my weak point . . . Well, good night."

They heard her clatter up the staircase and up the ladder. Mrs. Horseferry turned her gaze on to Tilly.

"I expect you'd like to go to bed too, now, wouldn't you, Tilly?" she said.

"No, thank you, ma'am," said Tilly, taking her seat on an upright chair near the fireplace.

Mrs. Horseferry hesitated, then, going to a cupboard in the wall, took out a bottle of gin and a glass.

"I don't touch spirits as a rule," she said with dignity, "but I have to take a glass in the evening on account of a certain stomatic complaint I suffer from. Nothing serious. Spirits hold it at bay."

She sat down on the rocking-chair by the window, poured out a glass of gin and began to sip it.

"The Culvertons will be your first experience of the Quality, I take it, Tilly?" she said.

"Yes, ma'am," said Tilly.

"Ah, well," said Mrs. Horseferry, "when you're as old as me and can look back. . . I know 'em inside out. I've seen and heard things you'd hardly believe." Miraculously, as it seemed, the glass was already empty and she refilled it. "There was one place I was at . . ."

There followed a series of reminiscences, growing more and more incoherent as the glass was filled and refilled. Mean Quality . . . dishonest Quality . . . eccentric Quality . . . spendthrift Quality . . . criminal Quality . . . heroic Quality. Anecdote after anecdote, swiftly succeeding each other, formed a series of kaleidoscopic pictures in Tilly's brain. But more surprising to Tilly even than the stories was the fact that slowly and by degrees Mrs. Horseferry's drooping eyelids lifted till she revealed the full stare of a pair of somewhat glazed brown eyes.

"Hushed up, of course. They said she'd gone to a finishing school in Paris . . . Spent money like water. Footmen. Parties. Dresses. Wines. Hadn't a penny when the crash came. He shot himself and she went off with the groom . . . Lived in her bedroom with the blinds down. No one ever saw her. Ate enormous meals, sent up on a lift. Went on for years, then suddenly she started throwing things out of the window and they took her away . . ."

As she talked Mrs. Horseferry's speech had gradually become more and more blurred. Suddenly her head dropped forward and she sat there motionless, her chin lost in the vast desert of her bosom. Loud snores issued from her body as if some wild animal had taken possession of it and were growling at Tilly.

Tilly stood up.

"I'll go to bed now if I may, ma'am," she said.

The only answer was a long rumbling snore.

Through all the events of the evening, Tilly had not lost sight of her determination to have a bath in the hip-bath.

She took one of the tall metal hot-water jugs that stood on the floor under the sink, filled it at the tap, then tiptoed across the kitchen and made her way upstairs to the attic.

Chapter Two

"They should be here any minute now," said Mrs. Horseferry.

She had been saying it at intervals for the last half-hour. She was very dignified, very aloof, very sleepy-eyed. Emmy had departed soon after breakfast, contemptuous to the last of Linden Rise and its surroundings.

"All those animal noises!" she said. "Common, I call it. If I want to hear cocks crowing, there's a man on the Halls can do it much better."

During the morning Mrs. Horseferry had initiated Tilly into her duties—the sweeping, the dusting, the "turning out" of the rooms, the laying of the table, the answering of bells, the carrying up of hot-water cans, the cleaning of lamps.

"They won't expect the same service as they get at home, of course," she said. "The Quality likes to rough it on a holiday. It helps to occupy their minds."

"Yes, ma'am," said Tilly.

She was wearing one of her new print dresses. It stood out stiffly all round her and reached almost to the ground. The white cap, coming low over her forehead, seemed to give the final touch of burlesque to the small squat figure.

Mrs. Horseferry, rubbing up the silver teapot at the kitchen table, looked at her with qualified approval.

"Raw," she commented. "Raw, but well-meaning."

"Yes, ma'am," said Tilly, feeling flattered by the description.

"I've left the front door open so that we shall see the conveyance arrive," said Mrs. Horseferry. "They ordered the wagonette from Tubbs' farm to meet the train. He's a reliable man, I understand, but of course the horses are sometimes needed for other duties and are not immediately available."

At that moment there came the sound of wheels and, looking through the open doorway, they saw a wagonette drawing up at the gate.

"I'll see to them, Tilly," said Mrs. Horseferry, her eyelids drooping still lower over her eyes, her voice becoming deeper and more majestic in her excitement. "You stay here. Put on the kettle and arrange the tea-things on the tray as I showed you."

"Yes, ma'am," said Tilly.

Mrs. Horseferry removed her apron, smoothed down her dress and took up her position at the front door as the little party trooped up from the gate—two women leading the way and four children straggling behind.

"Mrs. Horseferry?" said the taller of the two women.

"Yes, madam," said Mrs. Horseferry, her sleepy eyes making a swift survey of her employer.

Quality, she thought, noting the thin face with high-bridged nose, weary blue eyes and slightly disdainful mouth. Getting on, she thought, noting the strands of grey in the fair hair. Moneyed, she thought, noting the elegance of the blue skirt with its mauve bands and short Zouave jacket, the white frilled blouse, the blue hat with its mauve feather. The leg-of-mutton sleeves stood out stiffly; the tightly corseted waist gave the figure the fashionable hour-glass shape.

"I'm Mrs. Culverton. My husband is unable to come down till later in the week. This"—with a movement of her gloved hand towards the other woman—"is Miss Rossiter, my sister. She's come down with us to see the place and help us settle in. She won't be staying the night."

Miss Rossiter had stopped half-way up the path and was gazing at the cottage.

"It's simply fascinating," she cried. "I'd no idea it was going to be so fascinating. It's a duck of a place, darling. Simply charming. Look at it! Just *look*!"

Her face, large and highly coloured, glowed with enthusiasm, her hands flashed to and fro as she pointed out the green front door, the lavender-bordered path, the geraniums in the porch and the small arched windows, which seemed to gaze down at her with an air of pained surprise.

The children stood in a little group, looking about them with the wariness of young animals in unfamiliar surroundings. There was a dark, grave, handsome boy; a fair boy with a long mouth, a blunt nose and grey-blue eyes; a slender little girl with golden ringlets and blue eyes that sparkled with excitement, and a smaller girl with swarthy skin, black brows and straight, wiry, dark hair, who stood by herself a little way apart from the others.

"The driver will bring in the luggage," said Mrs. Culverton, ignoring her sister's outburst. "Perhaps you'll show us to our rooms now, will you, Mrs. Horseferry? We'll unpack before we have tea."

"Yes, madam. This way, madam."

They trooped up the narrow staircase and along the passage. "This is your room, madam . . . This is the young gentlemen's . . . and this the young ladies'."

"Thank you, Mrs. Horseferry," said Mrs. Culverton, a faint note of boredom underlying the graciousness of her voice. "It's all very nice. We shall live very simply, of course, while we're here. No late dinner. Just a plain supper. You have a young person from the neighbourhood to help you, I understand?" Yes, madam. Tilly Pound. She's in the kitchen now . . . There's a hand-basin in the bathroom, madam. The young ladies and gentlemen will wash there, I take it. I'll bring hot water up to your room, of course."

"Thank you," said Mrs. Culverton, again in a tone of dismissal.

When Mrs. Horseferry had gone, Mrs. Culverton drew the two long hatpins out of her hat and laid it on the bed, glanced round the room without interest, then sat down in the arm-chair by the window and gazed unseeingly over the sun-bathed countryside. She heard the murmur of voices from the children's bedrooms, and sharp exclamations of delight from Gertrude, who was darting about the house, discovering fresh outlets for her enthusiasm each moment, but her thoughts were so far away that the sounds made no impression on her mind.

She had looked forward to this holiday with secret happiness for months, and now it was all spoilt because Howard hadn't come. Till last night she had thought that he was coming, and last night he had looked at her, his handsome face wearing the furtive expression she knew so well, and had said: "I'm afraid I shan't be able to come down with you tomorrow, my dear, after all. I'll try and get down later, of course."

"Very well, Howard," she had replied in her cool, level voice, bending her head over her needlework, but her heart had contracted and her whole body had turned cold. It was that woman, of course. She'd only to raise her little finger and he went running to her. She must have known—or guessed—what hopes his wife was building on this holiday and have decided from spite or pure wanton mischief to disappoint them. She loved to show her power over Howard, to pit her beauty and allure against his wife's faded charms.

There was a knock at her door and Mrs. Horseferry entered with a polished brass can of hot water. ("I'll see to them this evening," she had said to Tilly, "just till they're settled. If there's any fault-finding, I'll be able to manage them better than you. You've not had the experience I've had in managing the Quality.")

"Is there anything further I can do for you, madam?" said Mrs. Horseferry, setting the hot-water can in the basin and covering it with a towel.

"No, thank you," said Mrs. Culverton. "I'll come to see you in the kitchen after tea."

"Very good, madam," said Mrs. Horseferry, with a note of grudging approval in her voice.

A real lady. No doubt about that. Even now, even in this little village even though she had retired from service long ago, it would have hurt Mrs. Horseferry's pride to cook for one of the "jumped-ups".

Mrs. Culverton washed her face and hands, dried them on the lavender-scented towel, then set to work on her unpacking, hanging her dresses in the wardrobe, laying her underclothes neatly in the drawers, putting her silver and tortoiseshell toilet set on the dressing-table. At the bottom of the trunk were the family photographs that she always took with her, more from habit than sentiment, even on the shortest absence from home—her mother and father, both now dead, the four children, Howard. She took up the photograph of Howard and put it on the dressing-table, trying to resist the stab of pain that shot through her heart as she looked at the pleasant, handsome face with the straight almost Grecian nose, the cleft chin and the hint of weakness in the smiling well-formed lips. Slowly, almost reluctantly, she turned her head to examine her own reflection in the mirror. The sunlight showed up mercilessly the crows' feet and pouches round her eyes, the greying hair, the deepening lines that ran from her nose to the corners of her lips. A gust of trembling seized her, and she replaced the photograph at the bottom of the trunk. Then she took up the photograph of her father and mother and put it on the chimney-piece, subjecting it to the same long scrutiny as she had given Howard's. Her father's face was strong and kindly, her mother's gentle and placid. That was what a marriage should be, what she had wanted her own marriage to be . . . the man strong and protective, the woman weak and yielding. She herself had been essentially weak and, till after their marriage, had taken Howard's strength for granted. It was only after their marriage that the discovery of his weakness had forced her to assume strength, to become, against her will and nature, hard and dominant and unyielding . . . and beneath her love she still felt a deep resentment against him for the role he had thrust upon her.

The sound of Richard's laugh from the next room roused her. She glanced at her watch, then began with quick deft movements to change into the dress of navy blue Surah, trimmed with white lace, that she had laid out ready on the bed.

Edmund and Richard were arranging their books in the bookshelf that stood beneath the bedroom window.

"What about this holiday governess?" said Richard. "It's going to be a bit of a bore having her, isn't it?"

"Oh, she's only for the girls," said Edmund. "Still—I'm going to do a little work every day on the subjects I'm weak at. I've brought my galleon set as a hobby, but I'm going to do some work as well."

Richard's long humorous mouth lengthened into a grin.

"I'm not going to waste a holiday swotting," he said.

"I think you ought to do a little work," said Edmund.

He spoke rather uncertainly. He was a deeply conscientious boy, and he was torn between a feeling of responsibility for his younger brother's moral progress and a slight unacknowledged jealousy of his young brother's mental progress. For Richard, though two years younger, lazy, cheerful, happy-go-lucky, passed all his examinations without difficulty and was already due for the "double move" that would bring him perilously near Edmund.

Richard was sitting on the floor beside the bookcase, his legs crossed, his head bent over a book. He had brushed his hair, but it stood up, as it always did, in loose, unruly waves.

Edmund placed his *History of England* carefully in the top shelf of the bookcase, then, as Richard made no answer, continued:

"We'd find six weeks of just lazing about rather"—he searched for a word and finally brought out—"demoralizing."

Richard raised his pointed Puck-like face from his book.

"I think I'd like to be demoralized," he said.

"There won't be much to do, you know, in a little place like this," said Edmund, placing his *French Grammar* beside his *History of England.*

"There'll be heaps to do" said Richard. "Didn't you notice as we came along in the wagonette? A river, farms, woods and a blacksmith's forge. They'll provide no end of occupation for idle hands."

Edmund smiled constrainedly.

"Don't get into mischief, old chap," he said. "It's a bit—worrying for Mother, not having Father here."

The responsibility for taking his father's place lay heavy on Edmund's spirit. He had a vague, unformulated idea that his mother's worries went further than the mere inability of her husband to be present for the first week of this holiday, but his mind shrank from probing more deeply.

"What's the fuss?" said Richard. "He's coming down later and she wouldn't thank us to sit round mooning at her. We've come away for a holiday. Holidays are things you're meant to enjoy." His eyes twinkled as he thought of an argument that would appeal to Edmund. "It's a waste of money not to, you know."

There was a knock at the door and Althea entered, wearing a clean frilled pinafore over a pink cashmere frock. She sat on the edge of the bed, her ringlets falling about her shoulders, swinging legs that were encased in long black stockings and button boots.

"Isn't it a darling cottage!" she said.

The boys' faces had softened at her entrance. Both felt for her the protective tenderness of the "big brother," and there was often, beneath the surface, a tacit rivalry for her affection.

"There's a farm down the road," she went on. "I can see it from our bedroom window. Darling baby chickens and a lovely little pony in the field. I'm going there after tea. I want to learn to ride a pony and I want to learn to milk a cow. Do you think they'll
    let me?"

"I expect so, Thea," said Edmund, "but—I've just been saying to Richard—we mustn't run too wild. Mother's tired and needs a rest. We must try not to worry her."

Althea's small lovely face reflected the gravity of his,

"Yes, I know. I won't worry her. I won't do anything without asking her. There'll be the holiday governess, too, won't there?"

"Miss Maple? Yes, but only in the mornings."

"Well, what I say is," said Richard, putting his books in an untidy heap on the windowsill, "if it's a holiday, it ought to *be* a holiday. Not asking permission and being careful all the time. Go out and milk cows, Thea." He gave her his impish grin. "Do anything you feel like doing. I'm going to."

Edmund was engaged in putting Richard's books tidily into the bookcase, and behind his back Althea gave Richard a demurely mischievous smile. From babyhood Althea had been the accepted darling of the household, and all the members of it had looked to find in her what they wanted. To Edmund she was a grave little sister, fit material for his moulding, to Richard a gay sprite of mischief, to Vere—but Vere didn't count. It was not always easy to accommodate herself to the conflicting claims, but practice had already given her a certain proficiency.

"I see you mean to do a little work after all, Richard," said Edmund, with kindly triumph in his voice.

Richard threw a careless glance at the book Edmund was holding.

"*Froissart's Chronicles?*" he said. "That's not work. It's fun."

Again the obscure jealousy stirred in Edmund's heart. It wasn't fair that what was work to him should be fun to Richard.

The door opened and Vere came in. She looked squat and bunchy in a starched holland pinafore. Her thick brows were drawn into their usual frown.

"I can't find my handkerchiefs, Thea," she said.

"You little stupid!" said Althea. "They're in the middle drawer of the dressing-table with mine."

"Oh," said Vere.

She advanced into the room and stood there uncertainly.

"Run off, kid," said Edmund shortly. "We don't want you."

"Fly away home, ladybird," said Richard.

Vere turned and went from the room.

"I hope she's not going to be a nuisance," said Althea. "We don't want her tagging round with us wherever we go."

"We needn't take her," said Edmund.

"Oh, I expect she'll be all right," said Richard vaguely. He went over to the window. "Look at Aunt Gertrude. She's going round the garden, smelling every single flower. She's going to be a bit of a bore if she stays."

"She's not staying," said Edmund. "She's going back tonight."

"You never know with Aunt Gertrude," said Althea.

"Come on," said Edmund. "Let's go down."

Mrs. Culverton was in the hall when the children came downstairs.

"Come along, children," she said. "Tea's all ready in the dining-room."

She spoke in the kindly, authoritative tone that she always used to them. She had—partially, if not entirely—shaken off her depression. Things were, after all, exactly as they had been for the last ten years. She didn't know why she had hoped that they would be different on this holiday. For the hundredth time she made up her mind to conquer her sentimental fondness for a husband who had long since tired of her.

They took their seats round the gate-legged table. Plates of sandwiches, scones, bread-and-butter and cakes were ranged round the bowl of marigolds in the centre. Mrs. Horseferry came in with a jug of yellow, creamy milk.

"I've cut some thin bread-and-butter, madam," she said, anxious to show her familiarity with the ways of the Quality, "and some thicker for the children. The sandwich cake is plain but wholesome. Four eggs in it. There are jam sandwiches for the children as being more digestible than savoury."

"Thank you, Mrs. Horseferry," said Mrs. Culverton. "That's very thoughtful of you."

Mrs. Horseferry's lids drooped more sleepily over her eyes at the praise.

"You'll ring if you want anything further, won't you, madam?" she said as she withdrew.

Mrs. Culverton took up the milk-jug and glanced round.

"Where's Vere?" she said.

Edmund went into the hall.

"Vere!" he called. "Come down to tea."

Then Aunt Gertrude burst into the room. She wore the slightly dishevelled look that excitement always gave her. Strands of dark hair had escaped the "bun," into which they had been coiled, and fell about her neck.

"My dear, it really *is* the most *fascinating* place. There's a dear little gate at the bottom of the back garden that goes into a field and up a hill into a darling little wood . . . And oh, my dear!" sitting down at the table. "What a tea! What a *tea*!"

"Yes, Mrs. Horseferry seems very capable," said Mrs. Culverton.

Aunt Gertrude gave a scream of laughter.

"What a name, my dear! What a *name*! And do *look* at that old Toby jug on the chimney-piece. Isn't it heavenly!"

"I should say it's a very ordinary modern reproduction," said Mrs. Culverton shortly.

With Gertrude's entrance all her newly found serenity had deserted her. Gertrude was her younger sister, and at the age of forty she still continued to cultivate the volatile girlishness that had once been her chief attraction. On their parents' death she had gone to live with an aunt, who was now bedridden and looked after by a professional nurse, so that Gertrude, unhampered by duties or ties, was free to indulge an impulsiveness that was fast degenerating into eccentricity. She would descend on her friends and relatives without warning and leave them as suddenly, fly off on mysterious journeys, abandon herself to emotional short-lived friendships . . . displaying throughout an eagerness and zest that embarrassed and exasperated her sister.

She had not known that Gertrude was coming with them today, till she descended unexpectedly on the household just as they were having breakfast.

"Darling, I *must* just run down with you and see that heavenly cottage you told me about . . . No, I can't stay the night there. I really haven't a minute, but I'm just managing to squeeze it in."

And throughout the journey she had not ceased to acclaim the passing scenery with shrill exclamations of delight.

Mrs. Culverton turned her gaze from Gertrude's heated, animated countenance to the children, trying to find comfort in them . . . but the shadow of her disappointment lay over them, too. In Richard's pleasant face she seemed to see her own weakness, the weakness to which she longed secretly to yield. In the lines of Edmund's mouth she saw the false strength that she had assumed like an ill-fitting garment. Only in Althea's small exquisite face did she find comfort. The coming of this child had delighted Howard. Two fine boys, then a fairy-like little girl, dainty and charming from babyhood. Their family seemed complete. And for the first two years of Althea's life had been years of unclouded happiness for Mrs. Culverton. Howard ceased his philandering, forgot his restlessness, and devoted himself to his wife and home and children. Because of those years she could never look at Althea without a stirring of tenderness—sweet and painful like the tingling of a nerve.

"Can we go out after tea, Mother?" said Edmund.

"Yes, dear," said. Mrs. Culverton. "Don't go too far away."

"To the river?" said Richard.

She smiled faintly.

"Don't get drowned."

Then Vere entered and stood just inside the doorway, her brows drawn into a scowl under her shock of thick straight hair.

"Come and sit down here, dear," said Mrs. Culverton, putting her hand on the empty chair next hers.

She always treated the child with studied kindness, trying to hide, even from herself, how little love she bore her. She hadn't wanted her . . . and she didn't want her now. It was because of Vere that she had finally and irrevocably lost Howard's love. She had been wretchedly ill during the months before the child came. The sight of her had, she knew, filled Howard with revulsion, and he had again turned to find his pleasure elsewhere. Even after Vere's birth she had been too ill to try to win him back (it was since Vere's birth that she had suffered from those devastating headaches that still prostrated her from time to time) and so the woman had finally secured her hold over him. Before that he had been merely a philanderer, flitting from one affair to another, ready always to return to her. "He's chock-full of charm, and he can't help using it," she would say to herself indulgently. Certainly it was the women's fault as much as his. Attracted by his good looks, flattered by the attentions that he could never resist paying to any woman under sixty, they had pursued him shamelessly. But Mrs. Brougham was different. He had given up philandering since she became his mistress. She possessed him utterly, body and soul . . .

Vere sat down and pushed the thick hair out of her eyes. Mrs. Culverton sighed. It didn't matter what you did to the child, she always seemed unkempt. Swarthy, scowling, ungainly, black-browed, with that shock of straight coarse hair falling over her eyes, she looked like a gypsy, a changeling. And she was so stupid and unresponsive that Mrs. Culverton sometimes wondered if she were actually a little "wanting".

"I'll go and get some more bread-and-butter," said Aunt Gertrude. "We ought to wait on ourselves, oughtn't we? I haven't dared to go into the kitchen yet, and I'm simply dying to see it."

She seized the empty plate and went from the room, with a trill of laughter and an eddy of flounced skirts.

A few minutes later she returned, holding the refilled plate of bread-and-butter. She closed the door and stood leaning against it, helpless with mirth.

"Oh, my dear!" she said at last. "Have you *seen* her?"

"Seen whom, Gertrude?" said Mrs. Culverton.

"Mrs. Noah. Mrs. Noah, straight out of that old Noah's Ark we used to have when we were children. Face, dress, everything. Mrs. Noah."

"What *are* you talking about, Gertrude?" said Mrs. Culverton.

"Tilly Pound. The 'help'. I've never seen anything so funny in my life. You *must* go in and see her."

"I shall be going there shortly in any case," said Mrs. Culverton, irritated, as usual, by Gertrude's exuberance. "There's no hurry."

"Well, you must go, then, children," said Gertrude, still laughing. "Don't go together, of course, or you'll simply not be able to control yourselves. Go one by one."

"Shall we?" said Richard, looking at his mother with a lift of his eyebrows.

"If you like," said Mrs. Culverton. "Finish your tea first."

"I've finished," said Edmund, getting up from his seat and going from the room.

It had occurred to him that, as his father's representative, he ought in any case to go into the kitchen and greet the servants. He paused for a moment outside the door, summoning his grown-up manner. He had been practising his grown-up manner at intervals ever since his fifteenth birthday and secretly he was very pleased with it. Then he opened the kitchen door and went in.

Tilly was sitting at the table eating a slice of bread-and-jam.

Mrs. Horseferry was not there. She had said that she did not want any tea and would go and rest in her bedroom till it was time to prepare the evening meal. She would do a little needlework, she added, to soothe her nerves, and she had taken her work-bag upstairs with her. It was a capacious work-bag, heavily laden in a manner that suggested a shrouded bottle of gin.

Tilly stopped eating at Edmund's entrance, holding a thick slice of bread-and-jam, with one enormous semi-circular bite taken out of it, in mid-air.

"Don't get up," said Edmund kindly.

The button eyes stared at him in what he took to be respectful admiration. Tilly put down her slice of bread-and-jam. Get up for a kid like that, she was thinking. Not likely!

"I hope you'll be happy with us these holidays," he continued. "We'll try to give you as little trouble as possible and, if there's anything we can do for you, you must let us know."

That, he thought, was what his father would have said—or rather (unconsciously he corrected the thought) what his father ought to have said. Actually his father would probably have said something free and easy that would have made Tilly laugh, but Edmund disapproved of freeness and easiness with servants.

"There are four of us, you know," he continued. "Myself— Master Edmund—and Master Richard and Miss Althea and Miss Vere." His well-cut lips flickered into a smile. "Quite an invasion for you, isn't it?"

"Yes," said Tilly and, remembering her manners and her aunt's injunctions, added, "Master Edmund."

Edmund hesitated a moment, wondering how to bring the interview to an end, then, deciding that it had come to an end already, turned and went from the room, well satisfied with the part he had played in it.

Sauce! thought Tilly, taking another large semi-circular bite out of her slice of bread-and-jam. No older than me, he isn't. I'd have clouted him one at school if he'd tried it on.

Before she had time, however, to construct an imaginary scene in which Edmund met the retribution meted out to sauce by her contemporaries, the door opened and Althea entered.

"You're Tilly, aren't you?" she said with an engaging smile.

"Yes, miss," said Tilly noncommittally.

"I'm Althea . . . Isn't this a darling place?"

"Yes, miss," said Tilly.

"We're going to have a lovely holiday here," said Althea. She gave a gay little peal of laughter. "I expect we'll be a terrible nuisance, but you won't mind that, will you?"

"No, miss," said Tilly, continuing stolidly to munch her bread-and-jam.

"Well, I won't worry you any more," said Althea, who had an uncomfortable feeling that the scene was falling flat. Servants generally adored her, but this odd-looking person wasn't even watching her. "I expect you're terribly busy, and we want to explore the garden. We're longing to explore everywhere. Goodbye."

She went from the room with quick light dancing steps.

Tilly cut another thick slice from the loaf. Airs and graces, she thought. Showing off . . . She sat there, munching bread-and-jam, her wooden face devoid of expression. Then suddenly something of humour lightened the ungainly features. My aunt'd've learnt her all right . . .

She was just cutting her third slice of bread when Richard entered.

"Hello," he said, closing the door behind him.

"Hello," said Tilly.

He sat down at the table and looked at her.

"Yes, you *are* like Mrs. Noah," he said.

"Am I?" said Tilly. "The one in the Bible?"

"Yes," said Richard.

"Fancy that!" said Tilly, impressed.

"Can I have some bread-and-jam? I'm still hungry. Everything in the dining-room was so thin."

"Well, better-class people like things thin," explained Tilly, spreading the slice of bread with jam, cutting it in two and handing

28

half to Richard, "and Mrs. Horseferry made some thick for you special."

"It wasn't thick enough," he said indistinctly as he bit into his piece of bread-and-jam. He gave her a long impersonal stare. "How old are you?"

"Fifteen. How old are you?"

"Thirteen. Where do you live?"

"I live here now. I used to live over at Pellborough."

She had an odd exciting feeling of friendship for this boy. He wasn't showing off like the others. He didn't care what she—or anyone—thought of him. In some strange way they were akin, the two of them.

"What was it like there? What were your father and mother like?"

"I hadn't any. I lived with an aunt and uncle."

"What were they like? Tell me about them."

He wasn't asking for the sake or asking, as the other two might have done. He really wanted to know . . . She began to tell him. She told him about her aunt and uncle, the schoolmaster, the Squire and the other people in the neighbourhood. She told him about the old woman who lived in the cottage next her aunt and who had ten cats, each with its own special footstool . . . of the man in the gypsy encampment who had a charmed snail that could cure warts and burns . . . of the piebald horse that always stopped outside the public-house and refused to go on till it had had its pint of beer.

"The Vicar didn't know about it when he bought it," she said, "and it made it sort of awkward for him. He'd got to go three miles out of his way to get from the village to the Vicarage so's not to pass The Goat an' Compasses or else go into the pub an' buy it its beer."

Richard's laugh rang out together with Tilly's rusty cackle.

"Which did he do?" said Richard, cutting another slice of bread and spreading it thickly with jam.

"He tried to break it of it gradual by waterin' its beer, but it soon found out an' wouldn't budge till they'd brought it a pint of the real stuff."

They were still sitting at the table, talking and eating bread-and-jam, when Mrs. Horseferry came down to begin her preparations for the evening meal.

Mrs. Horseferry crossed the kitchen without looking at them. She moved with slow deliberation, her eyes open in a wide fixed stare.

Chapter Three

Miss Maple was walking down the road towards Linden Rise, singing to herself beneath her breath. She generally sang to herself when she was alone, but she was singing today a little more loudly and discordantly than usual in order to convince herself that she was not feeling nervous. She was a small woman with a worn kindly face, a prominent nose and bright bird-like eyes. Her greying hair was coiled tightly at the back of her head beneath a black straw hat of indeterminate shape, the fashion of the short black jacket was that of several years ago, and the hand that held up the grey skirt clear of the dusty road showed neat darns in the black cotton glove.

Finding that her nervousness was overcoming her again, she quickened her pace and changed from "Drink to me only" to "Come, lasses, and lads," in order to rally her spirits. Secretly she was terrified of these Culvertons. She had often acted as holiday governess (her mother could not spare her to take a full-time post) to families in the neighbourhood, but these Culvertons were different. They were people from London. Bond Street and Piccadilly and the Tower were as familiar to them as the village green was to her. She had got up early in order to study the newspaper so that she could discuss the events of the day with them. She imagined that London people spent most of their time discussing the events of the day. She went over them in her mind . . . The dear Queen had given a dinner-party for the German Emperor at Osborne (so handsome, thought Miss Maple, admiringly, with those dashing up-turned moustaches). The leading article was rather long and involved, but Miss Maple had gathered from it that Mr. Gladstone's apparent preponderance in Parliament was devoid of all moral and intellectual weight. Perhaps she'd better keep off politics . . . The Culvertons might or might not be Home Rulers and people were apt to get somewhat heated on the subject. She must just feel her way. . . . A short paragraph that she had read as she put on her hat informed her that Sir Charles Freemantle favoured a restoration of the gold coinage. Sovereigns and half-sovereigns had evidently been allowed to subside to a point of lightness at which they had become a positive scandal. Miss Maple didn't see that this mattered as long as one had them, but she stored the information at the back of her mind. One might possibly be able to bring it into general conversation. There had been something about Mr. Balfour, too, but she'd forgotten what it was. She stopped singing in order to try to remember, then gave up the attempt.

"I'm going to love it," she said aloud brightly. "I'm going to love every minute of it. I'm looking forward to it."

Miss Maple had trained herself from childhood to look on the bright side. She saw things, not as they were, but as she would have liked them to be.

"I'm one of the lucky ones," she would say. "Everything always seems to go right with me."

At the gate of Linden Rise she stopped, tucked a few straying ends of hair beneath her hat, straightened the collar of her coat, moved the fingers of her gloves to conceal the darns, and, summoning all her courage, walked up to the front door. Mrs. Culverton, who happened to be coming out of the sitting-room, answered her knock. Her air of weary disillusionment had vanished. There was an almost girlish radiance about her. She had had a letter from Howard by this morning's post—a charming, affectionate letter, saying how sorry he was not to be with her and how much he was looking forward to joining her in a week's time. Her spirits had been caught up in a rush of happiness as she read it and she had tried to forget that Howard was always most charming and affectionate when he was betraying her most flagrantly.

The fact that Gertrude had departed last night added to her

sense of relief. Gertrude was so erratic that she might easily have decided at the last moment to spend the whole holiday with them.

"Miss Maple, isn't it?" she said with a pleasant smile. "Do come in. It's so good of you to give up your time to us like this."

The sun of her happiness wanted to warm even this withered little creature who stood looking at her so timidly.

She's—queenly, thought Miss Maple, who liked people to be neatly labelled and put into pigeon-holes in her mind. Queenly, she repeated to herself, and put her employer away into the pigeon-hole where she kept the Princess of Wales and the Queen of Roumania.

"Oh, no, Mrs. Culverton," she said earnestly. "I've been looking forward to it more than I can say. It's going to be the greatest pleasure. It is, indeed."

Her eyes had darted round the narrow hall and through the open door of the kitchen, where Mrs. Horseferry was mixing pastry at the table. Old Retainer, she said to herself, endowing Mrs. Horseferry with all the virtues of loyalty, devotion and integrity that went with Old Retainer.

"Come into the sitting-room," said Mrs. Culverton, "and then we can talk things over before you meet the children."

Miss Maple entered the sitting-room and looked round with approval. She knew Miss Lubbock, of course, the owner of the cottage, and had often been here to tea, but already the Culvertons had made it look different. There seemed to be bowls of flowers everywhere (Miss Lubbock had only had two or three flowers in a silver vase on the window-still), the furniture had been rearranged, the jar of gilded bulrushes had been removed.

"Do sit down," said Mrs. Culverton. "I hope you've not had far to come."

"Oh, no distance at all," said Miss Maple, sitting down on a small mahogany elbow chair, "and I always enjoy a walk." She drew in her breath and took the plunge. "What a magnificent spectacle the Queen's dinner-party to the German Emperor last night at Osborne must have been!"

"Yes," said Mrs. Culverton. "Now about our arrangements, Miss Maple . . ."

"Oh, yes, Mrs. Culverton," said Miss Maple, relieved that she needn't go on to Mr. Gladstone or the gold coinage. "I'm ready to fit in with any arrangements you like."

"I don't want you to give the children any actual lessons. I just want you to take charge of them during the mornings so as to leave me free. Edmund and Richard won't need much supervision. They are fifteen and thirteen years old. But I'd like you to be responsible for Althea and Vere. I don't think you'll find them any trouble."

"Oh, I know I shan't," Miss Maple assured her. "Indeed I shan't."

"Vere's rather stupid, but Althea's fairly intelligent . . . I thought that perhaps you'd take them for a walk this morning and show them the village. I believe that the church is quite interesting."

"Oh, yes, indeed," said Miss Maple, her face lighting up. "Perpendicular. Fan vaulting. A sixteenth-century tomb and new hassocks throughout only last year."

Mrs. Culverton smiled.

"Perhaps you'd like to come out and meet the children now. I think they're in the garden."

They went out into the garden. A burst of laughter led them to where the children were, at the bottom of the Orchard.

It was Vere who had gone there first. Beneath one of the apple trees she had found a discarded garden ornament—a stone owl about two feet high, covered with lichen. She had sat down by it, finding a curious comfort in it, then, after sitting there for some moments, she had picked some daisies, made a daisy chain and hung it round the thick stone neck.

Suddenly Althea, who was idly wandering about the garden, ran down to her with a cry of delight.

"Oh, isn't he a pet! Let's make him a buttercup chain as well . . . Richard!" she called. "There's a lovely stone owl down here. Come and help us to decorate him."

Richard and Edmund sauntered slowly down together. They had been wondering what to do, and this would fill in the time as well as anything else. They lent themselves to the pastime at first with a condescending air of "playing with the little ones," then became absorbed in festooning the figure with daisy and buttercup chains of varying length. Richard chose the largest nasturtium leaf he could find and placed it on the stone head for a hat, and Edmund tried to arrange a rhubarb leaf over the shoulders for a cloak, while Vere, withdrawing from them, stood watching them sombrely under her thick brows.

"Children!" called Mrs. Culverton.

They ran to her, slackening their pace as they caught sight of Miss Maple, whose face wore a set, bright smile. Mrs. Culverton introduced them, and they greeted the newcomer with constrained politeness.

"Miss Maple's kindly going to take you for a walk and show you the village and the church," said Mrs. Culverton. "Which of you would like to go?"

They all offered to go. They were in that slightly uncomfortable no-man's-land that lies between home life and holiday life, and they were glad to have some definite arrangement made for them.

Ten minutes later they were walking down the lane with Miss Maple—Edmund and Althea on one side of her, Richard and Vere on the other.

Miss Maple inspected them with an approval that already had something of proprietary pride in it. The boys looked neat and genteel in their dark suits, long black stockings and boots. Althea wore a pink cotton frock and Vere a rather bunchy frock of butcher-blue alpaca, piped with white.

"Now we must get to know each other," said Miss Maple, assuming the brisk manner that she always used with her young charges. "First of all I'm going to tell you about yourselves, and then I'm going to tell you about myself."

"How can you tell us about ourselves?" said Althea. "You've only just met us."

"Ah," said Miss Maple mysteriously, "I'm cleverer than you think. I can tell what people are like just by looking at them."

She had known the young Culvertons for a few minutes only,

but already they were, in her eyes, children of surpassing intelligence, surpassing charm, surpassing good looks. She had even decided that Vere was a little gypsy beauty, rather in the Italian fashion.

"All right," said Richard, with his one-sided smile. "Fire away."

Miss Maple turned her head to look at Edmund.

"I'll start with the eldest," she said. "Manly. Fond of games. Now, am I right?"

"Well . . ." said Edmund, who wasn't particularly fond of games.

"Conscientious and responsible. Always ready to strike a blow for the right and defend the weak."

This coincided so exactly with Edmund's idea of himself that he gave an embarrassed smile. The others were gazing at her with fascinated interest.

"And now for Richard," said Miss Maple, turning her head to study him. "Merry. An imp of mischief. Lovable. No one can be cross with him for long."

Richard's grin was devoid of self-consciousness. He was not sufficiently interested in himself even to wonder whether the description was a true one. Richard was only interested in other people. He was wondering now why Miss Maple sounded so bright and confident, when really she was shy and nervous. He could see the shyness and nervousness like a prisoner peeping out through the bars of a window. In fact, the description was entirely incorrect. Richard was indolent and happy-go-lucky, with a streak of the incalculable in him that made it impossible to predict his actions, but the suggestion of mischief in his Puck-like face was misleading.

"Not too fond of his lessons," went on Miss Maple archly, "are you, Richard?"

Richard made no answer. He had been reading in *Froissart's Chronicles* last night of the gathering of the English host for the war against France. "They were in number four thousand men-at-arms and ten thousand archers that followed the host afoot." And suddenly he seemed to see them flooding the narrow country lane—men-at-arms in bright armour, archers with green jerkins over their coat of mail. They reached as far as the eye could see, their helmets topping the distant hedges, their armour gleaming through the trees. They jostled one another as they walked. Their lusty laughter rose in eddies. The sound of their marching feet was like a call to battle.

"He's clever," said Edmund, "but he doesn't work as hard as he might. He's rotten at maths. He'll never really get on till he works harder at maths."

The words penetrated Richard's dream and he frowned, wondering how to explain to them that it didn't really matter to him whether he "got on" or not. Whatever it found congenial his mind fastened upon avidly. What it found uncongenial it rejected and could see no reason for not rejecting it.

"I don't like maths, you see," he said.

"And now for Althea," said Miss Maple, turning her bird-like gaze upon Althea. "I think that Althea's what I was at her age, aren't you, darling? Shy and sensitive. And"—glancing at Vere—"devoted to the little one."

Althea smiled. She was pleased with the description. It sounded like someone in a book.

"And now there's only Vere," said Miss Maple. Meeting Vere's scowling gaze, she felt suddenly disconcerted, but continued: "Well, Vere's just the baby. Everyone's pet, aren't you, darling?"

Vere pushed her hair out of her eyes and gave Miss Maple a blank stare.

"She's stupid," said Althea, then, remembering that she was "devoted to the little one," added kindly, "but we don't mind."

"Well, now I'll tell you about myself," said Miss Maple, glad, she could not have told why, to leave the subject of Vere. "I live in a darling little cottage with a sweetly pretty garden at the other end of the village. And I live with my mother. She's the dearest, kindest, loveliest old lady you ever met, witty and full of fun and so sympathetic that everyone brings their troubles to her."

Miss Maple was not trying to deceive herself. She actually saw the ugly pretentious little villa in which she lived as a "darling little cottage" and the disagreeable old woman who had tyrannized over her from childhood as "the dearest, kindest old lady".

"And now we know each other, don't we?" she ended with a little laugh.

Edmund and Althea looked impressed, Richard felt that they knew each other even less than when they started, and Vere had apparently not been listening.

They had reached a stile leading to a path that crossed a field and then vanished into a wood.

"Let's sit down on the stile and have a little rest," said Miss Maple, "and after that we'll go through the wood and back through the village. You must see the church and the farm. And Mr. Bailey at The Red Lion has about sixty rabbits. I think you'd like to see those."

"What does he want with sixty rabbits?" said Edmund.

"He has them for food and to sell, dear," said Miss Maple. "He kills them."

"Oh, how dreadful!" said Althea, remembering to be sensitive.

"Well, we won't think about that," said Miss Maple hastily. "He has some beautiful chinchilla ones that he keeps for pets. You'd love to see those. And he has two dear little girls . . . And now"—she took a paper bag from her pocket—"while you were putting on your things, I ran into the kitchen and wheedled some biscuits out of that darling old cook of yours, so we'll have a little picnic here before we go on, shall we?"

She handed round the bag of biscuits and they sat on the steps of the stile, munching them.

The young Culvertons had never stayed in the country before. Their lives had been divided between the big house at Streatham and—for the summer holidays—lodgings at the seaside. And Miss Maple knew all there was to know about the country. As they sat there eating biscuits, she told them the names of the wild flowers that grew near them in the hedgerows, the names of the trees by the roadside and of the birds and butterflies that flew past them.

"What's that?" said Edmund, as a brownish-grey bird with a white throat appeared for a moment on the top of the hedge, then slipped in among the leaves.

"A white-throat," said Miss Maple. "They won't be here much longer. They go away in the autumn."

"Where do they go?" said Vere.

It was the first time she had spoken.

"They go to Africa, dear," said Miss Maple.

"Africa . . ." repeated Vere slowly. "What's it like?"

Miss Maple considered.

"Open spaces," she said at last vaguely. "Great mountains and rivers. Enormous stretches of bushland. I've got a book at home with pictures of Africa and lots of other places. I'll bring it for you to look at."

"Thank you," said Vere.

"And now, if you've finished, we'll be going on," said Miss Maple, springing down from her seat. "We've got a lot more to see, and time and tide, you know, wait for no man."

They set off along the field path towards the wood. Althea turned round to see Vere still standing by the stile, staring down the road. She was going to call to her impatiently but remembered again that she was "devoted to the little one" and ran back her.

"Come along, darling," she said, taking her hand.

Vere pulled her hand away with a quick fierce movement, and Althea gave her a sharp pinch on the arm. Miss Maple wasn't looking, and Vere wouldn't cry. Vere never cried . . . Then she ran back to join the others, followed more slowly by Vere.

When they emerged from the wood to join the road again, they carried little bunches of wild flowers, whose structure and habits Miss Maple had carefully explained. Only Vere had taken so little interest in the flowers that Miss Maple had picked a bunch for her to carry and she carried it docilely with the others.

They trooped into the church behind Miss Maple and there Miss Maple, who knew the guide-book by heart, pointed out the perpendicular window, the fan vaulting the roof, the sixteenth-century tomb and the new hassocks.

Edmund, who was anxious to have a well-stored mind, listened carefully, storing up the words for future use. To Richard the tomb had turned into Saint Thomas's shrine and King Richard was there paying his devotions, together with a "noble company of lords, ladies and damosels." The gay throng filled the church with colour and movement, the rustle of silk and the clank of spurs. Althea studied the names in the visitors' book and furtively, when no one was looking, wrote "Miss Althea Culverton" in one of the back pages between two other names. Vere stared stolidly about her.

"I don't think there's time to visit the farm this morning," said Miss Maple, as, hot and a little dishevelled, she led her charges out again into the country road, "but we pass The Red Lion on our way home, so we might just call and see Mr. Bailey's rabbits."

The Red Lion lay back from the road behind a large chestnut tree, and Mr. Bailey himself, a genial red-faced man in shirt sleeves, was standing in the doorway.

"It's a public-house, of course," Miss Maple whispered as they approached, "but most respectable. Mr. Bailey gave five pounds towards the new hassocks and always provides oranges and sweets for the Sunday School summer outing. I feel sure that your parents would have no objection to your seeing his rabbits."

Mr. Bailey advanced upon them, his ruddy face beaming a welcome, and Miss Maple introduced the children.

"Yes, come along and look at the rabbits," said Mr. Bailey. "It's the chinchillas you'd like to see, isn't it? Pretty as pictures they are. This way."

He led them round to the back premises and opened a large shed full of rabbit-hutches. The children crowded round.

"Oh, *look* at the baby ones!" said Althea ecstatically.

"Would you two little ladies like to have a couple for pets?" said Mr. Bailey.

"Oh, we'd love it," said Althea.

"Tell you what I'll do, then," said Mr. Bailey. "I'll bring 'em over to Linden Rise this evening. Rare pets, they make. My little maids have one each, haven't you, ducks?"

They turned to see two little girls standing in the doorway. They were dimpled, chubby little girls with grey-blue eyes and dark curls, wearing white sun-bonnets and pinafores and blue-and-white check cotton frocks. They stood there, each with a finger in her mouth, staring at the other children.

"They're twins," said their father proudly. "Like as two peas, aren't they? Come on, Polly and Myrtle, and show the young ladies and gentlemen your pets."

As they advanced into the shed, one of them dropped the rag doll she was holding, and Richard picked it up.

"Which are you," he said, as he returned it, "Polly or Myrtle?"

The child clasped the rag doll and hung her head shyly, but the other child gave him a slow sweet smile that had a hint of roguishness in it.

"She be Myrtle," she said. "She be shy."

Miss Maple looked at her watch and gave a little scream.

"Good gracious!" she said. "We must fly or you'll be late for lunch. Come along, children. Helter-skelter home!"

Chapter Four

"Yes, Emmy was right," said Mrs. Horseferry. "Monied and genteel, but not the cream of Society. You can tell that from their correspondence."

"Yes, ma'am," said Tilly.

Tilly was stacking the lunch things in the sink, ready to wash them up, and Mrs. Horseferry, whose duty had ended with the cooking of the meal, was sitting in the rocking-chair watching her idly.

"No crests," said Mrs. Horseferry.

"No, ma'am," said Tilly after a moment's pause of mystification.

"But Quality," said Mrs. Horseferry. "Definitely Quality. They have the sort of manners that don't show. Jumped-ups have manners, but they show."

"She's got some lovely clothes," said Tilly.

"Y-yes," agreed Mrs. Horseferry. "From good exclusive shops but not the best houses. That's where Quality ends and Society begins."

"Yes, ma'am," said Tilly, furtively popping into her mouth a piece of lemon souffle that Vere had left on her plate.

The food at Linden Rise was a never failing source of amazement to Tilly. Her aunt had been a parsimonious housekeeper and an unimaginative cook. Mrs. Horseferry was an artist. Even today, though Mrs. Culverton and Althea were out to lunch, she had produced a meal for the three children that would have done credit to a London chef. She omitted no detail of flavouring or sauces or dressing that would enhance any dish. She had no thought of the individuals who were to eat the meal, or indeed of the eating

42

of it at all. It was an end in itself. Nothing in it, as far as Mrs. Horseferry could ensure this, must fall short of perfection.

The sweets in particular fascinated Tilly. From a respectful distance, her eyes wide with wonder, she would watch the beating of eggs, the whipping of cream, the dropping of essences . . . It had to be a respectful distance, for Mrs. Horseferry was jealous of the secrets of her craft. Even Tilly must not watch the processes that went to the making of her masterpieces. The lids would droop lower over the sleepy eyes and the voice would take on a deeper, more majestic note.

"Have you nothing better to do, Tilly, than to hang about here?" she would say, and Tilly would scuttle off to sweep the sitting-room floor or dust the bedrooms. Sometimes Tilly would settle herself to a task in the kitchen where she could watch the large deft hands flashing over the table among the eggs and flour and cream and butter, but always the sleepy eyes would turn to her and the deep voice would growl: "Leave that now, Tilly. It's time the landing window was cleaned."

Only this morning, when a new sweet was being prepared, Mrs. Horseferry had set Tilly to scrub the sink and draining-board and clean the taps, so that she must stand with her back to the kitchen-table. It was not that she suspected Tilly of any desire to learn her secrets. It was the ingrained habit of years.

"What was that pudding you made yesterday?" said Tilly, rubbing soap on the dish-cloth.

"Savarin," said Mrs. Horseferry, torn between her instinctive love of secrecy and the artist's longing to talk of her craft, "but you wouldn't find it in any cookery-book. Not as I make it. I met a chef once who'd cooked for foreign royalties and he told me—"

She stopped abruptly. "He told me a lot of things,"

"You made it in two parts, didn't you?" said Tilly reminiscently. "And you put one to stand by the fire while you—?"

Mrs. Horseferry's eyes had almost closed. Her voice seemed to come from the depth of her capacious bosom.

"Attend to your own business, Tilly," she said, "and I'll attend to mine."

"Yes, ma'am," said Tilly.

There was a silence, broken only by the rattle of crockery at the sink. Then Tilly said tentatively:

"I wonder what the children are doing?"

"The young gentlemen are, I believe, in their bedroom," said Mrs. Horseferry, speaking in a gracious voice that showed she accepted the overture. "Miss Vere is in the garden and Miss Althea, of course, is out to lunch with her mama. I don't suppose they'll be back for tea. In the country an invitation to lunch frequently includes tea. Not quite correct, but friendly and informal. They stay, admiring animals and looking at this and that in the grounds and cover considerable distances walking from one object to another till the time has slipped by and an invitation to tea is almost obligatory. Get tea here at the usual time, of course."

"Yes, ma'am," said Tilly, taking the tea-cloth from the rack and beginning to dry the cutlery.

Mrs. Horseferry rose slowly from her chair.

"Well, I'll go and rest now," she said. "When you've finished the washing up and had a wash yourself, Tilly, you may go and sit on the seat by the hedge in the back garden. Mrs. Culverton said that the staff might use that seat in the afternoon, and you ought to get what benefit you can from the sunshine. It"—she had intended to make some references to the bringing of roses into cheeks, but, glancing at the roses already blooming almost rampantly in Tilly's, stopped and ended rather lamely—"is supposed to be highly beneficial."

"Yes, ma'am," said Tilly.

"You might start hemming those dusters that are in the dresser drawer. They are obviously intended for our use, and if there's one thing I dislike in an establishment it's a scarcity of dusters."

She took the laden work-bag that lay on the floor by her chair and went up the stairs, past the boys' bedroom and up the narrow attic ladder.

Edmund was sitting at the table by the window busy with his galleon model. It stood, almost finished, waiting the final touches. Edmund was a slow and conscientious worker and he was working

44

now even more slowly than usual because he was reluctant to bring the work to a close. The last hour's work on a model always seemed to hold the accumulated pride and pleasure of the whole, and he liked to savour each moment of it.

Richard sat on the floor by the bookcase, surrounded by an untidy pile of books.

"What on earth made you bring all those books with you?" said Edmund, looking up from his model, with a note of impatience in his voice. "They're far more than you can possibly read in the time we're going to be here."

"I know," said Richard, "but I like to choose the book I'm going to read from a lot of other books. That's half the fun of reading."

"Well, you've not done much work so far," said Edmund.

Edmund himself had learnt a chapter of his history book, a page of French grammar and a page of Latin irregular verbs each day, and Miss Maple helped him by questioning him on the history chapter and hearing him recite the French grammar and Latin verbs.

"I never meant to," said Richard.

Edmund was conscious of the familiar feeling of mingled pride in his own conscientiousness and envy of Richard's lack of it. Craning his neck, he looked down at the book whose pages Richard was turning.

"What's that?" he said.

"Virgil."

"Virgil?" Edmund knit his brows. "But you aren't doing Virgil at school. You're doing Ovid."

"Yes, but Virgil's more exciting."

Edmund considered this in silence, his bewilderment increasing.

"Where did you get it?" he said at last.

"A secondhand bookshop. The fourpenny shelves."

"Has it got a vocabulary?"

"No, it's just the text. I can muddle along with it."

"It won't do you any good without a vocabulary or notes," said Edmund with a mixture of disapproval and satisfaction in his voice.

Richard gave his sudden Puck-like grin.

"I don't want it to do me good," he said. "I'd hate it to."

Edmund shrugged and returned to his galleon. Richard bundled the books back into the book-case, took up the Virgil and went down to the garden.

Vere lay stretched under an apple tree, an open book in front of her. Tilly was sitting on the wooden seat by the hedge at work on a little pile of dusters. At the end of the lawn stood the rabbit-hutch containing the baby rabbits that Mr. Bailey had given them. They were exactly alike, but Althea's was called Matty and wore a blue ribbon, and Vere's was called Patty and wore a pink ribbon. Both the children had been delighted by the new pets, but were now beginning to tire of them.

"They're terribly sweet," said Althea, "but they're a bit stupid, and it's a bother having to feed them."

Fortunately Polly and Myrtle still took a proprietary interest in the rabbits and would occasionally bring a bag of bran and a basket of lettuce leaves, standing shyly at the gate till someone asked them in.

Richard stopped to look at the book that Vere was gazing at so intently. It was the book that Miss Maple had lent her, *Pictures of Other Lands*. The picture she was looking at now was a brightly coloured representation of Egypt—an expanse of very yellow sand, with a very green oasis in the distance and a very neat pyramid on the horizon, all beneath a very blue sky.

"Well, you've seen that picture," said Richard at last. "Why do you go on looking at it?"

Vere answered without raising her head.

"Because it's far away," she said.

"What do you mean, far away?" said Richard.

"It's not here," she said.

He gave a puzzled smile and went over to the seat by the hedge to join Tilly, sitting on the grass at her feet.

"Hello, Mrs. Noah," he said.

"Hello, Master Richard."

"What are you doing?"

"Hemming dusters, Master Richard."

"Do you like hemming dusters?"

"No, Master Richard."

He opened his book and found his place, but part of his mind was still with Tilly.

"What would you like to do?" he said, looking up at her suddenly.

Tilly laid down her duster and gazed dreamily into the distance.

"I think I'd like to cook," she said.

"Yes," said Richard after a moment's consideration. "It would be fun. Mixing things . . ."

"She put a vanilla pod into the milk for that pudding she made on Sunday."

"Did she?" said Richard, laying down his book. Richard was always willing to have his interest taken from what he was doing to something else, and there were few things that failed to interest him. "What did she do after that?"

"I couldn't see it all, but she made a sort of custard with the milk and she poured it over some squashed-up apples—purry, she calls it—then she beat some more eggs and I didn't see what she did after that 'cause she sent me to clean the bath." She was silent for a few moments, then continued: "She made one with chestnuts and chocolate the other day, but she sent me up to dust the bedroom as soon as she'd started."

"I remember it. It was jolly good," said Richard.

"I saw most of the one she made with tapioca and red currant jelly. I think I could do that one."

"I'm sure you could," said Richard. "It would be fun to try."

"She's got some wrote down in a book," said Tilly, "but she keeps it in her bedroom. I had a look at it once. There's a pudding made of eggs and pork fat and lemon and cinnamon and port wine."

"It sounds awful," said Richard.

"It wouldn't be," said Tilly with simple conviction.

Richard returned to his book.

"Postera jamgue dies primo surgebat Eoo
umentumque Aurora polo dimoverat umbram"

47

"And now the next day was rising from the east," murmured Richard, "and Dawn had moved the shadow . . ." He didn't know what "polo" meant and he didn't know what "umentum" meant, but it didn't matter. He'd go on without them.

"cum subito e silvis . . . When suddenly out of the woods . . ."

He became aware that Tilly was looking down at his book, an expression of bewilderment on her face.

"I can't read it," she said. "Is it foreign?"

"Yes, it's foreign," said Richard.

"Is it a story?"

"Yes, it's a story."

"Is it exciting?"

"Yes."

"What's it about?"

"It's about a man called Aeneas who lost his home in a war and set out to find a new home in another country and it's about all the adventures he had on the way."

"What adventures did he have?"

"He met harpies."

"What's them?"

"Great birds with faces like women, who ate all his food."

"Crikey!" said Tilly, open-mouthed.

"Then he met a giant with one eye called Polyphemus who kept sheep and lived on men. He just took them up and crushed them on rocks and ate them then and there."

"Go on, Master Richard! He never!"

Richard laughed.

"Perhaps you're right," he said. "Perhaps he never."

"Tell me some more," she urged.

"I'll tell you more after tea. I'll tell you the whole story while you're washing up."

"Good gracious!" said Tilly. "What's the time?"

Richard took but the watch that Howard had given him on his last birthday.

"Half past four," he said.

"Goodness! I'll be late with tea," said Tilly. "It's supposed to be at four."

"I'll come and give you a hand," said Richard.

They passed the apple tree where Vere still lay—gazing now at a picture of the Himalayas, the peaks covered with froth-like snow beneath a sky of Reckitt's blue—and went in at the back door.

"The kettle's on," said Tilly in surprise.

"Pixies," said Richard. "Let's go and see if they've set the table."

They entered the dining-room and found Edmund putting the cups and saucers on the table. His lips were pursed, his brows drawn into a frown.

"You're a bit late with tea, aren't you, Tilly?" he said. "We're supposed to have it at four, you know. You shouldn't let yourself get slack just because your mistress is out."

It was an effort to say the words, but he had been rehearsing them as he put on the kettle and laid the cloth.

He did not particularly want his tea and would have preferred to remain upstairs working leisurely on his galleon model, but he considered it his duty as his mother's lieutenant to see that no advantage was taken of her absence. He might not actually have said the words if he had not seen Richard and Tilly talking together in the garden. Richard was too apt to be familiar with servants and the reproof he gave Tilly was meant to apply to Richard, too.

A sudden wave of anger surged over Tilly . . . Edmund's self-sufficiency had secretly irritated her for some time. Only a kid, she thought. No older than me. Giving himself airs. Sauce!

She stood now looking at him in silence, her bosom rising and faffing, a heavy flush spreading upwards from her neck, deepening the red of her cheeks.

"It's all right," said Edmund kindly, taking her emotion as a sign of guilt, "but don't let it happen again. You'd better go and cut the bread-and-butter now."

Tilly went back to the kitchen. Her face was as expressionless as ever, but her anger mounted as she cut the bread-and-butter and took the cake out of the tin. The sauce of it! The *sauce*!

Mrs. Culverton and Althea returned just as the three children were finishing their tea. Mrs. Culverton looked pale and tired. Little stabs of pain were shooting across her temples—the stabs that always heralded her headaches like the tuning up of an orchestra. She had written to Howard asking him to give her a definite date for his arrival at Linden Rise, and he had not replied. She had hoped to hear by this morning's post, but there had been no letter.

Althea, however, was radiant. Dressed in a white muslin frock with a pink sash and a leghorn hat trimmed with imitation daisies, her cheeks flushed with excitement, her eyes alight, she had been a great success at the luncheon party. All the guests had admired her. She had heard an old man call her a "little beauty" and an old lady had referred to her as "that angelic child". Responding to the atmosphere of adulation, she had given to each instinctively what each wanted of her. She had been roguish and kittenish with the old man, grave and wistful with the old lady, artless and tomboyish with a young man who obviously wanted her to be artless and tomboyish. She had believed in fairies with an elderly but childish spinster and had made a conquest of a local ornithologist by intelligent questions and an air of wide-eyed wonder. Elated by her success, she now chattered gaily to the others, describing the garden, the dogs, the guests . . . Edmund watched her with approval, Richard with amusement; Vere, who was in imagination climbing one of the snow-clad peaks of the Himalayas, stared at her vacantly, while Mrs. Culverton silently devised reasons for Howard's failure to answer her letter. The stress of business . . . the slowness of the country posts . . . Perhaps—her heart leapt and a sharp stab of pain shot through her temples—he hadn't written because he was coming himself. Perhaps he was on his way now . . .

In the kitchen Mrs. Horseferry was beginning her stately preparations for the evening meal.

"Get the tea-things out of the way as quickly as you can, Tilly," she said.

"Yes, ma'am," said Tilly.

Anger still smouldered in her. She repeated the words to herself,

"You mustn't let yourself get slack just because your mistress is out" . . . "don't let it happen again." Suddenly she laid down the tea-cloth she was holding.

"I'll just go up to Master Edmund's bedroom and put him out a clean towel," she said.

Mrs. Horseferry nodded majestic permission, and Tilly went upstairs, took a clean towel from the chest of drawers on the landing and entered Edmund's bedroom. There on the table was the almost finished galleon. She had examined it this morning when she made his bed and she was afraid that he might have finished it by now, but he hadn't done. There were still the last touches to be put to it, and Tilly understood the joy and pride of those last touches—a joy and pride that would be dimmed if anyone else played a part in it, however small. Quickly she set to work. The rigging was finished, the upper shrouds attached to the crow's nest, the flags were already glued round the pieces of thread. It only remained to tie the flags in place and lash the anchor to the bows. Just as she was replacing it completed on the exact spot on the table where she had found it, the door opened and Edmund entered. She turned her wooden face to him.

"I've finished it for you, Master Edmund," she said.

His eyes were fixed on the model. There were white patches on his cheeks and his nostrils were pinched.

"You beast!" he said hoarsely. "You *beast!*"

He hit out at her in blind rage, and she hit back, giving him a blow on the cheek-bone with her heavy fist. Then they stood, two angry children, glaring at each other and panting. Edmund broke the silence.

"I'll tell Mother," he said unsteadily. "I'll tell Mother and get you sent away."

He went from the room then, half-way downstairs, stopped . . . The scene that had taken place was so incredible that it couldn't have happened. He didn't lose his temper. He didn't strike girls. It couldn't have happened, and so it hadn't happened. The scene vanished from his mind like something being wiped from a slate.

He was standing in the hall when Tilly came downstairs.

"Don't think any more about it, Tilly," he said. There was graciousness and a faint amusement in his voice. "You meant to be helpful, I know, and I'm sorry I spoke hastily. We'll think no more about it, either of us."

"Yes, Master Edmund," said Tilly in her toneless voice, giving him her blank expressionless stare.

He went into the sitting-room, warmed by a glow of self-righteousness. Tilly had meddled with his things; he had reproved her sharply and then apologized. The whole incident redounded to his credit. He liked incidents to redound to his credit.

As Tilly set the omelet on the table for supper she was aware with quiet satisfaction of the faint blue shadows already gathering round Edmund's left eye.

Chapter Five

Vere walked slowly back from the village, carrying a bag of flour under her arm. Mrs. Horseferry had discovered, immediately after breakfast, that she was "out of flour" and had asked Vere to go to the village shop for her.

Vere was the only one of the children of whom she did not stand slightly in awe. They might be noisy, untidy, unruly—no different from a hundred children whose ears Mrs. Horseferry had boxed in her time—but they were still the Quality and, as such, objects of reluctant respect. About Vere, however, with her straight coarse hair, swarthy skin and generally uncouth appearance, there hung so little suggestion of Quality that Mrs. Horseferry would occasionally send her into the garden to pick mint or parsley or on an errand to the village shop.

On either side of the lane men were working in the fields, cutting and stooking the corn. A cart-horse passed her with three small boys sitting astride on its broad back. A young woman leant out of the upstairs window of a cottage gathering plums from a tree that grew against the house. An old man sat at his open doorway making ropes of onions.

Vere noticed none of these things. Mounted on a camel, she was traversing a boundless desert under a blazing sky. Arriving at an oasis, she dismounted, picked a bunch of dates, drank deeply from a sparkling well, rested a while, then, mounting her camel again, continued her journey towards the pyramids.

She didn't even see Richard, standing by the gate, till she was just opening it.

"Hello," he said.

She was silent for a few moments, while the desert faded away and the garden of Linden Rise took its place.

"Hello," she replied sulkily.

Richard gave her a puzzled glance. When first she looked at him, he had seemed to catch a glimpse of someone quite different from the Vere they knew, but it had vanished so quickly that he couldn't even be sure that he had seen it.

They walked along the path together towards the back of the cottage.

"Where have you been?" said Richard.

"To the shop for flour," said Vere.

The sulkiness lingered in her voice. The sun shone down on the cottage garden, but it was not the sun of the desert. It left her still cold inside, whereas the sun of the desert had filled her with a strange secret glow.

They heard whispers behind them and turned to see Polly and Myrtle standing at the gate with a basket of lettuce leaves. They were smiling shyly, heads lowered beneath dark curls, grey-blue eyes softly alight.

Richard went down to them. Myrtle kept her head lowered, but Polly looked up, her round cheeks dimpling.

"They're for Patty and Matty, please," she said.

"Thanks, so much," said Richard, taking the leaves from the basket. "I'll tell them you called—Patty and Matty, I mean. They often ask after you. Won't you come in and see them?"

But Polly and Myrtle, overcome by sudden shyness, were running back down the road towards The Red Lion as fast as their plump little legs could carry them.

Richard went down to the rabbit-hutch, and pushed the leaves through the netting for the two rabbits.

Edmund was sitting on the seat with Miss Maple, who was "hearing" him a page of Latin verbs. She was inclined to be lenient with him, giving hints or even whispering the right word, with the vague idea that if it wasn't said aloud it wasn't "telling." But Edmund refused to be lenient with himself. At his first mistake he took the book back and learnt the whole page again, while Miss

Maple devoted herself to a complicated piece of embroidery on which a wild tangle of unidentifiable flowers seemed to be struggling for existence against a background of drawn thread.

Althea was on the swing that Edmund had fixed up from a branch of one of the apple trees, pushing herself off the ground with her feet, bending the legs under her to make the swing go higher, wholly possessed by the joy of motion.

The stone owl had been brought up from the orchard and now stood in the middle of the little lawn. Every morning they decked him in fresh daisy chains, buttercup chains, nasturtium hat and rhubarb cloak. Only Vere took no part in it. This morning Richard had given him a Lord Mayor's chain of marigolds.

"Would you like to come and join us, Richard?" said Miss Maple, "We're doing Latin verbs. Not very interesting, of course, but a necessary part of groundwork. *Figo* . . ."

"Richard's lucky," said Edmund. "He can learn things by reading them over once . . . *Figo, figere, fixi, fixum*."

"There's such a thing as fatal facility, you know, Richard dear," said Miss Maple. "*Mergo* . . ."

"Yes, but there's moderation in all things," said Richard. "Edmund goes too far. He took his French grammar to cricket yesterday to learn while he waited to go in to bat."

"Well, I learnt it," said Edmund complacently. "*Mergo, mergere, mersi, mersum*."

The holiday had settled down into a regular pattern, and the children had been absorbed into the village life around them. They "helped" on the farm, had rides on the cart-horses, fished in the river and watched the blacksmith at work. Edmund and Richard played cricket in the evening with the village boys on the green. The freemasonry of established country life was something new to them, and they threw themselves into it wholeheartedly. Only Althea acted the little aristocrat, and she did it so charmingly that no one felt any resentment.

Miss Maple still came every morning as "holiday governess"—an elastic term that included hearing Edmund his lessons, arranging the flowers, doing the shopping, mending the children's clothes, taking the girls for walks and supervising the collections of pressed flowers that she had persuaded them to make.

"I don't like them all squashed up," Vere had objected. "I like them growing."

"But it's botany, dear," Miss Maple had explained, "and you can arrange them in pretty patterns."

"I don't like pretty patterns," Vere had said, and Miss Maple had sighed.

She was reconsidering most of the characteristics with which she had originally endowed the children.

Richard gave the swing a vigorous push that made Althea scream with delight, then went indoors to the sitting-room, where Mrs. Culverton was seated at the writing-table, surrounded by her correspondence.

She raised her head as he entered. Her usually pale cheeks were flushed and the weariness had left her eyes,

"I've just heard from your father, dear," she said. "He's coming down next week."

She tried to speak calmly, but Richard sensed the turmoil of her spirit, and his eyes slid away from hers in sudden embarrassment.

"Oh . . . he said, adding as an afterthought, "Good!"

He was fond of his father, but found something vaguely disturbing in the atmosphere when he was at home.

"And I've had a letter from Mrs. Entwistle," said Mrs. Culverton, taking up an envelope.

Richard gave a puzzled frown.

"Mrs. Entwistle?"

"Yes. You asked Entwistle to stay here, didn't you? His mother's written to ask if next week will be all right."

"I'd forgotten," said Richard slowly.

Entwistle . . . He remembered walking round the playing-field with Entwistle the day he received his mother's letter telling him that she had taken the cottage for the summer holidays.

"Invite any friend you like for a week," she had written, and on an impulse he had invited Entwistle.

Despite Richard's air of *bonhomie* and unfailing good humour, he did not make intimate friends. Entwistle was the closest friend he had, and the friendship was curiously devoid of intimacy. Their mental tastes were akin. Both had the quick keen brain of the scholar. They shared, too, a sense of humour less crude and obvious than that of most of their contemporaries. It was competition with Entwistle that had given the spur to Richard's work at school. Without competition he was apt to become indolent and dilettante. But the friendship remained impersonal. He knew nothing of Entwistle's family. Entwistle knew nothing of his. He had regretted the invitation as soon as he had given it. Somehow he didn't want the atmosphere of school to invade his home atmosphere.

"Let's put him off," he said. "Let's say there's no room."

"We can't do that, dear," said Mrs. Culverton. "We could easily set up a camp-bed in that little room at the end of the passage. Or we could get him a room in the village. He must come, now that he's been invited. I'll write to Mrs. Entwistle and tell her about trains. Perhaps we'd better postpone the expedition to Rotheram Hall till he comes—he and your father."

She tried to keep the note of girlish excitement out of her voice, but Richard was again conscious of that feeling of faint embarrassment.

Rotheram Hall was an Elizabethan house about five miles away that had lately been thrown open to the public, and the Culvertons, under Miss Maple's direction, had organized an expedition to it that was to take place the next day.

"Or perhaps not," she went on. "After all, there are a lot of other interesting places in the neighbourhood to go to. We're getting quite gay, aren't we? Tea at the Vicarage today and to Rotheram Hall tomorrow . . ."

From the kitchen came the sound of a man's voice followed by he rusty cackle that they recognized as Tilly's laugh.

"Tilly and the milkman," said Mrs. Culverton with a smile.

Tilly stood at the open kitchen door, holding the jug into which the milkman had just measured the milk. He was a youth of about nineteen, fair and stocky, with rather bulbous blue eyes and an ingenuous weather-beaten face.

"You all over, that!" said Tilly, pointing to a few drops of milk that had fallen on the doorstep. "Can't move without makin' a mess. Who d'you think's goin' to clean it up?"

"Your job, ain't it?" he grinned. "What you're here for, ain't it?"

He always enjoyed these verbal exchanges with the skivvy at Linden Rise. A queer piece to look at, but she'd got her wits about her.

"Oh, is it?" said Tilly tartly. "If you're so good at other people's business, pity you can't mind your own. Have you nothing better to do than stand about here, messing up people's doorsteps?"

"Not at the moment, I haven't," said the milkman easily. "Couldn't be in a better place, could I?"

Tilly's harsh cackle rang out.

"Depends," she said. "Some folks know better than to stay where they're not wanted."

"Go on!" said the milkman. "Cry your eyes out, you would, if I didn't turn up one morning."

"No, I'm not the sort that cries for joy," said Tilly.

The milkman took up his pail.

"I'll be under the tree on the green at six o'clock," he said, as he prepared to depart.

"Thanks for the warning," said Tilly. "And keep to the path," she called after his departing figure. "Don't go tramping over the lawn. It wasn't made for elephants."

"See you later," said the milkman, as he vanished round the side of the house.

"Not likely!" called Tilly.

She turned back into the kitchen, well pleased by the passage-at-arms. It was a language she had picked up since coming to the village and her progress in it gave her much secret satisfaction.

Mrs. Horseferry stood at the kitchen table, beating eggs. There was a faint smile on her sleepy face. She had listened to the little exchange with approval.

"That's right, Tilly," she said. "Hold your own with them. Always hold your own."

"I'll hold it with *him*," said Tilly, putting the milk-jug into the larder. "Saucebox!"

"But don't go meeting him, now."

"Not likely!" said Tilly.

"You're too young for that sort of thing, but not too young to learn to hold your own with them. Keep them at arm's length. That's the only way. Once you start giving in to them—well, one thing leads to another till, before you know where you are— well, there you are!"

"Yes, ma'am," said Tilly.

"I could tell you some things about men," said Mrs. Horseferry, compressing her lips and beating the eggs as vigorously as if they represented the whole male sex, "that'd make you so's you could never look at a man without shuddering for the rest of your life, but they aren't things I could tell to a young girl like you. Wolves in sheep's clothing, all of them, and some of them not even in sheep's clothing. Give them an inch and they'll take an ell. Hold your own and keep them at arm's length."

"Yes, ma'am," said Tilly.

"And now go and get me some parsley from the garden."

Tilly went into the garden.

Miss Maple was still hearing Edmund's Latin verbs on the seat, and Vere and Althea were playing "shop" on the little path, with sorrel seeds for tea, clover heads for cauliflowers and bunches of tiny leaves for lettuces and cabbages. Vere was the shopkeeper and Althea a succession of customers. Often the children would meet like this on the common ground of childish games and interests before withdrawing again behind the barriers that divided them.

"What do you want, Tilly?" said Althea.

"Some parsley for Mrs. Horseferry, miss," said Tilly.

"We'll sell it to you. Come to our shop to buy it. Get some parsley, Vere. I'll be the shopkeeper now. You be Mrs. Jones, Tilly." She adopted a high-pitched, affected voice. "And what can I do for you, Mrs. Jones?"

Tilly slipped back into the childhood that she had left so recently.

"I want some parsley," she said in a slow languid tone. "The best parsley. Not the rubbish you gave me last time."

"Of course, Mrs. Jones. Certainly, Mrs. Jones. It's the very best parsley."

"How much is it?" said Tilly, examining the chervil leaves that Vere had brought from the hedge.

Miss Maple looked at her watch and closed the Latin grammar book.

"I must be off now, Edmund," she said. "You'll learn the next page tonight, won't you, and I'll hear you tomorrow morning . . . What are you going to do this afternoon?"

"We're going to tea to the Vicarage," called Althea from her "shop". "We go to tea somewhere nearly every day now. It's fourpence a pound, Mrs. Jones."

"The Vicarage?" said Miss Maple, putting her embroidery away into her work-bag. "You pass our cottage on your way to the Vicarage. Start a little early and drop in and see us, will you? It would give us such pleasure. My mother's longing to meet you."

"Yes, we'd love to," said Althea eagerly.

It would be fun to meet Miss Maple's mother. At the mere thought of it a wistful gravity invaded the small exquisite face. Althea was always grave and wistful with old people.

"I'll have two pounds of it, please," said Tilly.

"Certainly, Mrs. Jones. May we deliver it? What's your address?"

Mrs. Horseferry's large form appeared at the kitchen door.

"Hurry up with that parsley, Tilly," she called. "Don't be all day."

Abruptly Tilly shed her childhood, picked a handful of parsley and scuttled back up the garden path.

Chapter Six

The children set off for Miss Maple's cottage soon after three o'clock. Edmund tried to put them through their paces as they walked along the lane, asking them the names of the flowers and trees that Miss Maple had taught them, but none of the three responded. Richard was dreamily watching the smoke of a garden fire that spread a blue mist, shifting and evanescent, across the road, Althea was already in imagination disporting herself at the Vicarage tea-party, Vere was traversing the open spaces and bushland of Africa.

At the bend of the road they were overtaken by the Vicar— a plump little man whose chubby face looked like a merry child's under the round clerical hat.

"And where are you off to this fine day?" he said as he drew abreast of them.

"We're going to tea with you," said Althea.

"Bless my soul! So you are!" he said. "I've been looking forward to it ever since I heard of it, but it just slipped my memory for the moment."

He took his watch from his pocket and consulted it.

"We've started out early," explained Edmund, "because we're going to call at Miss Maple's to see her mother."

"Splendid!" said the Vicar. "I ought to call there myself. I generally call on the old lady once a week and I've let a fortnight slip. Come along. We'll all go there together and then go on to the Vicarage for tea. What about your mother? I hope she's coming too."

"Yes," said Althea. "She's coming straight to the Vicarage at four.

She couldn't come to Miss Maple's with us because she had some letters to write. She's writing to Daddy. He's coming next week."

"Splendid! Splendid! Splendid!" said the Vicar. "Well, here's the cottage."

They stood for a moment or two looking at it in silence.

The only modern house in the village, it had been built fifty years ago by an ironmonger, who had made his small pile in Bellminster and had come out to settle in the country. Of yellow brick, relieved by highly ornamental stone-work, surmounted by a balustrade of disproportionate magnificence, its name, Blenheim Villa, carved above the front door, it struck a sharp note of discord among the mellow country cottages.

As they stood there the front door opened and Miss Maple came running down the short flight of steps. She was flustered and excited and just a little embarrassed. The children, too, felt faintly ill-at-ease. They were accustomed to Miss Maple at Linden Rise, but to meet her in her own home made both her and them in some way different people. They seemed to be meeting her as a stranger for the first time.

Althea, rising to the occasion, held out her hand and said, "How do you do," in a tone of formal politeness, and Edmund coughed to hide his self-consciousness.

"How do you do. Isn't this exciting!" said Miss Maple. "How nice of you to call, Vicar! Come along in, all of you . . . No, wait a minute. Just look at the cottage from here, children. Isn't it charming? A period charm, of course. Mannered and stylized but delightful—don't you think? Come right in and look at the garden."

They trooped through the gate, followed by the Vicar, and stood looking at the two squares of ragged grass, enclosed by privet and broken by patchy weed-infested flower beds. Miss Maple would have liked to make the little garden as trim and colourful as the other gardens in the village, but her mother could never bear to see her daughter engaged on anything that did not directly minister to her own comfort, so Miss Maple had compromised by seeing the garden as she would have liked it to be.

"A bit old-world, of course," she said. "I dislike those highly formal gardens, don't you? Just a suggestion of the wild about it. A combination of nature and formality. Restful, I think, don't you? . . . Now come into the house. Mother's longing to meet you. She adores children."

They went down the narrow stuffy hall to the sitting-room door that Miss Maple was holding open. It was a dark overcrowded little room, with thick damask curtains at the windows, damask hangings, looped and fringed, over the fireplace, a whatnot, a curio cabinet, a rosewood piano with pleated silk front, a bamboo fern-stand, a chiffonier, and, above the chimney-piece, an elaborate overmantel on which a flock of spindly little brackets and china ornaments seemed to be clinging precariously to the surface of the mirror.

Mrs. Maple sat in an arm-chair by the fireplace, huddled in a black shawl, wearing a lace cap trimmed with imitation violets. A pair of small dark malevolent eyes looked out from a maze of wrinkles, and the shrunken mouth was ominously set.

"What are all these children doing here?" she said as the party entered. "Send 'em away."

Miss Maple gave a gay little laugh in which could be discerned a faint note of apprehension.

"They're the young Culvertons, Mother," she said, bending down to speak loudly into the old lady's ear. "My pupils."

"Your what?" said the old lady grimly.

"Pupils, darling," shouted Miss Maple. "I teach them."

The old lady gave a sudden croaking laugh.

"How can you teach them when you don't know anything?" she said.

"There!" said Miss Maple, turning to the children. "I told you how witty she was, didn't I? Come right in and sit down. She wants to see you all. She loves children."

She planted the children on various small seats among the forest of furniture, and the Vicar took the arm-chair opposite Mrs. Maple. Something of the grimness of the old lady's expression relaxed as the small dark eyes rested on him. Miss Maple began to introduce the visitors.

"This is Edmund and this is Althea and this is Richard and this is Vere."

The old lady ignored her.

"Why didn't you come last week?" she said to the Vicar.

While the Vicar, raising his voice and repeating the words several times, was explaining that he had had to attend a conference last week, Miss Maple vanished for a moment and returned with a tin of biscuits, which she handed round to the children. Edmund, Althea and Vere refused, but Richard, seeing the disappointment on Miss Maple's face, took one and began to eat it. It was a dry and very flaky cracknel.

Mrs. Maple's small eyes darted in his direction.

"Who does he think's going to sweep up all those crumbs?" she demanded indignantly.

"That's just her joke," explained Miss Maple hastily to Richard. "She's full of fun," then, raising her voice, said, "ME, Mother."

"You!" said the old lady scornfully. "You, indeed! Thought you said you taught 'em. Well, can't you teach 'em manners?"

Miss Maple laughed merrily and, taking a brass shovel from the fender, began to gather up the crumbs from the carpet, assisted by Richard, who had swallowed the rest of his biscuit at one gulp in order to save further trouble.

"And now who's going to clean that brass?" demanded the old lady. She turned to the Vicar. "No good in the house, this girl of mine. No good at all. Brought home half a pound of rancid butter yesterday."

"It wasn't rancid, Mother," said Miss Maple, raising a flushed face from her crumb-sweeping. "It was only salted. The grocer gave it to me by mistake. It was quite good, but it was salted and you prefer it unsalted, you know."

"I hope you've been getting out of doors a little this fine weather, Mrs. Maple," said the Vicar, coming gallantly to Miss Maple's rescue.

"Oh, yes, indeed," said Miss Maple, slipping the shovel beneath the fern-stand to get it out of her mother's sight. "I took her to the end of the village in the bath-chair yesterday."

"I'm sure you enjoyed it," said the Vicar to Mrs. Maple. "It was a beautiful afternoon."

"Salted, indeed!" snapped Mrs. Maple. "It was rancid."

Althea had made her way over to the china cabinet and was kneeling on the floor examining its contents through the glass doors. The Vicar turned in his chair to share her scrutiny.

"There are some very interesting things there," he said. "Look at those carved peach stones. Do you see the tiny little faces and flowers on them? Wonderful, aren't they?"

"Oh, they're lovely," said Althea, widening her blue eyes and parting her lips in an expression of childish wonder.

The effect, of which she was fully aware, was attractive, and the Vicar was attracted. Smiling indulgently, he began to point out the other curios in the cabinet. Mrs. Maple shifted restlessly in her chair, fixing a baleful glare on Althea. Althea looked up to meet her eyes, and a sudden spark of rivalry passed between the old woman and the child.

"What's that darling little chair made of?" said Althea, deliberately holding the Vicar's attention.

"Ivory," he said.

"And what's that pink stuff?"

"Coral," said the Vicar.

"Ninety next year," said Mrs. Maple. "Not much longer for this world."

The Vicar turned to devote himself to his hostess. The short unequal contest was over, but Althea was well satisfied with the part she had played in it.

"Oh, you mustn't talk like that, Mrs. Maple," said the Vicar. "You're wonderful for your age, you know."

"Oh, well . . ." said Mrs. Maple. Elated by her small triumph, she drew her shawl about her coquettishly. "There's not many can get to ninety and keep their wits about them. I've always had my wits about me. Turned some heads in my time but always kept my own."

She gave her croaking laugh.

"Charming, isn't she?" whispered Miss Maple to Edmund. "I told you she was."

Althea remained kneeling on the floor, looking at the curios and making little exclamations of interest and delight. Mrs. Maple threw her another malevolent glance. Children . . . They were all the same. Stealing the limelight that belonged by right to old age. They ought to be put in their places . . .

"Stop that child breathing on the glass," she said sharply, putting Althea in her place.

The Vicar rose from his seat.

"I'm afraid I must be going now," he said.

"Oh, not yet," said the old lady, contorting her features into a roguish grimace. "You've only just come."

"I'm afraid I must," said the Vicar. "The conference has thrown me behind with all my work. I haven't written my letter for the parish magazine yet, and it ought to be in the printers' hands by tomorrow. There's a vestry meeting tonight and I have some notes to prepare for that and—well, I'm just about snowed under for the time being."

"You see, they all tell her their troubles," whispered Miss Maple to Vere. "I said they did."

The party took their leave, and Miss Maple saw them off at the gate with a brightness that was beginning—just beginning—to show signs of strain.

"What a nasty old woman!" said Vere clearly as they began to walk down the road.

Edmund said, "Vere!" in horrified reproach, Richard laughed and the Vicar hastily began to talk about the weather. Althea, who was tiring of her pose of childish wonder, decided suddenly to be intelligent, and for the rest of the walk asked earnest questions about ivory and coral and the carving of peach stones.

Mrs. Culverton was already seated on the Vicarage lawn when they arrived, looking slender and elegant in a beige *crépon* dress, with green velvet sleeves and a band of green velvet round the hem.

Her eyes rested with approval on Edmund, Richard and Althea, hardening slightly as they turned to Vere. Vere looked stockier and stumpier than ever. . . . Her frock was crumpled. A lock of thick coarse hair had escaped from her white frilled cambric hat and fallen over one eye. The hat was askew where Vere had evidently made an ineffectual effort to push back the lock of hair. The heavy brows were drawn together in their usual scowl. Mrs. Culverton sighed, and for comfort her eyes returned to Althea, fresh and dainty, in her white muslin frock and pale blue sash, smiling prettily as she greeted Mrs. Egerton, the Vicar's wife.

Mrs. Egerton was a pale, fragile-looking woman, with a willowy figure, dark cloudy hair, enormous eyes and a Burne-Jones neck and chin. She always dressed in severe tailor-made fashion, and her air of Pre-Raphaelite languor hid an inexhaustibly vitality and driving power. She sat now behind the tea-table, pouring water from the silver spirit kettle into the teapot, and her guests sat around in a semi-circle, the frills and trains of their light dresses foaming on the grass at their feet. The elder guests had gravitated to one side of the semi-circle, the younger to the other. The younger guests were shy and a little self-conscious. They talked together in lowered voices. The laughter of a gawky girl in red rang out frequently. Edmund set to work at once, handing round one of the wicker cake-stands. Althea sat down on the grass next to the only other little girl there—a plain child with protruding teeth and spectacles whom Althea surveyed with approval.

The elder guests were discussing the recent general election.

"I never thought that Gladstone would get back, but—well, there you are!"

"Disgraceful!" said a military-looking man with a luxuriant white moustache.

"I believe that Redmond and McCarthy have driven a pretty hard bargain with him."

"Yes, I heard that. He's undertaken, I believe, to reinstate all the evicted tenants and release all the political prisoners."

"It's an alliance he'll pay for dearly."

"Home Rule," said the military-looking man, "will be the ruin of the Empire."

"And how do you like Priors Green, Mrs. Culverton?" said a stout lady in a dress of black bengaline and a black lace mantle, heavily loaded with jet. The imitation grapes in her bonnet nodded when she spoke as if in polite interest.

"Very much, indeed," said Mrs. Culverton. "We haven't properly explored the countryside yet, but"—something seemed to glow and sparkle behind her quiet smile—"my husband is joining us next week and we shall probably get farther afield then."

"Splendid!" said the military-looking man. "It's not a bad little place, you know, Priors Green. Out of the world, of course, but none the worse for that."

The others joined in, praising the place with a faint undercurrent of apology as if deprecating the visitor's possible criticisms.

"So completely unspoilt."

"And of course one can always go up to London for a day or two if one wants to."

"London's just a *habit*. I stopped going there years ago."

"There's so little one *need* go to London for."

"Theatres and the Academy . . ."

"Of course. Ellaline Terriss is *wonderful* . . . I saw her in *Pantomime Rehearsal*."

"But our local amateur dramatic society is very good. Everyone said that their performance of *The Private Secretary* was as good as the West End show."

"And the shops in Bellminster are excellent. I must say I prefer to be served by people who know one's background and standing."

"And when you've seen one Academy, you've seen them all. I mean, they're only *pictures*, when all's said and done."

"There's an excellent golf course, you know," said a thick-set, muscular young man with ginger hair and an incipient ginger moustache, "and our village cricket team's the best for miles round."

"All the same," said a woman in lavender silk trimmed with guipure, "village life seems to lack a sort of *focus* when the Hall's empty. I did so hope that someone would have bought it this summer."

"There've been nibbles."

"We don't want a bachelor, of course."

"Oh, I don't know . . ." murmured the mother of the gawky girl.

"No, we want a family with children," said the mother of the plain little girl.

"A family who'll take an interest in sport," said the muscular young man.

"Intellectual, of course."

"Oh, yes. . . ."

"People who'll take part in everything and contribute to things."

"One's subscription lists get into a sad state when the Hall's empty."

"I suppose they'll want a large staff when they come. We may not find it so easy to get staff ourselves, then."

"Thank you for finding me my staff," said Mrs. Culverton to Mrs. Egerton.

"Oh, Miss Maple and Tilly . . ." said Mrs. Egerton. "Miss Maple's a dear and I'm always glad to find her little jobs. It gets her away from that dreadful old woman and gives her a chance of earning a little money, though I believe she isn't allowed to touch a penny of it . . . Actually, I didn't know Tilly, but the headmistress of her school asked me to find her a post and spoke quite well of her. I hope she's satisfactory?"

Mrs. Culverton smiled.

"Oh, yes. She's quite a little oddity, you know. The children call her Mrs. Noah, but she's very good, isn't she, Edmund?"

Edmund, who was passing with the cake-stand, stopped. For a moment an incredible scene flashed into his memory, vanishing almost as soon as it appeared.

"Yes," he said in a tone of amused superiority. "Very willing and anxious to please."

"Now what about a game of croquet?" said Mrs. Egerton, in that gentle weary voice that somehow had the effect of galvanizing everyone around her into immediate action.

The game was soon arranged and, as Mrs. Culverton sat watching it among the other guests, her thoughts went back to her husband.

The reaction from this morning's exultation was gathering over her spirit. Had she, in the letter she had posted on the way to the Vicarage, been over-effusive? Had she said too much . . . or too little? Had she, beneath her pleasure at his coming, shown the hint of reproach that she found it so hard to repress and that always alienated him?

The game was over now. Althea and the plain little girl were setting out for a tour of the grounds.

"It's the first time you've been here, isn't it?" the little girl had said importantly. "I've been here often and I know it quite well. There's a lovely little pond in the kitchen garden with goldfishes in it. Shall we go and look at it?"

"Oh, yes," said Althea gaily. She had enjoyed the game of croquet, during which she had flirted demurely with both the military-looking-man and the muscular youth, and she was ready now to be a child with other children.

The little girl turned to Vere, who was standing by them staring at them blankly and chewing her hat elastic.

"Would you like to come, too?" she said.

"Goodness, no!" said Althea. "We don't want *her.*"

Vere stood, still chewing her hat elastic, watching them impassively as they went away.

The Vicar, with Edmund and Richard, had joined Mrs. Culverton after the game.

"I made several silly mistakes," said Edmund with a preoccupied frown.

Edmund never minded losing a game, but, if he did a thing at all, he liked to do it well.

"Have another shot later," said the Vicar.

"Yes, thanks, I will," said Edmund, brightening.

"Do you think this glorious weather's going to last?" said Mrs. Culverton.

If it was wet, she was thinking, Howard would be bored. But, if it was fine, there would be picnics with the children, long leisurely walks in the evening . . . Her hopes of a second honeymoon were springing to life again, despite herself.

"I certainly hope it holds over tomorrow," said the Vicar. "We have our parish outing tomorrow."

"Where are you going?" said Richard.

"We're taking three wagonette loads over to Westering-on-Sea," said the Vicar with a smile. "Would you like to come?"

Richard looked at his mother.

"May I?" he said.

"If you like, darling," said Mrs. Culverton, "but we'd arranged to go to Rotheram Hall tomorrow, you know."

"Surely you hadn't forgotten that, Richard?" said Edmund reproachfully.

For days past, under Miss Maple's direction, they had been reading the history of Rotheram Hall in an assortment of guidebooks, looking at photographs, studying plans. Miss Maple had also shown them reproductions of the many old masters the house contained, with lectures on the life and work of each artist. All this had inflamed Edmund's desire to see the Hall and destroyed Richard's. He now knew so much about it that he had lost interest in it.

"What are you going to do at Westering-on-Sea?" he said.

"I don't think we've any idea," said the Vicar.

Richard grinned. The expected held no charm for Richard. It was the unexpected that lured him.

"All right," he said. "I'll come with you if I may."

Chapter Seven

Howard arrived on the Friday afternoon. He came by an earlier train than the one he had mentioned in his letter and walked up to the cottage from the station.

Mrs. Culverton had gone up to her bedroom after lunch to rearrange her hair and change into a dress of rose-coloured silk, with a white lace fichu, which he had once carelessly admired, when, happening to glance out of the window, she saw him at the gate and ran downstairs to meet him.

"Well, Edith, my dear," he said, putting his hands on her shoulders and touching her forehead with his lips. "How nice to see you again!"

She responded on a carefully casual note. Any display of emotion, she knew, put him at once on the defensive.

"I hope you had a good journey," she said. "Come along in and look at the place. We like it so much."

And, as soon as he entered, his all-pervading charm filled the little cottage like a burst of sunshine. Tilly gazed open-mouthed at the tall, handsome stranger. Mrs. Horseferry's lids drooped still lower over her eyes as she replied respectfully to his easy, pleasant greeting. Her mind was already at work, burrowing among the hidden secrets of her craft. There were dishes that her pride would not have allowed her to prepare for a woman and a handful of children, but now that the master had come . . . The children shared the general excitement, welcoming the new element that Howard's arrival brought to the holiday, aware that, while he was with them, discipline would be relaxed, misdemeanours pardoned.

"I've done my best to look after Mother and the children," said

Edmund, with the air of a viceroy handing over the insignia of office to the reigning sovereign.

"Good for you, old chap!" said Howard, in a manner that Edmund secretly considered inadequate to the occasion.

"Mother's had one or two bad headaches," said Edmund.

"Yes, she does," said Howard without emotion.

At Howard's coming the whole holiday became keyed up to a quicker tempo. His good looks and charm caused a small flutter in the neighbourhood. There were picnics, tea parties, dinner parties. Each day was now marked by some small festivity, and Miss Maple's duties were largely confined to looking after Vere when the others went out.

"It's too far for you, darling," Mrs. Culverton would say. "It would only tire you."

She would not have admitted, even to herself, that Vere's presence spoilt what was otherwise a delightful family picture—herself and Howard and three good-looking, high-spirited children.

Howard treated all his children with effortless geniality. Althea was his favourite; to Vere he was completely indifferent; his two sons, whom he had found amusing as small boys, now bored him considerably, though he was careful to conceal all signs of his boredom. Howard, who was essentially a simple man, had made a sort of pact with life. He was prepared to be pleasant even in the most difficult circumstances if life in return would be pleasant to him, and, when life broke the compact, as it frequently did, he felt aggrieved and cheated.

With the passing weeks Mrs. Culverton began to show signs of strain. The shadows deepened round her blue eyes. Her cheeks grew thin and hollowed beneath their transparent flush of happiness.

"You're looking very tired, my dear," said Howard. "Why don't you take a day or two in bed?"

But she couldn't do that. Even here, even in this remote country village, she seemed to be surrounded by enemies. The doctor's eldest daughter was a beauty, though hardly out of her teens. Mrs. Redburn, the widow who lived in the bungalow just outside the village, was handsome in the full-figured, dark-eyed fashion that appealed so irresistibly to Howard. She had to be always in evidence, always on her guard. Behind the part of her that talked and smiled and tried to give Howard the pleasant uncritical atmosphere he loved, lurked a spy—watching, listening, taking notes. Desperately she strove to keep the spy hidden from him, aware that at the first signs of its presence he would take to flight. And it wasn't only the casual, social contacts of Priors Green that she felt she must watch unceasingly. Always in the background was the thought of—that woman. Through their most casual conversation suspicion twined itself like a dark thread . . . *She* must have told him that . . . He must have been there with *her* . . . He must have heard from *her* this morning . . .

So far, however, Howard was enjoying the holiday. He liked the countryside, was amused by the round of local gaiety and was agreeably surprised by the standard of comfort at the cottage. For Mrs. Horseferry, who had never felt quite happy about offering the Quality a "light supper," began to prepare a series of carefully thought-out, perfectly cooked dinners. She made heavy inroads into the store of wine that was kept in the cupboard under the stairs, putting Madeira into the beefsteak stew, claret into the casseroled mullet, sherry into the whiting *au gratin*. Her own private stock of gin needed now constant replenishing. Each evening her eyes became a little more widely open, a little more glassy, her movements a little more deliberate, the dignity with which she received Howard's compliments a little more stately. Absorbed in her tasks, she had less attention to spare for Tilly, and Tilly would creep near her to watch the various stages of each process . . . till the glassy eyes would turn on her and the sleepy voice would say, "Have you no work of your own to attend to, Tilly, that you must poke and pry into mine?" and Tilly would retire, abashed, to sweep the floor or wash up the tea-things.

Entwistle arrived the week after Howard. He was a fair, slightly built boy with a face that seemed to be set in a pattern of immutable gravity. He had, it seemed, come to Linden Rise for the sole purpose of writing a magazine in collaboration with Richard, and he allowed nothing to interfere with his purpose. The two made the little box-room their headquarters and would retire there immediately after breakfast, spending the morning in the composition of poems, stories, articles. The rest of the family he ignored. Edmund was relieved at not being expected to fraternize with a schoolfellow of lower standing, but Althea was puzzled and mortified by the situation. All the other friends of Edmund's and Richard's who had visited the family had made much of her, but Entwistle seemed neither to see nor hear her. As Tilly, watching with slightly malicious interest, put it, "She brought out her whole bag o' tricks and he didn't even know she was there." Gradually it became a matter of supreme importance to Althea that he should yield to her charm. As the days went by and still he showed no signs of recognizing her presence, she began, for no particular reason, to fix all her hopes on the day of the expedition to Bellminster. On that day, she decided, he would capitulate . . .

The expedition to Bellminster had been planned in a vague fashion ever since the beginning of the holiday, and it was finally arranged for the last Saturday of Entwistle's visit. They made their plans on the Friday evening, sitting in the garden after tea. Miss Maple had drawn up a time-table for them—an hour in the twelfth-century parish church, half an hour in the public gardens, an hour for the ruins of the castle, two hours for a visit to the Roman villa just outside the town . . . but the Culvertons' thoughts turned chiefly to the shops in High Street.

"I must get some new gloves," said Mrs. Culverton, "and replace that milk-jug that Tilly's broken. She's rather clumsy."

She spoke absently. Howard had gone into the village as soon as he had finished his tea and she was tortured by a suspicion that he had gone to post a letter to his mistress.

"Yes, but she's a well-meaning little creature," said Edmund.

It gave him deep satisfaction to hear anyone criticizing Tilly, though he always put in a good word for her when they did—and that, too, gave him deep satisfaction.

"I've got a shilling," said Althea. "I'd like to buy a little present to give to Miss Maple."

She threw Entwistle a glance to see if he was touched, but apparently he wasn't.

"I've got five shillings," said Edmund. "I want a new pencil-box. I'd like to get one with a picture of the castle or the church on it. It would make a nice souvenir. How much money have you got, Richard?"

"None," said Richard.

"You were an idiot to spend all your money on that silly parish outing," said Edmund.

Richard grinned.

"I'll borrow from you if I want any," he said. "You won't need all that five shillings for a pencil-box."

Richard had enjoyed the parish outing. He had played cricket and joined in races on the beach and had helped Polly and Myrtle hunt for shrimps in the pools. They had gone the round of the little shops on the front, and Richard had bought for each of the twins a necklace and a little box made of shells. When Richard had money he always spent it and didn't much care whom or what he spent it on.

"I'll see," said Edmund. "It's rather a bad habit to get into, you know, borrowing money."

"Perhaps," said Richard, "but lending's a good one. It says in the Psalms that the good man is merciful and lendeth, so I'll let you be the good man and I'll be the bad one."

Edmund gave a constrained smile.

"Well, of course," he said, "that was written a long time ago, and the words probably mean something quite different in the original."

"I'd like to buy something for Mrs. Horseferry and Tilly, too," said Althea.

She threw another glance at Entwistle as she spoke, but he wasn't listening. He hadn't been listening to any of it. He'd been composing the last few lines of a poem called "The Wood" that he was writing for the magazine, which they had now named *The Torch*.

> "*And dim mysterious sunlight filled the wood,*
> *Piercing the trees like arrows . . .*"

76

He said the words to himself, then knit his brows, wondering if "mysterious" was right . . .

Mrs. Culverton looked out of the window.

"Your father's a long time," she said, trying to speak casually. Entwistle rose to his feet.

"Come on, Richard," he said. "Let's go for a walk and then get to work on *The Torch*. There isn't much time left."

"Right," said Richard. "Where shall we go?"

"Up the field and through the wood," said Entwistle. He was a conscientious craftsman and thought that the walk might suggest a better adjective than "mysterious".

As they were going through the orchard, Entwistle stopped suddenly.

"You know, Richard. . ."

"Yes?"

"I wonder if we ought to have a scientific article. Most magazines have scientific articles."

"What sort of a scientific article?" said Richard.

"Well, we might have one on sound waves."

"We don't know anything about them."

"I was reading something about them the other day. There are probably hundreds of sound waves that we don't catch and this means there are hundreds of sounds that we don't hear. I might make a poem of it."

"I don't think I should," counselled Richard. Though he possessed little of the creative instinct, he had a keenly critical mind, and secretly found Entwistle's poetry somewhat flat. "I think an article would be better."

"Perhaps," said Entwistle. Suddenly he noticed Vere sitting in the long grass of the orchard near them. "Hello . . . What are you doing there?"

"I'm thinking," said Vere.

"What about?"

"I've been listening to what you said . . . Perhaps the flowers are singing as well as the birds. Perhaps the trees are singing . . ."

Entwistle gave a short amused laugh and the two went out through the gate at the bottom of the garden.

Althea had seen the little exchange from the dining-room window. She went down the orchard to Vere, her small face tight and set.

"You've got mud on your pinafore," she said, "and your face is dirty and your hair's untidy. Aren't you ashamed of looking like a scarecrow?"

"No," said Vere simply.

The memory of the kindly smile that Entwistle had given Vere had added a sting of rivalry to Althea's determination to win his friendship. She made her plans as she went to bed. Entwistle's bedroom overlooked the garden. She would get up early the next day—the day of the expedition to Bellminster—put on her new frock of peach-coloured alpaca with the white lace collar and go down to the garden. Entwistle would hear her singing to herself and would look out of his window to see her standing by the rabbit-hutch, feeding Patty and Matty. She would stop singing to talk to them . . . Happiness bubbled up in her as she considered the picture through Entwistle's eyes. It was a simple plan, but Althea had often found that simple plans were best.

She awoke early, dressed quickly, brushed her fringe to a shining smoothness, took out the "curl rags" in which her hair was done up for the night, combed out the ringlets, twisted them round a small but expert finger and put on the new peach-coloured dress. It buttoned up the back and was difficult to fasten, but she managed it at last and ran down to the rabbit-hutch. And there she stopped short with a gasp of dismay. For one of the rabbits lay dead on the floor of the hutch. And it was the one with the blue ribbon— the one that belonged to her, She stood for a few moments staring at the stiff inert ball of fur. She wasn't particularly fond of Matty, but Matty's death threw out her plans. She couldn't very well start singing to herself now . . . Then suddenly another plan occurred to her, and her eyes brightened. Glancing up to make sure that Entwistle was not at his window, she quickly changed the ribbons and ran back to her bedroom.

Matty's death was not discovered by the others till after breakfast.

It was Richard who discovered it, going down to start the daily embellishment of the stone owl.

"We mustn't let the old chap think we've forgotten him," he said, "just because we're going on the spree."

Then suddenly he saw Matty lying stiffly on the floor of the hutch.

"Edmund!" he called.

Edmund came down with Entwistle. Vere followed them slowly.

"Look!" said Richard. "I'm terribly afraid it's dead. Is it yours, Vere?"

"Yes," said Vere.

And then, when the stage was set, Althea arrived, running down the garden, her ringlets flying out behind her.

"I'm afraid that Vere's rabbit's dead, Thea," said Edmund solemnly.

A look of concern flashed into Althea's face, followed by a look of tenderness and compassion.

"Oh, darling," she said, "I'm so sorry. You must have mine instead. I don't want it. I want you to have it. You will have it, won't you?"

Vere's answer was drowned by a chorus of appreciation. Mr. and Mrs. Culverton had joined the group.

"Althea, how kind of you!"

"How sweet of you, darling!"

"Aren't you grateful, Vere?"

Althea threw a swift glance at Entwistle, then lowered her eyes. The plan had succeeded. He was looking at her with a sudden kindling of interest. For the first time he was conscious of her as an individual.

"That's decent of you," he said in his clipped curt accents. "Terribly decent."

At that moment Tilly came down to report that the fishmonger had called.

"And, please, ma'am, Mrs. Horseferry says would you like salmon or turbot for tonight?"

"I'll come and see to it," said Mrs. Culverton.

She rested her hand for a moment on Althea's shoulder before she went indoors.

"We won't forget this, Thea," said Mr. Culverton as he turned to follow his wife.

"Let's bury it," said Richard, taking Matty out of the hutch. "Come on."

"I don't think I want to come," said Althea in a small, unsteady voice.

"No, of course not," said Edmund sympathetically.

"It was jolly decent of you," said Entwistle again.

The three boys took the rabbit down to the end of the orchard. Vere trailed slowly behind them. Althea was left alone with Tilly.

"Vere's rabbit died," explained Althea a little condescendingly, "and I was so sorry for her that I gave her mine."

Tilly gave her a long expressionless stare.

"I was looking out of the kitchen window," she said, "and I saw you change the ribbons."

Althea's face went white, then crimson, but she said nothing. They stood staring at each other in silence. Althea's eyes were hard and dry like pebbles. Neither of them blinked or flinched. Then Mrs. Culverton called, "Come and get ready, Althea," and Althea turned and ran back to the house.

They were all ready when the cab that was to take them to the station drew up at the door. Mrs. Culverton had taken particular pains with her appearance, putting on a new tailored dress of grey tweed with Eton jacket and yellow silk waistcoat, giving nearly half an hour to the arrangement of her hair beneath the black straw hat trimmed with cowslips. She had hoped that Howard would make some comment on it, but he had made none.

It wasn't till the cab was just drawing up that they noticed Vere. She had joined them, looking unusually neat, wearing her best hat and clutching her purse in her hand. She evidently took for granted that she would be going with them, while they had taken for granted that she would be staying at home.

"Oh, darling," said Mrs. Culverton in dismay. "I hadn't—I mean, I think you'd find it too tiring."

"There isn't room for her in the cab," said Althea.

"We might just squeeze her in," said Richard.

"Not in this heat, my dear boy," said Mr. Culverton. "One of you will have to go up beside the cabman, anyway."

"I could walk to the station and get the next train," said Entwistle.

"Nonsense!"

"It will be a long day, darling," said Mrs. Culverton, "and much too tiring for you. You'll be far happier at home. Miss Maple will probably be coming along later and you could go for a nice walk with her. You don't mind staying at home, do you?"

"No," said Vere.

Mrs. Culverton gathered up her skirts with an elegantly gloved hand to enter the cab.

"Good-bye, darling."

"Good-bye."

Vere watched them till they were out of sight then went back into the cottage.

Tilly set about her morning's work. There was a lot of tidying up to be done. They left things all over the place, but that was one of the privileges of the Quality, to leave things all over the place. She thought of Miss Althea—mean little thing! Then suddenly she thought of Vere. She had felt slightly worried at the thought of the child's not going to Bellminster with the others. She had an idea that she had been looking forward to it, counting on it. She hoped she wasn't fretting. Miss Maple, supposing that all her charges were included in the expedition, had stayed at home with her mother, and Tilly had an uneasy sense of responsibility. On pretext of fetching some mint, she went into the garden to see what the child was doing. She found her sitting on the grass in the orchard. She had taken off her hat and was sitting motionless, staring in front of her.

"What are you doing, Miss Vere?" said Tilly kindly.

"I'm listening," said Vere, her eyes still fixed on the distance.

"But there's nothing to listen to," said Tilly.

"Yes, there is. Quietness has a sort of sound," said Vere slowly. "A sound all of its own. I'm listening to it."

"Oh," said Tilly. She still stood there uncertainly.

Vere turned to her with a faint smile.

"It's all right," she said. "I don't mind not going with the others. I'm beginning to like being alone. I'm beginning to make friends with it."

Tilly picked her mint and returned to the kitchen.

"Funny kid, Miss Vere," she said to Mrs. Horseferry.

Mrs. Horseferry made no comment. She had been silent and withdrawn all mornings steering an unsteady course across the kitchen, speaking, when she had to speak, in a blurred, indistinct voice.

"Are you not feeling well, ma'am?" said Tilly.

Mrs, Horseferry turned bloodshot eyes on her.

"I'm feeling extremely ill," she said, "but that," with dignity, "does not concern you. Kindly mind your own business."

"Yes, ma'am," said Tilly.

She had learnt to accept every manifestation of Mrs. Horseferry's humour—good or bad—without question, but she still felt a little worried about Miss Vere. Later in the morning she went into the garden again. Vere was sitting in the same place, but she had her box of crayons by her side and a large exercise-book on her knee. She was working absorbedly . . . a stretch of yellow sand . . . a cluster of trees . . . a red sun . . . a grey pile on the horizon. The whole had a strength and certainty about it that held Tilly motionless for some minutes. Then:

"Nothing I can do for you, is there, Miss Vere?"

Vere shook her head and Tilly returned to the kitchen.

The party returned soon after five o'clock. They had seen the castle and the Roman villa, had lunch at The Blue Dragon and done their shopping in High Street. The children had spent all their money (Richard had borrowed two shillings from Edmund to buy a copy of Defoe's *Memoirs of a Cavalier* at a secondhand bookshop) and were tired, happy and slightly bemused by the day's events. They had all treated Althea with special consideration (Entwistle had sat next her at lunch and waited on her assiduously) and her lips were curved into a little smile of triumph as she walked up the path, carrying her parcels.

On Mrs. Culverton's delicate face the lines of strain were deeply etched. She had felt proud and happy as she sat opposite Howard at the lunch-table in the dining-room of The Blue Dragon, with the children around them, but even then, beneath the happiness, nagged the familiar pain of jealousy, as she noted other women— younger, smarter, better-looking than she was— and caught the glances of casual admiration that Howard sent them. He was bored with her already, she told herself . . . perhaps even now, even as he smiled amusedly at Althea's chatter and teased Edmund about the tie that he had bought instead of the pencil-box, his thoughts were with that woman . . . Perhaps he was planning to return to her tonight . . . tomorrow . . . the next day.

She stopped at the bottom of the stairs and handed two small parcels to Richard.

"Will you take Mrs. Horseferry and Tilly their presents, Richard?" she said, "I'm too tired to face them."

Richard went to the kitchen. It was empty. He took the two china brooches from their wrappings and put them on the table. Then the door opened and Tilly entered. Her round wooden face wore a comical expression of dismay.

"Look, Tilly," said Richard, handing her one of the brooches. "Mother's bought you this."

"Oh, Master Richard!" said Tilly mournfully.

She didn't see the china brooch. She only saw Mrs. Horseferry stretched on her bed in the attic bedroom, breathing stertorously, an empty gin bottle on the floor beside her.

"What's the matter?" said Richard.

"Oh, Master Richard, I couldn't think why she wasn't down starting of the dinner, and I've just been up to see and—and she's dead drunk. I can't rouse her nohow."

"Drunk?" said Richard. "Who?"

"Mrs. Horseferry, Master Richard . . . Oh, Master Richard, they mustn't know. It'd shame her if they knew and—and they might send her away."

"But what can we do?" said Richard.

A light of resolution shone in Tilly's round black eyes.

"I dunno what she was going to make, but there's some veal in the larder and we could make what she calls a frikassy of it. I know how to do it 'cause I've watched her. You cut it into little bits and put it in a casserole with white sauce and pepper and nutmeg and what-not and a bay leaf and some lemon slices. Then you put a mushroom in and when it's done you put in a tablespoonful of cream and the yokes of two eggs beat up in cream and you boil it up and take out the bay leaf and lemon and—"

"Sounds a bit complicated," said Richard doubtfully.

"No, it isn't. It's all in the book and she's left it downstairs in her drawer. Look!" She took a tattered notebook out of one of the drawers in the dresser. "She'd kill me if she knew I'd touched it, but she's too far gone to know anything. Let's try and do it, Master Richard."

"All right," said Richard, infected by her eagerness. "We can have a shot, can't we?"

Tilly put the book on the table and turned over the pages.

"Here it is . . ."

The door opened and Althea entered. She had put on a white pinafore over the peach-coloured frock.

"Mother's gone to bed with a headache, Tilly," she said distantly. "She doesn't want anything to eat. The rest of us will have dinner at the usual time, please."

The small childish face above the starched frills wore a comical expression of hauteur.

"What's the matter with *her*?" said Richard in amused surprise as the door closed behind her.

"Never mind her," said Tilly. "Listen. 'Blanch in salted water two pounds of lean veal, then cut into one-and-a-half inch squares' . . ."

Elbows on table, heads together, they read the directions with frowning concentration.

Chapter Eight

It was the last day of the holiday and a sense of unreality was beginning to invade the pleasant, timeless atmosphere of life at Linden Rise. Once more the children had the feeling of entering the bleak no-man's-land that stretches between one existence and another . . . between holidays and home . . . between home and school.

Entwistle had departed, taking his copy of *The Torch* with him.

"I'll make another copy out for you, Richard," he said, "and send it to you."

"Don't bother," said Richard. "I don't want one." Entwhistle had stared at him uncomprehendingly. He couldn't understand that the magazine now belonged to the past, and Richard had no interest in the past.

After the day of their visit to Bellminster Entwistle had treated Althea with grave politeness and an air of distant admiration that slightly disconcerted her. She had won her triumph, however, and was well content with it. She would have found it difficult to live up to the standard she had set herself and felt no regret at his departure.

The general atmosphere of restlessness extended to the kitchen. Mrs. Horseferry's good humour had vanished. Drinking more heavily, she became morose and silent. Since the evening when Richard and Tilly had cooked the dinner (Tilly had, in her excitement, picked a laurel leaf instead of a bay leaf and even dropped it into the *fricassée,* but Richard had retrieved it in time and none of the others had suspected that the meal had not been cooked by Mrs. Horseferry herself) she had never again been incapable of carrying out her duties, but sometimes it was all she could do to steer her erratic course across the kitchen floor. Her zest had worn itself out. She allowed Tilly to take a hand in the cooking without comment and even Howard's appreciation now failed to thrill her. She was counting the days before she could return to her snug bed-sitting-room in Bellminster.

It was Howard's idea to give a party in the garden on the last Saturday of their visit, and for that afternoon the disintegrating threads of the holiday seemed to gather themselves together again into a pattern. The afternoon was fine and sunny. From the garden they could see the hills rising up from the valley like a curtain, and above them fleecy clouds hung motionless in the blue sky. London sweltered in a heat wave, but here the air was fresh and keen, with a hint of autumn in its crispness.

As if determined to give his wife no cause for complaint, Howard devoted himself chiefly to Mrs. Maple, who arrived in a monumental bath-chair that completely hid the small panting form of Miss Maple and appeared from the front to be self-propelled.

"She's wonderful today," said Miss Maple breathlessly, as she manoeuvred the chair into the shade of an apple tree. "Quite at her best."

The old lady snarled as the wheels of her chair hit the trunk of the tree. Then she caught sight of Howard and twisted her wizened features into an arch grimace. Howard obeyed the invitation and set himself to wait on her, fetching her tea and raspberries and cream, responding gallantly to her ogress-like advances.

Miss Maple flitted about among the guests, proudly displaying her familiarity with the family and her knowledge of their ways. . . . "Oh, yes, we clipped the hedge last week, Edmund and Richard and I. We had great fun doing it." . . . "The children put daisy-chains on the owl every day." . . . "We call her Mrs. Noah." . . . "Do you remember, Althea darling?" . . . "Wasn't it funny, Richard, when . . .?" The thought of the Culvertons' departure was like a black tunnel at the end of a sun-lit patch. She was, of course, more than half in love with Howard; no one had ever been as dignified and aristocratic as Mrs. Culverton, no children as delightful as

Edmund and Richard and Althea and Vere. Already she was forgetting Edmund's pomposity, Richard's irresponsibility, Althea's vanity and Vere's sullenness. In any case she had only half glimpsed these failings and blamed herself for seeing them more than the children for possessing them. Certainly the children looked their best this afternoon—handsome (even Vere looked less unkempt than usual), charming, unaffected and well-mannered.

The group round Mrs. Culverton at the tea-table was discussing her imminent departure.

"I'm so sorry you're going. We shall miss you."

"You'll come again next year, won't you?"

"Perhaps . . ." said Mrs. Culverton.

But she knew that she wouldn't come again next year. She didn't quite know what she had expected of the holiday, but, whatever it was, it had not been given her.

Mrs. Egerton was leaning back languidly in her basket-chair. She wore a tailored suit of dark blue linen. Beneath the plain straw hat the thick coils of her hair seemed too heavy for the slender white column of her neck. Her great dark eyes seemed almost to fill the pale oval of her face.

"I always think," she said in her dreamy, wistful voice as she looked round the garden, "that that seat would look better under the apple tree."

As if impelled by a sudden irresistible force, half a dozen of the guests sprang to their feet to move the seat.

Tilly passed with a tray of cakes and sandwiches.

"Oh, Tilly," said Mrs. Egerton gently.

"Yes, ma'am," said Tilly, stopping short in her progress.

"When Miss Lubbock comes back I've arranged for you to stay here as her maid. The maid she had before has got married, you know, and I think you'll suit each other excellently."

Questions, comments, expostulations rose to Tilly's lips and died away. Meeting those gentle, wistful eyes, she knew that questions, comments, expostulations would be useless. The thing was settled.

"Yes, ma'am," she said and proceeded on her way.

When the guests had gone, Mrs. Culverton went up to her

bedroom to change into a warmer dress. As the sun dipped westwards, a chill had begun to invade the air and a mist was rising from the river. In her bedroom she sank down wearily into the chair by the window and let her gaze rest idly on the distant horizon. She did not turn her head even when Howard came into the room.

"Tired, my dear?" he said as he closed the door.

She made no answer. He went to the other window and stood there, his hands in his pockets.

Suddenly she turned to him.

"Why don't you go to her?" she said unsteadily. "You're thinking of her all the time, aren't you? You're bored to death here with me. You never wanted to come. You only came because you were sorry for me . . . Go to her," she continued, her voice rising hysterically. "I can't bear it any longer. I'm so sick of it all . . ."

She dropped her face into her arms. He came and stood by her. The furrows in his cheeks were deeply graven.

"Don't, Edith," he said. "Please don't."

She raised her ravaged face.

"All these years . . . I can't go on with it . . . It's killing me . . ."

Her voice broke into sobs. He hesitated then went from the room.

After a few moments she followed him. He was in the box-room taking his suitcase from a pile of boxes. She laid a hand on his arm.

"Don't leave me, Howard," she said. Her face was blotched with tears, but she had regained her self-control. "There are only a few more days left. Stay with us for those."

He put his suitcase back without speaking.

"Howard," she said, making an effort to keep her voice steady, "I promise I'll never ask you this again, but—won't you give her up?"

There was a long silence.

"I can't," he said at last.

Looking into his eyes, she saw an unhappiness as deep as hers. She turned from him and went back to her bedroom. He descended the staircase and, going to the sitting-room, took up the newspaper, fixing his eyes on it unseeingly. He looked old and tired, his face stripped of its easy charm.

Tilly entered the kitchen with a laden tray.

"They've had a row," Mrs. Horseferry said, interest in the family flickering again into momentary life.

"Who?" said Tilly, setting the tray on the table,

"Him and her," said Mrs. Horseferry. "Not much of one," she added regretfully, "and I couldn't hear what they said. He didn't say much. She did the talking. Gave it him good and proper."

"What a shame!" said Tilly. "And him such a lovely gentleman!"

"It's the lovely ones that cause the trouble," said Mrs. Horseferry.

Then the children, who had been wheeling Mrs. Maple back to Blenheim Villa, returned and scattered over the garden helping to clear up the debris of the party.

"By the way, Richard," said Edmund suddenly, "what about those two shillings you borrowed from me?"

"What about them?" said Richard.

"When are you going to pay me back?

"I don't know."

"How much money have you got?"

"None."

Edmund put down the chair he was carrying and considered the matter.

"It isn't that I want the money. I don't. But you oughtn't to borrow money and not pay it back. It's a very bad habit to form."

Richard quirked an eyebrow.

"What shall I do, then?"

"I'll think about it," said Edmund, "and let you know."

The next day the children began to collect their possessions ready for packing—their pressed flower collections, the things they had bought at the village shop, the books that lay scattered over the house. They embellished the stone owl with a tiara of dahlias and sweet peas ("Let's give the old chap something to remember us by all his life," said Richard), and arranged that Polly and Myrtle should come in the evening to take Patty back to The Red Lion.

89

Mrs. Culverton was in bed with a headache, and Howard wandered aimlessly about the cottage, rousing himself occasionally to talk with mechanical cheerfulness to the children.

"Daddy looks worried," said Althea.

"Yes, he does rather," agreed Edmund.

"Perhaps he's lost all his money," said Althea.

In stories where the head of the household lost his money, one of the children always rose nobly to the occasion, getting work, earning money and being generally admired and loved . . . and Althea intended to be that one.

"No, I don't think he has," said Edmund slowly.

"What is it, then?"

"I don't know," said Edmund.

He didn't know, but he was secretly a little troubled—less on his parents' account than his own—by the atmosphere of tension. He felt vaguely that any open breach between them would affect his own dignity and position, and he was keeping an anxious eye on the situation.

Richard went into the kitchen after tea and found Tilly sitting at the table slicing runner beans.

"She's passed out again," said Tilly, "but it's only chops, so it doesn't matter."

"They know, anyway," said Richard. "I heard Father say to mother that the woman drank like a fish, but she was an artist and artists must be allowed their vagaries." He took a knife from the dresser and, sitting down at the table, set to work on the beans. "I'm doing them better now, aren't I? Mine are almost as thin as yours. But it's dull once you've got the knack. I wish they popped like peas."

"More than the pop, you like," said Tilly with her hoarse cackle. "You didn't leave me enough to cook, not the last time you did them for me."

"They were too good to cook," said Richard. "There's poetry in peas. There's none in beans . . . How are you going to do the chops?"

"I could do 'em devilled," said Tilly thoughtfully. "I watched her do 'em that way last week. You want cream and cornflour and mustard and cayenne and Worcester sauce. And butter, of course. But I think I'll do 'em plain."

"Yes, do them plain," said Richard. "We've gourmandized enough.

> *"Persicos odi, puer, apparatus;*
> *Displicent nexae philyra coronae;*
> *Mitte sectari, rosa quo locorum*
> *Sera moretur."*

"You and your double Dutch!" said Tilly with an indulgent smile.

"It's Horace. We had it for an unseen last term, and I liked it, so I learnt it by heart." He looked round the kitchen. "I'm sorry we're leaving here. Are you glad you're going to stay on with Miss Lubbock?"

"That's as may be," said Tilly non-committally. Her wooden face seemed to flicker for a moment as she added, "Sauce-box!"

"Who?" said Richard. "Me?"

"No, Jim. The milkman. Told me this mornin' he knew I'd never be able to tear myself away from him. Said it jus' as he was goin', he did, so's I couldn't tell him what I thought of him. I'll tell him tomorrow all right."

Then the door opened and Edmund entered.

"Oh, there you are, Richard," he said. "What on earth are you doing here?"

"Slicing beans," said Richard simply.

"Oh," said Edmund with a note of disapproval in his voice. "I've been thinking over the two shillings you owe me, and I've decided to buy the book back from you, as it were. It will do for me to give to the form library. They like you to give a book when you leave the form and I shall be moved up next term, so you can give me back the book and that will cancel the two shillings you owe me."

Richard was conscious of a swift surge of anger, then his lazy good nature triumphed. He'd read the book and didn't particularly want to keep it. And there was something vaguely satisfactory about the episode. It was so exactly Edmund . . .

"All right," he said. "It's upstairs. I'll get it."

When he returned, Edmund was standing by the kitchen window, looking out at the garden with an air of detachment.

"Thanks," said Edmund, putting a two-shilling piece on the table and taking it up again. "Now it's as if I'd paid you two shillings for the book and you'd given me the two shillings back to pay your debt. Do you understand?"

"Yes," said Richard.

Edmund slipped the book into his pocket with a smile.

"And I'm sure you feel happier about it, don't you?"

"Not noticeably," said Richard after a moment's consideration.

"But I told you I didn't want the money," said Edmund, speaking earnestly and a little pompously, "and I don't. I only don't want you to get into the habit of borrowing money and not paying it back. Now this is what I'm going to do." He reached up to the chimney-piece, took down an ancient and discoloured missionary-box that stood between a pewter mug and a tea canister, and slowly dropped the two-shilling piece through the slot. It was, he felt, a noble and impressive gesture, worthy of a more appreciative reception than that shown by Tilly's hard stare and the amused quirk of Richard's eyebrow.

"Thank you, Edmund," said Richard gravely. "You've behaved like a gentleman over the whole affair."

"That's all right, old boy," said Edmund as he replaced the box on the chimney-piece. "It's just a question of what's right and what's wrong."

"And now we've both done what's right."

"Quite," said Edmund, then, feeling that to stay any longer would be something of an anticlimax, made a dignified, unhurried exit.

"Sauce!" said Tilly. She reached up and took the box down. "We can get it out again easy."

"Can we?" said Richard, interested. "How?"

"Like this," said Tilly. She took a knife from the table drawer and put it in the slot. After a little manipulation the two-shilling piece and three pennies rolled out.

"Take the lot," said Tilly generously.

"No, I can't do that," said Richard, dropping the three pennies back through the slot. "The box must keep its three pence. It's probably had it for years."

"Well, you can buy another book now, can't you?" said Tilly.

"No, I don't think I can do that," said Richard.

He looked out of the window. Polly and Myrtle stood by the rabbit-hutch, Polly holding Patty in her arms. Richard went down to them.

"We're taking Patty home," said Polly and Myrtle gave him her slow, sweet smile.

"Good!" said Richard. "I'm sorry we let the other one die," He plunged his hand into his pocket and brought out the two-shilling piece. "Look! Would you like this to buy some sweets with?"

Their eyes shone with delight.

"Oo, *thank* you," they gasped, taking the coin, then, overcome by shyness, ran back to the gate.

"What are you goin' to do with that two shillings?" said Tilly as he re-entered the kitchen.

"I've given it to Polly and Myrtle to buy sweets with," he said.

They looked at each other and began to laugh.

Chapter Nine

Tilly bustled about the cottage, putting on the clean chair-covers, polishing the silver, making up the beds, getting ready again for the Culvertons. It was nine years since their former visit, but the time had slipped by so quickly and uneventfully that it seemed only yesterday she had waited in the kitchen in her new print dress while Mrs. Horseferry received them at the front door. The events of that summer stood out more vividly in her mind than anything that had happened since. Certainly the highlights of Miss Lubbock's existence—the spring cleaning, the bottling season, the jam-making season, the church bazaar were not things to impress themselves on the memory, and Miss Lubbock herself was so colourless, so timid, so devoid of any spark of initiative or imagination that to Tilly, even after nine years, she was hardly more real than the furniture she dusted every morning.

Miss Lubbock had not been away since the summer she had let the cottage to the Culvertons. It was a mistake, she said, to go away in the summer because one missed so much in the garden, and it was a mistake to go away in the winter because one was so much more comfortable at home. It had never occurred to her—or to Tilly—that Tilly should go away, so for nine years Tilly had swept and dusted Linden Rise, cooked the vague, sketchy dishes that Miss Lubbock liked and that consisted chiefly in "using up bits", done a little gardening under Miss Lubbock's directions and generally accommodated herself to Miss Lubbock's gentle spinster way of life.

But this summer Miss Lubbock had gone away—not on a holiday, but in a spirit of resolute martyrdom—to nurse a sister in

Cumberland who had been taken ill with bronchitis. Mrs. Egerton, on hearing the news, had come at once to the cottage to take charge of the situation. She had looked up the trains, made the luncheon arrangements (a packed luncheon and there'd just be time for tea at Lancaster), and even decided which of her clothes Miss Lubbock should take.

"Yes . . . yes . . . yes, I'll do that," Miss Lubbock agreed meekly.

She was a flabby little woman with a small mouth, pendulous cheeks, and white hair so thin that her scalp showed pinkly through it.

"And now what about the arrangements for the cottage?" said Mrs. Egerton.

"Tilly will be here," said Miss Lubbock. "She'll look after it."

"Oh, I don't think I'd just leave it," said Mrs. Egerton in her quiet, diffident voice. "I think that's not wise. I find that both maid and house run to seed when they're left to themselves. I think it would be much better to let it. The money would be useful, too."

"Oh, no, I don't want to let it," pleaded Miss Lubbock.

"There are the Culvertons, you know," said Mrs. Egerton dreamily. "The family that was here before. They left everything in order, didn't they?"

"Yes, but—"

"I expect they'd like to come again. They'd probably be glad to get out of London. The Queen's death must have cast such a gloom over it."

"I've forgotten their address," said Miss Lubbock in a vain attempt to stem the tide of Mrs. Egerton's gentle persistence.

"I think I've got it," said Mrs. Egerton vaguely. "I'll write to Mrs. Culverton tonight."

"But—"

"And about your sister . . . There's nothing like a mustard leaf on the chest for bronchitis. And I should give her chest a good rubbing with equal parts of turpentine and olive oil last thing at night. An occasional teaspoonful of ipecacuanha wine is an excellent thing, too."

Miss Lubbock wanted to return to the subject of letting the

cottage, to discuss it, to argue about it, but she knew that the attempt would be useless.

And something of the same feeling came over Mrs. Culverton as she read the letter that Mrs. Egerton wrote to her that evening. Its suggestion of renting the cottage for the summer was vague and almost apologetic, but Mrs. Culverton had a curious conviction as she read it that the final arrangements had now been reached and it was too late to draw back. In any case the Streatham house was to be decorated this summer and Linden Rise would make a family headquarters while it was in the hands of the workmen. She wrote to Mrs. Egerton agreeing to her suggestions (for Mrs. Egerton's letter, beneath its note of vagueness and apology, had been quite concise about terms and conditions) and, somewhat to the surprise of everyone but Mrs. Egerton, the thing was fixed up.

Only in her encounter with Tilly did Mrs. Egerton meet defeat. She came to tea to Linden Rise one afternoon and followed Tilly into the kitchen when she carried out the tea-tray.

"There'll be more work than you can manage when the Culvertons are here, Tilly," she said, "so I've arranged for Nellie Durban to come and help you in the mornings."

Tilly turned round from the cupboard where she was putting away the sugar. Her face looked more expressionless than ever.

"I'm having no one else in my kitchen, madam," she said.

Mrs. Egerton's beautiful dreamy eyes rested on her in silence for a moment. Then she said:

"But, Tilly, you can't possibly manage everything. There'll be cooking for six as well as the cleaning."

"That's my business, madam," said Tilly. Her mouth was a thin line across her round wooden face, her eyes hard and black and bright as sloes.

"But, Tilly," said Mrs. Egerton. Her vagueness and dreaminess had vanished. She spoke urgently, imperiously—in itself, she knew, a confession of defeat. "You can't *possibly* manage. Anyway, I've asked Nellie Durban to come every morning from nine to one."

Tilly put the cake away in the cake-tin before she answered. Then she said:

96

"The minute Nellie Durban or anyone else sets foot in my kitchen, out I goes, madam, and I goes for good."

Then she busied herself with stacking the crockery in the sink.

Mrs. Egerton drifted back to the sitting-room. It wasn't often that she had to admit defeat, but she admitted it now.

"On second thoughts, dear," she said to Miss Lubbock, "I think I'll put Nellie Durban off. I don't really think that Tilly could get on with her—or with anyone else for that matter. If she finds the work too much it may teach her a lesson."

"It may, of course," said Miss Lubbock a little doubtfully.

Mrs. Egerton gathered up bag and scarf and gloves.

"And I must run away now," she said. "I've got the G.F.S. at six, and it's such a lovely evening I think I'll take the longer way home through the wood."

She felt a little shaken and wanted to have time to recover herself before she met the G.F.S.

So Tilly had packed off Miss Lubbock—protesting, complaining, changing her plans every minute, leaving Tilly detailed instructions for dealing with the peas, the raspberries, the beans, the ravages of slugs in the celery and moth in the blankets—and was now preparing the house for the Culvertons. So vividly did she remember them that, oddly, she expected them to be just the same as when she had last seen them. Edmund would be twenty-four, Richard twenty-two, Althea twenty and Vere eighteen . . . but somehow she couldn't believe it. When she thought of their coming she saw again the wagonette at the door and the four children getting down from it. They would stand in a little group, looking about them, and soon they would be hanging daisy-chains on the stone owl in the garden, playing "shop", swinging on the swing, going to the farm to watch the cows being milked, to the blacksmith's to watch a horse being shod, running down to the village shop to spend their pennies . . .

She had stayed in the background on their last arrival, wearing her new ill-fitting print dress, while Mrs. Horseferry stood at the front door to receive them. Now she had an "afternoon uniform"—a long black dress, a white apron and a white cap with streamers—

and she would stand at the door to receive them instead of Mrs. Horseferry. These nine years had not, after all, gone for nothing. They had brought her to the stage where she could stand at the front door to receive the Culvertons.

Actually their second arrival was not unlike their first. They arrived in the horse-drawn wagonette from Tubbs' farm. Mrs. Culverton got out of it first and walked up to the door followed by two young men and two young women.

"Well, Tilly," said Mrs. Culverton graciously, "this is very nice. How are you?"

She looked older, more tired, more worn, but the air of aristocracy that had impressed Tilly so deeply nine years ago was as marked as ever. Her figure was still slender and graceful in the dress of grey moiré silk with grey cloth pelisse, and the small grey hat, trimmed with ostrich feathers, was tilted forward to throw a soft shade over her eyes.

"You remember us all, don't you?" she went on, waving a gloved hand in the direction of the four young people. "Mr. Edmund, Mr. Richard, Miss Althea and Miss Vere."

Tilly was vaguely aware of a handsome, dark, well-proportioned young man, a fair girl and a dark girl . . . but Richard was the only one she really saw—Richard, his hair as fair and unruly as it had been nine years ago, with the familiar twinkle in the grey-blue eyes, the familiar twist at the corner of the long mouth.

"Well, Mrs. Noah," he said, and a wave of emotion that she couldn't have explained swept over her. She swallowed, gulped and stared at him.

They were trooping into the cottage just as they had done nine years ago.

"I wrote to you, Mrs. Noah," said Richard, "and you never answered."

She remembered the letter that Richard had written to her the first Christmas after their visit. She still had it in a drawer upstairs under her handkerchiefs. It had never occurred to her to answer it.

"I hadn't no paper," she said, "nor no stamps."

He laughed.

"I'll get you some," he said. "I'll have a nice crest of the ark engraved at the top."

She gave him the grin he remembered so well—the grin that came and vanished almost at once, hardly seeming to disturb the wooden gravity of her features.

"Now, Richard, don't stand talking nonsense," said Mrs. Culverton with a hint of impatience in her voice. "Are our bedrooms the same as we had last time, Tilly?"

"Yes, madam," said Tilly.

"Mr. Culverton has been abroad on business, but he's returning today. He should be here tomorrow."

"Yes, madam."

Mrs. Culverton went up to her bedroom and looked around. Not a detail had altered in the nine years. The crocheted hairtidy still hung from the mirror; "God is Love" still looked down at her from its green plush frame. The curtains and the bedspread looked a little more washed-out and faded, but that was all. Her thoughts went back to the former visit and she remembered the turmoil of spirit with which she had first looked round this room, hoping for a miracle that had never happened . . . and her lips tightened. She had hardened herself since then, no longer expected miracles. And it gave her a certain bitter satisfaction to know that Howard, in his turn, was suffering something of the torture that he had inflicted on her. His mistress was tiring of him and turning to a younger lover, and Howard now occupied the ignominious position of ex-favourite, the recipient of favours given in pity, retained chiefly because of his usefulness, to be sent on errands, to fetch and carry. She knew that he suffered deeply and sometimes a pang of compassion for him would shoot through her heart, but she steeled herself against it, aware that even now the woman only had to raise her little finger and he would go running back to her.

On her last visit she had set the stage for a second honeymoon. She was asking less of this visit. She had decided that Howard should be made to assume his proper responsibilities towards his children. It was natural that when they were younger he should have left them to her, but, now they were growing up, it was time that he shouldered his fair share of the burden. She intended to take the opportunity of this holiday at Linden Rise to impress his duty upon him. Edmund and Althea gave no cause for worry or concern. Edmund, after a satisfactory, if undistinguished, career at school and college, was now comfortably settled in the Civil Service. He seemed to have altered little with the years. He was conscientious, hard-working, kind and considerate. He would make, thought Mrs. Culverton with a touch of bitterness, an excellent husband to some nice girl. And Althea . . . The hardness round Mrs. Culverton's heart melted at the thought of Althea. Althea at twenty retained the fairy-like loveliness of her childhood with the added poise of an expensive finishing school. She had a delicate childlike charm, a Watteau-like grace that suggested the fragrance of a spring morning. Mrs. Culverton could see no flaw in Althea. The child was, perhaps, a little oversensitive. Things hurt her more than they hurt other people, and sometimes the hurt could only be assuaged by the expenditure of a good deal of time and trouble and even money, but Mrs. Culverton never grudged time, trouble or money where Althea was concerned. She had received a proposal at her coming-out dance and had received two more since then, but she had refused them. Mrs. Culverton approved of the refusals. None of the young men had been in any way worthy of Althea. The only day-dream that she allowed herself now was the day-dream of Althea's future, a future in which she enjoyed vicariously all the happiness that life had failed to give her. In Althea she would know unclouded marriage and children as perfect as Althea herself.

Richard, of course, should have been the most satisfactory of the children, but somehow he wasn't. He had gained a scholarship to Oxford, won prizes and distinctions during his college course and finally obtained a first-class Honours Degree. A dozen roads lay open to him, but he would have none of them. He agreed vaguely to every suggestion she made and evaded all her efforts to tie him down to a definite decision.

Vere was hardly more satisfactory. She had left school last term and should now begin to play her part on the stage where Althea was winning her triumphs. The way had been prepared by Althea. Her beauty and the friends she had made at the finishing school had drawn round her a set of young people whom Mrs. Culverton mentally designated as "useful" and who were willing to accept Vere without question. Moreover, Vere herself, surprisingly, was not bad-looking. So gradual had been the change by which the dumpy, childish figure had attained grace and slenderness, the sallowness of skin turned to a warm olive, enhancing the large dark eyes, that Mrs. Culverton still could not quite accustom herself to the fact that Vere was "presentable". Even the thick dark brows added a touch of distinction, and the dark wiry hair could be disciplined to a shining sleekness that suited the smoothness of the oval face. But Vere, instead of seizing the advantages offered by this transformation, was growing increasingly difficult. She had refused to follow Althea to the finishing school. She now refused to have a coming-out dance, though Mrs. Culverton's plans for it were well under way. Mrs. Culverton had indeed begun to plan the dance before Vere left school and it had never occurred to her to consult the child. Curiously, in all her mental pictures of Vere's coming-out dance it was Althea, not Vere, whom she saw as the central figure. Vere was only a vague shadow in the background.

There was a knock at the door, and Edmund entered. He had put on a country suit of tweed but he looked as neat and well-groomed as he did in his town clothes. His shoes shone, his collar gleamed, his tie was carefully knotted. His handsome, regular-featured face wore an expression of kindly solicitude.

"Not too tired, are you, Mother?" he said.

Mrs. Culverton roused herself.

"No, thank you," she said with a faint smile. "I'm merely being lazy. I'm going to unpack now."

"Is there anything I can do for you?"

"No, thank you."

"I'll go out for a walk then. I think I'll try and get a good walk every day while we're here. It's foolish to come to the country and not get all the benefit you can from it, isn't it?"

"Of course, dear. Where are the others?"

"Richard's in the bedroom. Messing about with books, as usual."

There was the old mixture of amusement and irritation in his voice, but the envy was no longer there. Edmund had set his feet on a road that led from promotion to promotion. He was completely satisfied with himself. He envied no one.

"And I think the girls are still unpacking," he went on. "There's nothing I can get you in the village, is there?"

"No, thank you."

"No letters to post?"

"No, thank you. I've hardly had time to write any yet."

"I'll try and rake old Richard out," he said pleasantly as he turned to go. "He's too fond of frowsting."

She heard him return to the bedroom and heard Richard say: "All right. I'll just go as far as the orchard and see if the stone owl's still there."

She went to the landing window and watched the two walk down the garden together. Beside Edmund's solid frame, Richard's figure looked slight and undersized; his fair hair was, as usual, a little too long; he walked with a slouch, hands thrust deep in the pockets of his shabby college blazer, a pipe in the corner of his long mouth. Edmund frequently remonstrated with him about both pipe and blazer. Edmund was always generous of advice, continuing to offer it long after it had been rejected.

At the end of the orchard they stopped and stood looking down at something in the long grass. They had evidently found the stone owl. Richard made a low bow, his hand at his heart, then Edmund went through the little gate into the field and Richard returned to the house, glancing about him with lazy interest.

They're so different and they both irritate me so, thought Mrs. Culverton. I think I'd have liked one son who was a mixture of the two.

Then she went down the little passage again and entered the girls' room.

Althea turned from the wardrobe where she was hanging up a dress. Her dresses covered the bed, filmy muslins, voiles, silks, cascades of flounces, frills of lace. Her lovely face was alight with eagerness.

"Isn't it thrilling to be back here!" she said. "I expect there'll be heaps of fresh people now. They all asked us out, didn't they? Parties and things."

Althea drifted on the surface of life. She liked change and excitement—new people, new interests, new clothes, new impressions.

"I hope you'll have a nice time, darling," said Mrs. Culverton tenderly. "Let me help you put your things away." She turned to Vere, who was standing by the open window. "Have you started your unpacking yet, Vere?"

"Not yet . . ."

Richard's voice floated up from the garden.

"The stone owl's still here."

"I'm so glad," said Vere.

"You'd better start, hadn't you, dear?" said Mrs. Culverton. "I'd like to get all the boxes cleared out of the way before tea."

There was the sound of a knock at the front door, voices in the hall, then Tilly came upstairs.

"Mrs. Egerton to see you, madam," she said.

"Oh, dear!" said Mrs. Culverton.

"She's wasting no time," said Althea with a gay little laugh. "Perhaps she's come to ask us to a party."

When Mrs. Culverton had gone Althea continued to hang up her dresses, singing softly to herself, and Vere knelt down on the floor to open her box. Her wardrobe was still a schoolgirl's wardrobe, and her unpacking would be a simple affair compared with Althea's.

"I think it's going to be fun here, don't you?" said Althea.

"I don't know," said Vere.

Althea threw her a quick glance. Her relations with Vere were uncertain. They had gone to the same boarding-school, but, being in different forms, had had little contact with each other. Even in the holidays Vere had been to Althea merely a younger sister to be snubbed and ignored. But now that Vere had left school and was coming out—for Althea did not take Vere's protests against the coming-out dance seriously—they would be going to the same parties, sharing the same friends. Althea was willing to come to an understanding with her, and had already made several tacit offers of friendship to which Vere had so far shown herself obtuse. Althea would rather like to take a younger sister under her wing, introduce her to the right people, have her in the background as a witness of her own triumphs. It would be fun to talk things over after parties, exchange confidences, devise little plots against rivals and enemies, give each other the unobtrusive help that can so often send an affair running smoothly on its course. And Vere was no longer a disgrace to her. Slender, olive-skinned with smooth dark hair and lustrous dark eyes, she was now undeniably a credit. Not pretty enough to be a rival, but no longer so plain as to be a humiliation . . . She looked at the white nun's veiling frock that Vere was taking from her trunk (the "one plain white dress" of the school inventory) and said:

"That awful thing! You haven't any decent clothes, have you, coming straight from school like this?"

Vere made no comment.

"I tell you what!" said Althea. "When we're back at home again I'll get Mother to give me some money and we'll go on a shopping expedition and buy you some decent clothes—just the two of us. You'd like that, wouldn't you?"

Vere put down the white frock and knelt motionless for a few moments, gazing into space as if considering the proposition. "No," she said at last in her quiet detached voice. "No, I don't think I should," and added, "thank you," in a tone of formal politeness.

All Althea's newly found kindness vanished and the old dislike surged up in her. Beneath the dislike was an obscure jealousy. Though she would not have admitted it she was jealous of some quality in Vere that she didn't understand. Her features sharpened. Her mouth took a tight line.

"Don't put any of your things on the dressing-table," she said. "I shall want that. You can do your hair at the mirror on the chest-of-drawers. And there isn't any room for your dresses in the wardrobe. You can keep them in that bottom long drawer."

"All right," said Vere without interest or resentment.

For a few minutes there was silence, broken only by the sound of Mrs. Egerton's voice from the room below.

"I wonder what she's come about?" said Althea.

Mrs. Egerton had greeted Mrs. Culverton with her usual deprecating apologetic air.

"I'm so sorry to invade you the minute you arrive like this," she said, "but I was just passing the gate and I thought I'd look in and see if there was anything I could do for you."

"How kind of you!" said Mrs. Culverton. "No, I don't think there is, thank you. We're in the process of settling in. The girls are just unpacking."

"I think we can give you quite a gay time this summer," said Mrs. Egerton. "The Hall's been taken at last and by very nice people. Sir Godfrey and Lady Lynneker. They have two sons, Piers and Roddy. Piers is twenty-four and Roddy twenty-two. And two very nice girls, Mabel and Dorothy, as well as an adopted niece, Lindsay Moreton. I told Lady Lynneker about you and she's going to call as soon as they get home. They're in Scotland at present."

"You're all so kind," murmured Mrs. Culverton. Her thoughts had seized eagerly on Piers and Roddy—just the right ages for Althea and Vere—but her tired blue eyes betrayed no flicker of interest. "It seems like coming home to come back to Linden Rise. It was so nice to find Tilly still here."

"Yes, Tilly . ." said Mrs. Egerton. A blank look came into her eyes as she remembered her defeat at Tilly's hands. "I thought of getting you a girl from the village as well, but on second thoughts I decided that Tilly would probably manage better on her own. So often when there are two of them they waste their time gossiping."

"We had a Mrs. Horseferry, I remember, the last time we were here."

"Y-yes. She still lives in Bellminster. You can always get her over to cook a meal for any special occasion, but—well, she's not very reliable these days. Intermittently she's still a very good cook, but, if you arrange a day beforehand, as you generally have to, you might just hit on one of her lapses."

"Yes, I remember her lapses . . . Then there was a Miss Maple who came as the children's governess."

"She's still here. Her mother's dead and she's quite well off now. The old woman was evidently one of those misers who enjoy pinching and scraping and starving themselves and everyone around them. Poor Miss Maple simply couldn't believe; it when the lawyer told her how much money she had. She still doesn't believe it. She lives exactly as she used to live in the old woman's time except that she's bought a dog, but she still feels guilty about it because her mother didn't like dogs. It's a shaggy sort of creature without a face and, to judge by the state of Miss Maple's clothes, in a state of perpetual moult. I expect she'll be coming round to see you. She's been talking about you all these years."

"How boring for you!" smiled Mrs. Culverton.

"Oh, no," said Mrs. Egerton. "There's so little present in a small country place like this that we all enjoy browsing on the past." She rose and drew on her gloves. "Well, I mustn't keep you any longer. I'm sure you've a lot to do." She turned to the door then stopped. "Oh, there's one other little thing . . ."

"Yes?" said Mrs. Culverton.

"It's not very important, but"—Mrs. Egerton's manner became even vaguer than usual. Her eyes wandered dreamily round the room—"Miss Lubbock's sister will be a permanent invalid, I'm afraid, so Miss Lubbock has decided to make her home with her. Miss Lubbock's not very well off, and it will really simplify things for both of them. I've written to suggest that she sells Linden Rise at once with its contents. Her sister has quite a large house and they won't need any of this furniture. Don't you agree?"

"Yes, but—"

"It would be so nice for you to have a holiday cottage, wouldn't it?"

"Yes, but—"

"You could keep Tilly here and then, any week-end that any of you could come down, the cottage would be ready for you. A week-end cottage is such a convenience, I think."

"I know, but—"

"I'll write to her tonight. She's prepared to sell it quite reasonably. Don't bother to see me out. You must be so busy . . . By the way, did you notice the valerian growing in the church-yard wall as you passed? It's a wonderful touch of colour against the grey stone wall. I love those lines of Tennyson, don't you?

> "Flower in the crannied wall,
> I pluck you out of the crannies;
> Hold you here, root and all, in my hand,
> Little flower . . ."

Continuing the quotation in a voice so languid that it seemed part of the sleepy summer afternoon, she drifted down to the gate and out into the road.

Mrs. Culverton stood at the door, watching her, trying to shake off the spell of dreamy inertia that the visitor had laid on her. Then she heard the sound of horses' hooves and turned her head sharply.

The station cab was breasting the little rise.

It drew up at the gate and Howard got down from it.

Chapter Ten

"Well, my dear," he said. "How are you? I managed to catch the night boat and get here today, after all."

He spoke with the impersonal cheerfulness that he had always used as a defence against her.

I wonder if he met her over there, she thought, if they've patched it up . . . and, before she could guard against it, the old familiar pain had her in its grip.

The cabman was carrying his box upstairs, and Tilly was supervising its passage up the narrow stairway.

"No need to knock the whole place down," she was saying. "When we want an earthquake we'll let you know."

Howard paid the man and followed his wife into the bedroom.

"We only arrived about an hour ago," she said. "We haven't finished unpacking yet." As if to punish him for the breakdown of her guard, momentary as it had been, she decided to set him to his task at once. "Howard . . ."

"Yes?"

"I want you to speak seriously to Richard."

He took his keys from his pocket and unlocked his box.

"What about?" he said shortly.

"He's come down from college and he ought to be deciding what he's going to do."

"Well, it's for him to decide that, isn't it?"

"He doesn't seem to take any interest in it."

"I expect he'll settle to something when he's looked round a bit."

"He won't, Howard. You must talk to him about it."

"As you wish, my dear. I shall probably find an opportunity while we're down here."

"No, Howard. You must do it today. It's no good putting things off."

He was silent, hunting for escape and finding none.

"Very well," he said at last.

Her lips flickered into a thin line of triumph.

"I'll send him to you when you've gone downstairs," she said. "And then there's Vere . . ."

He fastened his empty suitcase and put it by the door.

"What about Vere?"

"She's being difficult."

"Vere's your business, surely."

"Why? She's your daughter as much as mine."

He shrugged.

"And how is Vere being difficult?"

"She's left school but she won't fit into any of the arrangements I've made for her. I'm willing to give her a coming-out dance like Althea's, so that she'll get to know the right people and have a good start, but—she's just being stupid about it. As stupid as Richard. She did quite well at school. Her drawing reports were excellent."

"And what of Edmund and Althea? Any complaints about them?"

"No."

"Let's thank heaven for Edmund and Althea."

"I do," said Mrs. Culverton devoutly.

In the little sitting-room, Howard took out the evening paper that he had bought on the journey and, sitting down by the window, opened it with the vague idea that it might serve as a bulwark. Even when he heard his wife's "Your father wants to speak to you, Richard," he continued to turn over the pages with an air of abstraction.

"Here's Richard, Howard," said Mrs. Culverton.

Richard followed her into the room. She shut the door and sat down at the writing-table. She intended to be present at the interview. She couldn't trust either of them not to wriggle out of it.

"Sit down, my boy," said Howard.

Richard sat down in the small chintz-covered chair by the fireplace. He looked young and pleasant and politely interested in whatever was coming.

"Have a cigarette?" said Howard, handing him his cigarette-case.

"No, thanks," said Richard, lugging a pipe from a crowded pocket. "Do you mind if I smoke this?"

"Not if your mother doesn't."

Mrs. Culverton made an impatient gesture of consent.

"Your mother feels that we ought to have a little talk about your future," said Howard.

His mantle of *paterfamilias* sat uneasily upon him, and he always felt faintly ridiculous when he assumed it. He tried to hide his self-consciousness under a bantering manner.

"You've carried everything before you up to now. Quite a conquering hero's progress. Your mother and I are proud of you. So far so good." He avoided Richard's eye and continued: "But the question is, what are you going to do now? Have you any suggestions?"

Richard considered.

"No, I don't think I have," he said at last.

"But you want to get down to work of some sort?"

"I suppose so," said Richard with a note of uncertainty in voice.

"You must have worked hard enough for your scholarship and degree," put in Mrs. Culverton sharply.

"Yes," said Richard, and added vaguely: "There was Entwistle . . ."

He couldn't have explained how it was that everything had changed now that Entwistle had gone abroad. They had worked together and in competition, and the mixture of rivalry and cooperation had given a zest to the work and kept Richard on the high road of endeavour. Without it, he knew, he would have wandered down every alluring bypath. Their friendship had remained impersonal, based chiefly on a love of Ancient Greece and focussed less on each other than on their common work and interests. And now Entwistle had gone out to a Government post in Uganda. Richard didn't miss his companionship, but the mainspring of his ambition seemed to have been broken with Entwistle's departure.

"He's gone out to East Africa, you see," he added lamely.

"Would you like a post of that sort?" said Howard.

"No, I don't think I should," said Richard.

"What about schoolmastering?"

"I don't think I'd be any good at that," said Richard.

"There's writing . . ." Howard made an attempt to be jocular. "One gathers from your career so far that you possess a certain amount of brain—you got a particularly brilliant First—so why not let others have the benefit of it ?"

Richard appeared to give the suggestion earnest consideration.

"I'm not creative," he said. "I suppose I've got a certain critical faculty, but I haven't any creative powers at all."

"What about medicine?"

"Oh, no. I'd make a frightful mess of that."

"There's the Civil Service."

"I don't think I could manage that," said Richard. "I'm not methodical."

"There's the Diplomatic Service."

Richard puffed meditatively at his pipe.

"I don't think I'm diplomatic, either."

"There's the business," said Howard doubtfully. Howard was junior partner in a flourishing firm of paper manufacturers, but the senior partner already had five sons firmly established in it. "I don't think that would be much good to you, though."

"And I probably shouldn't be much good to it," said Richard.

"You surely wouldn't be content just to drift through life, would you, Richard?" said Mrs. Culverton.

Richard contemplated that idea, too, with polite interest.

"I don't know," he said, "I rather think I should."

Howard smiled.

"Well, there's a Chinese proverb: 'He who is contented with being contented will always be contented'."

"There's a lot in that," said Richard.

Mrs. Culverton's fingers beat an impatient tattoo on the writing-table. Son and husband threw her guilty glances.

"Haven't you any ambition at all, Richard?" she said.

"I don't think I have," said Richard apologetically. "Not much, anyway."

"There's always the Bar," said Howard.

"Of course," said Richard. His long mouth twisted into a half-smile. "I'm sorry. I feel I'm behaving absurdly like Richard Carstone."

"You are, rather," agreed Howard. "Perhaps we'd better keep you clear of the law. He died of it, didn't he?"

"Yes. And Miss Flite let her birds free."

"Tulkinghorn didn't fare much better, if I remember rightly."

"You know, I never could cotton to Esther."

"Dame Burden? No, she's a bit of a bore. But the Smallweeds, the Jellabys, Skimpole and Chadband . . . They're a grand crowd."

Mrs. Culverton could contain her irritation no longer. How futile Howard was! Almost as futile as Richard himself.

"You have to earn your living, Richard," she said, "so you may as well set about it."

"Quite," said Richard in hasty propitiation. "I realize that."

"Have you any objection to reading for the Bar?"

"Oh, none," said Richard.

"Very well, then," said Mrs. Culverton. "We'll make arrangements for you to start as soon as possible. That's settled. And now will you please tell Vere that we'd like to speak to her?"

Richard departed, still wearing his air of unruffled indolence.

"He's infuriating," said Mrs. Culverton.

"Don't be hard on the boy," said Howard. "He's not done badly so far."

But he spoke absently. His thoughts had obviously not been with her or Richard in the interview in which he had played so ignominious a part.

"Was Mrs. Brougham with you in Paris, Howard?" she said suddenly.

He turned his eyes to her, his face emptied of expression. "No," he said. "She's with her husband. He had a bad heart attack and she was sent for suddenly."

She thought of Mr. Brougham, moneyed, assured, a cynical *mari complaisant,* giving his wife a free hand on condition that he, too, should go his way unquestioned.

"Whatever happens, Howard, I won't divorce you," she said in a low unsteady voice.

He gave a twisted smile.

"As things are, you have no grounds, my dear."

Then Vere came in. She stood just inside the door, wearing the navy blue dress with white, collar and cuffs that was part of her school outfit. Her smooth hair was parted in the middle and fell down to her waist in a long plait. She fixed her eyes on her parents with a mixture of courage and timidity. There was something poignantly young and defenceless about her. Howard looked at her as if seeing her for the first time—as indeed he was. Mrs. Culverton had buckled on her armour again. She would conduct this interview herself. Howard was hopeless. She even regretted the impulse that had made her try to enlist his help.

She had been wondering how to deal with Vere and, as the door opened, a plan had suddenly occurred to her.

"Your father and I have been having a talk about you, Vere," she said. "Your drawing shows promise and we are willing to allow you to go to the Slade School of Art on condition that you fall in with my plans for a coming-out dance and my other arrangements. Do you agree to that?"

Vere looked from one to the other. She didn't want to go to the Slade School and she didn't want to have a coming-out dance, but she was overwhelmed by the solemnity of the occasion (never before had she been summoned into the presence of both her parents together) and abashed by the kindness in Howard's eyes.

"Yes," she said on a quick intake of breath.

"Very well," said Mrs. Culverton. "You may go now."

"It's dreadful the way these children shilly-shally," she added as the door closed on Vere.

"It's dreadful for them to be in our power like this," said Howard slowly.

"I don't know what you mean," said Mrs. Culverton.

She rose from the writing-table and went towards the door. Then she stopped, struck by a sudden thought.

"By the way," she said, "Mrs. Egerton was here this morning. The Vicar's wife, you know."

"I remember. The mailed fist in the velvet glove."

"I don't know about that," said Mrs. Culverton, "but she said that Miss Lubbock wanted to sell the cottage and that we might like it for a holiday and week-end cottage."

"And what did you say?"

"Well, it would be useful . . ."

"Did you actually agree that we should buy it?"

Mrs. Culverton considered. She'd forgotten exactly what had been said, but she had an idea that it was all settled except the final details.

"I don't really know why I agreed to it, but I believe I did."

"What about price?"

"She said that Miss Lubbock was prepared to sell it reasonably."

"Oh, well," said Howard, "it would be nice for you and the children."

Her mouth tightened and she made no comment.

Richard was in the kitchen handing china from the packing-case that stood on the floor to Tilly, who was arranging it on the shelves.

"You needn't bother with it, Mr. Richard," Tilly had protested. "I can do it easy."

"I like doing it," said Richard. "I find it much more congenial than the other occupations that my parents have just been suggesting to me."

"What do they want you to do?"

"All sorts of things, and I shouldn't be any good at any of them . . . I'm a misfit, Tilly."

"Never you mind, Mr. Richard."

"I don't mind. That's the worst of it. Misfits ought to mind." He sat back on his haunches and contemplated her with lazy interest. "What have you been doing with yourself all these nine years, Mrs. Noah?"

"Nothing," she said, dusting a vegetable dish and putting it on the shelf.

"You must have done something," he persisted. "Aren't you promised in marriage to anyone or anything of that sort?"

Tilly shrugged.

"Sort of," she said.

"To whom?"

"Jim. The milkman. Takes a lot for granted, he does."

"Let's forget him," said Richard. "No one should take you for granted. You're unique . . . Who's going to do the cooking while we're here?"

"Me."

"Good! What are we going to have tonight?"

Tilly considered.

"I've got a leg of mutton and I'm going to do it the ordinary way 'cause there isn't time to do anything else, but—"

She stopped, and something seemed to glow into life behind the stolid wooden features.

"Yes?"

"There's a lot of things I'd like to try. I copied them out of her book before she went. I tried some of 'em on Miss Lubbock but," scornfully, "they only scared her, so I gave up, but I'd like to try some of 'em while you're here."

"Which shall we try?" said Richard.

"There's one with rump steak," said Tilly, sinking her voice to a conspiratorial whisper. "You half roast it and then you put it in a saucepan with water and red wine and a shallot and some lemon and walnut ketchup. Then you stew it for two hours, then you put in half a pint of mushrooms and you serve it with forcemeat balls and horse-radish. We could do it tomorrow, but I've not got no mushrooms nor no red wine."

"I'll get you some," said Richard. "I'll go into Bellminster tomorrow morning and get you some."

"Oh, Mr. Richard!" said Tilly. "Will you really?"

"You look like Joan of Arc."

"What was she? Was she a cook?"

"Not exactly." He gave her a long scrutiny as he handed her a white fluted milk jug. "You know, you haven't changed at all, Mrs. Noah."

"Neither have you, Mr. Richard."

"We must have changed really, you know. It would be terrible if we hadn't. 'Change is a condition of reality'. Heraclitus said that more than two thousand years ago and it's still true."

"Do you read them old Latin books all over the place same as you used to?" said Tilly.

"Latin!" he said contemptuously. "It's a barbarous language. There's only been one civilized language since the world began, Tilly, and it's Greek. It makes every other language sound like Animal Grab. Listen."

She listened for a few minutes in silence then broke in.

"What does it mean?"

"It's describing a grove in Colonos, where the nightingale sings and the narcissus and the golden crocus grow and the river of Cephisus is fed by streams that never sleep."

"But what's the story about?" said Tilly. "Go on. Tell me the story. Same as you did about that giant with one eye that kept sheep."

"All right," said Richard, "Once upon a time there was a king called Cadmus and he was warned by a fortune-teller that he would be killed by his son."

"I wouldn't have taken no notice," said Tilly. "They talk a lot of nonsense, them fortune-tellers. I had mine done by a gypsy at the fair last year and she told me I'd be left a fortune by a dark man and the only thing I got left by a dark man was a dustbin full of rubbish what the dustman never cleared that week. Go on."

"Well, anyway, he believed it and when his wife had a son he gave the baby to one of his shepherds and told him to take the baby up to the hills and leave it there to die."

"Murder, that was," said Tilly. "I'd have set the Cruelty man on him."

116

"It didn't die, but before he gave it to the shepherd he—"

The kitchen door opened very slowly and Miss Maple entered, preceded by a shaggy brown dog that sat down in the middle of the hearth-rug and began to scratch its ear. The short black jacket that Miss Maple wore might have been the same one she wore nine years ago; her gloves were still darned, her hat worn and shapeless.

She tiptoed into the room, her finger at her lips.

"It's Richard, isn't it?" she whispered. "How nice to see you again, dear boy! I don't want the others to know I'm here. You've only just arrived and aren't ready for callers, but I just wanted to find out from Tilly if there was anything I could do for you. Have you got everything you need, Tilly? I could easily spare you some cutlery or linen or saucepans."

"No, thank you, Miss Maple," said Tilly. "We've got everything. They sent all that sort of thing off beforehand. It arrived this morning and we're just finishing unpacking it now."

"I see. . . but remember to call on me for anything you want. Anything at all."

"Well, it's grand to see you again, Miss Maple," said Richard. He drew forward the rocking-chair. "Do sit down."

Miss Maple hesitated, then sat down. The brown dog shifted its position, leaving a patch of brown fur on the rug.

"He's moulting," exclaimed Miss Maple. "He's getting ready for his winter coat." The brown dog elevated his head and began to scratch his neck. "He hasn't really got fleas, dear. He does it to pass the time." She looked at Richard. "And now, dear boy, tell me all your news."

"I haven't any," said Richard. "Tell me yours."

"Well, I lost my dear mother, you know, last year. It was a shattering blow. She was such a wonderful saint-like character, you remember."

"Yes, I remember," said Richard. "I'm terribly sorry."

"I try to keep things going exactly as she would have liked," said Miss Maple. "I feel that's the least I can do for her memory. Of course, I oughtn't to have had Major"—she shot an affectionate glance at the scratching dog—"because dear Mother didn't like dogs, but she had a dog called Major when she was a child, so I've called him Major, which makes it seem a little less insulting to her memory."

The brown dog stood up, stretched, then went and put its front paws on Miss Maple's knee.

"No, Major," said Miss Maple weakly.

Ignoring her protest the brown dog jumped on to her knee and sat there, bolt upright, completely hiding its mistress.

"What sort of a dog is it?" said Richard.

Miss Maple's small face peeped round the large woolly head.

"A poodle, dear. At least, mainly a poodle. I mean, he's larger than a poodle, of course, but I think the poodle strain predominates. I haven't had him clipped because I think that the effect is just a little indelicate. They always remind me of chorus girls, though, of course, I've never seen a chorus girl." She glanced at the clock, "Oh, dear! I must be going now."

"But why?" said Richard. "You can't run away like this the minute you've come. We've got nine years to make up."

"Yes, indeed, but Mother always liked to have tea at four o'clock promptly, and I always try not to be late." She gently pushed the brown dog on to the floor and made an ineffectual attempt to brush the patch of brown fur from her skirt. "Anyway, it's been such a joy to see you, dear, and I'll look in to see the others in the course of a day or so when you're settled. I was feeling so depressed, and this little visit has quite cheered me up."

"Why were you feeling depressed?" said Richard.

Miss Maple, who had got up, sat down again.

"I've been so *worried*, Richard," she said, lowering her voice, "and it would be such a relief to confide in someone. No, you needn't go, Tilly. You can listen, too. After all, three heads are even better than one or two are."

Tilly, who was spreading butter on bread on the table by the window, nodded agreement. The brown dog went to investigate the dark recesses beneath the sink. Miss Maple continued.

"You see, ever since I was a girl I've been subscribing half a crown a year to something called The Friendship League. For quite a long time I thought that it was comforts for lighthouse-men and then I found that it was a Home for Rest for Animals, but that's neither here nor there. The point is that early in the summer a man came down from their headquarters and asked me to form a branch of the Society here in Priors Green and be its secretary and collect subscriptions and he just talked and talked and when he'd gone I found that I'd said I would without meaning to and it was too late to say I wouldn't, so—"

She stopped.

"Yes?" said Richard.

"Well, I've been trying to. I've been so worried I haven't been able to eat or sleep. You see . . . I made a list of people to ask in Priors Green, but—I can't ask them. I just *can't,* Richard. I get as far as the gate and then I go back. Sometimes I get right inside the house, and then I pretend I've come about something quite different. I simply can't ask them for subscriptions. I haven't got the courage. I've tried and tried and I can't. And I had a letter from the man yesterday asking for my list of subscribers and—well, I don't know what to do. I can't write back and say I haven't got any."

"What does he want exactly?" said Richard.

"He'd like about ten subscribers and he doesn't expect more than half a crown from any of them. It's only about twenty-five shillings, and I'd willingly pay it myself."

"Why not pay it yourself?"

"Oh, I can't do that, Richard. He wants public interest." Richard's mouth lengthened into a grin. He burrowed in his pockets and brought out a pencil and an envelope.

"All right," he said. "Let's give him public interest."

"What are you writing, Richard?"

"Your list of subscribers . . . 'Mrs. Smith, Belle View, Priors Green' . . . There isn't a Belle View, is there, Tilly?"

"No," said Tilly.

"'Mrs. Brown, Cosy Nook, Priors Green'. There isn't a Cosy Nook, is there, Tilly?"

"No."

"'Mrs. Merryweather, Vane House, Priors Green'."

"No, Richard," protested Miss Maple.

Richard continued to make his list.

"Let's have 'Mrs. Egerton, The Vicarage', just for a joke. She'll never know."

"No, Richard. It's not right."

"The end justifies the means," said Richard. "The Jesuits believed that and they were better people than we can ever hope to be . . . That's an idea. 'Mrs. Jesuit, Pope Villa, Priors Green'."

"Oh, dear!" said Miss Maple, torn between dismay and a certain fearsome excitement.

"'Mrs. Noah'. . ."

"No, Richard! . . . I must go now. This is all nonsense, dear boy. Of course I don't take it seriously. I'll be late for tea if I don't hurry. Good-bye, dear boy. Come, Major."

She went out through the kitchen door and hurried along the path to the gate. The brown dog ambled a few paces behind her, then sat down heavily on the path and began to scratch its underside.

Chapter Eleven

"Well, don't take all day about it," said Tilly sharply to the milkman as he stood measuring the milk into the milk-jugs at the kitchen table. "I've not got till the middle of next week if you have."

Jim was evidently not in the mood for the usual volley of back-chat. He looked at her dourly.

"You're different since they came," he said.

" 'Course I'm different," she said. "I'm busy. I've got a good deal more to do, let me tell you, than when I only had Miss Lubbock to see to."

"It's not that," he said. "You're different."

"Don't be daft," she said.

But she knew that she was different. Her life before the Culvertons returned to Linden Rise held now in her mind a strange dream-like quality and both Jim and his courtship shared in it. Her promise to marry Jim seemed no more real than the "spills" that Miss Lubbock had set her to make in her spare time. "You're daft," she said again.

"No, I'm not," he said. "I know when a person's different."

"I tell you, I'm busy," she said. "The Lynnekers are back from Scotland and they're giving a garden party at the Hall this afternoon and they're all going to it. I've got to iron out Miss Althea's dress and they're having lunch early and I'm that busy I don't know which way to turn."

His eyes searched her wooden features.

"You're different," he persisted.

"I'm not," she muttered sullenly.

"You're promised to me, you know, Tilly."

"I know."

"Don't you think it's time we fixed the day?"

"Where's the hurry?"

"Why not next month?"

"I'll be too busy."

He closed his mouth in a long firm line.

"I'll go to parson about it tonight and get the banns fixed up."

She shrugged, and he plodded slowly down the path.

Tilly put away the milk and returned to her ironing, taking a glowing red iron from the heart of the fire, slipping it into an ironing shoe and running it smoothly over the folds of organdie on the kitchen table.

A few minutes later she went up to Althea's and Vere's bedroom. Althea was standing at the dressing-table and Vere was sitting on the bed.

"Here's your dress, Miss Althea," said Tilly.

"Thank you, Tilly," said Althea in the tone of distant graciousness that she always used to Tilly. "Put it on the bed."

Tilly laid the dress on the bed and went downstairs. Althea spread out the folds with slow caressing touches. The dress was of white organdie, printed with pale blue flowers, trimmed at the hem with a small lace flounce and a ruching of pale blue ribbon.

"I'm going to wear my white lace hat with it. I threaded it with blue ribbon last night." She took from a drawer a pair of white open-work silk stockings and laid them on the bed with the dress, then took a pair of white kid shoes from the wardrobe and put them on the floor by the bed. "Get your dress out, too, Vere. Put out all the things you'll need so as to be ready to change into. You don't want to have to hunt for things at the last minute."

She spoke kindly. She was the elder sister initiating the younger sister into the intricacies, of the social maze. And Vere was in a mood to be initiated. Hanging in the wardrobe was the dress of primrose-coloured linen that Mrs. Culverton had sent for from Schoolbred's for the occasion of the Hall garden party. Though Vere was not to put her hair up till her coming-out dance, the dress was almost a grown-up dress. It reached almost to her ankles.

There was a little black velvet bow at the neck to match the black velvet sash.

"And don't scrape your hair back as you usually do," said Althea. "If you back-comb it a little and fix it with combs before you plait it, it'll suit you much better. I'll do it for you if you like."

"Thank you," said Vere, taking her dress from the wardrobe (for Althea had relented about the wardrobe and had allotted Vere three hooks in it) and laying it on the bed by Althea's.

Till now she had taken little interest in her appearance or her clothes but the primrose-coloured linen dress had wrought a sudden change in her. She saw herself in it as plainly as if it had been the picture of someone else. The long dark plait rather spoilt the picture, but soon her hair would lie in smooth coils in the nape of her neck. Soon she would be really grown-up . . . and at the thought excitement stirred in her heart.

"And don't go for a walk this morning," said Althea. "You should always take things easy on the day of a party. Otherwise you don't look your best. It's awful to feel that one's looking pale and off-colour. I wish they'd let us use rouge, but geranium petals are quite useful. Just rub them on your cheeks, you know. Dulcie Grey told me about them . . . We both ought to rest after lunch till it's time to get ready."

"Yes," agreed Vere, almost humble in her new role as Althea's disciple.

Althea opened another drawer and took out a flounced petticoat and lace-trimmed camisole, both threaded with pale blue baby-ribbon, and put them on the bed.

"I hope that Edmund will remember to call at the shop for those safety-pins. I forgot to pack any, and I want to pin my petticoat on to my corsets at the back and make sure that it doesn't dip. . . . Besides, I never really trust tape. Molly Kempton's came right off at the Morrisons' dance. It was frightful."

This holiday, like the former one, had now settled down into a regular pattern. Edmund divided his time between golf and reading. He made a conscientious study of what he called "current affairs", read three daily newspapers and several weekly reviews, and had brought away with him a selection of books dealing with political and economic problems. Richard "mooned about", as Mrs. Culverton put it, gossiping with the villagers, pottering in the garden, taking his place with the harvesters in the fields, helping Tilly in the kitchen. He read a good deal, too, but with less discrimination than Edmund, interspersing Plotinus' *Enneades* with the novelettes that Tilly kept in the drawer in the dresser. "He seems to have no sense of dignity," said Mrs. Culverton to Edmund, and Edmund agreed. Even the delicious dinners that Tilly served up night after night were spoilt for Mrs. Culverton by the knowledge that Richard had had a hand in their preparation.

Howard had suddenly left the cottage on the pretext of a business trip to Norway. He had grown more and more restless as the days went by and had suddenly announced his decision one morning at breakfast, packing his things and departing before his wife could rally her forces to remonstrate. As if to salve her pride and compensate for the slight of Howard's defection, she had begun to admit Althea into a new and more confidential relationship, taking her on shopping expeditions into Bellminster or on visits to houses in the neighbourhood, buying her presents of clothes and jewellery, consulting her about their arrangements, deferring to her judgment. At first Althea had been delighted by this new position of importance, but of late she, too, had been showing signs of restiveness. And Vere—till the Hall party and the new; dress had drawn her nearer—had stood aloof from the family circle. She went for long solitary walks over the countryside, her sketching block in her pocket, or lay on the grass in the orchard, absorbed in the books of travel that alone seemed to interest her.

"I'll lend you my gold locket," said Althea, opening her jewel-case and examining its contents. "It will go with your dress, and I'm wearing my aquamarine pendant."

"Thank you," said Vere again.

Althea went to the window and looked out at a blue sky flecked with lavender clouds.

"I shall kill myself if it rains," she said.

But it didn't rain. . . . The sun shone down brightly upon the smooth green lawns and ordered flower-beds of the Hall. The Hall itself was a pleasant rambling house—two long low wings on either side of a taller main building with a wide porticoed entrance. It was of no particular style of architecture, so inconvenient and badly planned that it needed an army of servants to ensure even the minimum of comfort, but it had an air of dignity and elegance; it suggested a placid, unhurried existence of culture and kindliness; within its walls, one felt, the good things of life had been both enjoyed and shared.

Sir Godfrey and Lady Lynneker stood at one end of the main lawn receiving their guests. At the other end a red-coated band, installed in an improvized bandstand, played a selection of Strauss waltzes.

Sir Godfrey Lynneker was talking to Mrs. Culverton. His tall, erect figure, well groomed grey moustache, the carnation in his buttonhole and the studied angle of his grey top hat gave him a slightly dandified air, but his blue eyes were keen and shrewd and his mouth was as firm as it was good-humoured.

"We're so much off the beaten track here," he was saying, that your coming makes local history. My wife will try to drag you onto all her pet committees. You mustn't let her absorb you, though actually, of course, it's Mrs. Egerton who manages us all."

He looked across the lawn to where his wife stood talking to Mrs. Egerton. Lady Lynneker was short and plump and placid-looking. Her two daughters, Mabel and Dorothy, stood near her. They were of heavier build than their mother, but their smiles, like hers, radiated a warm expansive kindlinesss. Both wore dresses of pale pink silk with accordion-pleated flounces and hats of elaborately frilled tulle that sat rather oddly above the plain, pleasant faces.

"Yes, I can believe that," said Mrs. Culverton. "It was Mrs. Egerton who made us buy Linden Rise. At least she suggested it . . ."

Sir Godfrey laughed.

"I know those suggestions. They're worse than the laws of the Medes and Persians . . . But, seriously, we're very glad to have you here. There seems to be a dearth of young people in this particular neighbourhood. And our young people and yours should get on well together—two boys and two girls of much the same age. Yours are cleverer than ours, of course."

"Oh, surely not," said Mrs. Culverton, a hint of motherly complacency peeping through the disclaimer.

"I had a talk with Edmund in the village yesterday, and I've never come across a boy of that age so well informed, and as to Richard—well, a First in Classics isn't got so easily."

"Yes, I suppose he's clever," said Mrs. Culverton a little dubiously.

She was still feeling worried about Richard. Only yesterday she and Althea and Vere had come in from a day's shopping in Bellminster to find Richard having tea with Tilly at the kitchen table.

"When you're alone here for tea, Richard," she had said to him afterwards, "Tilly must bring it in to you in the sitting-room on a tray."

He had looked at her with his lazy smile.

"But why?" he had said. "It seems so silly."

Lady Lynneker came across the lawn to join them.

"I'm just telling Mrs. Culverton what an acquisition her young people are going to be to Priors Green," said Sir Godfrey.

"Yes, indeed," said Lady Lynneker. "I love young people. I always collect as many as I can around me."

She hasn't suffered as I have, thought Mrs. Culverton with a pang of bitterness, or she couldn't look like that, smile like that.

. . . Self-pity closed over her, hiding the sunny lawn and the groups of chattering guests.

"They're the same ages, too," said Lady Lynneker, "but of course they're not so clever."

"I've just been saying that," said her husband, "though, mind you, Piers is clever in his own way."

Lady Lynneker's eyes went to where a tall young man, with a fine-drawn, sensitive face was talking to a slender girl with violet blue eyes and dark hair.

"That's Lindsay, my niece," she said. "Her parents died when she was a child and she's lived with us ever since." A shadow passed over her face. "She's not very strong."

"Old Roddy hasn't any brains at all," said Roddy's father, his face beaming with pride as he looked at a fair stocky boy who had just joined the group round Althea. "He only comes to life on a horse or playing with a ball."

Lady Lynneker smiled.

"Your daughter seems to have brought him to life," she said to Mrs. Culverton.

Althea stood in the centre of her little group, laughing and talking. Beneath her eagerness was a faint appealing shyness, a delicious hint of immaturity.

"How lovely she is!" said Lady Lynneker. "And Vere, too. Such a dear pretty child!"

Kindliness overflowed her heart, leaving no room for envy on behalf of her own homely daughters.

Mrs. Culverton's eyes narrowed slightly as they sought and found Vere, sitting on a seat under the shade of a cedar tree with a young man.

"That's the doctor's new assistant," said Lady Lynneker. "He's our most eligible bachelor. Your little girl has snatched him from under the very noses of the Corbett girls. There are four of them, and I heard that first of all they had decided to draw lots for him but had later agreed to open the fight to all four and let the best one win."

"Well, it's delightful for my young people to be here," said Mrs. Culverton. "We've always lived in a London suburb and this is a most refreshing change."

The strains of *Die Fledermaus* died away and *The Blue Danube* took its place. Sir Godfrey nodded approvingly.

"I always insist on that," he said. "They played it at the dance where we got engaged, so I always say 'Play any other tunes you like but you *must* play *The Blue Danube*'!"

Edmund passed, carrying a deck-chair, looking purposeful and competent.

"They're bringing out tea," said Lady Lynneker. "Find Mrs. Culverton a chair, dear, and see that she gets some."

Vere, sitting with the young man in the shadow of the cedar tree, was conscious chiefly of a feeling of bewilderment, but beneath the bewilderment excitement fluttered at her heart like a bird. In the last few minutes she had been rapt into a new world —a world in which young men gazed at one in ardent admiration and a dress of primrose-coloured linen made one look pretty and almost grown-up.

"I hope that we're going to see a lot of each other," the young man was saying. "It seemed such a dead-alive hole till you came to it, but as soon as I saw you I knew that it wasn't going to be dead-alive any longer."

He was an earnest, ingenuous young man . . . Meeting his eyes, hearing the deep tones of his voice against the sensuous strains of *The Blue Danube*, caught up in the atmosphere of gaiety and colour and movement and laughter, Vere felt something frozen in her turning to warmth and fluidity, felt a strange new languor stealing over her body. He put his hand on the seat by hers and the languor sharpened to delight.

"Don't you think it possible," he was saying, "for two people to meet and—and to know each other at once? I mean, to feel that they've always known each other . . . to sort of belong to each other. Does it seem absurd to you?"

She turned her head away. A flush dyed the smooth olive of her cheek.

"No," she whispered so low that he could only just hear.

"I've heard of it," he said, "but I never believed it till now, did you?"

"No . . . not till now."

"You're very young, aren't you?"

"I'm eighteen."

"Come and give us a hand with these tables, Larry," called someone. "Lady Lynneker wants them moved out of the sun." He rose with reluctance, his eyes still fixed on Vere.

"They're arranging croquet after tea," he said. "Will you be my partner?"

"Yes."

"You won't forget?" he persisted. "If anyone else asks you to be their partner, you'll say you've promised me, won't you?"

"Yes."

He went away and she sat gazing in front of her.

The crowd surged to and fro, the women's dresses making a gaily coloured pattern as they moved about—padded lace-frilled bosoms, tightly fitted waists and hips, cascades of flounces . . . gossamer trains sweeping the grass, feather boas floating gracefully, parasols archly twirled. Isolated pieces of conversation reached her as the groups passed and re-passed.

"So sad, the Empress Frederick's death!"

"Yes . . . Our dear Princess Royal. Her father's favourite child,"

"Of course the war's over to all intents and purposes, but the Boers won't admit it. The arrogance of that fellow Kruger is colossal."

"Chamberlain was so right to say that we'd fight them to a finish. It's the only sort of treatment that they understand."

"We saw Ellen Terry in *The Merry Wives of Windsor*. And of course the Academy."

Vere heard and saw none, of it. She still sat gazing in front of her, but she now sat rigid, her hands tightly clenched. Gradually the glow was fading, leaving her cold and frightened. It was like the goblin feasts one read of, whose fruit, so pleasant to the taste, turned to wormwood in the throat. She looked round at the rainbow-hued guests, the bright flower-beds, the sun-chequered lawn. It had all become sinister and treacherous and, despite the sunshine, dark. The words that floated from the groups around her turned to the words, "Come buy, come buy . . ." She looked down at the dress that had filled her with pride and joy only a few hours ago. That, too, was part of the trap. . . Panic mounted in her . . . She sprang to her feet, but before she could escape Larry returned.

"Look," he said, "they're starting the first game of croquet now. Will you come?"

She stared at him, her eyes dilated, the muscles of her face taut. "I don't want to play," she said breathlessly. "I don't like the game."

Then she turned from him abruptly and went away.

She had seen the hurt and resentment in his eyes and was conscious of a pang of compunction, but it was drowned immediately in a surging flood of gladness and relief. She'd broken free. She belonged to herself once more. I'll never let it happen to me again, she said to herself. Never, never, never . . .

When next Mrs. Culverton looked round for her, she saw to her dismay that she was standing by herself, watching the crowd, sullen and scowling, her underlip thrust out—the Vere of her childhood.

Althea didn't know how it was that she found herself sitting at a little table with Mrs. Redburn. Mrs. Redburn was a small, seductive-looking woman with a mouth like a cupid's bow and eyes like black plums. There was a sort of bloom about her, thought Althea, studying her, but there was a snake-like quality about her, too. She wore a dress of violet-coloured silk that revealed the curves of hip and bosom a little too plainly and a close-fitting toque of artificial violets.

"You don't remember me, do you?" she said.

Althea searched her memory.

"I don't think I do . . ."

"Oh, I remember you so well," said Mrs. Redburn. "Such a lovely child you were! I knew you were going to turn into a beauty, but I didn't know quite *what* a beauty."

The flattery was so crude that even Althea, who loved flattery, had a feeling of embarrassment. She gave a constrained smile.

"The men were all round you this afternoon like bees round a honey-pot," said Mrs. Redburn.

She had a smooth silky voice that seemed to creep along one's nerves even after she had finished speaking.

"Oh, I don't know," said Althea uneasily.

"Your father's not here?"

"No, he's had to go away on business."

Mrs. Redburn laughed softly, showing a red-pointed tongue between very white teeth.

"On business!" she repeated, as if lingering over an excellent joke. "I think he's the most handsome man I've ever seen."

"Yes, he's very good-looking," agreed Althea vaguely.

"I hear you've bought Linden Rise."

"Yes."

"So you're one of us now . . . I suppose you know everyone here?"

Althea's eyes wandered among the crowd.

"Not quite everyone."

"No, of course. The Lynnekers cast a wide net for these occasions. And, my dear, I don't suppose you know even the people you've met . . . Now tell me whom you've met."

At each name Althea mentioned, the smooth silky tongue set to work. Sneers . . . innuendoes . . . dark hints. Something in Althea made her shrink away from it, but something else attracted her towards it. She could have stopped it, she knew, but she didn't want to stop it. Repelled and fascinated, she made the right comments, asked the right questions, drew Mrs. Redburn on from revelation to revelation, ignoring her secret distaste. The red venom-tipped tongue shot out between the smiling lips.

"As to the Lynnekers . . . of course they're my hosts, so I shouldn't say anything against them, but—"

"Yes?" encouraged Althea. "Just fools," said Mrs. Redbum a little flatly. "Thinking so much of themselves. Giving themselves airs. So gracious and patronizing. That clodhopper, Roddy. Those, great plain horsy girls."

"What about Piers?" said Althea.

Her glance went to where Piers stood on the terrace outside the house, talking to the girl with violet-blue eyes and dark hair. He was tall and good-looking and he had been the centre of all the day-dreams she had woven round this afternoon. He would be Sir Piers Lynneker. He would own this house and estate. His wife would queen it over the neighbourhood. And not only over the neighbourhood. London . . . the season . . . money . . . jewels . . .

admiration . . . As she put on the organdie dress and lace hat, she had seen herself through his eyes, had lived in eager anticipation of their meeting. And the meeting had disappointed and humiliated her. He had greeted her courteously, but as if he did not really see her. Not once had he joined the group that clustered round her. Not once had his eyes strayed in her direction. It was clear that to him she was no different from any of the other guests who thronged the lawns. Roddy had hovered about her, beaming ingenuous admiration, but it was not the younger brother she was interested in.

"That's his cousin, isn't it?" she said, "the girl who lives with them . . ."

"Yes." The silky voice grew lower. The violet toque drew nearer. "My dear, I could tell you something about *her*. If he knew what she *was* . . ."

"Tell me," pleaded Althea. "Do tell me."

"Well, he's adored her ever since she was a child. It's common knowledge that he's proposed to her over and over again."

"Won't she accept him?" said Althea, vague hopes rising again in her heart.

Mrs. Redburn shrugged.

"She's clever," she said. "She holds him off. She'll take him in the end, of course, but if he knew what she *was* . . ."

"Do tell me," pleaded Althea again.

"Well," the silky voice was only a whisper now, "it happened last summer. She gave out that she was going to the South of France with a friend for three months. Everyone believed it, but I found out that she'd never been near the South of France."

"Where had she been?"

"She'd been to a nursing-home in London. I found it out quite by chance. He'd no idea of it. Neither had anyone else."

"But why?" said Althea. "What did it mean?"

Again Mrs. Redburn shrugged, spreading out plump ringed hands.

"My dear, what does it mean when a girl goes into a nursing-home for several months and doesn't tell anyone? Surely you know."

The colour flamed into Althea's cheeks.

"You mean—that?" she gasped.

"Of course I do."

"But doesn't he know? Surely he ought to know?"

"Of course he ought," said Mrs. Redburn, "but I'm the only person who knows and I daren't tell him." She gave a short laugh. "I can dare a lot but not that."

Althea looked at her for a moment in silence.

"Why did you tell me?" she said.

One part of her had seized avidly on the piece of scandal, but the other part—the child who still lived in her—felt ashamed and besmirched.

"I thought it would amuse you," said Mrs. Redburn lightly, "You hardly know them, so it can't mean much to you. People here are such toadies. It's high treason to say a word against the Lynnekers here. I often watch those two and have a good laugh to myself thinking of it. If only he *knew* . . . Watch them now."

Althea turned her head to look at the couple on the terrace, but as she looked they went towards the long french window and vanished into the house.

Chapter Twelve

"What's the matter, Lindsay?" said Piers.

The room was high and dim and cool. Drawn curtains at the windows kept out the sun, and the air was sweet with the scent of the roses that were massed in an old Delft soup tureen on a low chest against the wall. The sounds from the lawn—the chatter and laughter and strains of the band—were muted and distant.

Lindsay had gone to a settee in the farthest corner of the room. Piers followed and sat down by her.

"What is it, darling?"

"I've got a headache. It's the heat, I think. Don't stay with me, Piers. I shall be all right."

"You shouldn't have gone riding this morning. You should have rested."

"I can't rest. You know I can't rest."

He knew that she couldn't rest. She was either upheld by surging excitement or plunged into black depression. Her moods changed so suddenly that, however hard one tried to be prepared for the change, it took one always by surprise.

She had removed her hat and her dark hair fell softly over her high blue-veined forehead. Her eyes were shadowed, yet curiously bright and glancing. They moved around the room now, darting here and there in quick, aimless scrutiny. Her mouth was long and beautifully arched, but it was set in a line of strain, and every now and then the corners gave a quick nervous twitch. Her hands, resting on the settee, clenched and unclenched themselves. He laid his hand on the one that was near him.

"Don't, Lindsay," he said.

She gave a faint, uncertain smile.

"I'm sorry. I'm all on edge this afternoon. I don't know why."

"Stop worrying about things, Lindsay. Say you'll marry me. I'll look after you."

"Piers, we've been over it so often. It wouldn't be any use."

"Why not?"

She looked at his thin sensitive face.

"We're too much alike. We'd wear each other out. The more we loved each other the more we'd wear each other out. And we're both—frightened."

"Frightened?"

" Yes. Frightened of everything. Of people and things and—life."

"I'm not frightened, Lindsay," he said gently, holding her hand and intertwining his fingers with hers.

"Yes, you are. You won't face it, but you know in your heart that you're frightened. I've had to face it because—" She turned her head away with a sudden sharp movement.

"Don't, Lindsay. Don't think of it."

"We'd tear each other to shreds without meaning to. You'd be hurt for days because of the way I'd looked or spoken . . . and I'd be the same. We'd torture each other, although we loved each other . . . because we loved each other. We each ought to marry someone stolid and stupid and insensitive."

He laughed shortly.

"How terrible!"

"If I marry at all, that's the sort of man I'm going to marry," she said.

"No, you're not. You're going to marry me." He took both her hands. "You love me, Lindsay. You know in your heart that you love me."

"I love you more than anyone in the world, Piers, but—not that way. I'm not going to marry you."

He heard his mother's voice on the terrace outside, "Where's Piers?" He rose. Then he bent over the settee, put his hands on her shoulders and pushed her gently against the cushions.

135

"Rest, darling," he said. "Rest and relax. I'll be back as soon as I can."

Left alone, she sat up again with a quick jerk of her slender body, and her violet-blue eyes widened with fear as they moved round the room. In the half-light the shadows seemed to take on a life of their own, hostile and sinister, gathering together in the corners. The ticking of the Sèvres clock on the chimney-piece lost its sleepy note and became sharp with menace. Her fear intensified till it was beyond control. She rose quickly and made her way out again to the terrace. Piers was not there. In front of her was the lawn with its crowds of guests and she shrank from the thought of joining them, but behind her lay the empty room with the gathering shadows and the ticking clock. Then suddenly came the memory of the cool quiet spot beneath the trees at the other side of the kitchen garden that was her favourite refuge. None of the guests would be there. She took one of the deckchairs that were stacked at the end of the terrace and stood hesitating. To reach her refuge she would have to cross the lawn, to face the hordes of people who seemed to be her enemies, who seemed already to be watching her malevolently. And then, while she hesitated, a young man appeared, walking across the terrace with an air of quiet purpose. She had met him earlier in the afternoon. He was the elder of the two Culverton boys—the good-looking one. He stopped.

"May I carry that for you, Miss Moreton?" he said, taking the chair from her.

Their eyes met. He saw nothing of her indecision, her secret fear. She was just a girl who wanted a chair taken somewhere. And, with his quiet earnest gaze upon her, she became just a girl who wanted a chair taken somewhere.

"Oh, thank you," she said. "I'm trying to find a place away from the crowd. I'm feeling rather tired and it's so hot on the lawn."

He considered the question for a moment with frowning concentration.

"Why not go and watch the croquet on the other lawn?" he said. "Actually, I was just going to watch it myself. I'll put your chair in the shade and away from the other seats so that you can watch the game without interruption."

She drew a long deep sigh. This was what she wanted, someone to take decisions out of her hands—those small, trivial, everyday decisions that wore down her spirit—to tell her what to do in this calm authoritative manner.

"I'm afraid that I haven't played croquet since I was here as a child nine years ago," he said as he walked beside her, carrying the chair, "but I'm very anxious to learn, and I think that one can learn a game best by watching it carefully."

He set the chair up for her in the shadow of some trees on the edge of the croquet lawn. A short distance away was a group of chairs filled by laughing, chattering young people.

"We'll stay here, I think," said Edmund. "You can't watch a game properly if you're distracted by people talking to you. I'll sit here with you if you don't mind."

"No, please do," said Lindsay.

He fetched another deck-chair and sat in it by her side, leaning forward, watching the game intently and in silence. He wasn't like Piers. He didn't throw her anxious sidelong glances wondering what was in her mind, if anything had happened to upset her, hurting her by his anxiety and receiving hurt in his turn from her hurt. This man wasn't even interested in her. He hardly knew she was there. He only wanted to learn how to play croquet. And while he was there she was safe. No one could worry her . . . nothing could frighten her. She relaxed peacefully in her chair.

Miss Maple and Richard were sitting at a small table near the buffet. Miss Maple wore the dress that she had worn at garden parties for the last six years. It was a dress of foulard silk with a beige ground and flowers climbing about it in all directions. Her faded panama hat was contemporary with the dress, but was refurbished each summer by a trimming of fresh ribbon to match the flowers. This year it was red to match the red flowers, last year it had been blue to match the blue flowers and the year before it had been green to match the green flowers. She wore a pair of white kid gloves, yellowed by age, black cotton stockings and stout black leather walking shoes.

"Seed cake?" she said, looking at the plate of cakes that Richard was handing to her. "It's a great favourite of mine, but I don't think I'd better. Mother didn't like it and I make it a rule never to have any in the house." She hesitated, selected a small currant bun, then, lowering her voice, said, "Richard . . ."

"Yes?"

"I sent that list in—the one you did in the kitchen."

"Good for you!"

"And I had such a nice letter from the man, thanking me for rousing public interest in the cause. You know . . ."

"Yes?" said Richard again.

"It's my first incursion into crime and—well, I really find it rather thrilling, Of course, I feel guilty, too, but I can understand the—the sort of *thrill,* that international spies and people like that get out of it."

"That's grand," said Richard.

"It gives one a strange feeling of *daring.* I think I'll have that piece of seed cake, after all."

Richard passed her the plate of cakes.

"As long as you stop on the right side of the law," he said, "the possibilities are endless."

"Yes, indeed," said Miss Maple, "and it's true what they say in tracts. After the first downward step the rest is easy. There's a sort of *lure* in it. Since I sent in that list I've had temptations that I never had before."

"What sort of temptations?" said Richard.

"Well, yesterday I was suddenly tempted to buy some new clothes. It's wrong to care what you look like, and, of course, the price even of a new hat would buy food for a starving family, but I don't know any starving families, and I contribute regularly anyway to the Sick and Poor Fund, but Mother allowed me ten pounds a year for clothes, and it seems an insult to her memory to spend more now that she's gone."

"It would be fun," said Richard, his glance travelling from her deplorable hat to her deplorable shoes. "Let's do it together. Let's go into Bellminster and get you a whole new outfit. You could try the things on and I could tell you if you looked nice in them."

"Oh, *no,* Richard. I resisted the temptation. I decided quite finally not to buy any new clothes . . . but it shows how true it is that once you start—slipping, you simply can't stop, because no sooner had I resisted that temptation than I had another one."

"What was the other one?" said Richard.

"You'd hardly believe it. I simply don't know how, to tell you."

"You can tell me," said Richard. "I can believe most things, and I'm as silent as the grave."

"It was much worse than the first one, and I'm sure I shouldn't have had either of them if I hadn't sent that list."

"What was it?" persisted Richard.

"It sounds dreadful, put into words, Richard. It was—well, I was lying in bed this morning and I had a sudden temptation to go abroad."

"Go abroad?"

"Yes. To Paris or Rome or the Channel Islands. Just to see what they're like."

"But why shouldn't you?"

"Oh, Richard, it would be an insult to Mother's memory. She couldn't bear foreigners. She never went abroad in her life."

"Yes, but—" began Richard.

Miss Maple interrupted him,

"I didn't feel quite happy about going to church after sending that list, but still I haven't done anything as bad as the people in the Bible did."

"And they seemed to get away with it all right," said Richard.

"Yes, indeed," agreed Miss Maple earnestly. "Look at David. He's held up to us as an example and he did far worse things than making up a list of people out of his head."

"Or eating seed cake," said Richard, and they both laughed.

"Come along," he continued. "Let's have a game of croquet."

"Oh, no, Richard. I couldn't. I must be going home now. Mother always used to get upset if I wasn't back from a garden party by six."

"All right," said Richard. "I'll see you to the gate."

"Thank you, dear boy. I'll just go and say good-bye to Lady Lynneker . . . Richard, it *is* rather exciting, isn't it?"

Mrs. Egerton, sitting beside the Vicar's warden and gently suggesting several improvements in the organization of the next church social, looked up as Richard and Miss Maple passed her chair. Miss Maple's eyes were bright and her cheeks were flushed. She was laughing and the panama hat was slightly askew. If I hadn't known her for fourteen years, thought Mrs. Egerton, I'd think she was tipsy.

The guests were gradually departing on foot or in carriages. The Culvertons collected themselves together and took their leave of Lady Lynneker. The Lynneker girls accompanied them to the gate. A host of dogs had been released as the party ended and were leaping round the two girls.

"Down, Rover! They're so rough that we kept them in the kennels till people began to go because they *will* jump up and people don't like it in their best clothes. To heel, Prince! He's no idea what 'heel' means, the darling, and I've spent months trying to teach him. It *has* been lovely to see you . . . *No*, Ranger! . . . You must come again soon . . . *Quiet*, Hector! . . . Let's all have a picnic sometime . . . It's been such fun."

They waved good-bye at the gate, and the Culvertons walked slowly down the road towards the village.

"I suppose we might have had a cab," said Mrs. Culverton, "but it didn't seem worth it."

"Oh, no," said Edmund, "it's much better for us to walk—especially after all those rich cakes they had for tea."

"Did you enjoy it, Edmund?" said Mrs. Culverton.

"Yes, thank you," said Edmund. "It was very pleasant. I really think I've got the hang of the thing now. Croquet, I mean. I think I could face a game in public now without making a fool of myself. I hadn't even seen it played since that time we were here before."

"You were sitting with Miss Moreton, weren't you?"

"Yes," said Edmund. "A nice quiet girl."

"And what about you, darling?" said Mrs. Culverton, turning to Althea, who was walking on the other side of her. "You enjoyed it, didn't you?"

"Yes . . ." said Althea.

Her eyes were starry and there was a little secret smile on her lips.

"Roddy Lynneker was very attentive, wasn't he?" said Mrs. Culverton, a note of archness in her voice.

Mentally she had made up a list of "eligibles" for Althea from their London acquaintances, but now mentally she tore it up. The Lynneker connection would be much more satisfactory. They had breeding, money and an assured position. They could give Althea everything she wanted.

"Yes, he was, wasn't he?" said Althea with just the right mixture of pleasure, amusement and diffidence in her voice.

"Whenever I looked at you, he was hovering round," said Mrs. Culverton with a fond smile.

"The main thing is not to use too much force," said Edmund, "and, of course, to manoeuvre into a favourable position."

"He's very good-looking," said Mrs. Culverton.

Althea was silent. She wasn't thinking of Roddy. She was thinking of Piers. Choosing her moment, stalking him with admirable finesse, she had waylaid him on the terrace in front of the house. He told her that he was looking for Lindsay and she had begun to talk to him about Lindsay, praising her with a mixture of naive enthusiasm and childlike shyness, feeling her way, acquiring a new and deeper guilefulness beneath the surface ingenuousness that served her so well. And at once his interest had been aroused. He had responded with a sort of eager gratitude . . . And you couldn't lay it on too thick, she thought with faint contempt. He'd swallow any flattery of Lindsay . . . She wasn't, of course, sure of the success of her tactics. They might lead nowhere at all. But at least it was a step in the right direction to have roused his interest in her, to have made him see her as a definite person and connect her with Lindsay in his mind.

"And he's a wonderful sportsman, I gather," continued Mrs Culverton.

"It's a great mistake to make games an end in themselves," said Edmund. "As a relaxation they're in their right place, and one's justified in trying to play them as well as one can, but they shouldn't take the place of the serious business of life."

Mrs. Culverton looked at Richard and Vere, who were walking together in silence.

"I didn't see you talking to anyone in particular, Richard," she said dryly.

Richard threw his mind back over the afternoon.

"I talked to Miss Maple," he said.

"Oh, Miss Maple!" said Mrs. Culverton, dismissing Miss Maple with a shrug.

Tilly was sitting at the table chopping almonds when Richard entered the kitchen a few minutes later.

"Can I give you a hand with anything, Mrs. Noah?" he said. "No, thank you, Mr. Richard," said Tilly. "It's curried fowl and I've just put the minced apple in the sauce and it's got to simmer for half an hour and I've got the fowl frying nicely and then it's got to cook half an hour more after I've got the almonds and the sauce in."

"Yes, I remember," said Richard, inspecting stew-pan and casserole. "Don't forget the lemon juice and cream."

"Not likely!" said Tilly.

"Well, if you don't really need me, I'll go out for a walk. I want to work the whole thing out of my system—chatter and *The Blue Danube* and people wearing their best clothes."

"Well, you're not doing that," said Tilly, glancing at the shabby tweed coat he had put on. "Where are you going?"

"I'm going to Elston Woods. I've found a place there straight out of the seventh Idyll. There's a spring with a poplar beside it, and the elm trees form a shadowy glade, arched overhead, woven with green leaves."

"One of your old books?"

"Theocritus."

"Go on. Tell me the story of it," she said. "I can listen while the fowl's frying. I've got everything ready."

"There isn't a story. There's only Lycidas, the goat-herd. He wears a goat skin and an old cloak, buckled with a plaited belt, and he carries a crooked stick of wild olive. He's the finest flute player among all the herdsmen and reapers and he'll drive all the frills and flounces and feather boas out of my system. He's much more real than Lady Lynneker or Mrs. Egerton."

"Get away with you, Mr. Richard," said Tilly with her rusty laugh.

Richard took his pipe from his pocket, lit it with a spill from the kitchen fire, then set out along the narrow lane between tangled hedges fragrant with late honeysuckle. Already the green of the elm trees was fading to russet and golden tassels hung from the sycamores. When he reached the brow of the hill, he slackened his pace and, taking his battered Theocritus from his pocket, began to read as he walked. Suddenly he stopped short . . . He had thought that the lane was empty, but now he saw a girl in a cotton dress standing at a gate in the shadow of a tree, gazing down into the valley. She turned to him and he recognized the grey-blue eyes, fringed with dark lashes, and the soft sweet childish mouth.

"It's Polly," he said.

She shook her head. The colour had crept into her creamy cheeks.

"No, it's Myrtle," she corrected.

He laughed.

"So you're still just alike."

She nodded shyly. He saw again the little girl with her finger in her mouth.

"We've been here three weeks," he said, "and I've not seen you till now."

"I've seen you," she said.

"Then why haven't I seen you?"

"I hid."

"Where?"

"Anywhere. When I saw you I hid."

"Why?"

"I thought I wouldn't know what to say to you."

"But you do."'

Again the slow sweet smile.

"Yes . . . I don't feel shy now I'm with you, but I wouldn't have spoke to you if you hadn't spoke to me . . . Where are you going?"

"I was going to Elston Woods. Where are you going?"

"Nowhere. I came to see if I could see the fair."

"What fair?"

"The fair over at Horden. It comes every year. You can't see it because it's just round the bend of the hills, but you can hear it. Listen."

Richard listened and caught a sound so faint that it could hardly be detached from the other sounds of the summer evening. "Merry-go-rounds," he said.

She nodded.

"Polly and me's always gone there together till this year."

"Where's Polly, then?"

"She's gone to Hurst Farm over at Mallingford to help aunt. Uncle's ill and aunt wants help. She'll be there six weeks, maybe."

"You miss her?"

She nodded.

"Her and me always did things together."

"Did you share your sweethearts?" he teased.

"We didn't want no sweethearts, Polly and me," she said solemnly.

"How did you go to the fair?"

"By bus from the green . . . There's swings and hoop-la."

"And coconut shies?"

"Yes."

"And Aunt Sallies?"

"Yes."

"And shooting at balls?"

"Yes."

"And a Fat Woman?"

"Yes."

"And a Strong Man?"

"Yes . . . and there's a goat that draws a little go-cart with a monkey driving it."

He shut his book and put it into his pocket.

"Come on," he said. "Let's go."

Chapter Thirteen

It was a few weeks later that Aunt Gertrude arrived unexpectedly from a cruise, accompanied by a fiancé. There was nothing unusual in this. Aunt Gertrude was always arriving from cruises accompanied by fiancés. Great-aunt Lucy had died six years ago, leaving all her money to Aunt Gertrude, and Aunt Gertrude was now a wealthy woman. She could afford cruises and she could afford fiancés. The fiancés were generally much younger than Aunt Gertrude. They wore the air of victims decked out for sacrifice—with the gold cigarette-cases, the gold watches, the rings, the pearl studs, the Savile Row outfits that Aunt Gertrude always showered upon them. They looked startled and a little anxious, and they generally managed to make good their escape just as Aunt Gertrude was setting about the preparations for the wedding. Aunt Gertrude was never unduly perturbed by this. She spent her life going on one cruise after another, and the fiancé-hunt added zest to an existence that might otherwise have become slightly monotonous. Her latest fiancé was a member of a Shakespearean touring company, whom she had captured in Sydney and brought home in triumph by the next boat.

She arrived at Linden Rise just as Mrs. Culverton, Althea and Vere were having tea. In the nine years since her last visit she had grown much fatter; her untidy hair was grey, her features thick and heavy, but her vitality was unimpaired. She burst in upon them with a scream of excitement.

"I heard you were here, so I just *had* to come. No, you mustn't get up and you mustn't put yourselves out in the teeniest bit because we've booked rooms at The Blue Dragon in Bellminster, and we're terribly busy and we're only just darting in and out on you."

"We?" said Mrs. Culverton faintly.

"Yes," said Aunt Gertrude, with an air of faintly mischievous triumph. She went to the door, which she had closed behind her, and threw it open.

"Come in, Herbert."

A tall thin man entered the room with an air of impressive dignity. His greying hair receded from prominent temples. He had deep-set eyes, an aquiline nose, a long flexible mouth and a well-formed chin. He shone with Aunt Gertrude's offerings. His gold watch-and-chain were new, his pearl tie-pin was new, his suit and shoes were new, his embroidered waistcoat gleamed with virgin blue and gold.

"This is Herbert," said Aunt Gertrude. "Herbert Partridge. I'm sure you must have heard of him. He's played several parts in the West End."

Herbert, in no way embarrassed by the Culvertons' scrutiny, bowed gracefully. It was a curtain-call bow—assured, unsmiling, debonair.

"Now whom does he remind you of?" said Aunt Gertrude, cutting short the murmur of greeting. "Look at him. Whom does he remind you of? The living image."

Herbert turned his profile to them, gazing absently out of the window. They stared at his profile in a bewildered silence.

"Yes, Henry Irving," said Aunt Gertrude, though no one had spoken. "Everyone notices it, don't they, Herbert?"

"It's a likeness," said Herbert, bringing his full face to bear on them with a faint smile, "that is frequently commented on."

He had a deep resonant voice that seemed to make his most trivial utterances pregnant with hidden meaning.

"Do sit down and have some tea," said Mrs. Culverton, recovering her scattered forces.

"No, thank you," said Aunt Gertrude. "I've had tea at the hotel and Herbert doesn't take tea. Now tell me all your news."

"There isn't much to tell," said Mrs. Culverton. "I'm sorry the boys aren't here. They both go up to London every day, now that Edmund's back at work and Richard's studying for the Bar. It's your news we want to hear."

Herbert had lowered his tall figure into a small arm-chair, where he sat with his profile turned on them and his chin slightly raised. Aunt Gertrude gazed at him with proprietary pride.

"We're going to be married quite soon, aren't we, dearest?" she said. Herbert inclined his head, then raised it to the angle that best concealed the slightly sagging chin. "In the late autumn or early winter, probably. Herbert's a well-known Shakespearean actor, you know. He was playing Shakespeare in Australia when we met. He's played Shakespeare all over the world—in Jamaica, Trinidad, South Africa, the Bahamas, the Canaries, everywhere. You did bring your press-cutting album, didn't you, dear?"

"I left it in the hall," said Herbert, rising from his chair to make a graceful, unhurried exit. He returned a few moments later with a brief-case, standing for a second or two in the doorway to collect their glances before moving slowly and impressively back to his chair.

"There they are, my dear," he said, handing the case to Aunt Gertrude with a deprecating smile. "Hopelessly exaggerated, some of them, of course."

"Oh, no, darling," protested Aunt Gertrude. "Not exaggerated in the least."

She took an album from the case and, sitting down by Mrs. Culverton, began to turn over the pages, reading the notices aloud.

Vere moved her chair nearer the actor's, fixing her dark eyes on him intently.

"Tell me about them," she said. "About Trinidad and Jamaica and South Africa . . ."

The lure of far distant places still drew her like a will-o'-the-wisp, seeming to hold some magic that would give life the meaning and. completion it now lacked. She wandered in a sort of waste land between her tormented adolescence and a maturity that evaded her. On the afternoon of the Hall garden party she had crossed the boundary that divided them and had turned back in panic.

Since then she had again withdrawn herself—silent and aloof—from the life around her. But, for all her appearance of self-sufficiency, her defences were failing her. She had so encased herself in her childhood's armour that her adolescence had been retarded, but when it came it brought a new receptivity. People, things, ideas impinged violently on her consciousness. She could no longer hide from them. But she fought savagely to hide from them, to belong wholly to herself as she used to belong, ever striving to build up her defences as they crumbled around her. She had lost interest in her drawing since it had been arranged for her to go to the Slade School. It had been her refuge, but now it had become one of the forces from outside that threatened her. She had come across an Arabic grammar in a secondhand shop in Bellminster and was studying it when alone in her bedroom or on her solitary walks. The thought of it was a secret comfort to her as she plodded her way through the routine of household duties and social functions on which Mrs. Culverton insisted. She was becoming known as "the shy Miss Culverton" or, more unkindly, as "the dull Miss Culverton".

"Trinidad . . ." said Herbert thoughtfully. "Forests . . . green valleys . . . lakes . . . Port of Spain is specially beautiful. A wonderful waterfall falling from the woods into a rocky pool with trees around and a most gratifying reception of my Polonius."

Vere was silent, clothing the bare bones of the description with her imagination, seeing a fairy glen of unforgettable loveliness echoing to the music of falling water.

"And Egypt . . ." she said breathlessly. "Have you ever been to Egypt?"

"I was in Cairo once." He turned his head towards the group gathered round the press-cutting album. "You won't overlook the Horatio ones, will you? They are, I think, the kindest of all." He turned back to Vere. "Egypt? . . . The gold of the desert, the blue of the sky . . . They gave my Theseus a wonderful ovation."

"Well, there you are!" said Aunt Gertrude, closing the book. That shows what an actor he is, doesn't it? He's had his ups and downs, of course . . ."

"'The affairs of men rest still uncertain'," said Herbert, and added, *"Julius Caesar."*

"But—I don't want him to do any more touring. They all *want* him, of course, all over the world, but I think it's time he concentrated on the West End. He'd have been a West End star long before now if he hadn't stood down to let other people have their chance. Of course, success isn't everything—"

"'Oh, fortune, fortune, all men call thee fickle'," said Herbert and added, *"Romeo and Juliet."*

"He's got a quotation for everything," said Aunt Gertrude with a fond smile, "but, as I say, I want to get him back on the West End stage. I'm arranging some readings for him. I've approached several literary societies and they've agreed to let him do readings. I was wondering whether there was one here that would let him."

"Yes, I think there is one," said Mrs. Culverton vaguely. "I know they've approached Edmund about giving them a Talk of some kind."

"We're not charging anything at the moment," said Aunt Gertrude, "because we want to get him *known* again. Then probably the West End will approach him." Herbert gazed out of the window as if the conversation did not concern him. "He can do whole scenes, taking all the characters in different voices. Well, that shows he's better than the ordinary actor who can only just take one part, doesn't it? Do that scene from *Twelfth Night* that you know by heart, Herbert."

"Oh, no, my dear," said Herbert with his deprecating smile. "They wouldn't want to listen to that."

"But you would, wouldn't you?" said Aunt Gertrude.

The Culvertons gave a vague murmur of assent.

"Besides, it will be practice for you, darling," went on Aunt Gertrude, "because you know you're going to read *Twelfth Night* at the Eastgate Literary Society meeting next month."

"Well, of course," said Herbert, yielding, "if you all *insist.*" He stood for a moment in an attitude suggestive of an Entrance, then launched into the scene, adopting a deep voice for Sir Toby, a high-pitched voice for Sir Andrew Aguecheek, a lisping voice for Malvolio and a throaty contralto for Maria.

Mrs. Culverton did not trouble to conceal her boredom, pursing her lips, tapping her fingers on the arm of her chair. Althea listened and watched with a disdainful curl of her lips.

Althea was feeling depressed and unhappy and vaguely angry, and it was a relief to vent her irritation on this ridiculous fiancé of Aunt Gertrude's. Her affairs seemed to have reached an *impasse* and she didn't know what to do about it. She had attached herself firmly to Piers and Lindsay. Edmund, too, had joined the party, and there it had stopped. The four of them played tennis and croquet and went for walks together. Lindsay turned to Edmund for advice and reassurance, but there was something so impersonal about Edmund's attentions that not even Piers could feel jealous. The situation had become static and irksome. Something ought to be done about it, Althea felt, but she couldn't think what to do. It was plain that Piers liked her, but, as long as he saw Lindsay enshrined above all others and worshipped at her shrine, the affair couldn't progress. It was a humiliating position, and Althea wasn't accustomed to humiliating positions. It made her bad-tempered and she vented her bad temper freely on everyone around her.

Herbert, as Malvolio, was doing a bit of comedy business with the letter, pretending to drop it and picking it up. Althea stared at him blankly in a manner that was intended to be offensive. Herbert, apparently absorbed by his comedy business, missed neither the stare nor the offensiveness. Only Vere followed his every word and movement with a rapt, intent gaze. She didn't hear a word he said. She didn't even know—or care—what scene he was acting. He was someone who had been to Trinidad, Cairo, Jamaica . . . who had seen the golden glow of the desert against the blue sky, the grandeur of tropical forests, of majestic waterfalls, of deep still lakes, walled by green foliage. Her eyes were fixed on him as though, by the very intensity of her gaze, she could wrest his knowledge from him.

The scene was over and Herbert stood, bowing modestly and mopping his brow with a delicately perfumed handkerchief. Mrs.

Culverton clapped languidly, Althea gave a scornful smile and Vere continued to gaze at him absorbedly.

"How delightful!" said Mrs. Culverton. "So kind of you!"

"Well, you'll remember, won't you?" said Aunt Gertrude. "He's open to engagements any time from now on. Dramatic and literary societies and things like that. The only condition, is, of course, that if he gets a West End offer he'll have to throw up any other engagement to accept it. They'll have to take the risk of that . . . And now, darlings, we must fly. No, we haven't even time to look round the garden. We'll be seeing you again, of course, but this evening we're going to be terribly busy. We've got the secretary of Bellminster Dramatic Society coming to dinner. I think they're going to snap Herbert up for their autumn programme. Come along, Herbert darling." Herbert gathered himself together for his Exit. "I'm so sorry we've missed the boys."

"They catch a London connection together at Bellminster each morning," said Mrs. Culverton, "but they return at different times. Edmund doesn't get back till later, but you may meet Richard on his way from the bus stop."

"We'll look out for him," said Aunt Gertrude. "He may be able to introduce Herbert's work to the Bar."

Chapter Fourteen

They didn't meet Richard, however. Richard had gone straight from the bus stop to Blenheim Villa. He found Miss Maple sitting alone in her overcrowded little sitting-room, knitting socks for seamen. She knitted a good many socks for seamen these days as a sort of sop to her conscience.

"How nice to see you, dear boy!" she said. "I was hoping you'd call."

"I've brought you some papers," said Richard. He sat down by her and took a sheaf of leaflets from his pockets. "They give you all the particulars of trips to Paris, Rome, Norway, Belgium and any amount of other places."

Miss Maple laid aside her sock, glanced at them, then thrust them aside.

"Oh, Richard, I couldn't! What would people think? It would look so *odd*."

"Why odd?" said Richard.

"Well, I never *have* gone abroad. Dear Mother never went abroad."

Richard smiled.

"Well, read them and think them over," he said. He gave her a disapproving scrutiny. "You've not got it on."

"Oh, Richard, I couldn't. Not just sitting alone in the house like this."

"Have you worn it out of doors?"

"Oh, I couldn't do that, Richard. Not out of doors. Everyone would see it. They'd be staring at it and talking about it. It cost more than what dear Mother allowed me for clothes in a whole year. I was *mad* to let you talk me into it."

"Now look here," said Richard, "you've got to promise me to put it on first thing in the morning and wear it all day."

"Wear it all day?" gasped Miss Maple. "A lovely new dress like that?"

"Yes. You bought it to wear, didn't you?"

"No, I didn't," said Miss Maple with spirit. "I bought it because you *forced* me to."

"Well, will you promise to wear it tomorrow?"

"Not actually tomorrow," said Miss Maple. "I must have a little more time to get used to it," then, her face brightening: "It really *is* rather nice, you know. I tried it on again last night. But I'm still terrified of it. The first night after I'd bought it I kept waking up and thinking of it hanging there in the wardrobe—with the new coat as well—I just *perspired* with remorse, if you'll pardon the expression, dear boy. It seemed even worse than that list of names. Richard . . ."

"Yes?"

"I was thinking about that list this afternoon and I decided to put some five shilling names in. I think I'd feel better if I did. I mean, even if it's doing wrong, they're getting money from it, so it sorts of cancels out. Or does it, Richard?"

"I shouldn't worry about that," said Richard. "Let's just enjoy it."

"Oh, Richard! Shall I put in a ten-shilling subscription or would that be going too far? I mean, I know that the whole thing's a sin, but I can't make up my mind whether ten shillings is less of a sin than five shillings or more."

"I don't think it matters. Let's have one or two ten shillings, anyway. Ten shilling subscribers must have double-barrelled names, of course. Let's think of some. Pettigrew Smith . . . Plantagenet-Brown . . . D'Arcy-Jones . . ."

Miss Maple laughed. It occurred to her suddenly that she had laughed more often since entering her life of crime than she had ever laughed before.

Richard was looking round the room.

"You know, you ought to clear some of this junk out," he said.

"Junk?" said Miss Maple indignantly.

"Yes. All those ornaments and the bamboo fern-stand and the what-not and the chiffonier. That's a lovely little writing-desk, but you can't see it for junk. That card-table's a beauty, too, and so is that little mahogany chest-of-drawers. If you turned almost everything else out, the room would look just right."

Miss Maple gave a gasp of horror.

"Oh, Richard, I couldn't. It's always been like this. Ever since I can remember. Ever since I was a child. Some of the things were dear Mother's wedding presents." She looked thoughtfully round the room. "I see what you mean, of course."

"Well, think about it," said Richard. "And now I must be getting on." He stood up. "What are you going to have for supper? Porridge or a boiled egg?"

"Well, actually I'm going to have a poached egg, dear."

"You ought to have a nice little maid to look after you and cook for you."

"*Richard!*" said Miss Maple in horror. "Go away at once. I won't listen to another word."

"Well, think about it," said Richard as he went down to the gate.

Myrtle was waiting for him at the corner of the road. She smiled shyly as he approached.

"I thought you wouldn't be coming tonight," she said.

"Why not? I said I would."

"I never believe it till I see you," she said with her soft country burr.

"But you always see me."

She gave her slow sweet smile again.

"I know. I don't mind even scrubbing the bar floor as long as I've got that to look forward to. I think on it all day . . . Where do you want to go?"

"Let's go to Elston Wood. I'll forget *Winfield's Torts* and you shall forget the bar floor."

155

"Do you hate being learnt law, Richard?"

"Oh, no," he said vaguely. "It's quite interesting in a way. A bit uninspiring, but it does as well as anything else, I suppose."

They walked up the hill towards the stile that led into Elston Wood. She was sweet and gentle like the summer twilight. Her voice was soft and low, her eyes dark and limpid in the shadow of her hair. They climbed the stile and walked down the dim mossy path between the trees. Their fingers intertwined. Her head drew near his shoulder.

"Do your folks know you come out with me?" she said suddenly.

"They wouldn't care," said Richard. "They're too busy with their own affairs to care what anyone else does. Mother's wondering what Father's up to; Edmund's thoughts are all tied neatly with red tape and labelled Sport, the Office, General Culture, and they fill his mind so completely that there isn't room for anything else; Vere hides away from us all and Althea snaps all our heads off."

"Why does she snap your heads off?"

"I don't know, but she does. One hardly dares speak to her these days."

But when he reached home Althea wasn't snapping people's heads off. Her eyes were bright, her cheeks flushed and there was an air of suppressed excitement about her. She laughed gaily as she gave him an account of Herbert's Shakespeare recital and hummed to herself as she sat threading baby-ribbon through the lace trimming of a camisole.

Her excitement still upheld her the next morning.

"You aren't feverish, are you, darling?" said Mrs. Culverton anxiously at breakfast.

"No, of course not," said Althea with a high-pitched laugh.

Mrs. Culverton had arranged to take Althea into Bellminster to do some shopping, but at the last minute Althea excused herself from accompanying her. She was tired, she said. She wanted to get on with her embroidery. Mrs. Culverton was disappointed. More and more she was coming to rely on Althea. Aloof and peremptory with the other children, she accepted Althea's snubs humbly and sometimes wept a little in secret when Althea showed too plainly her preference for companions of her own age.

It had been a morning of mellow autumn sunshine, but dark clouds had gathered and the rain was beginning to fall when Tilly showed Piers into the little sitting-room, where Althea sat, working on a piece of embroidery. His face looked strained and pale.

"Forgive me for coming at this unearthly hour," he said, "but I wanted to see you and I hoped I'd find you alone."

"I am alone," she said.

Her voice was a little unsteady and bright patches of colour burnt in her cheeks. Beneath her excitement was a suggestion of apprehension, as if she had brought about a situation that she did not quite know how to handle.

"All the others are out," she went on with a forced laugh. "It was such a lovely morning. What a pity it's turned to rain! But I think it's only a shower. Do sit down."

He sat down facing her on the other side of the hearth.

"I want to talk to you about Lindsay," he said.

Althea made no reply. A gust of trembling seized her, but she stiffened her body to control it.

"You're fond of Lindsay," he went on, "and you understand her. You understand her better than anyone does, I think, except me. And there's something I want to tell you."

"Yes?"

"You see"—he leant forward, his elbows on his knees, his frowning gaze fixed on the fireplace—"you're her friend, but you're a newcomer here. You aren't mixed up with the life of the place as everyone else is. You belong and yet you don't belong. One can—tell you things and know that they won't go any further. They wouldn't mean much to you, anyway. They mean too much to people here. That's why I can tell you this, though I couldn't tell it to anyone else. You're sweet and kind and understanding."

Althea lowered her eyes to hide the hope that had sprung up in them and clenched her hands to keep them steady.

"You know that Lindsay's—highly strung, don't you?"

She nodded.

"Well, last year she was very ill. Mentally ill, I mean. And she had to go into a home for some months. We didn't want people to know about it—Lindsay couldn't have faced life here if people had known about it—so we pretended that she'd gone on a holiday to the South of France. This is in strictest confidence, of course. Lindsay doesn't know I'm telling you, but I had to consult someone and you seemed—near to us somehow. You'll give me your word not to tell this to anyone, won't you?"

Again she nodded. Her throat was too dry to speak.

"She came back cured," he went on. "She's still highly strung, of course, but there's been no more trouble. She's terribly shy and—afraid. If she thought people knew . . ." He put his hand into his pocket and brought out a letter. His voice grew so harsh that she hardly recognized it. "I received this by the morning's post. It's an anonymous letter and it contains such a foul suggestion that I feel I haven't even the right to show it to you." He handed it to her. She read it, moistening her white lips. "It was posted in Priors Green. Someone in the village must have written it. There's not a word of truth in it, of course, but if Lindsay knew about it I think it would kill her. I'm determined to find out who wrote it. The handwriting's disguised, but—will you help me, Thea? Have you ever heard even a whisper of this?"

She shook her head, her gaze still fixed on the letter. She dared not let him see the terror in her eyes.

"If you do hear even a whisper of it, I want you to let me know at once. Meantime—"

Then Tilly came in. She stood square and squat in the doorway, her boot-button eyes fixed on them.

"The window in your bedroom's jammed, Miss Althea," she said. "I can't get it up nor down nohow and the rain's coming in all over your things."

Althea was about to dismiss her impatiently, but Piers had risen from his chair.

"Let me see what I can do," she said.

They went up the staircase, followed by Tilly. Althea was

conscious of a certain relief. Tilly's clumsy interruption gave her a respite in which she could rally her forces.

Piers strode across the bedroom to the open window and pushed it up. Then he stood motionless, his eyes fixed on the little writing-desk beneath the window. On the desk was a blotting-pad and on the top of the blotting-pad lay a crumpled sheet of blotting-paper. A letter had been blotted on it recently, and a word here and there was plainly legible. He stood staring at it, his eyes blank with horror, then turned slowly to Althea.

"*You* wrote it," he said in a whisper that hardly seemed to break the silence of the room.

Althea's youth and loveliness had dropped from her. Her face was grey and blotchy, her eyes hard and dry like pebbles.

"I—" she began, but he had gone from the room."

They heard the slamming of the front door and quick footsteps down the path as he fled from the house.

Althea looked at Tilly, who stood there, her face wearing its most wooden expression.

"You put it back," she said, and like Piers she whispered so that the words were barely audible.

"Yes, miss," said Tilly in a cheerful resonant voice. "You'd throwed it away in the waste-paper basket and I thought it was a pity to waste it. A good piece like that—hardly used."

"You knew," said Althea, her voice choking with anger. "You knew . . ."

"I could read what you'd wrote," admitted Tilly, as she turned to go. "Enough to guess . . ." She stopped at the door and added: "He's good, miss. He's good and you're bad. You'd have hurt him cruel if you'd got him."

Then, before Althea could gather breath to reply, she went down to the kitchen again and set to work peeling the potatoes.

Upstairs Althea lay on her bed sobbing convulsively.

I'm not bad, she was saying to herself. I'm not bad. I'm good. I was trying to do what was right. If it was true, he ought to have been told. And now I've lost him. He'll marry Lindsay.

Then her sobs died away and she lay staring at the ceiling, her tear-stained face set in harsh, unlovely lines.

At that moment the last lingering traces of her childhood left her.

Chapter Fifteen

The summer was drawing to a close and the Culvertons were beginning to consider their return to London. They discussed vaguely and inconclusively the idea of giving up the London house altogether. The train journey to London which Edmund and Richard made each day from Priors Green was tedious but not impossible. The project of a coming-out dance for Vere seemed to have died from lack of real interest on the part of everyone concerned, and, if Vere went to the Slade School, she too could go each day by train.

Mrs. Culverton herself shrank from returning to the London house. She had read in the paper of Mr. Brougham's death and shortly afterwards had received a letter from Howard asking her to give him a divorce. Mrs. Brougham, sobered and distressed by her husband's death (for there had been between them a friendship that, though tinged with cynicism, was none the less sincere), had turned again to Howard and was willing to marry him if his wife would agree to a divorce. Mrs. Culverton had replied by a short, curt note refusing even to consider the suggestion and there the matter had ended.

The children were shocked but not deeply affected by the situation. They had been fond of Howard, but he had never formed an integral part of the family life. He had been a shadowy if charming figure in the background and, now that he had faded out of the picture altogether, he left no great blank in their existence.

Mrs. Culverton continued to try to dull her pain by concentrating all her affection on Althea, as if determined to rebuild on Althea's happiness the ruins of her own. Althea must have the best "chance" that could be found for her and she was prepared to expend herself without stint in the pursuit of it. At one time it had seemed that Piers Lynneker was transferring his affection from his cousin to Althea, but Piers had left Priors Green to join a friend on a yachting cruise of indefinite duration. It was said in the village that he had proposed again to Lindsay and that Lindsay had rejected his proposal so finally that he had gone away in the accepted fashion of rejected suitors to forget his grief in fresh scenes and new experiences. This had been a disappointment to Mrs. Culverton, but it had its redeeming features. One was that Roddy, who had from the beginning openly shown an ingenuous admiration for Althea, now constituted himself her escort on all public occasions and called at the cottage on every excuse he could invent. Though good-looking in a heavy blond fashion, he lacked Piers's air of distinction, and, of course, would not inherit the title or the Hall, but, if Althea married him, she would have the Lynneker background, the Lynneker protection and, presumably, a considerable share of the Lynneker money. Piers, of course, would have been a better match, but Althea had met all her mother's discreet enquiries on the subject with a curtness that had quelled all further hopes.

So Mrs. Culverton, shutting Howard out of her mind, filled it with Althea . . . She lay awake through the long nights, turning the problem over and over in her mind. Would she be doing better for Althea by staying at Linden Rise or by going back to London? If they went back to London it would leave the Priors Green field open to the girls who flocked round Roddy on the tennis courts and golf course, but by staying away from London were they missing something better? Then Mrs. Culverton would turn her mind to another redeeming feature in the situation. There was no doubt that Lindsay was attracted by Edmund. Edmund himself, immersed in his immediate interests and engagements, seemed not to be aware of this, but Mrs. Culverton knew and recognized the signs. She did little in the affair, however, beyond treating Lindsay with a special, if somewhat impersonal, kindness. The girl was lovely and charming but oddly variable. Sometimes she was so shy and withdrawn that it was difficult to form any contact with her, sometimes gay and eager and volatile as a child. Mrs. Culverton left the affair to Edmund. Edmund was capable of managing his own concerns and if he wanted her help he would let her know.

So taken up were Mrs. Culverton's thoughts by Althea and Edmund that she had few to spare for Vere and Richard. It never occurred to her to wonder what went on behind the hardening front that Vere turned to the world, to wonder what Richard did on the long mellow autumn evenings. He was seldom in the cottage, but that was just as well. The place seemed rather small when they were all there, though it would make an ideal home for her when they were all married.

Edmund might have noticed the signs of Lindsay's growing dependence on him, if his mind had not been taken up by his "Talk" to the Priors Green and District Literary Society. From a vague suggestion (it was difficult to get speakers in a little country place and Edmund's informal dissertations on the political situation had impressed, all his hearers) it had now become a definite engagement with a definite evening booked at the church hall. Secretly Edmund felt disconcerted. When first the idea had been suggested to him he had let it be understood that he was a competent speaker merely because it was becoming more and more difficult for him to admit incompetency in any field at all. He had made various unsuccessful attempts to get out of it . . . He would be particularly busy at the office during the next few months . . . He had engagements on the evenings suggested . . . But the Literary Society was embarrassingly accommodating. It was willing to put off the meeting for as long as Edmund wanted it put off, to agree to any date suggested by Edmund himself . . . till Edmund, to his secret dismay, found himself finally committed to give his address at the church hall at eight o'clock on the evening of the last Saturday in September.

He discussed the matter with Richard.

"Of course, I've made a study of political science," he said, "and it occurs to me that I could base my speech on that. I thought that, if I did it from the angle of the origin of our modern political ideas, I could take it back to the eighteenth century. That's the point from which most of our modern constitutional government with Prime Minister and the rest of it really originated. Anyway, I haven't read much earlier than that."

"The eighteenth century . . ." said Richard slowly. "It's the only age of civilization that England's ever known. It had elegance and graciousness and taste and culture. Look at their furniture, their houses, their poets, their philosophers. It's the only age when the English knew how to live. They had wit and culture—as well as money. Wit and culture don't exist any more and we don't know how to use money even when we've got it."

"Quite," said Edmund a little blankly.

"I was reading *Lady Holland's Journal* the other day and her reading in six months would simply astound you—*Juvenal, Arioso, Tasso, Ovid, Montaigne, Burnet's History, Hearn's Travels, Lazaritto de Tormes, Let's Life of Sextus the Fifth, Cook's Voyages, Wolf 's Ceylon, Bayle,* and a dozen more I've forgotten together with innumerable French and German novels. And she was a busy Society hostess, not a recluse."

"Quite," said Edmund again. "Well, I'd thought of taking the whole thing from a political angle."

"Yes, go ahead," said Richard, puffing at his pipe. "I expect that's the best way. I don't know much about politics."

"Perhaps you'll read it for me when I've got it into shape and tell me what you think of it?"

"Certainly," said Richard.

About a week later Edmund handed Richard a sheaf of closely written papers.

"If you'd just read it through," he said, "and correct any slips I've made, I'd be grateful. I've done the whole thing rather quickly and there may be one or two mistakes."

Richard took it up to his bedroom and read it. It was as dull and pompous as Edmund himself. Sentence after sentence of statement and comment—flat, unoriginal, undistinguished.

As Edmund was setting off for the train the next morning Richard handed him a small folded manuscript. There was a faint light of mischief in his eyes.

"I've copied it out again, Edmund," he said, "altering a point here and there. I've put the one you wrote on the table in your bedroom."

"Thanks," said Edmund, slipping the manuscript into his pocket.

He didn't look at it till his lunch hour. Then, sitting at his corner table in the small select restaurant he patronized, he took it out of his pocket and began to read it through. It wasn't his paper at all. It wasn't even headed "Politics in the Eighteenth Century." It was headed simply "The Eighteenth Century," and a quick glance down the pages showed that hardly a word of his original manuscript remained. Anger surged up in him . . . then he began to read it more carefully and the cloud cleared from his brow. It was interesting; it was amusing; it was, here and there, pointedly witty, in a modest unobtrusive fashion, it was erudite. There were quotations from diaries, poems and journals. Its surface was light and sparkling over a solid basis of knowledge and critical judgment. He read it to the end, then put it in his pocket with a smile of satisfaction.

When he reached home that evening, Richard was standing on the verandah, pipe in mouth, gazing idly over the garden.

"I've decided to use your additions," said Edmund with only a slight hint of constraint in his manner. "I think that the paper, as you've amended it, is more suitable to the type of audience I'm likely to get here than my original script. That"—he smiled faintly—"would have been a little above their heads, I think."

"Quite," said Richard.

The tentacles of the Priors Green and District Literary Society spread far and wide among the surrounding villages. (It owed its origin to a tentative suggestion of Mrs. Egerton's and still retained something of the impetus of that origin.) Everyone of any standing at all was a member. It took away the feeling of isolation and inferiority that living in the country was apt to give, and was not only the excuse for an occasional social gathering but made the members feel that they were "keeping abreast of intellectual movements". The last intellectual movement they had kept abreast of had been a cycling tour in Cornwall undertaken by one of the

Bellminster Parish Church curates. His lecture had been accompanied by lantern slides, which had appeared with monotonous regularity upside down, but they had all enjoyed the evening and it was clear that there was going to be a large attendance at Edmund's talk on "The Eighteenth Century."

Mrs. Culverton grew somewhat nervous as the day approached, but Edmund seemed unaffected, by nervousness or apprehension.

"You've got your lecture ready, haven't you, dear?" said Mrs. Culverton on the Tuesday morning.

"Lecture?" said Edmund, looking puzzled.

"For Saturday."

"Oh, that!" said Edmund with a smile. "Yes, I've got the thing somewhere, if I haven't lost it. I must rout it out and look through it. Thanks for reminding me."

Despite his show of nonchalance, Edmund was both elated and apprehensive. He built high hopes on the evening, though he couldn't have told quite what the hopes were. But, just as he laboured to perfect himself in everything else he undertook, so he laboured to perfect himself in this. He knew the speech by heart. Every day during his lunch hour in London he went to an elocution teacher to practise it. Each inflection of his voice, each movement of his hands was carefully studied and rehearsed.

It was a relief to him that Richard was in bed with a feverish cold when the day arrived. The fine weather had been broken by a thunderstorm the night before and Richard had arrived home soaked.

"Where on earth have you been?" said Edmund.

"In Elston Woods."

"You're a silly ass to go mooching about the countryside alone like that," said Edmund. "If you'd been playing tennis or cricket you'd have been near shelter of some sort."

"How do you know I was alone?" Richard had said, and Edmund had laughed as at a puerile joke.

Edmund's only fear with regard to the lecture had been lest the sight of Richard's face, wearing its familiar quizzical smile, should distract him or make him feel self-conscious, So relieved was he by Richard's indisposition that he cycled into Bellminster on Saturday morning and brought him a pound of grapes and half a dozen peaches.

"It's awfully good of you, old chap," said Richard, who was sitting up in bed, wrapped in a dressing-gown. "I shall be sorry to miss your lecture."

"I'm sorry you won't be there," said Edmund. "After all, you gave me the idea."

The Culvertons were among the first arrivals at the church hall, which rapidly began to fill. Mrs. Culverton sat in the front row watching Edmund, composed and impassive, on the platform. The Vicar made a short speech of introduction, then Edmund rose to his feet. There was a moment when it seemed as if his opening might be wrecked by Miss Maple, who arrived several minutes late and walked up to a vacant seat in the front row, wearing a new coat of incredibly fashionable cut and a new and very becoming hat. Beneath the hat her small face was set and tense and flushed. There was a gasp of amazement as she took her seat, then the audience settled down to listen to Edmund. And at once they were gripped. He had a clear, resonant, if slightly harsh, voice, and, thanks to his intensive training at the hands of the elocution teacher, every word and expression had the effect of spontaneity. He halted every now and then as if searching for the right word. The witty turns that Richard had given to so many of the sentences appeared to be jokes made on the spur of the moment. He held a paper of notes in his hand and occasionally looked at it as if to consult it. His voice flowed on—incisive, clear, compelling, holding the attention of the audience without apparent effort. Or at least of most of the audience. Roddy Lynneker's eyes were fastened on Althea, merely because when he was near Althea he couldn't help looking at her. Althea's eyes were fixed on Edmund, but her thoughts were far away. She had not seen Piers since that moment in her bedroom when he had turned to her and said, "*You* wrote it"—he had left Priors Green two days later—but she had written to him, explaining that someone (she couldn't in honour tell him who it was) had come to see her the day before his visit and while in her bedroom had asked if she might write a note at the writing-table and it was she who must have written the letter whose impression was left on the blotting-paper. She had received an answer—a short formal note, accepting her explanation and apologizing for his outburst . . . but she knew that he would never marry her now.

Mrs. Culverton, glancing at Althea's face, felt a sudden stab of dismay as she noted the sharpening of the lovely features and the tight lines of the mouth. Were Althea's looks, after all, the sort that "went off" early? She must get her settled quickly. She mustn't take any risks. Then her glance travelled to Lindsay, sitting forward in her seat, eyes fixed on Edmund, following his every word and movement. She didn't even try to hide her secret. She was openly, unashamedly, in love.

The lecture came to an end in a burst of applause. Edmund stood there acknowledging it with a slight bow. His smile showed only modest appreciation of his reception, but inwardly he was conscious of a sudden surge of excitement, a strange new sense of power. He came down from the platform to be surrounded by an eager crowd.

"The best lecture we've ever had."

"It was wonderful. And perfectly delivered."

"Congratulations, my boy! Congratulations!"

"My brother helped me with it," said Edmund, but he said it with the air of one generously giving credit where in fact little credit was due.

Miss Maple had spent the lecture steeling herself against the glances that had been turned in her direction. At the end her courage had failed her and she had scuttled home as quickly as she could. Everyone who was not discussing the lecture was discussing Miss Maple.

"My dear, did you *see* her coat? *And* the dress!"

"What she must have *spent* on them!"

The general attitude was one of disapproval, with a faint underlying note of injury. Miss Maple had been Miss Maple for so long that she had no right to change. The sight of the fashionable new coat and dress had given them a curious feeling of insecurity. If Miss Maple could change, so might everything else. . . .

"So unsuitable!" said the eldest Miss Corbett.

"I do hope she's not going to turn peculiar," said Mrs. Egerton.

Edmund found himself standing alone with Lindsay in the doorway.

"It was lovely, Edmund," she said, with an excited little laugh, "but just at first it was all I could do not to giggle. You looked so comical, somehow, standing up there on the platform, clearing your throat before you began to speak."

Edmund's face darkened and the smile left his lips. For some time now the easy good nature of Edmund's boyhood had been leaving him. He took himself seriously and expected other people to take him seriously too.

"I'm sorry you found me comical," he said stiffly.

"Oh, Edmund!" said Lindsay in quick contrition. "I didn't mean—I only . . ."

She gazed at him, her blue eyes dismayed, her mouth tremulous, and in that moment it was as if an electric spark passed between them. To Edmund it was the culminating peak of the evening. I'm in love with her, he thought, and she's in love with me. We shall be married, have children, grow old together . . .

The Hall carriage had come to fetch the Lynnekers, but Lindsay said that she would prefer to walk, and she and Edmund walked down the lane to the big stone gates of the Hall and up the long avenue of beech trees. They discussed the evening, the lecture, the audience, people's comments . . . but the undercurrent of excitement made everything they said seem meaningless and unreal, like the sound of wind or water accompanying what they were saying to each other without words.

"I'll go in by the side door," said Lindsay, and they walked along the terrace to a side door, shadowed by fall shrubs. There they stopped, and Lindsay turned her glowing face to him.

"I don't want to go in," she said. "I'd like to go for a long walk."

He smiled at her—a tender, protective smile.

"Never mind what you want," he said. "It's time you were in bed. Run along."

She thrilled to the easy masterfulness of his tone and made a half movement towards him. He knew that she wanted him to take her in his arms and kiss her and he felt a strong impulse to do so, but he resisted it. He intended to conduct the affair correctly. He would call on her uncle tomorrow morning and propose to her in the course of the afternoon.

"Run along," he said again, his smile robbing the words of brusqueness.

She laughed—a sweet, high-pitched, childish laugh—and went indoors.

Mrs. Culverton, Althea and Vere had walked home after the lecture, accompanied by Roddy Lynneker, who left them with reluctance at the gate of the cottage. Tilly had prepared sandwiches and coffee in the dining-room.

"Thank you, Tilly," said Mrs. Culverton, dropping her cloak on to a chair. "How kind of you!"

She was feeling proud and happy. Everyone had praised Edmund's speech, and Althea had looked radiant as she stood talking to Roddy at the gate. That curious impression of the sharpening of her features must have been due to the inadequate lighting of the church hall.

"How's Mr. Richard, Tilly?"

"He's better, madam. He's sitting up in bed reading his old Plato."

"How dull!" smiled Mrs. Culverton.

"Yes, madam," said Tilly, placing the coffee-pot on the table and arranging the cups. "There's no story in that old Plato same as there is in some of the others. Euripides, now, he's different. He wrote some good stories, did Euripides. And Aeschylus, he did, too. He wrote one about a woman murdering her husband that's as good as anything you'd find in the newspapers."

"I suppose nothing's happened here while we've been away?" said Althea without looking at Tilly. Since the episode of the letter she had never looked at Tilly when she spoke to her. She spoke in a carefully casual tone.

Whenever she returned to the cottage even after a short absence, she always had a wild hope that Piers might have sent a message or even appeared in person to beg her to forgive him and to tell her that he couldn't live without her.

Tilly considered. Jim had appeared at the kitchen door just as she was washing up the dinner things.

"Well, aren't you ready?" he had said.

"Ready for what?" Tilly had said, standing with a vegetable dish in one hand and a tea-cloth in the other.

"It's your evening off, ain't it?" said Jim. "Aren't you comin' out with me?"

"Evenin' off!" jeered Tilly. "I told you las' week——"

"Last week they was havin' Vicar an' his wife to dinner," said Jim. "They've had their dinner early tonight an' gone off to this ruddy lecture, so you can come out."

"I've got all their dinner-things to wash up," said Tilly.

He glanced round.

"You've finished them."

"Mr. Richard's ill in bed."

"Ill in bed! He's got a cold, that's all. I've bin about my work with a worse cold than what he's got. Don't pretend you can't leave him."

"He might want something."

"Let him want, then."

"They had veal for dinner and he couldn't eat it. I'm going to get him an omelet."

"An omelet won't take long."

"That's all you know. And I've got the sandwiches to make. They like somethin' when they come in."

"Let them like, then."

Tilly began to put the china on the shelves in silence.

"Come on, Tilly," he coaxed.

Tilly set her mouth stubbornly.

"I'm not leavin' Mr. Richard with him ill in bed."

"Just to the end of the lane and back, then?"

"I'm too busy, I tell you."

"You're too busy every week. Las' week it was the Vic'rage to dinner and the week before it was darnin' Mr. Richard's socks."

"He's got to have them darned, hasn't he?"

"Not by you, he hasn't. He's got a mother and sisters, hasn't he?"

"Well, they don't do 'em. He can't go about lookin' like a tramp."

"What's it matter to you what he looks like, the crazy loon!"

A flash of anger came into her face.

"You leave Mr. Richard alone," she said sharply. "If we start calling names, I could call you a few."

"Now listen," said Jim portentously. "You can choose between them Culvertons an' me an' you can choose here an' now. I shan't ask you again. There's other pebbles on the beach, let me tell you, as good as you or better. Are you comin' out with me?"

"No," said Tilly shortly.

"Right!" said Jim and strode off, shutting the garden gate smartly behind him.

Tilly finished putting the cutlery away. She was conscious of no other feeling than one of relief that now she could get on with Mr. Richard's omelet without fear of interruption.

Her mind went back over the incident as she ranged the coffee-cups on the table.

"No, miss," she said, "nothin's happened here."

Chapter Sixteen

Aunt Gertrude was married in the middle of November, and Mrs. Culverton went up to London for a week before the wedding to see to the letting of the Streatham house. She had decided to let it for a year, at the end of which time, she thought, events might have made her path clearer than it seemed at present. Edmund and Lindsay were unofficially engaged, for Sir Godfrey had insisted on waiting till Lindsay was twenty-one before sanctioning a formal engagement. Roddy was still paying court to Althea, but, either from diffidence or because he did not consider that he had yet sufficiently paved the way, had not yet proposed.

Mrs. Culverton shrank from returning to the Streatham house, full of memories of Howard, while to give it up altogether seemed such a complete break with the past that she could not bring herself to face it, so that the year's "let" seemed the best solution of the problem. She had heard indirectly that Howard and Mrs. Brougham had taken an old farmhouse in Essex and that Howard, devoting all his time to his mistress, was now little more than a sleeping partner in the business. She received the usual allowance from her solicitors but had not heard from Howard since the letter in which he had asked for a divorce.

The day of Aunt Gertrude's wedding was bleak and foggy, and Aunt Gertrude looked outrageous in a white woollen dress heavily trimmed with marabou, a white feather boa and a white feathered hat. Since her engagement to Herbert she had grown enormously fat while Herbert had become almost cadaverous. He had made several attempts to evade the marriage. He had said that he wasn't worthy of her, but she had replied that that didn't matter. He had said that he hadn't been justified in asking her to share his meagre bachelor existence, and she had replied that that didn't matter either because it wouldn't be a meagre bachelor existence any longer.

There was a slight glaze of anxiety in her eyes as she entered the church, but it cleared as she saw Herbert—tall and thin and tragic-looking, wearing his new morning suit—awaiting her by the chancel rails. During the service Herbert had a good deal of difficulty with his profile. He didn't like standing with his back to the audience, in any case, and he felt that, whichever way he turned his profile, only a limited number of people could see it. His "I will", however, did much to restore his complacency. It rang through the church—deep, sonorous, vibrant with feeling startling Aunt Gertrude so much that she nearly dropped her bouquet. Even the officiating clergyman was a little taken aback, and there was a moment's pause before he turned towards Aunt Gertrude to continue the service. After that something of Herbert's aplomb returned to him and he displayed his profile to the congregation majestically, first on one side then on the other, at his favourite angle.

The reception was held at the Savoy. A large and rather noisy crowd of Herbert's old cronies attended it, watched disapprovingly by a group of Aunt Gertrude's connections. The noisier Herbert's cronies became, the more disapproving became Aunt Gertrude's connections. Edmund constituted himself a sort of liaison officer between the two groups, but, as fast as he introduced them to each other, they gravitated back into their respective camps. Richard mingled with both groups indiscriminately, his Puck-like face alight with interest and amusement. He hadn't wanted to come, but now that he had come he was enjoying it. Althea, of course, was the centre of a crowd of gay young people. She looked radiantly lovely and Mrs. Culverton's eyes strayed to her with pride as she followed Aunt Gertrude about, picking up her bouquet and bag and boa at frequent intervals. Aunt Gertrude was volubly expansive.

"We're going to Bognor for the honeymoon," she said. "We'd rather have gone to somewhere like Venice, of course, but I can't get Herbert Shakespeare readings at Venice and I can at Bognor, so it seemed a pity to miss the opportunity. There's a man on the Bognor *Advertiser* who knows a man on the London *Times* and it might lead to something."

Herbert, under the influence of champagne and the general atmosphere, of congratulation, was growing more and more tragic.

"Here's luck, old chap," said a man with so prominent a nose that he had spent his entire professional life playing Shylock, "and may tomorrow be as happy as yesterday."

> "'And all our yesterdays have lighted fools
> The way to dusty death','"

quoted Herbert mournfully as he drained his glass.

Vere stood in the shade of a potted palm watching the scene with the familiar ache of loneliness at her heart. Everyone but herself seemed to be at their ease, to be able to talk to people freely, happily, confidently. Only she was held bound in an isolation that had once been a defence and was now a prison. Even with her fellow pupils at the Slade School she could not free herself from it. She repelled advances that she would have liked to accept. She fled from the school in a sort of panic as soon as the classes ended. She looked round now at her mother, Edmund, Richard, Althea . . . and the old pain of being unwanted swept over her. They wouldn't mind if I wasn't here at all, she thought. Nobody would mind . . . And she had recourse to the childish daydreams in which she gave her life in dramatic circumstances for her family and they wept disconsolately around her grave.

Aunt Gertrude darted across the room to her.

"I've been wanting to speak to you, Vere," she said mysteriously. "We appreciated it so much, Herbert and I. We want you to know how much we appreciated it. We shall never forget it. Never!"

"Forget what, Aunt Gertrude?" said Vere.

"When he gave that recital in the sitting-room at your cottage, dear. Althea and your mother were bored—just bored—and they didn't even try to hide it. But you! You sat there, your dear little face so full of interest, carried away by it, drinking it in."

Vere remembered the afternoon when she had sat watching Herbert, thinking of Trinidad, Jamaica, Cairo . . .

"We shall never forget it, dear," said Aunt Gertrude again. "Herbert's often spoken of it. The whole thing would have been so discouraging for him if it hadn't been for your little dear face carried away by it, drinking it in. He'll always remember it, dear, no matter what heights he climbs to."

Then someone called Aunt Gertrude and she darted off again.

Going home with the children, Mrs. Culverton felt happier than she had felt for a long time. Edmund was engaged to Lindsay, Richard was (presumably) reading hard for the Bar, Althea would soon be engaged to Roddy and Vere—well, at any rate, Vere was quiet and well behaved and fairly presentable. She could tackle the problem of Vere when she'd got Althea off her hands. They were good-looking, delightful children and, studying their faces as they sat together on the opposite seat of the first-class carriage, Mrs. Culverton was conscious of a rare thrill of maternal pride. She could—for the moment—even think of Howard without bitterness. Howard had eluded her from the beginning. Her children couldn't do that. They, at any rate, belonged to her.

But she felt tired when she reached home, and the sight of an envelope on the little table in the hall, addressed to her, with the word "Private" written at the top in large letters, sent a wave of apprehension over her spirit.

She opened it and read:

Dear Mrs. Culverton,

    May I come and speak to you tomorrow morning on a very private—and I am afraid, distressing—matter? It concerns Richard. Please don't tell him that you have received this note.

                    Yours sincerely,
                    Viola Egerton.

She read it again, frowning in perplexity. It couldn't be anything serious. Her mind went over the obvious pitfalls of youth. Drink . . . Debt . . . Women . . . No, not Richard. Richard was vague and ineffectual, but there was a fastidiousness, an integrity about him that had always made her feel that she could safely leave Richard's morals to Richard himself. It couldn't be anything serious. . . .

Richard came home the next evening by an earlier train than usual. Myrtle was not waiting for him in the lane, but he knew that she couldn't always escape her duties at home in time to meet him and he walked on slowly towards the cottage, enjoying the freshness of the autumn evening.

Crossing the village green, he met Miss Maple with Major at her heels. She wore the new coat and hat. There was an air of well-being, even a slight suggestion of assurance about her.

"Good!" said Richard, surveying her with approval.

"Oh, yes, Richard," said Miss Maple. "Yes, indeed. I can wear them now almost without a qualm. I passed the Rubicon the night of Edmund's lecture. I nearly *died* of shame that night when I went in wearing them, with everyone looking at me. Everyone still looks at me, but—do you know, Richard?— I'm beginning to enjoy it."

"That's grand," said Richard, "and when are you going to Paris?"

"Oh, Richard, no! Never! But—well, we are going to do something rather daring—Major and I."

"What?" said Richard.

Miss Maple lowered her voice confidentially.

"I haven't told anyone about it yet, but we're going to Broadstairs. To an hotel. I've never stayed at an hotel before."

"Why Broadstairs?"

"Well, you see, Mother once stayed there as a child, so it makes it seem a little less *flagrant*, don't you think? And, Richard . . ."

"Yes?"

"I *have* added a ten-shilling subscriber to the list. I've called him Mr. Croxton, The Crossways. Do you think that's all right?"

"I think it's fine, but let's put him in the army," said Richard. "We haven't got anyone in the army. Let's call him Major Croxton."

"Yes, that's a good idea, Richard," said Miss Maple with a

conspiratorial smile, "and we might have a colonel next, mightn't we?"

"Why not a Field Marshal?"

"Oh, *no, Richard!* And now"—anxiously, as she glanced at her watch—"I must fly, or I'll be late for supper."

"Toad-in-the-hole or a rissole?"

"Neither, Richard. Curried egg. There was a recipe of it in that little cookery book you gave me and I tried it last week and it was delicious and I'm going to try it again."

Richard walked on, smiling to himself. Almost as soon as he opened the door of the cottage his mother called from upstairs.

"Will you come up to my bedroom, Richard? I want to speak to you."

He went upstairs, feeling a little puzzled. There was something vaguely ominous in the tone of her voice. He entered her bedroom and stood uncertainly on the threshold. She was sitting in the arm-chair by the window, an unopened book on her knee. She turned her head to him unsmiling.

"Sit down, Richard. I want to speak to you."

"You aren't ill, are you?" he said with kindly anxiety as he took his seat on the bed.

"No, Richard. I asked you to come up here because I didn't want to be interrupted . . . Richard, I saw Mrs. Egerton today and she says that people are talking."

"They generally do, don't they?" said Richard mildly. "What about?"

"Is it true, Richard, that you have been seen in the village and in the woods with Myrtle Bailey?"

Richard considered. He seemed in no way discomposed.

"Well, I've been in the village and in the woods with Myrtle Bailey," he said at last, "so I suppose it's quite possible that I've been seen there."

"Richard!" said Mrs. Culverton in deep reproach. "If you didn't think of yourself you might have thought of the girl's reputation."

"How do you mean, her reputation?" said Richard with his maddening air of impersonal interest.

"Well . . . do you think that any young man of her class is going to marry her if her name's been coupled with yours?"

"Oh, but I'm going to marry her," said Richard. He spoke as if surprised that Mrs. Culverton had not drawn the obvious conclusion. "Of course, I'm going to marry her."

"Richard!" Mrs. Culverton had gone very pale. "She's—she's not going to have a baby, is she?"

"No," said Richard easily. "Why should she? . . . Oh, I see what you mean. No, there hasn't been anything of that sort."

A smile flickered over his thin face. "You needn't turn me out into the snow."

She made an impatient gesture.

"Don't joke about it, Richard. You *can't* marry this girl."

"Why not?"

"Think of your career."

"I don't see how that will affect it. She loves me and I love her."

"But, Richard, think of your position. A wife like that would be a hopeless handicap."

Again he considered, his brows drawn into a puzzled frown. "You know," he said apologetically, "it doesn't mean terribly much to me—position and that sort of thing. I'm sorry. I can't help it. It's just the way I'm made."

"But, Richard, for an educated man trained for the Bar to marry a girl like that!"

Again the note of apology sounded in Richard's voice.

"I don't consider myself educated, and I'm afraid I'm not going to be very much good at the Bar. I'm not the type."

"You're not going to give it up, Richard?"

"Oh, no, of course not. No, I'll go on with it, but—well, I just don't think I'm the type, that's all."

"You're clever."

"I hope not," he said with a faint smile. "It's the last thing I want to be."

"You won all those scholarships and prizes and you got a brilliant First."

"Yes, but it's all so childish and uncivilized."

"What is?"

"The whole system. Examinations. Cramming up a lot of stuff simply and solely to show that you've crammed it up. It's a desecration of real learning. I feel ashamed whenever I think of it. I felt guilty about it at the time."

Her feeling of helplessness increased. She made an effort to rally her forces.

"Richard," she said slowly, "you must not marry this girl."

His smile was gentle and a little unhappy.

"I'm sorry you mind so much," he said, "but I'm going to."

"You can't afford to marry at all."

"Not yet, I know. We'll have to wait. We're both willing to."

"You might consider the others. What do you think Edmund will say to this—or Althea?"

"I don't know," said Richard. "It'll be rather interesting to find out."

"You definitely refuse to give her up?"

"Yes."

Mrs. Culverton rose, still trying to appear mistress of the situation.

"It's no use continuing the conversation, she said. "I'll think it over and let you have my decision later.

Richard went slowly downstairs.

Tilly came out of the kitchen, a saucepan in one hand and a pepper-pot in the other. "What's it all about, Mr. Richard?" she said.

"I want to marry Myrtle Bailey," said Richard, "and Mother doesn't want me to."

"If you want to marry Myrtle Bailey, Mr. Richard," said Tilly, "you marry her. Your mother can't stop you."

"I don't think she can," said Richard, "but she's going to try."

"What's she going to do?"

"I don't know."

"I do," said Tilly. "She's going to see Mrs. Egerton again."

Chapter Seventeen

Tilly was right. Mrs. Culverton set off to the Vicarage soon after breakfast the next morning. She found Mrs. Egerton sitting at her bureau, drawing up a list of tentative suggestions that she meant to make at the next meeting of the Mothers' Union.

"Well?" said Mrs. Egerton as Mrs. Culverton entered.

"It's worse than we thought," said Mrs. Culverton.

"Oh, dear!" said Mrs. Egerton, horrified.

"No, not in that way," said Mrs. Culverton hastily. "I mean, he wants to marry her."

"Oh, dear!" said Mrs. Egerton again, less horrified but more deeply perturbed. "Have you—talked to him?"

"You can't talk to him," said Mrs. Culverton. "There's nothing you can appeal to in him. I'm sorry to have to say it about my own son, but he seems to lack the ordinary standards of ordinary, well-bred people."

"He's absolutely set on this marriage?"

"Yes."

"It will make a lot of talk. It's made a lot already. It would have made more if it hadn't been for Miss Maple."

"Miss Maple?"

"Yes. People have had her to talk about and it's taken the brunt off Richard. Suddenly coming out in all those new clothes. And so strange in her manner. Not a bit like *our* Miss Maple. Almost"— she searched for a word and ended—"almost independent. However, that's by the way. It's Richard we have to think of."

"Could we buy the girl off, do you think?" said Mrs. Culverton.

"I somehow don't think so," said Mrs. Egerton. "Richard wouldn't agree to it in any case, would he?"

"I'm afraid not."

"And the Baileys . . ."

"Public-house people!" said Mrs. Culverton with a shudder. "How he could ever have been attracted by a girl of that type!'

"They're good country stock," said Mrs. Egerton thoughtfully. "Uneducated, of course, but the Baileys have owned Hurst Farm at Mallingford for hundreds of years. I was thinking of the girl just before you came in. There's something *about* her."

"Common," said Mrs. Culverton.

"Common, of course," agreed Mrs. Egerton, "but if you're certain that Richard won't give her up I have another suggestion."

"Yes?"

"A friend of mine has a sort of finishing school at Tunbridge Wells, and she makes a speciality of putting a polish on girls from humble surroundings. I remember a case very like yours. The boy was of good family and the girl was from the working class and when the parents found that it was impossible to make him give her up they sent the girl to Miss Fortescue. She was there for two years and you'd never have believed at the end that the girl wasn't of gentle birth. Her accent, her manners, everything. And she'd got that smattering of education that is really all one wants for practical purposes. I mean, she could discuss things—art, literature, politics. There were gaps, of course, but the girl had been trained to cover the gaps in a way that was a triumph in itself. She could change the conversation the moment she felt that she was getting out of her depth. And that's not the only case. It's amazing the amount of polish that Miss Fortescue can put on even in a few months. She's a genius."

"It's difficult to know what to do," said Mrs. Culverton, knitting her brows. "As I said, there's nothing in Richard that you can appeal to. He lacks the most elementary standards. He has no ambition and no sense of fitness . . . And, of course, I do owe something to Althea and Edmund. A sister-in-law like Myrtle Bailey would be a terrible handicap—especially to Althea. Roddy hasn't proposed yet, but the thing's obvious."

"Quite obvious," agreed Mrs. Egerton. Her voice took on its gentlest, most diffident note. "Well, I suggest that we put the matter in Miss Fortescue's hands . . . Her terms aren't exorbitant, but I assume that you're prepared to pay a reasonable sum for Richard's happiness?"

"Certainly," said Mrs. Culverton with a sigh.

"The girl should probably go at once. And, of course, she won't have the ordinary school holidays. I mean, Miss Fortescue likes to keep them right away from the surroundings that have been the cause of the trouble. Even a short visit, she finds, sets them back. We can safely leave clothes and things to her. It only wastes time buying them in advance. In fact she likes to use the buying of the outfit as a first lesson in taste."

"Yes, but wait a moment," said Mrs. Culverton, feeling that she was being hustled along at too breathless a pace. "What about the girl's father? What about Richard? What about the girl herself? They'll have to be consulted, surely."

"Oh, yes," said Mrs. Egerton. "I was coming to that. I suggest that we all have a little conference on the subject here tomorrow afternoon. It will need tact, of course. It may be rather difficult."

It was rather difficult. The Vicar, though summoned to the conference by his wife, made the excuse of an urgent pastoral visit and escaped immediately after lunch. Mr. Bailey arrived first. He looked ill-at-ease in his Sunday suit of navy blue serge and stiff white collar, and he sat on the edge of his chair, rubbing his hands up and down his knees, a look of worry and bewilderment on his round red face. Mrs. Culverton and Richard arrived shortly afterwards, Richard looked sulky and resentful. He slumped into a chair and sat with his legs stretched out in front of him, his eyes fixed on his boots. Mrs. Egerton opened proceedings shortly, then Mr. Bailey spoke in a slow, deep voice.

"I'm not pleased about this marriage idea," he said, "an' I won't pretend I am. I'd rather the girl married into her own class, I don't hold with people marrying out of their class. We're not gentlefolks an' we've never set up to be." He had nearly expended his eloquence. His face had gone brick-red with the effort. He took out his handkerchief and mopped his brow. "I knew nothin' of all this till Mrs. Egerton here come along an' told me, but when I taxed Myrtle with it she didn't deny it. I've sent her to her aunt at Hurst Farm an' got Polly back till things are fixed up regular. I'm havin' no girl of mine talked about."

"I don't see why there's all this fuss," said Richard impatiently. "Myrtle and I want to marry each other and that'll be all there is to it."

"Not quite so fast, young man," said Mr. Bailey, eyeing his prospective son-in-law with disfavour. "Myrtle's got no mother an' it's up to me to do what's best for her." He turned to Mrs. Culverton. "I take it you're no more anxious for this marriage than I am, ma'am?"

"I'm afraid I'm not," said Mrs. Culverton.

"If we could stop it, we would, both of us," said Mr. Bailey, "but, if the young people are set on it as they seem to be, it's best to have it settled and above-board than goin' on in secret. We all know what *that* leads to."

"Quite," said Mrs. Egerton.

"An' I'm havin' no girl of mine looked down on one way or another. She'll be looked down on if she don't marry now all the talk's started an' she'll be looked down on if she do—you bein' gentlefolk an' her not bein.' I wish to heaven she'd never clap eyes on you."

Richard raised his scowling gaze from his boots.

"If we love each other, it doesn't matter a halfpenny cuss about being what you call gentlefolk."

"Yes, it does, young man," said Mr. Bailey grimly. "She'll speak different from your friends and act different." He turned to Mrs. Culverton. "I'm right, aren't I, ma'am?"

"Yes," said Mrs. Culverton.

"Your friends'd look down on her an' I'm havin' no girl of mine looked down on."

"Now listen to me," said Mrs. Egerton, raising a languid white hand. "You'll have to wait in any case, Richard dear, because you're hardly in a position to marry yet. And I think that in the peculiar circumstances it would be well if Myrtle didn't continue to live in the village. As her father rightly says, once talk has started there's no telling where it will stop and we have the girl's reputation to consider."

"Reputation!" exploded Richard furiously.

"Yes, reputation, Richard," said Mrs. Egerton. "A girl's reputation is a very precious and delicate thing. It never recovers from even the faintest—blemish. The slightest indiscretion is remembered against her all her life. I'm right, aren't I, Mrs. Culverton?"

"You are, indeed," said Mrs. Culverton.

"Indiscretion!" muttered Richard savagely.

"Please don't interrupt, Richard," said Mrs. Egerton softly. "I think that if Myrtle spent this time of waiting, which is inevitable in any case, in the happy cultured atmosphere of Miss Fortescue's establishment, it would be time well spent. It would put an end to these daily meetings with Richard in which we all agree that there is a certain danger, and it would enable her to do Richard credit as his wife, no matter how high he soared in his profession."

"Oh, good lord!" groaned Richard, dropping his head into his hands.

"What do you think, Mr. Bailey?" said Mrs. Egerton, ignoring Richard's outburst.

Mr. Bailey made a gesture of helplessness.

"It's right beyond me, Mrs. Egerton," he said. "I want to do what's best for the girl. I want to do what her mother would I think right if she was alive."

"I'm quite sure," said Mrs. Egerton, "that this is what Myrtle's mother would think right."

"I'll leave it to you then, Mrs. Egerton," he said gloomily, "but I'm not being beholden to no one. Any money that's got to be paid out on it, I'll pay."

"We can discuss that later," said Mrs. Egerton. "The main thing is to make the immediate arrangements."

"Shall I write to Miss Fortescue?" said Mrs. Culverton.

"Actually, I have written," said Mrs. Egerton, gazing dreamily into the distance, "and I had a wire this morning to say that she's expecting Myrtle at the end of the week."

Mrs. Culverton lingered at the gate waiting for Richard to accompany her home, but Richard, with a muttered excuse, strode off by himself in the opposite direction. Mr. Bailey allowed a decent time to elapse, during which he pretended to interest himself in the dahlias that flourished bleakly on the edge of the Vicarage shrubbery, then, as soon as he thought that Mrs. Culverton would be well on her way to Linden Rise, he set off for The Red Lion to get into his working clothes.

Richard walked aimlessly over the countryside till he had driven out of his mind every other emotion but weariness and a feeling of exasperated helplessness. Coming down from the hills towards the valley, he was surprised to see the familiar figure standing in the shadow of the trees at the entrance of the lane that led to the woods.

"Myrtle!" he said.

The figure stepped forward from the shade.

"It isn't Myrtle," she said with a low laugh. "It's Polly. Dad's sent Myrtle off to aunt at Hurst Farm over at Mallingford an' got me back home. I've got a note for you from Myrtle."

"But—I'd forgotten how exactly alike you were," said Richard, stammering a little in his surprise.

"We're nearly alike but not quite," smiled Polly.

"I suppose so," said Richard, studying her face.

Polly handed him a crumpled half-sheet of paper.

"She told me to give you this."

Richard opened it, straining his eyes to read it in the fading light. It was scrawled hurriedly and illegibly.

Richard, darling, I love you and I'll always love you. Whatever—

He stopped. "I can't read the next word. "H-a-q—"

They bent their heads over it together.

"'Happens'," said Polly. "It's a p, not a q."

186

"Why does she make her p's like q's?" said Richard, vaguely irritated.

"I don't know. She always does."

Whatever happens (he read), *I shall never stop loving you. My heart is yours till death do us part.*

"Thanks," said Richard a little flatly.

A Myrtle writing letters like that seemed different somehow from the soft, sweet Myrtle who had wandered with him down the mossy woodland paths and nestled against him beneath the shadowy trees.

"They're going to send her to school, you know," he said.

Polly gave a low gurgle of laughter.

"They'll learn her her p's an' q's there all right, won't they?" she said. "I must go now. Dad'd be furious if he knew I'd come at all."

She ran from him down the darkening road. He stood gazing after her, the crumpled half-sheet of paper still in his hand. No, they weren't quite alike. There was a sparkle of fun, a glimmer of mischief in Polly that there never had been in Myrtle.

Chapter Eighteen

"Lindsay will be twenty-one next week," said Sir Godfrey, "so we thought we'd better tell you the whole story."

He was standing in front of the fireplace, his hands clasped behind him, his kindly blue eyes fixed on Mrs. Culverton, who was sitting opposite on the chintz-covered settee. Lady Lynneker sat next her, watching her husband, a hint of anxiety behind the usual serenity of her expression.

Mrs. Culverton, Althea and Edmund had come to tea to the Hall. The young people had met early in order to go for a walk, and Mrs. Culverton had been fetched later by the Hall carriage. She had gathered that Sir Godfrey wished to discuss some matter with her in private before the young people returned, but had taken for granted that the matter would concern the practical details of Edmund's marriage to Lindsay.

"It was a very bad nervous breakdown," said Sir Godfrey, "and she had to go into—a sort of home."

"She was there for three months," said Lady Lynneker. "There has been no return of the trouble," said Sir Godfrey. "She's highly strung, of course, and if Edmund, when he knows all the facts, still wants to go on with the engagement—"

"Oh, I'm sure he will," put in Mrs. Culverton.

"—he must be prepared to use the utmost gentleness and tact with her."

"You need have no fear about that," said Mrs. Culverton with a touch of maternal pride in her voice. "Edmund's a good boy. He's been a wonderful son to me and a wonderful elder brother to the other children."

"This is in absolute confidence, of course," said Lady Lynneker. "Lindsay would be most distressed if people knew about it. The secret has been well kept. Everyone thought that she was in the South of France. You've—heard no rumours of it, have you?"

"None whatever," Mrs. Culverton assured her.

"The doctor says that there should be no return of the trouble except under circumstances of exceptional strain," said Sir Godfrey.

"And she can quite safely have children," said his wife. "In fact, he says that having children would be the best thing for her. She'll always be shy and sensitive, of course, but she has such a gay and happy side to her. She's such a dear, sweet child."

"She's charming," said Mrs. Culverton.

"Piers wanted to marry her, you know," said Sir Godfrey ruminatively, "but I wasn't really sorry when she refused him. I don't like the idea of cousins marrying. It weakens the stock."

"It would have been lovely to have kept her in the family," said Lady Lynneker wistfully.

"Better for her to go to fresh surroundings," said Sir Godfrey. "Give the child a clean break."

"Yes," said Lady Lynneker, "and perhaps when she's gone Piers will settle down again. He's been so restless since she definitely refused him. He's hardly been home at all."

"Well, that's the situation, Mrs. Culverton," said Sir Godfrey. "We wanted you to know exactly how things stood before we let these young people become definitely engaged. If you feel inclined to advise your son against the marriage we shall quite understand."

"No," said Mrs. Culverton, "I certainly shan't advise Edmund against it. I think that they're ideally suited to each other. Edmund's kind and capable and he likes looking after people. And Lindsay's so gentle and yielding."

"Y-yes," said Lady Lynneker thoughtfully. "She has her faults, of course. She's vague and forgetful and—incalculable. She'll always need patience and understanding."

Mrs. Culverton nodded.

"Edmund has patience and he'll understand her." She looked at Sir Godfrey. "Have you told Edmund?"

"No," said Sir Godfrey. "Lindsay wanted to tell him herself. She would have liked to tell him before, but we advised her to wait till we'd had this talk with you."

"She's probably telling him now," said Lady Lynneker. "And Roddy . . ." She smiled. "It seems that we're going to have a double family connection, Mrs. Culverton."

"Roddy came to see you last night?" said Sir Godfrey. "Yes."

"I understand that he's going to propose to Althea today. I take it that you have no objection."

"None," said Mrs. Culverton, adding generously: "Althea's a lucky girl."

"Well, that's as may be," said Sir Godfrey. "Roddy's a good boy. Not clever like your boys, but he'll make a good husband. That is, if she accepts him."

"I think she'll accept him," said Mrs. Culverton. She was silent for a moment or two, then went on with a slight effort: "I'm sorry about Richard and that Bailey girl. I mean, your position here—"

Sir Godfrey waved the matter aside.

"Oh, these things sort themselves out," he said vaguely. "No need to take them too seriously. We've got these other two sets of young people to think of first. Roddy, of course, will have to get down to a job. The boy can't spend the rest of his life playing games, and I can't afford to allow him enough to support a wife and family. As it happens, a cousin of my wife's was staying here last week-end and he offered to take Roddy into his business. The boy would have to go through the mill in the Birmingham factory first and then he'd be put in the London office with, eventually, the possibility of a partnership. Not very interesting, of course, but the boy hasn't the brains for a profession, and it seemed an offer that oughtn't to be turned down without good reason."

"Of course," said Mrs. Culverton.

She was feeling secretly a little disappointed. Somehow she hadn't thought of Althea's husband being "in trade." Still, there would always be the background of the Hall and the title . . .

"We can leave settlements and that sort of thing to the lawyers," said Sir Godfrey. "We needn't go into that now." He turned to look at the clock on the chimney-piece. "The young people should be here soon."

"Yes," said Lady Lynneker. "The girls said they'd be in by half past four."

"The girls" were striding over the crown of the hill. They wore well-cut coats and skirts of country tweed, stout leather boots and plain felt hats. Their faces were whipped to a glowing freshness by the cool crisp air.

"It was a clever idea of yours to pretend that we wanted to call at Langley Farm, Mabel," said Dorothy.

Mabel smiled proudly.

"Well, I knew they'd want to be alone."

"Still—it leaves the four of them together even so."

"Oh, they'll split up." She looked down into the valley. "Yes, Roddy and Althea are getting over the stile into the woods. Do you see them?"

"Yes. So that's all right. He's going to propose, isn't he? Do you think she'll have him?"

"Yes, I do."

"She's a good sort. I hope they'll be happy."

"And Lindsay's going to tell Edmund about her—illness."

"I don't think it'll make any difference, do you?"

"I'm sure it won't. She's such a good sort."

"So is he."

"Yes."

"I never feel I know the other two very well—Vere and Richard."

"But they're good sorts."

"Oh, yes. They're all good sorts."

With secret reservations that they did not voice even to each other, the girls had accepted the Culvertons. They were to be "Roddy's in-laws" and "Lindsay's in-laws" and as such the girls were prepared with dogged loyalty to defend them against the world.

Lindsay and Edmund were walking down the shadowy lane that skirted the Hall park.

"I wanted to tell you myself," Lindsay was saying in her sweet, tremulous voice. "I never think of it now. It's like a bad dream. I just—went to pieces, I don't know why. I—got frightened. Of everything. Every little thing seemed just more than I could bear. People speaking to me frightened me. I couldn't go into the village or out to tea or anything. I'd lie awake all night feeling frightened. Of everything and nothing. And I used to cry and I didn't even know myself what I was crying about."

"Darling." Edmund's hand found hers and held it firmly.

"You're never going to be frightened again."

"I shan't be now I've got you. You don't—mind about it? I mean, about my having been away."

"Of course not, my darling."

The slight shock that Edmund had experienced on hearing the news had been quickly followed by a curious feeling of elation. He wouldn't have admitted—he didn't even realize that this gave him a hold over her which he would not have had otherwise. He loved her passionately and longed to protect her, but the price of his protection must be absolute surrender, and he felt that by her confession she had surrendered herself so absolutely that she could never afterwards dispute his supremacy.

"Uncle's telling your mother now," she said, "and then let's never think of it again, shall we? Let's forget it as if it had never happened. Just now—just here with you—I feel as if it had never happened. I've felt—safe ever since I first met you. Do you remember? I was carrying a deck-chair and not knowing where to go."

He smiled.

"Yes, I remember."

"We'll be able to live somewhere near here, won't we? And you can go up to London every day."

"Well, I don't know," he said slowly. "I don't suppose that I shall be staying in the Civil Service for ever. It might be more useful to live in London."

"I don't care where I live as long as I'm with you." She gave her sweet, breathless laugh. "I do love you so, Edmund."

He looked down at her violet-blue eyes and long beautiful mouth.

"I love you, Lindsay, he said, "with all my heart and soul."

They had reached the gate of the Hall now and stood there, waiting. Roddy and Althea could be seen coming down the lane from the wood. Althea looked flushed and happy and a little bewildered. She had felt calm and sure of herself till Roddy kissed her in the shade of the gnarled old oak tree in Elston Woods. Till that moment she had been sexually unawakened. Partners at dances had snatched occasional furtive kisses in "sitting-out places"—beneath potted palms or on the staircase—but Roddy's kiss had jolted her out of her complacency, left her spent and breathless. Even so, her forces were not so shattered that she did not instinctively adopt the pose most likely to appeal to Roddy. Roddy didn't want a playmate. He had playmates in plenty, friends in plenty. He wanted someone to worship—some remote and perfect being of exquisite beauty and purity and charm and Althea, now that the position of Roddy's future wife was securely hers, set to work to build stone by stone the pedestal on which she was to stand.

"I suppose I'm one of those people who *give* out all the time," she said, as they walked back through the wood, Roddy's arm around her, her head on Roddy's shoulder, "and naturally people take it for granted. They depend on me so—Mother, Vere and everyone."

"Time you were taken away from it all," said Roddy.

"It's because of—Father, I suppose," said Althea. "I've had to try to make up for it to them. Vere's so terribly selfish and so is Richard. It's made it so hard for me. Mother doesn't mean to be selfish, but she turns to me for everything."

"You're wonderful, darling," said Roddy fervently.

"I suppose I'm too conscientious," said Althea, "and too sensitive. I take things too hard. But it *has* been a strain to help them and keep cheerful all the time. Even Edmund . . . He's kind and he means well, but he's out at work all day and he's naturally wrapped up in his own affairs. And Richard and Vere never think of anyone but themselves . . . Richard and that dreadful girl!"

"Well, when I marry you and take you away," said Roddy cheerfully, "they'll just have to get on with it, won't they?"

"Yes . . . I think I—minded about Father more than any of the Others. I've not had a happy childhood, Roddy."

"Well, you're going to be happy from now on," said Roddy. A disconsolate expression came over his face. "I dunno how I'm going to get through those two years at Birmingham. Think of me being stuck out there and you here meeting other men every day. You're sure to meet someone you like better than me. I'm such a hopeless bore and I've no brains at all. Never have had."

She smiled at him tenderly.

"Darling!" she said.

"It's going to be hell waiting two whole years."

"It'll soon pass, Roddy."

He stopped and looked down at her. Her fairness seemed to shine in the dim shadow of the trees. Again he gathered her into his arms and kissed her. She was pale and trembling when he released her. Then slowly, very slowly, they walked across the field and down the lane to the Hall gates, where Edmund and Lindsay were waiting for them.

Roddy's face beamed with ingenuous delight as he approached. "Allow me to present to you the future Mrs. Lynneker," he said.

"Oh, Roddy," laughed Lindsay affectionately, "you *would* say that! Congratulations, darlings!"

Edmund's congratulations were tendered solemnly and at some length.

"You *are* an old sober-sides, aren't you, darling?" teased Lindsay, and Edmund laughed, but a little constrainedly.

"Come along in," said Roddy, "and break the news to the parents. I expect the girls are there already."

"It's a real family party," said Lindsay. "Are the other two coming—Vere and Richard?"

"No," said Edmund. "They don't get home till after tea, anyway. I'm here because I'm taking a slice of my official holiday."

Richard generally got home about six o'clock, but Vere got home, as Tilly put it, "at all hours". As soon as her work at the Slade was over, she went on what she thought of as "voyages of discovery" through London, walking at random, finding everywhere odd bits of loveliness and interest—Staple Inn, Clifford's Inn, Pickering Place, Fig Tree Court, Godwin Court, St. Mark's Lane . . . She explored Limehouse and the docks. The docks in particular fascinated her. She would stand, motionless and enraptured, her eyes fixed on the strange craft with their dark-skinned crews or, taking her sketching-block from her pocket, make quick vivid sketches of them. She wandered round secondhand bookshops, poring over old books of travel, bringing her purchases home and keeping them hidden in her bedroom. The small box-room had now been turned into a bedroom for her. And still she alternated between a fierce joy in the fact that these new experiences were hers and hers alone, and a wistful desire to share them with someone.

"Where's everyone?" said Richard, entering the kitchen, where Tilly sat beating eggs at the kitchen table.

"Your ma and Miss Althea and Mr. Edmund's at the Hall," said Tilly, "fixin' up about gettin' married, and Miss Vere's not back yet."

"I hope they'll fix it up satisfactorily," said Richard. "Edmund should make the world's best husband. He's the only man I know without any faults at all. And Althea will make an excellent wife as long as things go smoothly. Althea is one of those plants that flourish in the sunshine. In the sunshine she's adorable."

"Huh!" sniffed Tilly.

"What do you mean by 'Huh!', Mrs. Noah?"

"I mean, it's all wrong," said Tilly, setting her lips grimly. "They're both marrying people they can hurt, and they ought to marry people that can hurt them. I'd rather have seen you an' Myrtle Bailey married than them four."

"So would I," said Richard.

"Well, why did you let them send her away to get made clever?" said Tilly. "She was all right like she was."

"I thought so," said Richard.

"Why didn't you stand up to them?"

"I don't seem much use at standing up to people."

"She won't be no good to you clever," said Tilly, adding her beaten eggs to a bowl of cream and pouring the mixture into a saucepan on the kitchen range. "You're clever an' that's enough. Clever people need stupid people to give them a rest from bein' clever, an' stupid people need clever people to give them a rest from bein' stupid."

"I never thought of it that way," said Richard.

"No good'll come of it," said Tilly. "You mark my words, it won't. Interferin' with God-given things like cleverness an stupidness!"

"I see your point," said Richard. "And when are you going to get married yourself?"

"When I find someone stupid enough," said Tilly with her sudden wooden grin. She had told him nothing of the breaking off of her engagement to Jim. "Have you had your tea?"

"Yes, thanks . . . I think I'll go and do some gardening."

Of late Richard had begun to take an interest in the garden. He found a curious comfort and stimulus in the work of digging and planting, a sense of achievement in the contemplation of his finished labours that little else in life had seemed to give him. He frequently spent the whole evening working in the garden. Or else he would go to the lane that led to the wood to see if Polly was there. Myrtle wrote him stilted little letters—beautifully written and perfectly spelt—once a week, but she wrote more frequently and more naturally to Polly, and when Polly had had a letter she would wait in the lane for Richard and they would walk through the wood together discussing it. Walking through the wood with Polly, listening to her soft gentle voice, he might have been with Myrtle again, except for the quick flashes of humour that Myrtle had never shown.

When he returned to the kitchen, after digging over the vegetable patch, he found Tilly cutting strips of angelica at the table. He watched for a few moments in silence.

"What's that for?" he said at last.

"It's for the top of the pudding. It's Apple Amber."

"I'll do it for you."

"No, I've got nothing else to do just now." She looked at the book that protruded from his pocket. "What have you been reading?"

"The *Timaeus*."

"That old Plato?"

"Yes."

"It's dull then."

"No, it isn't. It's about the creation of the world."

"Adam and Eve?"

"No." He took his seat on the edge of the kitchen table. "The world, Tilly, is a living creature with a soul and a body just like you. The sun and the moon and the stars have souls and bodies, too."

"It's a lot of stuff and nonsense," said Tilly. "I don't hold with it."

"You've been reading Aristotle," he accused her.

"Oo, I never!" said Tilly indignantly. "All I been reading is the cookery notes in *Home Pages*, an' it never tells you nothin' you didn't know before. Go on. Never mind old Plato. Tell me one of your Greek tales, Mr. Richard."

"Which one?"

She took the pudding out of the oven, dredged it with sugar and began to decorate it with cherries and the strips of angelica.

"Not the one about the man that got his liver pecked at by birds nor the one about the man that smelled on a desert island . . . Tell me the one about the woman what a giant fetched back from the grave. I like that one best."

"*Alcestis*," said Richard. "All right."

He lit his pipe and began the story.

Chapter Nineteen

Lindsay and Edmund were married in May, and in June Mrs. Culverton sold the London house. She kept a few pieces of furniture but most of it was too big for the cottage and she was glad to be rid of things that she had chosen as a bride and that held now only unhappy memories. She had little hope of Howard returning to her. A friend had informed her that he and Mrs. Brougham had left the Essex farmhouse and taken a villa in Rapallo, and that—she couldn't have told why—had seemed to set the final seal on his desertion.

In order to occupy her thoughts she had thrown herself with zest into the business of house-hunting for Edmund and Lindsay, helping them choose furniture and fittings—inspiring terror in agents, upholsterers and decorators by her air of cold authority—and now the two were comfortably settled in a small discreet house in a small discreet square in the neighbourhood of Westminster. Discretion, indeed, was the keynote of the establishment. Even the odd-job boy (who wore a page's uniform in the afternoon) had a correct and circumspect air.

Much to everyone's surprise, Edmund had left the Civil Service and taken a post as private secretary to a prominent Member of Parliament. He had begun his campaign quietly and resolutely soon after his marriage. The first step had been to get to know the right people and with a persistence that was impervious to snubs and set-backs he had got to know the right people. Among them was the prominent Member of Parliament, who had gradually come to value Edmund's competent, unobtrusive help so greatly that he had offered him the post of secretary.

Roddy was "going through the mill" in Birmingham, bewildered, homesick, but determined to master the work that was to give him Althea as the final reward, Althea received a letter from him every morning, written in schoolboy handwriting, couched in schoolboy phraseology, protesting his love and giving her a bald account of his doings. He had joined a tennis club; he had joined a cricket club; he had joined a golf club. His landlady was decent but he hated the place. He thought of Althea every moment of every day. He missed her terribly. She was the most wonderful girl in the world. He loved her more than ever. Would she write at once and tell him that she still loved him? He was such a dull boring ass that he couldn't believe that she did, but if ever she stopped loving him it would be the end of life for him . . . He sent her frequent presents—for the most part tasteless and ill-chosen—and carried her photograph about with him in his breast pocket. Everyone he had shown it to, he told her, had agreed that she was the *most* wonderful girl in the world.

Richard and Vere went up to London by an early train each morning, and Mrs. Culverton and Althea were alone together all day at Linden Rise. To Mrs. Culverton Althea still held the key to the lost world of romance and hope and youth, and she could not bear to let go her hold on it. There were days when the two lived on terms of happy intimacy—shopping in Bellminster, planning clothes and outings, discussing local events, sharing little jokes from which Richard and Vere were excluded, but Althea's irritability was never far from the surface. "An engaged girl's nerves," Mrs. Culverton would say in extenuation after an outburst. And certainly the glamour was fading from the engagement. Kicking my heels in Priors Green for two years, Althea would say savagely to herself. The Lynnekers made much of her, but she was beginning to find the Lynnekers a little boring. Piers had come home again and was helping his father with the management of the small estate. Though punctiliously polite to Althea when they met, he avoided her as far as possible. Althea was still in love with Roddy, but a vague discontent possessed her, and Mrs. Culverton was the obvious outlet for it. She was irritated especially by Mrs. Culverton's attempts to attach herself to her when she was going out with her friends.

"What are your plans today, dear?" Mrs. Culverton would say at breakfast.

"I'm going into Bellminster with Ella Corbett," Althea would reply shortly. "I have some shopping to do."

"There are several things I want in Bellminster. I could come with you."

"We're starting too early for you. We're starting almost immediately. You'll have things to see to here.

"I could join you for lunch."

"Oh, no, Mother. We don't know where we're having it or what time we're having it. Ella has to go to her dressmaker's.

"I could come in later and meet you for tea."

"Oh, *no,* Mother. We've got things to talk about . . ."

There was something pathetic in the way Mrs. Culverton would humble her pride to plead for Althea's companionship, but that was in itself to Althea an added irritation. Sometimes the scene would end in tearful reproaches. There were days when the two were barely on speaking terms, and then Mrs. Culverton would turn to Richard and Vere for comfort, but they had gone so far from her that they did not even realize she was asking their help.

Small local festivities succeeded one another through the summer. Old friends of the Culvertons from the Streatham days came down for occasional week-ends. Aunt Gertrude arrived and remained for a fortnight, heavily draped in widow's weeds. For Herbert had not long stayed the course. After a Shakespearean reading in which he had worked himself up into such a frenzy of emotion that perspiration streamed from every pore, he had walked home through a heavy shower of rain, caught pneumonia and died within a week. Aunt Gertrude accepted his loss with fortitude, draping her ample form in such a profusion of weeds that she resembled, from the distance, an ancient funeral horse. Even her handkerchiefs had an inch and a half of black round the hem, and the thick black edging of her envelopes barely left room for the address. There was a new poise and dignity about her. Her old exuberance had vanished.

"I'm quite enjoying being a widow," she confided to Richard. "It has the status of a married woman without the uncertainty."

To Vere she still threw out mysterious hints whenever they were alone together.

"I'll never forget it, dear. You'll see, I'll never forget it. Your dear little face drinking it in! Herbert never forgot it. He often spoke of it."

She was now so stout that the little wooden staircase creaked beneath her weight, and the small frilled arm-chair in the sitting-room could no longer contain her. Even the settee had a smothered panic-stricken look when she sank into it.

"It's my blood pressure that makes me so fat," she explained complacently.

She seemed to take the same quiet pride in her blood pressure and obesity as she took in her new status of widowhood.

It was on the last evening of Aunt Gertrude's stay that Miss Maple electrified the village by giving a sherry party.

"Someone gave one at the hotel at Broadstairs while I was staying there," she explained to Richard, "and it seemed a very pleasant way of passing the evening."

There had been a subtle change in Miss Maple since her return from the Broadstairs hotel. She had returned with another new hat, two new dresses and her hair groomed and waved. Even Major was now brushed and trimmed and walked at her heels with an air of modest consequence. Miss Maple was still shy, but behind the shyness was a new suggestion of assurance that infuriated some people and amused others. She herself was beginning to take the change for granted. She no longer apologized for it abjectly in every tone and glance, no longer appeared openly ashamed of her excesses.

It was the first sherry party that had been given in Priors Green and everybody who was asked to it went. And there a fresh shock awaited them. Miss Maple's drawing-room was stripped of its fern-stands and knitted mats and Victorian ornaments. The whatnot and chiffonier had vanished. A bowl of roses stood on the polished surface of the card-table that had previously supported a stuffed bird in a glass case and a massed array of family photographs. The voluminous draperies had been removed from the chimney-piece. Light chintz curtains hung at the window.

"Well, this is delightful," said Richard, raising his glass to her. "Congratulations!"

"I'm so glad you like it, Richard," said Miss Maple. "I don't approve of drinking in the ordinary way, but you could hardly call this drinking, could you?"

"Assuredly not," said Richard.

"And, as I told you, once you start slipping, you just go on. One thing seems to lead to another."

"It began with the list, didn't it?" said Richard. "How is it getting on? Have you included a bishop yet?"

"Oh, Richard," said Miss Maple ruefully. "That's all over. Something dreadful happened,"

"What?"

"Well, I kept adding new names, you know, just to salve my conscience and I ended by adding several guinea subscribers and then—Richard, you could have knocked me down with a feather when the letter came."

"What letter?"

"They wrote to say that as I'd got such a splendid body of supporters in Priors Green they were sending a special speaker from headquarters to address them, and they sent me a choice of dates and asked me to book a room for it."

Richard chuckled.

"Did you say you were leaving England for an indefinite period?"

"No, Richard, I never thought of that. I said that since I last wrote half the subscribers had left the neighbourhood and the other half had died."

Richard spluttered over his glass of sherry.

"What did they say to that?"

"They wrote rather a stiff letter. Reading between the lines, I could see that they didn't believe me. But it's rather a relief to be rid of the whole thing."

"Yes," said Richard. "Still, I'm sorry we didn't have a bishop."

"Actually I had put an archdeacon in. I was getting rather foolhardy towards the end. It's just as well it's stopped. I might have landed myself in trouble. I mean, if I'd started on Court circles. . ."

"You'd probably have involved yourself in high treason," said. Richard.

Mrs. Egerton came up and manoeuvred Richard into a corner.

"I've been trying to speak to you all evening, Richard," she said.

Richard looked round for escape and saw none.

"I've had a letter from Miss Fortescue."

"Oh, yes," said Richard a little apprehensively.

"She's very pleased with Myrtle's progress. Of course it's bound to be slow. One mustn't expect miracles, but she thinks that when Myrtle's finished her education she'll be a real credit to you."

Richard looked at her gloomily and made no answer.

''Now I always go to visit Miss Fortescue once a year and I'm going next Saturday," said Mrs. Egerton, "and Miss Fortescue suggests that you go with me to see Myrtle. Miss Fortescue thinks that in the circumstances you ought to keep in touch with her. It Mull be a help to you both. I've written to say that we'll arrive by the three-thirty from Charing Cross. There's a good connection from Bellingham."

Richard had armed himself for the journey with an assortment of periodicals, afraid of being drawn into the desultory conversation that can make even the shortest railway journey an acute nervous strain, but Mrs. Egerton, who evidently shared his views on the subject, settled down in a corner opposite him, opened a copy of *The Channings,* explaining that it was the book she always read on railway journeys, and did not raise her eyes from it till the train drew in at Tunbridge Wells station.

Miss Fortescue's establishment was a large Victorian house on the outskirts of the town. Its lace window curtains hung symmetrically, its Venetian blinds were exactly level, its brass knocker shone, its white doorstep gleamed. On the front lawn geraniums and calceolarias grew in neat rows in diamond-shaped beds within the confines of neat edgings of lobelia.

Miss Fortescue received them in a small, austerely furnished room that opened off the hall. She was a tall, grey-haired, rather stout woman dressed in purple silk, and her manner was an expertly blended mixture of majesty and affability.

"This is delightful," she said, looking at Richard's stooping untidy figure with faint disapproval. "Simply delightful! . . . Now I thought that Mrs. Egerton and I would have tea in my sitting-room and leave the drawing-room for you and Myrtle. I may call you Richard, may I not?"

"Please do," said Richard.

"Now, Richard, you mustn't expect to find Myrtle—finished as it were. My work is only half done yet, but she's getting on very nicely. Very nicely indeed. You'll find a definite improvement. I suggested this meeting *because* I want you to keep in touch with each other, and for the same reason I'm allowing Myrtle to have tea without the presence of a chaperone, which is perhaps a little unorthodox, but"—with a sudden effusion of affability—"I can trust you, can't I, Richard?"

Richard stared at her uncomprehendingly. The affability vanished and majesty took its place.

"There must be no attempt at—dalliance, you understand."

"Oh, yes. Yes, of course," said Richard, embarrassed.

"Well, now come to the drawing-room and I'll send Myrtle to you."

She took Richard upstairs to the drawing-room and closed the door on him. It was a terrible room. It ran the whole length of the house and had at each end large bay windows swathed in lace curtains and draped in damask. The door was draped in damask, the chimney-piece was draped in damask, the grand piano was draped in damask. On a desert of rich Aubusson carpet stood small oases of spindly gilt chairs and gold-upholstered settees. From the corners of the room potted palms sent out an earthy smell. It was a room that was evidently used only on formal occasions. Affability lurked slyly in the blue ribbons that tied back the lace curtains and in the peacocks' feathers in the empty grate, but the general effect was one of majesty. A small gilt-legged settee stood against the wall and in front of it was a tea-table covered by a lace cloth and supporting the tea equipment—gleaming silver, egg-shell china, wafer-thin bread-and-butter and savoy fingers.

Richard was gazing at it sombrely when the door opened to admit Myrtle. Just at first he did not recognize her. Her rather plump figure was tightly corsetted. She wore a well-cut dress of pale blue with a lace collar. Her hair was fashionably dressed.

"Oh Richard, isn't this lovely!" she said.

Her voice was not much altered. Its country burr was less discernible but it was still there. She sat down at the tea-table, making room for him beside her on the settee.

"Sit down, Richard . . . I'll pour out. They teach us how to pour out, you know . . . Cream? . . . Sugar? . . . Do have some bread-and-butter?"

"Well, how are you enjoying it?" said Richard.

"Oh, Richard, it's lovely. We have such fun. One of the girls, Maddy, is so funny. Her real name's Madeleine but we call her Maddy. She can take off all the governesses and she does it to their faces. It'd make you die of laughing." She broke off to giggle, then went on, "One day she went into Miss Plummer's bedroom and sewed up the sleeves of her nightdress, and another time she put a little rubber duck into the milk jug and Miss May poured it out." She dissolved into giggles again.

"So you're—quite comfortable here?" said Richard for want of anything else to say.

"Yes. It's proper grand, too. There's a butler and all. She won't let me say 'proper' but she's not here so I'll say it. I like all the governesses but Miss Wraxham. We call her Waxy. She's a fussy old-fashioned thing, but we get a lot of fun out of her because she's so absent-minded and short-sighted. One day Maddy changed her coat to Miss Plummer's hook and put Miss Plummer's on hers and Waxy put it on and went out in Miss Plummer's coat. We nearly died with laughing . . . Miss Laurence is ever so sweet—*she* wouldn't let me say 'ever so' either, but she's not here—and she's in love with one of the parish church curates. He's called Samuel and we have such fun singing that hymn line 'Oh, give me Samuel's heart' when she's anywhere around. She goes as red as red. Maddy thinks they're secretly engaged. She got a lovely Valentine from him on St. Valentine's day. We had such fun on St. Valentine's day. We each sent one to Waxy and signed them with boys' names."

Again her voice broke into giggles. Richard looked at her with growing dismay. All her gentleness and stillness had gone. She had become a giggling schoolgirl.

"Oh, dear!" she said, suddenly remembering her duties as hostess. "Have some more bread-and-butter? . . . A savoy finger? . . . More tea? . . . Was your tea as you like it?"

"Yes, thank you."

"You've eaten nothing."

"I'm not very hungry. What do you do with yourself all day?"

"Oh, lots of things. We have dancing lessons. I like them. Are you a good dancer, Richard?"

"I don't dance at all."

"What a pity! But you could learn, couldn't you? And we have Indian club exercises for our figures and singing lessons and botany lessons and lessons in general culture and politics and art and literature. And last week we went to London and saw the shops in Bond Street. I could have looked at them for ever. We went to the British Museum, too, but that was dull. Richard, shall we live in London when we're married?"

"I don't know where we shall live."

"Maddy's people live in London. So do Poppy's. Poppy's father's a barrister. You're going to be a barrister, aren't you, Richard?"

"I'm reading for the Bar."

"They have a big house and a carriage. Shall we have a big house and a carriage?"

"It's highly improbable," said Richard.

"She's here because she's a bit backward and couldn't go to an ordinary boarding-school. Her father comes to see her sometimes. He's ever so handsome and he wears suits like people in the advertisements in the papers." She gave a critical glance at Richard's slack, untidy figure. "I thought you'd be wearing your best suit, Richard."

"I haven't got a best suit," said Richard. "I have three suits and this is the one I happen to be wearing today."

"It looks—crumpled," she said.

"It is crumpled," said Richard.

"I don't mind for myself," said Myrtle hastily, "but the other girls will all be looking at you out of the windows." He glanced at his watch. "Oh, don't go yet, Richard. We haven't had a proper talk at all."

"No." He roused himself. "I suppose you want to hear all the news of Priors Green?"

"Oh, no, I don't think so, but there are heaps of things to talk about." She assumed what was evidently meant to be the air of a society hostess. "What do you think of the peace treaty?"

"I don't think of it at all," said Richard. "What do you think of it?"

"From a military point of view," said Myrtle, "we are spared two or three months' further campaigning and from a political point of view it gives us the advantage of beginning the work of reconstruction sooner."

"I see," said Richard.

"Oh, and I forgot to tell you that we went to London to see the Academy."

"And what did you think of that?" said Richard.

"It's the stronghold of traditional art," said Myrtle. "A safeguard against the experimentalist and the icon—icon . . ."

"Iconoclast?" suggested Richard.

"Yes, that was it . . . She told us what it meant but I've forgotten. Oo, and there was a lovely picture of the new King by Luke Fildes. You could get a reproduction for ten guineas and Miss Fortescue's getting one for the hall . . . We read poetry, too," she added with; a touch of pride.

"What poetry?" said Richard.

"Not the vulgar ones. Kipling's vulgar and so is Shelley. She reads us lots of Tennyson. He's all right. I mean, he isn't vulgar. He has the vision of the poet with the exactitude of the scientist.

That's right, isn't it?" she said a little anxiously. "I haven't got him muddled with someone else, have I?"

He looked down at the shadowed grey-blue eyes, the soft full mouth, then gently slipped his arm around her and bent his lips to hers. She broke away with a little scream of horror.

"No, Richard. Not here. I'd simply *die* if anyone came."

"All right," said Richard, slouching back in his corner of the settee again, his hands in his pockets. "Go on telling me about Tennyson."

"There's no more to tell," said Myrtle. "Miss Fortescue says there's a new one called Shaw, but he outrages the sanctity of the home and defiles the glory of womanhood or else the other way round I forget which—and, anyway, he's a Socialist, so he doesn't count."

At that moment the door opened and Miss Fortescue came in.

"I'm afraid you must say good-bye to Richard now, Myrtle," she said.

Myrtle took a decorous farewell and withdrew.

"Well," said Miss Fortescue with majestic pride when she and Richard were alone together, "you find a definite change in her, don't you?"

"I do," said Richard. "A very definite change."

"I'm so glad. Of course I haven't really worked on her accent yet. Or rather, I'm working on it gradually. It wasn't bad to start with, and I find that to work on an accent too quickly gives an effect of self-consciousness and affectation."

Then Mrs. Egerton came into the room.

"Richard, dear, we must fly or we'll miss our train. The cab's at the door."

They drove through the streets of the town towards the station.

"I didn't see Myrtle myself," said Mrs. Egerton, "because Miss Fortescue thought that no good purpose would be served by it at this half-way stage, but she assures me that already there's hardly a trace of the working class left in her. Do you agree?"

"I do," said Richard. "In fact, there's none at all."

He was afraid that Mrs. Egerton would discuss the subject for the rest of the journey, but she opened *The Channings* as soon as the train started and did not speak again till they reached Bellminster station. They were separated on the bus and at Priors Green Richard, with a muttered excuse, set off alone to the corner of the lane where Polly was waiting for him in the dusk.

"Well, did you see her?" she said.

"Yes."

"What's she like? Have they stopped her being common?"

"She wasn't common before. They've made her common.

She sensed something of his dejection.

"Never mind, Richard," she said, slipping her hand into his.

They entered the wood and walked down the shadowy winding path. She did not speak again, but her serenity and sweetness seemed to shed themselves into his spirit till all its unrest was stilled.

Stopping suddenly at a point where an overhanging beech tree made an archway across the path, he took her in his arms and pressed his lips on hers.

Chapter Twenty

Althea's wedding was to take place at the end of the summer. Roddy had served his apprenticeship and was now installed in the London office. Sir Godfrey had bought a small Regency house in Chelsea for the young couple, and Mrs. Culverton was once more busy with the furnishing and equipment of an "establishment."

Althea, during the weeks preceding the wedding, bloomed into a new radiance. Her petulance and restlessness vanished. She was the bride-to-be, fêted and courted by everyone, and she responded instinctively to the atmosphere, becoming gay and light-hearted and girlishly excited. Now that she was approaching the status of matron a new intimate relationship sprang up between her and her mother, and Vere's feeling of isolation increased as the other two grew closer together. They held long confidential conversations, lowering their voices to whispers when Vere entered the room, or breaking off the discussion abruptly and waiting with obvious impatience for her to go away. As if in self-defence Vere adopted a manner of pert nonchalance that exasperated Mrs. Culverton. Assured now of Althea's allegiance, she became harsher in her treatment of Vere, reproving her for faults that she had previously ignored. There were nights when, bewildered and unhappy, Vere cried herself to sleep with childish abandon.

The news of Aunt Gertrude's death (from an apoplectic stroke) crashed like a bombshell into the atmosphere of wedding preparations. The telegram announcing it arrived while Mrs. Culverton, Althea and Vere were having lunch, and Mrs. Culverton threw it on to the table with a gesture of annoyance.

"How exasperating!" she said. "We can't possibly go into mourning at a time like this."

"Mourning?" screamed Althea. "Of course we can't."

"Or postpone the wedding."

"Of course not."

"The week-end, too!" said Mrs. Culverton, pointing out this further proof of Aunt Gertrude's thoughtlessness.

"When's the funeral?"

"Tuesday," said Mrs. Culverton, looking at the telegram again. "Richard could go up for it, I suppose, but I really don't see that I can."

"And there'll be all her affairs to settle up," said Althea. "What a nuisance!"

"There's no hurry about that. I could go down for a day or so later."

"I could go," said Vere.

She felt a sudden longing to identify herself with the family, to carry her share of family responsibility.

"Don't be so foolish, Vere," said Mrs. Culverton sharply, glad of the opportunity of venting her irritation on someone. "Of course you couldn't go. You wouldn't be of the slightest use if you went. You're too stupid and careless and unbusiness-like to be any help at all."

Vere rose from her seat and went from the room. The rebuff had brought the sting of tears to her throat, and, impelled by an impulse of flight, she took her hat and coat from the hatstand and set off towards the woods.

"Sulking!" said Mrs. Culverton, as she heard the front door close. "She's always been a difficult child . . . Well, now, Althea, let's get this business of the church decorations fixed up before anything else. We can discuss what to do about Aunt Gertrude later."

Vere walked through the wood, checkered green and gold with the sunshine, then up to the top of the hill. There she sat, on a small hummock, gazing down into the valley . . . A hay-cart was lumbering along the lane between hedges afoam with Queen Anne's

Lace . . . Some children ran shouting round a pump in the farmyard . . . In the meadows cattle stood motionless beneath the shade of the elm trees . . .

She took her sketching-block from her pocket and began to sketch the farther end of the valley, where a clump of alders marked the stone bridge that spanned the river and the tiled roof of a barn, gilded with lichen in the sunshine, showed through the trees. Sketching generally brought her a sense of comfort, but today the hurt of her spirit remained unassuaged. Putting the sketch, half finished, into her pocket, she rose and, descending the farther side of the hill, walked across the fields to the next village. She stopped for tea at a little cottage, hoping vaguely that her absence would cause some slight anxiety at home. Even now, half unconsciously, her mind took refuge in the old childish pictures of a penitent family mourning her loss.

It was six o'clock when she returned to Linden Rise. From the hall she heard the sound of Mrs. Culverton's and Althea's voices followed by a sudden silence as her footsteps approached the sitting-room door. She entered the room and stood in the doorway.

"Come in, Vere," said Mrs. Culverton. "I want to speak to you."

Vere advanced slowly and sat down opposite Mrs. Culverton.

"Mr. Jackson came while you were out, Vere" said Mrs. Culverton.

"Mr. Jackson?"

"He's Aunt Gertrude's solicitor. She must have grown more eccentric than ever in these last few years. She made him promise to come down here immediately on her death to tell you the news himself. He didn't stay till you returned as he would have missed his train to London. He asked me to tell you in his place."

Glancing from one to the other, Vere was conscious of a new hostility, a new resentment. Althea's eyes were hard, her mouth set. Mrs. Culverton's voice was cold and distant.

"What news?" said Vere.

"Except for a few small legacies, Aunt Gertrude has left you all her money. I must say it's rather strange, considering that I am her only sister and Althea her eldest niece."

"It's more than thirty thousand pounds," said Althea.

"Whatever are you going to do with it?"

Vere drew in her breath.

"I'd like to go away and live somewhere by myself," she said.

She hadn't known that she was going to say it till she heard the words. She turned white as she waited for their response. She couldn't have told exactly what she hoped for—protestations of affection, assurances that they needed her, entreaties not to leave them. It was to be a pale reflection of the death-bed scene of her childish dreams.

Mrs. Culverton shrugged.

"There's no reason why you shouldn't," she said. "You'll be of age next month."

Vere rose jerkily from her seat.

"I'll go and take my things off," she said unsteadily.

She wanted to hide her emotion from them. It was so confused that she didn't understand it herself. Beneath the desolation of the lost child was a strange new excitement. She'd be free. At last she'd be free . . .

She went upstairs to her bedroom, where Tilly was turning down the sheets on her bed.

"Is anything the matter, Miss Vere?" said Tilly. Her wooden face was as expressionless as ever, but her harsh voice was softened to a note of solicitude.

"No, thank you," said Vere. "I—I just feel a bit sick."

"Have a lay down," said Tilly.

"Tilly," said Vere, turning her head away and speaking in a small flat voice. The exultation had faded, leaving only the desolation of the lost child. "Aunt Gertrude's left me a lot of money and I've just told them that I want to go away and live by myself . . . I don't know . . . I'm not sure . . . Perhaps—perhaps they really want me, after all. I—I won't go away if they do . . . Perhaps they'll ask me to stay. If they do ask me . . ."

"You stick to it, Miss Vere," said Tilly, closing her trap-like mouth. "Whatever they ask you, you stick to it."

Vere went to the window and stood for a moment in silence, looking down at the garden.

"Yes, Tilly," she said at last. "Yes, I think I will."

But the sensation of Vere's legacy faded quickly into the background in the gathering momentum of Althea's wedding preparations.

Edmund and Lindsay came over from London, and Edmund gave away the bride with an air of impressive dignity and played the part of host at the reception with punctilious correctness. Bride and bridegroom departed for the honeymoon in North Italy and Edmund and Lindsay settled down for a week's stay at Linden Rise. It was Edmund who had suggested this. Lindsay had had a miscarriage early in the year from which she had not yet quite recovered, and he hoped that the country air would do her good. She was pale and listless but seemed still to be deeply in love with Edmund, while Edmund on his side treated her with a protective kindness that held more than a hint of the schoolmaster in it. Despite the surface amity, however, there was a suggestion of tension in the atmosphere between them that made Mrs. Culverton vaguely uneasy. At times Lindsay would seem to rouse herself to be gay and lively, but there was a brittle edge to her gaiety and an undertone of hysteria in her laughter.

Edmund had brought down with him a case full of pamphlets and blue books and spent each morning reading and making notes. He was taking himself more seriously than ever. After further training from his elocution teacher he had made several speeches at political meetings. His speeches were concise, apt and ably delivered. The eyes of his superiors were turned on him with interest and speculation, and Edmund considered that in a few years' time he would be in a position to stand for Parliament himself. Already he was beginning to treat everyone he met as if they were his constituents—in a friendly and affable fashion, but with the reserve of one who could reveal momentous secrets if he would.

Lindsay spent a good deal of time at the Hall, but Piers had left Priors Green for Scotland the day after the wedding. It had never occurred to Edmund to be jealous of Piers, though he knew that Piers had been in love with Lindsay. His own perfection had become a fetish with him and he expected everyone around him—his wife most of all—to pay homage to it.

On the last day of their visit they had been invited to a garden party given by Sir Giles Chadwick, the squire of one of the neighbouring villages. Sir Giles was a Member of Parliament and brother-in-law of a Cabinet Minister, and it was rumoured that the Cabinet Minister himself would be present. Lindsay didn't want to go. She pleaded a headache, said she was too tired, but Edmund was insistent. Lindsay's beauty and charm were an asset of which, he considered, she had no right to deprive him. They should, on formal occasions, be as much at his disposal as his top hat and buttonhole.

She yielded reluctantly and set off with him in the Victoria that he had hired from Bellminster. She wore a dress of pastel blue with a broad-brimmed hat that threw a soft shadow over her face. Edmund looked at her with approval.

"You'll be your nicest to Sir Giles, won't you, darling?" he said, as the carriage set off along the country road, "and, of course, specially nice to Mr. Anstruthers if he's there."

She glanced restlessly from one dusty hedgerow to the other and made no answer.

Mrs. Culverton was waiting for them in the little sitting-room when they returned. She saw at once that something had gone wrong. Lindsay's eyes were feverishly bright, Edmund's handsome face grimly set. Lindsay sank down on to the settee; Edmund stood—tall and formidable in his grey frock-coat—looking down at her.

"I didn't like to say much to you coming home," he said.

"You said enough," said Lindsay.

Then suddenly she laughed—a peal of childish laughter, bubbling, irrepressible.

"What happened, Edmund?" said Mrs. Culverton.

Lindsay's laughter had died on a high note and she sat watching them, her hand at her throat.

"Lindsay behaved disgracefully," said Edmund.

Lindsay had certainly behaved disgracefully. It was as if, for that afternoon, her youth, repressed so long by her own fears and Edmund's guiding hand, had risen and taken its revenge on her. There had been at the party a crowd of young people whom Lindsay had known when she lived at the Hall. They were high-spirited, irresponsible young people, and suddenly Lindsay, with one of her swift incalculable changes of mood, had lost her shyness and joined them, chattering as animatedly as they chattered, laughing, teasing, being teased. It would not have mattered, of course, if they had been young people who counted, but they were not. They belonged to the class that Edmund summarized as "people of no account". People of account were present in large numbers— heavy, pompous, elderly—but Lindsay, caught up suddenly in the ebullience of youth, treated them with scant courtesy, making her excuses almost immediately the introductions were over and returning to the crowd of young people, drawn to their carefree, light-hearted company as by some new magnetic force. She had evaded introduction to the Cabinet Minister altogether.

"What happened, Edmund?" said Mrs. Culverton again.

"Nothing," said Edmund, setting his lips, "except that Lindsay did not behave as I have a right to expect my wife to behave."

"I hardly ever do, do I?" said Lindsay, the lingering aftermath of youthful defiance fighting with her habitual fear of Edmund's displeasure. "What did I do wrong this time?"

"You know quite well what you did wrong," said Edmund. "You were barely civil to your host and hostess."

"They were dull," said Lindsay, relaxing against the cushions. "It seemed such a lovely afternoon. I didn't want to spoil it."

"You behaved like a silly schoolgirl," he said. "I was ashamed of you."

Lindsay sat up suddenly, her figure tense, her eyes feverishly bright.

"Can't you leave me alone?" she flamed. "Why won't you ever let me be myself?"

Edmund's face darkened. His brows drew ominously together.

"When your conduct displeases me," he said, "it is my duty to tell you so."

"Oh, Edmund," put in Mrs. Culverton pacifically.

"You knew that I wanted you to meet Mr. Anstruthers," went on Edmund, "and you deliberately avoided him."

"I disliked him," said Lindsay. "He was like a walking Baptist chapel."

"It's immaterial whether you liked him or disliked him," said Edmund. "You must learn to behave with civility to people. I expect certain standards from you as my wife and—"

Suddenly Lindsay's precarious self-control broke down. She dropped her head on to her hands.

"Oh, be quiet!" she cried between her sobs. "I won't listen . . . I can't bear any more of it . . . It goes on and on and on . . . Leave me alone . . . I hate you . . . You're cruel and mean and selfish . . . You don't love me . . . You don't love anyone but yourself . . ."

Edmund strode up to her and pulled her hands down.

"Stop behaving like a hysterical child," he said, a note of cold fury in his voice.

She wrenched herself free and ran to the door.

"I shall expect an apology for this," said Edmund as she flung open the door and vanished.

When she had gone he stood with lowering brow and protruding underlip, staring in front of him. They heard the sound of Lindsay's footsteps ascending the stairs, then the closing of her bedroom door.

"Edmund, you ought to be more careful in your treatment of Lindsay," said Mrs. Culverton.

He turned to her, his face stiff with anger.

"Will you kindly leave me to manage my own affairs, Mother?" he said.

Mrs. Culverton looked at him in silence. Her feeling was one bewilderment rather than resentment. This was an Edmund she did not know, had never known. She wondered by what secret and imperceptible stages he had emerged from the docile, good-natured boy she remembered.

217

Lindsay did not come down again that evening, but the next morning all seemed well . . . Lindsay was pale and quiet, her manner held a fine-drawn intensity that made Mrs. Culverton watch her anxiously, but she appeared calm and happy, while Edmund, on his side, was kind and almost lover-like. A reconciliation had evidently taken place.

They set off for the station in the musty-smelling station cab, and Mrs. Culverton watched them go with a heavy heart.

She was sitting at her writing-desk going over her household accounts when Richard came home that evening.

"Can you spare me a moment, Mother? he said.

She turned round from the desk, pen in hand.

"What is it, Richard?"

"I've decided to give up the Bar, he said.

She laid down her pen.

"Richard!" she said. "Why?"

"Entwistle's back from Uganda, he said. 'I had lunch with him today. He's given up his job there. The climate doesn't suit him. He's starting a new literary journal and he wants me to help him edit it."

"But, Richard," said Mrs. Culverton helplessly, "think of all the trouble we've taken with—well, with Myrtle for one thing."

"I couldn't marry Myrtle in any case now," said Richard.

"Why not?"

"That's another thing I have to tell you," said Richard. "I married Polly last week."

Chapter Twenty-One

Mrs. Culverton came slowly downstairs. She wore one of the trailing black dresses that she had worn ever since Howard's death and a short black woollen shawl over her shoulders. She made her way down the narrow passage and opened the kitchen door.

"Aren't you going to get the tea, Tilly?" she said. "It's five minutes past four."

"No, it isn't, madam," said Tilly, setting her lips. "That there clock in the hall's fast. It's five to four an' tea'll be in at four as usual."

"Oh, very well," said Mrs. Culverton peevishly and turned back towards the sitting-room.

Tilly and Mrs. Culverton had been together at Linden Green now for three years. There were days when Tilly was difficult and there were days when Mrs. Culverton was difficult and there were days when both were difficult together. Occasionally Tilly would give notice and occasionally Mrs. Culverton would dismiss her, but this was accepted on both sides as a gesture of independence and never referred to again.

Mrs. Culverton had received the news of her husband's death two years ago, and though at the time she had shown little emotion she had aged quickly since receiving it. It was as if some tension that had kept her whole being taut and elastic till then had vanished. She grew slack and listless. Even her once slender figure was now flabby and shapeless and a querulous note had invaded her once cool authoritative voice. She spent a good deal of time in self-pity and derived an obscure satisfaction from it—so much so that she was apt to resent and depreciate any small pieces of good fortune that came her way. She pottered about the house and village and took her part in the various local festivities and on the various local committees and the months slipped by unnoticed. The Lynnekers still lived at the Hall but "the girls" had married. Both had married into neighbouring county families and were busy playing the part of beneficent overseer in their respective villages. Piers, too, had married, outraging public opinion by marrying a foreigner—a gentle, slender Italian girl, whose dark hair and wide-spaced blue eyes gave her a faint likeness to Lindsay. He paid flying visits to Priors Green but spent most of his time in Florence, where his wife's people lived. There were changes in the village, as well. Mr. Egerton was now an Archdeacon in charge of a large North Country parish, and a young bachelor, shy and diffident, held the living of Priors Green. Gradually, imperceptibly, Miss Maple had taken the reins into her hands. By now she "ran" most of the parish activities and exercised a kindly sway over the Vicar himself, protecting him from the over-eager attentions of his unmarried parishioners and guiding him with skilful hands along the thorny path of local prejudice. The Vicar was pathetically grateful and felt towards Miss Maple rather as he had felt towards his nurse when he was a small boy. She still lived at Blenheim Villa, but a trim uniformed maid was now in attendance, and Major, who had died last year, had been replaced by a dapper Sealyham.

When Tilly entered with the tea-tray, both she and Mrs. Culverton glanced at the clock—Tilly triumphantly, Mrs. Culverton a little resentfully. The hands stood at four o'clock precisely. Mrs. Culverton did not really mind whether she had tea at four o'clock or not, but she enjoyed catching Tilly out. The two of them spent a good deal of time and trouble trying to catch each other out, enjoying a short-lived triumph till the scales were turned. Beneath the surface relations of authority on Mrs. Culverton's part and respect on Tilly's a quiet warfare was carried on that added zest to both their lives.

"Here's your tea," said Tilly, setting the tray on the table by Mrs. Culverton's arm-chair. "I've made you some hot scones, so don't let them get cold."

She spoke kindly, refraining from dwelling on her little triumph, refraining even from adding to it by drawing Mrs. Culverton's attention to the fact that she had forgotten to alter the calendar on her writing-desk—a day-to-day calendar that she would never allow Tilly to touch.

"I'll pour your tea out for you," she went on.

"Thank you, Tilly," said Mrs. Culverton, leaning back in her chair and heaving a long deep sigh as she watched the golden stream issue from the silver teapot into the Wedgwood cup.

"What's the matter?" said Tilly bluntly. 'Got your head bad again?"

"No," said Mrs. Culverton. "It's only that I'm a miserable old woman, Tilly."

"Go on!" said Tilly, putting down the tea-pot and standing, arms akimbo. "There's lots worse off than you."

"Nobody loves me," said Mrs. Culverton. "Not even my own children."

"Don't be daft," said Tilly. "Didn't they all write to you on your birthday?"

Mrs. Culverton waved that aside and drew her shawl around her with a mournful gesture.

"I've given my life for them," she said, "and what do I get in return?"

"Well, they've turned out all right," said Tilly stoutly. "There's Mr. Edmund a Member of Parliament and Miss Althea going to parties and things in London and Miss Vere—well, Miss Vere's done the best of the lot, hasn't she?"

"Yes," said Mrs. Culverton with a certain reluctant gratification. "There's something about her book in this morning's paper."

Mrs. Culverton still felt bewildered at the thought of Vere—Vere with her new air of poise and sophistication and her flat in London; Vere who had just published a book, highly praised by critics, describing her journey through the mystery cities of Lubaantun. The illustrations, water colours by Vere herself, seemed to Mrs. Culverton to be meaningless splashes of colour, but the critics had praised them too.

She sighed again.

"She owes it all to me," she said. "I suggested her going to the Slade. I encouraged and helped her, but I get no thanks, no gratitude."

"Well, never mind," said Tilly. "Drink your tea before it gets cold an' them scones won't stay hot till Christmas. I'm goin' out after tea an' I want to get the washin'-up done."

"Where are you going?" said Mrs. Culverton with an interest she tried to conceal.

"I'm going round to Mr. Richard's," said Tilly.

Mrs. Culverton's lips tightened. She had never forgiven Richard and she never would forgive him. So utterly had he disgraced the family that forgiveness, she considered, was out of the question. Whenever she thought of him, living in Priors Green in an ordinary working-class cottage with Polly and their child, making a scanty living by growing vegetables (for the literary venture with Entwistle had soon come to grief), even helping Mr. Bailey in the bar of The Red Lion, shame and bitterness flooded her soul. The fact that the other residents of Priors Green remained on friendly terms with him (as far as he allowed friendly relations) increased her bitterness.

"Now don't start on Mr. Richard," said Tilly, noticing the tightening of her lips. "He's all right."

"All right!" echoed Mrs. Culverton. "Do you call it all right to treat a girl as he treated Myrtle Bailey?"

"She didn't mind," said Tilly easily. "She's as happy as a sandboy at Didsbury's."

Mrs. Culverton's mind went back to the interview that had taken place between herself, Myrtle and Mrs. Egerton among the palms and brocade hangings of Miss Fortescue's drawing-room. They had gone to tell Myrtle of Richard's marriage, expecting tears and reproaches, but there had been neither. Myrtle had received the news with a quietness that had in it something of relief.

"I liked him till I got educated," she explained, "but after I got educated—well, I couldn't help seeing how dull he was. Between you and me and the lamp-post I've been wondering for some time how I could get out of it. He bored me something awful the last time he came here."

"But, Myrtle," said Mrs. Egerton, "what are you going to do?"
Myrtle had apparently thought it all out.

"I don't want to marry anyone yet," she said. "I can do better for myself than that. I've got looks and style and education and I'd like to get a job at Didsbury's."

"Didsbury's?" said Mrs. Egerton. She thought of the large draper's shop that dominated the market square in Bellminster and suddenly realized that Myrtle, gleaming with newly acquired polish, would fit into the atmosphere very well.

"They want refined girls," said Myrtle, "and I'm refined now, so I should stand a good chance."

"But Miss Fortescue would be horrified," said Mrs. Egerton. "Oh, her!" said Myrtle carelessly. "Her and her museums and stuff. She ought to be in one herself."

Miss Fortescue, too, received the news with fortitude.

"One has one's failures," she said. "Fortunately they are few, but it is best to admit them honestly. Myrtle is quick in picking up tricks of manner and style, but there is in her an innate disinclination for Culture that is a great stumbling-block. I have done with her all that can be done. She will now pass muster in genteel circles among the less discerning, and that is all that I—or anyone—would be able to accomplish in this particular case."

So Myrtle returned to The Red Lion. Mr. Bailey's attitude to the situation was one of slightly sardonic amusement. He was fond of the two girls and had come to like Richard, and he found Myrtle's new mannerisms intensely diverting. The whole affair gave him food for much philosophic reflection.

Myrtle, well groomed, well dressed, with high heels and clipped, refined accents, obtained a post in Didsbury's millinery department and was soon promoted to head assistant. She was a great favourite with the customers. ("Such a superior girl." "I always wait till Miss Bailey can attend to me, however long I have to wait.") She enjoyed the work and had refused several offers of marriage. She was accommodating and good-natured, slipping back into the country ways and speech as soon as she returned home, serving in the bar in the evening and speaking with the old, soft country burr.

Mrs. Culverton was relieved that the affair had not developed into tragedy, but at the same time felt obscurely aggrieved that it had not done so. Someone (either Richard or Polly or Myrtle— she wasn't sure which) ought to have been taught a salutary lesson, and no one seemed to have been taught any lesson at all. Perhaps the plump baby that had been born to Richard and Polly was her greatest grievance, and the secret reason for the grievance (though she would not have admitted it even to herself) was that Althea, the beloved, was still childless. She would glance through the hedge as she passed the cottage and see the sunburnt, half-naked child toddling about the tiny garden and her heart would contract with sudden pain. She paid Richard and Polly ceremonial visits, behaving with frigid politeness, sitting upright and unrelaxing in her chair, but even that failed apparently to stir in them any sense of shame or compunction. They were kind to her, but behind their kindness was a hint of compassion that affronted Mrs. Culverton most deeply.

"I want to see Nigger before he goes to bed," said Tilly.

"Nigger!" echoed Mrs. Culverton. "They might at least call the child by his real name, outrageous though it is."

It was when Richard had called his son Dominic that she had finally washed her hands of the family.

"Well, he's so brown he's like a nigger," said Tilly.

But Mrs. Culverton's thoughts had gone to Althea.

"You'll be going to Miss Althea next month as usual, won't you, Tilly?" she said. "She hasn't written about it but I know that she's counting on you."

Every summer Mrs. Culverton "lent" Tilly to Althea for the fortnight during which Althea's cook was on holiday, and while Tilly was away Mrs. Culverton generally went to rooms in Folkestone where she spent most of her time sitting at her bedroom window, watching the passers-by and thinking over her grievances.

"I suppose so," said Tilly, setting her lips, then added: "Why don't you come too?"

"No . . . no," said Mrs. Culverton. Her form grew rigid and she trembled slightly. "No, I'd rather not."

Alone here she could dream of Althea, the beloved; could see her as a devoted daughter, her loving thoughts and anxiety centred on the lonely figure in Linden Rise, but contact with Althea dispelled the dream and she could not bear to have it dispelled. Althea impatient, slightly contemptuous, finding her mother's presence an encumbrance, making no secret of her relief when Mrs. Culverton suggested an earlier day for her departure than had been fixed . . . No, she wouldn't think of it . . . wouldn't remember it.

"I find the journey too tiring," she said. "It was a very nice tea, Tilly. You may take it away now."

"Come along with me to Mr. Richard's," coaxed Tilly. "The walk will do you good."

"No, thank you, Tilly," said Mrs. Culverton with dignity. "It grieves me more than I can say to see the depth to which Richard has sunk. I never thought that any son of mine would turn out a wastrel."

The word "wastrel" annoyed Tilly.

"Very good, madam," she said. She took up the tray and went to the door. "You've forgot that there date thing again," she said with a note of quiet triumph in her voice as she left the room.

Briar Cottage, where Richard lived, was a small tumble-down cottage that appeared to be held together by the climbing roses, honeysuckle and jasmine that covered it. At the side of the cottage stretched the field that Richard worked as a nursery garden, with its ordered lines of vegetables and a row of greenhouses at the bottom. The rickety van in which he took his produce into Bellminster was parked near the gate.

Tilly made her way round the cottage to the sloping garden at the back a garden consisting chiefly of rough grass and gnarled old apple trees. Beneath one of them Richard lay outstretched on his stomach, wearing battered corduroy trousers and an open-necked shirt. His head was propped on his hands and he was reading a book. A litter of other books covered the grass around him. Nigger—a chubby brown baby in faded blue rompers—sat astride his back. Occasionally Nigger would shout "Gee-up!" and then Richard, still absorbed in his book, would jerk his thin body up and down, while Nigger roared with delight. Polly sat on a kitchen chair near them at work on a pile of house-hold mending. In her print overall with bare legs and sandals and a blue ribbon tied round her dark hair, she looked like a little girl.

Tilly, standing for a moment unnoticed by them, was aware of an atmosphere of deep contentment. They're happy, she thought with a rush of thanksgiving.

Then they saw her . . . Richard sat up, Polly rose from her chair, and Nigger began to toddle towards her across the orchard.

"You sit here," said Polly. "I'll sit on the grass."

"No, I'll sit on the grass," said Tilly. "I want to play with Nigger."

"Well, Mrs. Noah," said Richard with the old quirk of his eyebrow, "how's everything?"

"Pretty good," said Tilly, sitting on the grass and tickling Nigger's dimpled knees with a clover leaf, at which Nigger laughed uproariously. "You go on reading your old Greek and I'll give Polly a hand with the mending."

"I'm not reading my old Greek," said Richard. "At least not exclusively." He glanced at the litter of books around him. "I'm browsing among Wordsworth and Boswell and Montaigne and Chaucer, but at the moment I'm reading Virgil's *Georgics*—his weather portents are pretty sound, you know—after which I shall return refreshed to the hoe."

"He's got some grand onions," said Polly proudly. "I wanted him to show them but he wouldn't."

"The competitive element is incompatible with true husbandry," said Richard. "It vulgarizes it. Why should we puny mortals take credit for Nature's handiwork?"

"The nonsense he talks!" said Polly with an indulgent smile.

"But all the same he's done grand with everything this year."

Richard was a good gardener. He felt an affection—even a respect—for all growing things and took a deep delight in tending them.

"You'd think they were alive, the way he goes on with them," said Polly. "I hear him talking to them sometimes."

"They are alive," said Richard, his eyes twinkling. "Plotinus tells us that they each have a share of the Universal Soul. They respond to love and reach up after the Divine, which is more than some humans do."

"Oh, you and your stuff!" said Tilly, and she and Polly laughed again, Nigger joining in with an exultant crow.

"Here's Miss Maple," said Polly, as Miss Maple came round the corner of the cottage.

"Well, come and tell us your traveller's tales," said Richard, for Miss Maple had just returned from a Mediterranean cruise.

"No, they wouldn't interest you, Richard," said Miss Maple, taking the chair that Polly had vacated to sit on the grass with Tilly. "It was all very obvious and insular and luxurious and a little vulgar, but I thoroughly enjoyed it. I liked the luxury, and one could ignore the vulgarity, and I haven't got beyond the obvious in sight-seeing yet, but—well, I'm going to try to get away from the insularity the next time I go abroad."

"What do you mean by the insularity?" said Richard.

"People flocking to English tea-rooms wherever they go. And going in a herd to see local night life and being thrilled when the local nightlifers sing English songs for them. I'm going to strike out a more individual line the next time."

"Like Vere?"

"Oh, no, dear. Not quite so individual as that. I'm only going so stay by myself at some hotel where they don't speak English and just hope for the best. I'm going to make an *adventure* of it."

"That's the spirit," said Richard. "And what did you do with yourself when you weren't drinking tea in English tea-rooms and eating six-course dinners?"

"Seven, Richard," said Miss Maple with quiet pride, counting cheese and dessert. I knitted for Nigger. I knitted him four little coats and six vests." She opened the parcel she was carrying and brought out a bundle of tiny garments. Then she looked at her godson, her eyes clouding with sudden anxiety. "I forgot that he'd be growing all the time I was away. I do hope they won't be too small for him."

Wool stretches," said Polly reassuringly.

Miss Maple seized Nigger and took him on her knee, tickling and kissing him and drawing off his rompers. He laughed and kicked and plunged.

"Thank heaven!" said Miss Maple piously, as she drew the knitted vest over his sturdy brown body. "They fit . . ."

Tilly had slipped indoors. One of her greatest joys was putting the little cottage to rights. Polly was happy-go-lucky, Richard completely unaware of his surroundings, and Nigger seemed to thrive on disorder.

She swept and dusted and polished. From the garden they heard the sound of her voice upraised untunefully in snatches of song.

"You know, Richard," said Miss Maple when she had restored Nigger to his rompers and set him down on the grass again, "I met Sir Godfrey in the village this morning and he was talking about you. He says that as you've made such a success of this small piece of ground he doesn't see why you shouldn't employ more help and go in for nursery work in a big way."

Richard sat up, folding his arms round his knees.

"I don't like big ways," he said. "I scratch a living from the soil and that's my highest ambition. I belong to a long line of soil-scratchers, going back to Adam himself. We have a dignity and distinction that we should lose if we went in for big ways. It would besmirch a great tradition."

"The nonsense!" murmured Polly fondly, rolling over on the grass and letting Nigger climb on to her back and pull her hair.

Then Myrtle came round the side of the cottage and joined them, sitting on the grass, seizing Nigger and bouncing him up and down, till he roared with excitement. She wore her town clothes and high heels, her hair was newly waved, but she had left Miss Fortescue's Myrtle in Bellminster and spoke with the old country accent.

"Dad says could you come and give us a hand tonight, Richard?" she said. "There'll only be me and dad and we're expectin' a bit of a crowd after the cricket match."

"Right!" said Richard. "I'll be there."

Next to working his land he enjoyed serving in the bar of The Red Lion.

Tilly came out of the cottage with an armful of dusters and tea-cloths that she had washed and began to hang them on the line.

"How's Mother, Mrs. Noah?" said Richard.

"She's all right," said Tilly. "A bit cantankerous."

"Tell me if I can do anything for her," said Richard. "Whenever I offer to do anything she snaps my head off."

"That's your own fault," said Tilly. "Marrying a publican's daughter!"

Myrtle and Polly laughed—low sweet gurgles of laughter like the sound of woodland streams.

"When are you going to Althea's, Tilly?" said Miss Maple.

A cloud came over Tilly's square face.

"Next month, I suppose," she said sombrely.

Chapter Twenty-Two

The house that Roddy and Althea occupied was one of a row of small compact Regency houses in a backwater of Chelsea. Curved balustrades led up short flights of steps to gaily painted front doors, whose fanlights showed delicate tracery of wrought-iron work. Balustrades of wrought-iron enclosed tiny balconies outside the upstairs windows. The front door of Roddy's and Althea's house was painted red and there were boxes of geraniums at the windows.

Althea had at first been delighted with the little house, enjoying her new position of importance, the deference of the tradespeople and the flattering interest of the neighbours. Mrs. Culverton had engaged two excellent maids and there was an odd-job man who came in the mornings, wearing a bowler hat and a green baize apron, to "do" the fires and clean the boots.

And then, very very gradually, the whole thing began to pall. She became bored with the house, she became bored with housekeeping, she became bored with Roddy. When she married Roddy she had been in love with him, but over her love hung the glamour of the Lynneker connection. And both Roddy and the Lynneker connection had seemed to change with the change from Priors Green. Roddy became dull, stupid and ordinary. He was still handsome, of course, but she had grown so much accustomed to his good looks that she no longer noticed them. She only noticed the clumsiness of his thick-set figure and the slowness of his thought and speech. She had imagined that the Lynneker connection would give her the *entreé* to what she vaguely thought of as "Society", but, outside Priors Green, no one seemed to have heard of them. She had wanted to entertain, to be a well-known hostess, but there wasn't anyone to entertain except friends of Roddy's—stocky young rugger enthusiasts or pallid businessmen. The cousin of Lady Lynneker's who had given Roddy the job lived out at Teddington, where he and his wife devoted all their free time to cultivating roses and attending spiritualist séances. As social assets they were useless. The neighbours were not much better. They were either Bohemian and over-friendly or already members of a social group that discouraged intruders.

Althea made several short-lived friendships (she was "touchy" and her idea of friendship was one-sided) and gave a succession of parties where the guests were so ill-assorted that they evaded all her somewhat amateurish attempts to unite them. She had hoped that Edmund would help her, but Edmund was so busy carving out his political career that he had little time for anything else. So she abandoned, for the time, her social ambitions and turned her attention to Roddy. Roddy, it seemed, was getting too much out of life. He was the centre of a crowd of hearty, carefree, athletic friends with whom he was, as Althea considered, surprisingly popular . . . His week-ends were generally taken up by games or matches. He always seemed to be setting out with a crowd of hilarious friends, armed with golf, tennis or cricket equipment. And Althea decided to remedy this state of affairs. She became wistful and delicate and almost incredibly sensitive. She managed to make Roddy feel guilty whenever he left her alone.

"It's right, darling," she would say. "It's silly of me to mind so much, but I feel so lonely when you aren't here and I had so looked forward to having all this week-end with you. But don't take any notice of me, darling. Do go."

And always he stayed . . . His presence bored and irritated her, but at least she had the satisfaction of knowing that he wasn't enjoying himself without her. She found her "delicacy" particularly useful and would lie on the couch in a mysterious state of nervous prostration while Roddy hovered about her, waiting on her with clumsy tenderness—distressed, anxious, ineffectual. She was no longer in love with him, but it had become a matter of supreme importance that all his tune and thought should be devoted to her.

He sent so many last-minute telegrams, cancelling engagements, that his friends began to consider him a little unreliable. Althea's "delicacy" was useful in other ways too. It absolved her from all unwelcome duties—particularly that of providing Roddy with a child.

"Not yet, darling," she would plead. "Wait till I'm a little stronger."

She spent a good deal of money on clothes and beauty treatments. She was not quite so lovely as she had been. Her features were sharpening and the rosebud mouth, which had always been just a little too small, seemed to grow smaller. Sometimes, when she stressed her loneliness and nervousness in his absence, he would suggest her going home for the week-end.

"Oh, no, Roddy," she would say, seeming to shrink into herself. "I don't want to. You don't understand."

"Yes, I do, darling," he would say sympathetically.

Her "unhappy childhood" was one of her strongest delusions. She honestly believed that the strained relations between her father and mother had thrown a shadow over her childhood from which she had never recovered. Actually, the harm went deeper than that. She had thrived on the disharmony, deriving zest and excitement from it, learning from her earliest years to play off the unhappy man who was her father against the unhappy woman who was her mother.

"It reminds me of the old days," she would add pathetically. "The others weren't hurt by it as I was. I—*cared* so."

"I know, darling . . . but what about running down to the Hall? They'd love to have you and you needn't see much of your mother."

Again she seemed to shrink into herself.

"Oh, no, Roddy . . ."

She had stayed with him at the Hall soon after their marriage, and, although Piers had been away, the visit had been torture to her. Roddy had slipped back easily into his old position. Lady Lynneker claimed him as her son, the girls as their brother. The conversation was full of references she didn't understand, jokes that had no meaning for her. She felt isolated and of no importance and had made him cut short the visit by several days, refusing ever to go there again.

"Piers is abroad, you know," said Roddy.

A shadow came over his face as he spoke. He didn't know what had happened to cause the breach between Piers and Althea. Piers had said nothing of it, but from Althea's evasive references he had gathered that Piers had tried to make love to her. Roddy felt regret but no rancour. Althea was so lovely . . . Piers must have lost his head and, of course, Althea was so inexperienced and—and pure that it would affect her more than it would affect an ordinary girl. He missed his home and would have liked to visit it, but, as long as Althea felt as she did, it was best to stay away. Perhaps the girls had been a little casual with her (he knew that she thought they had) and perhaps his mother hadn't done all she could to make her welcome (Althea had been "hurt" several times during the visit). Anyway, there it was and couldn't be helped now. No use going there, however much he longed to, if it made Althea unhappy. Sometimes he felt depressed and bewildered and vaguely disillusioned, but he was still convinced that Althea was the most wonderful girl in the world and that he was wholly unworthy of her. Without that conviction life would not have been worth living.

Tilly arrived at the Chelsea house late one Friday afternoon. She wore, as always, a shapeless navy blue coat and a hat that completely engulfed head and forehead, and she carried her belongings in the old rush hold-all with which she had first come to Linden Rise. The housemaid opened the door to her.

"Oh, there you are," she said.

She was a tall fair girl with thin features and a high pompadour of coarse blonde hair. She had been with Althea for several years and had met Tilly on her previous visits. She felt for her a contempt that gave her a pleasant sense of superiority and a respect that secretly she tried to conquer.

"Come along in. Glad to see you, I'm sure. I cooked the lunch but not a word of thanks. Oh, no! Grumbled because the carrots was 'ard. Well, I can't help the nature of carrots, can I? I'm not the Almighty."

Tilly ignored this and plodded on towards the stairs.

"Same room, I suppose," she said.

Ivy gave a shrill giggle.

"Oh, yes," she said. "We've not 'ad another wing built on, as far as I know."

In a few minutes Tilly was back in the kitchen in print dress and apron busy with the preparations for the dinner. Ivy sat at the table, rubbing up the cutlery, a paper-backed novel propped up in front of her, to which she gave intermittent attention.

"'E was goin' out this afternoon," she said, "but she wouldn't let him. Oh, no! Said she'd be lonely. Said she'd got a headache. No use for him reelly but got to keep him tied to her apron-strings. Can't bear to think of anyone enjoyin' thesselves but 'er."

"Now that's enough," said Tilly.

She had no delusions about Althea—or indeed about any of the Culvertons—but no outsider should criticize them while she was there. Ivy shrugged and returned to her novelette. For a few moments there was silence, but she couldn't keep away from the fascinating subject for long.

"Got him to take her to tea at the Savoy in the end. 'E's gotter be 'angin' round her all day or she goes off into the sulks. She's lucky, you know, catchin' a mug like 'im. Wish I had the chance. Not but what 'e isn't nice. A real gentleman, 'e is. Always tries to smooth you down when she's been on at you. Good-looking, too, if you like that sort. I like 'em thinner an' taller an more 'atchet-faced meself. But how 'e puts up with her beats me."

"I've told you that's enough," said Tilly, setting the scales on the table with a clatter.

Again Ivy shrugged and returned to *Fetters of Love*, but only for a few minutes.

"What she *spends!* she broke out. "Dresses an' hats an coats an' what not! An' havin' her face an' hair done up. Pretty in a way, of course, but she's gettin' a bad-tempered look. You can't go on bein' bad-tempered without it comin' out on your face same as measles. An' those 'eadaches of hers! Comes when she wants 'em an' goes when she's got 'er way, if you asks me."

At that moment there was the sound of a key in the lock and voices in the hall. Ivy craned her neck with an expression of eager interest.

"'Ark at 'er! All merry an' bright! You'd think butter wouldn't melt in 'er mouth . . . Listen! . . . There's somebody else with them, That'll be another for dinner. 'Ark at 'er laughin'. Proper little ray of sunshine, you'd think she was, wouldn't you?"

They heard Roddy's voice. "Come along in here, Nigel. I'll get a drink. Then a peal of laughter from Althea, which Ivy mimicked beneath her breath. Soon Althea came into the kitchen.

She wore a dress of grey moiré silk, a white fox boa, and a small grey hat. The air of listlessness that she had cultivated recently had gone. She looked radiant. Her eyes were bright, her cheeks flushed. But her eyes hardened as they rested on Tilly. She had erased from her mind the memory of the anonymous letter, but there remained a cold hatred of the dumpy, wooden little figure, a longing to hurt and humiliate it.

"Oh, you've arrived, Tilly," she said.

Tilly rose from her chair at the table.

"Yes, madam," she said.

She was always punctiliously correct in her behaviour as Althea's employee.

"How's my mother?"

"Quite well, thank you, madam."

"We met an old school friend of the master's at the Savoy," said Althea, "and he's come home with us. So there'll be an extra one for dinner."

"Very good, madam," said Tilly.

Althea's eyes went up and down Tilly's dumpy figure.

"You still wear those comical old-fashioned print dresses," she said, with a look of amused contempt.

"Yes, madam," said Tilly in her expressionless voice.

Althea turned to Ivy, and both her look and manner conveyed a condescending kindness that was intended to emphasize the coldness of her manner to Tilly.

"You'll put the best dinner service, won't you, Ivy?" she said, "and open that box of sugar almonds that's in the dining-room cupboard and put them out on the silver bon-bon dishes." What a good thing I did the flowers freshly this morning! A pity I didn't get some smilax for the table . . . The grapes and pineapple will do for desert." She stopped and her excitement bubbled up in a gay little trill of laughter. "I mustn't forget anything in this last-minute hurry, must I? The Worcester dessert service, of course, and the Crown Derby coffee-cups."

She went back to the drawing-room, and they heard voices and laughter as she joined the other two.

". . . the village idiot," they heard her say, "but a wonderful cook," then someone closed the door.

Ivy looked at Tilly curiously.

"She don't like you, do she?" she said.

"Never mind who likes who," said Tilly, who had felt only a faint amusement at hearing herself described as the "village idiot." "You'll have your work cut out with that dinner table, so you'd better start on it."

Captain Carruthers, the school friend of Roddy's whom they had met accidentally at the Savoy, was a tall young man with an elegant figure, fair hair and a fair moustache. Ivy, waiting at table, grew more ecstatic after each course.

"'E's lovely," she said. " 'Is eyes! Looked at me straight, 'e did when I handed him the potatoes an' me bones turned to water. An' 'is smile! 'E's put me off 'atchet-faced men for the rest of me life. Aristocrat to 'is finger-tips,'e is."

"Never mind his finger-tips," said Tilly. "Get busy with your own."

"She's togged herself up no end for him, said Ivy a little wistfully. "She's put on that new white chiffong an' 'er white lace bridge coat."

"Never mind bridge coats," said Tilly. "Here's the savoury. Take it in quick."

Roddy came into the kitchen to see her later in the evening when the guest had gone and Ivy had retired to bed with *Fetters of Love* and a cup of hot milk.

"Nice to see you back here, Tilly," he said, standing by the kitchen table, his hands in his pockets. His good-looking face wore the slightly worried expression that was becoming habitual to it, but the honest, friendly smile he turned on her sent a glow of warmth into Tilly's heart.

"Thank you, sir," she said, laying down the coat she was knitting for Nigger and standing up.

"Sit down," said Roddy, sitting down himself opposite her at the kitchen table. "What's that you're making? It's a jolly colour."

"It's a coat for Nigger, sir—Mr. Richard's little boy."

"Oh, yes . . . How are things at Priors Green? Seen anything of my people lately?"

There was a wistfulness in his voice that turned him suddenly into a homesick little boy, and Tilly began to tell him all the news of home, becoming almost garrulous in her desire to comfort and reassure him. She told him of the garden party that Lady Lynneker had given in the summer, the prizes that Sir Godfrey had won at the Agricultural Show, the new conservatory that was being built on to the breakfast-room at the Hall.

"They're quite fit, I hope, are they?" he said.

"Oh, yes, sir," said Tilly, her needles flashing over the red wool. "Her ladyship had bronchitis last winter, you know, but she's quite well again now. Sir Godfrey still has his sciatica sometimes . . ."

"They're getting on, of course," said Roddy with a sigh.

"Yes, sir," said Tilly.

"How do you think Miss Althea's looking?"

"Looks the same as usual to me, sir," said Tilly shortly.

The worried look on Roddy's face deepened.

"She's not strong, you know," he said, "and things here must be pretty dull for her . . . You knew her as a child, didn't you?"

"Yes, sir."

His face had softened to tenderness. He took a deep pleasure in talking to someone who had known Althea as a child.

"I've got some photographs of her as a child. Her mother gave them to me when we married. There's one at the seaside . . ."

Tilly remembered it. Althea, holding a bucket and spade, her lovely face looking grave and wistful in the shade of a frilled sun-bonnet.

"And there's one on a rocking-horse," said Tilly, mentioning the only photograph of Althea in which she looked a plain and rather disagreeable child.

"Yes, I've got that, too," said Roddy, and it was clear from his expression that even the one on the rocking-horse was bathed in glamour for him.

"She didn't have a happy childhood, of course," he went on. "I know her mother's a well-meaning woman, but she never understood Althea. And the trouble between her father and mother went very deep with her. She was so much more intelligent and sensitive than the others. That's why I feel that we ought to do all we can to make things easy and—happy for her now." He smiled a little ruefully. "She ought to have married a better chap than me, of course, but we love each other and that's all that matters."

"Yes, sir," said Tilly.

"She seems much brighter tonight. It's done her good, going out and meeting people . . ."

Then the door opened and Althea came in . . . Her lips tightened as she saw them. Richard used to sit in the kitchen with Tilly like this and it had always exasperated her.

"Oh, *there* you are!" she said. "I couldn't think where you'd got to."

Roddy rose with his pleasant smile.

"I've been hearing the latest news of Priors Green," he said. He turned to Tilly. "Well, good night, Tilly. If there's anything you want, you'll let us know, won't you?"

They went out and closed the kitchen door.

"Really, Roddy," said Althea with a short laugh, there's no need to fraternize with the woman quite to that extent.

"Well, it's decent of her to come down and give us a hand," said Roddy mildly.

"Nonsense! She's only doing a job she's paid to do."

As the days went on Althea's mood of happiness continued to

uphold her. Gone was her wistfulness, her discontent, her irritability. Roddy basked in her kindness and began to lose his air of bewilderment and worry. Captain Carruthers was a constant visitor. On leave from his regiment in India, he would have found time hanging somewhat heavy on his hands had it not been for the pleasant little house in Chelsea and for Althea, gay and charming, blooming into the old radiance and good looks. Roddy was delighted with the friendship.

"You've made a conquest of old Nigel, he said proudly to Althea. "Bowled him clean off his feet."

Setting off for the office every morning directly after breakfast, sitting at his desk, working with conscientious deliberation throughout the day, Roddy was glad to think of Althea lunching with Nigel, going to matinees, to Ranelagh, for country drives with Nigel; glad to return to the new bright atmosphere of the little house, to Althea's laughter and Nigel's amusing anecdotes.

"It's good of you to give us so much of your time, old chap," he said gratefully. "It's done Althea no end of good."

There were few nights when Nigel did not dine with them. Sometimes Roddy joined them on their week-end expeditions, but Althea had suddenly become solicitous about his neglect of his games.

"No, darling, don't give up your golf. I know you like to get your golf at the week-ends. I shall be all right."

And she was all right. Her eyes lost their hardness, growing limpid and starry, her lips relaxed into soft seductive curves. She was deeply, passionately in love for the first time in her life.

"Playing with fire, that's what she is," said Ivy darkly. "She'd better be careful."

And suddenly Althea became careful. Though Roddy was still wholly unsuspicious, she grew evasive about her meetings with Nigel, and Nigel came less frequently to the Chelsea house. She would give Roddy elaborate accounts of her day's doings that contained no mention of Nigel.

"Oh, well," said Roddy, "I suppose he's got a lot of other people to look up. We're lucky to have seen as much of him as we have done."

Tilly was kept busy in the kitchen. It was difficult to please young Mrs. Lynneker these days. Her moods alternated between excitement and irritability. There were days when nothing was wrong and there were days when nothing was right. Her mood seemed to depend chiefly on the number of times that Captain Carruthers had rung her up on the telephone or called for her in the slightly furtive fashion that their acquaintanceship had begun to assume. With Nigel she was always gay and cheerful. She had early learnt that the pose of delicacy and hypersensitiveness, so successful with Roddy, bored and irritated him. But there were times when, parting from him in laughing good spirits at the door, she ran upstairs to throw herself on to her bed in a storm of tears.

"Breaking 'er 'eart," said Ivy. "Met Mr. Right too late. Well, 'e's lucky, that's all I can say. Better break 'er 'eart than 'is."

"And what do you know about broken hearts if I may be so bold as to ask?" jeered Tilly, who was rolling thin beef steaks round partridges and tying them with quick deft movements.

"Ah!" sighed Ivy. "I've 'ad me own broke more than once. Now you . . ." She looked at Tilly's wooden dumpy figure and round expressionless face. "You're lucky, you are. In a way, I mean. You aren't the sort as goes to men's heads. I don't suppose you've ever 'ad a proposal in your life.

"Don't you?" said Tilly, thinking of the milkman with faint detached interest. The milkman was now married and had three children. Tilly sometimes went to tea with them on her afternoon off.

"Cryin' 'er 'eart out," said Ivy, "along of bein crossed in 'opeless love."

"Crying for temper, more like," said Tilly, "along of her new dress not a-fittin' proper or meetin' someone else in the same hat. Now you get on with your work."

But gradually Tilly became aware that some definite project was afoot. A new suggestion of secrecy and purpose invaded Althea's manner. The telephone conversations were quick and business-like, without the old suggestion of easy dalliance, cut off abruptly with, "I won't say anything else now." . . . "Yes, the usual place." . . . "Don't ring me up tonight."

Her manner to Roddy became more tender and affectionate. She seemed anxious for his comfort and enjoyment, anxious that he should not sacrifice his convenience to hers.

"Roddy, darling, you are going up to Wheatley next weekend aren't you?" she said one evening as they were having dinner.

Tilly, who was waiting at table because it was Ivy's "evening out" threw her a curious glance then lowered her lids over her boot-button eyes. Roddy, too, looked at her in surprise.

At Wheatley lived some cousins of Roddy's who each summer got up a cricket match against another family that lived in the same district. Both families were keen cricketers, and Roddy used to go each year to join the Lynneker team. There had been a small scene when the invitation arrived this year. Althea had protested tearfully, telling him that she couldn't face the loneliness of a week-end without him, had accused him of caring for nothing but his own pleasure . . . and in the end he had written to refuse the invitation.

"No, darling," he said. "You remember, surely. I wrote to say I couldn't go. You said that you didn't want to be left alone."

"Oh, Roddy, did I?" she said in rueful penitence. "I didn't mean it. You shouldn't have taken me seriously. I quite thought you were going. Couldn't you fix it up even now?"

"Well, yes," he said slowly, "I could. I heard from them yesterday that they're still a man short. Of course they may have got one by now."

"But, even if they have, you'd like to go for the week-end and meet them all again, wouldn't you? I hate to think of your giving it up for my sake."

"That's awfully sweet of you, dear," he said, touched by the unusual note of kindness in her voice.

"You *will* go, then, won't you ?" she persisted. Her eyes were feverishly bright. Her hands trembled so much that she laid down her knife and fork. "You *will*, won't you? I'd hate you not to go because of me."

Roddy did not notice her agitation. He enjoyed the Wheatley week-end so much that this year he had tried not to think of it. Now the thought of it flooded his mind with joyful anticipation and a half-conscious sense of release. Freedom and easy companionship with the old friends . . . Not treading warily, watching Althea's moods . . . A blessed, carefree, convivial week-end with the boys.

"But what about you, darling?" he said. "Won't you be lonely?"

Her eyes slid away from his.

"I'll run down to Mother at Folkestone for the week-end," she said breathlessly. Then she caught Tilly's boot-button eyes fixed on her and gathered herself together, tense and rigid.

"You can go now, Tilly," she said. "We shan't need you any more."

After that the tempo of the little house seemed to quicken.

Roddy began his preparations for the week-end, for it turned out that they were still short of a man at Wheatley. Whistling light-heartedly he set to work cleaning cricket boots and pads, introducing a new zest into his early morning exercises. If Althea had had time to notice it, it would have irritated her, but she had no time to notice it. She was too busy with her own preparations—rather elaborate preparations, it would seem, for a weekend with her mother in quiet rooms in Folkestone, including new dresses, new underclothes and a new nightdress of the sheerest silk. Captain Carruthers seemed to have faded out of the picture altogether.

"'Spect he'll look in on us before he sails," said Roddy vaguely. "It'll be nice to see the old chap again."

He was overcome by compunction before he set out for Wheatley.

"Are you sure you'll be all right, darling? You've been so sweet about it all, but—if you like I can get out of it even now. I can send a wire."

"Oh, no, Roddy," said Althea with a catch of her breath. "Of course I'll be all right."

"Well, it'll be nice for your mother to have you."

"Yes."

"And the sea air'll do you good."

"Yes."

So, holding himself with a new alertness, a look of eager, boyish expectation on his pleasant young face, Roddy stepped into the cab that was to take him to the station.

And then Althea began her packing. She had given Ivy the day off.

"There'll be no one at home," she had said kindly, "so you can have the whole day. Tilly can see to things here."

Tilly took up a cup of coffee to Althea's bedroom half-way through the morning.

Althea was standing in front of the mirror. She wore a new dress of pale green cloth with a waistcoat of brown velvet. Her hands were raised to fasten an emerald pendant over the chemisette of Irish crochet, and the lace ruffles that edged the short sleeves fell back gracefully from her elbows, showing the smooth soft curves of her arms. Her box stood packed on the floor in a sea of tissue paper. A long green coat, matching the dress, and a brown hat with a sweeping green feather lay on the bed.

"Can I do anything to help you, madam?" said Tilly.

"No, thank you," said Althea. Her voice was unsteady, but she tried to speak coldly and distantly.

Tilly had reached the door when Althea spoke again in the same quick, unsteady voice.

"Oh, Tilly . . ."

Tilly turned and met her eyes. She's just remembered I'll find out she's not been to her mother's, she thought with a flash of insight.

"Yes, madam?"

I'm not going to Folkestone after all," said Althea. "I've heard from an old school friend who's been ill and is convalescing and wants me to go and stay with her, so I'm going there instead."

"Yes, madam. What station are you going from?"

"I'm going by motor-car," said Althea.

Tilly fixed her boot-button eyes on her in a hard, unblinking stare. The blue eyes met them, dilated and defiant.

"You're going with him, aren't you?" said Tilly. "With the Captain?"

The colour faded from Althea's face, leaving white patches.

"How *dare* you?" she said.

And suddenly a wave of ungovernable anger swept over Tilly. She'd put up with a lot from these Culvertons, but she wasn't going to put up with this. The boot-button eyes snapped. The hard red colour in her cheeks became harder and redder.

"You're not going," she said.

"What do you mean?" said Althea.

"You're not going," repeated Tilly. "I won't have it. I won't have it in the family. Not that, not in the family. I don't care for you and I don't care all that much for Mr. Roddy, but I'm not having that in the family."

"Leave the room at once!" said Althea, her voice strangled by rage.

There came the sound of a car drawing up at the front door and the sound of the front-door bell. Althea snatched up her suitcase.

"Let me pass," she said.

Tilly stood there, stolid and immovable, a hand on each doorpost.

"You're not going," she said again.

Althea sprang forward, but, before she knew what was happening, Tilly had taken the key from the door and was out in the passage turning it in the lock. Althea beat her hands on the door, crying shrilly and incoherently. Tilly plodded downstairs and opened the front door. Captain Carruthers stood there, smiling pleasantly and amusedly at the comical wooden figure in shapeless print dress and apron.

"Will you tell your mistress that I've called for her?" he said.

"She's not coming," said Tilly doggedly.

The smile dropped from his face.

"What do you mean?" he said.

"She's not coming," repeated Tilly.

He stared at her open-mouthed, in perplexity and dismay. Tilly had raised her voice as she repeated the words, and a handful of passers-by had stopped to watch the little scene.

"Stand on one side," he ordered in a high-pitched, peremptory voice. "Let me pass."

"She's not coming," said Tilly, placing a hand on each doorpost as she had done upstairs. "I'm not having it."

At that moment the upstairs window was thrown open and Althea appeared on the little balcony. She was distraught and wild-eyed, her hair dishevelled, her dress in disorder. She ignored the gathering crowd and called down to Captain Carruthers in a sobbing hysterical voice.

"She's locked me in," she said. "She's locked me in my room. She's gone mad. She—"

And then suddenly Tilly came to herself. She realized with horror that she had committed the unforgivable sin. She'd forgotten her place. After all, it was nothing to her what these Culvertons did.

"Come in, sir," she said respectfully, standing aside.

Captain Carruthers plunged upstairs. The key was still in the lock of Althea's door. He turned it and entered.

"Come away from that window," he ordered harshly. "Are you out of your mind?"

Althea crossed the room to him; arms outstretched.

"Oh, Nigel, it was like a bad dream. She's a wicked woman . . . Let's go away now quickly."

He recoiled from her. His face was yellow with fear.

"The whole street heard," he said. "There's a crowd out there still. The people next door . . . they were watching through the window. They heard everything, saw everything."

"What does it matter?"

"What does it matter!" he echoed. He had been pleased at the thought of enlivening his leave by the seduction of Roddy's pretty wife, but a public scandal was a very different thing. "It means my career, I tell you. Roddy'll get to hear of this and there'll be the deuce to pay if I don't clear out at once."

"No, no," she pleaded. "Don't, Nigel . . . Don't . . . Roddy won't hear of it. If he does, what does it matter? I can manage him. Don't be so cruel. I love you so . . ."

He disengaged her clinging hands with a rough movement. His good looks had vanished. His eyes seemed to have grown closer together and his lips were drawn back in a sort of snarl.

"It's no use, Althea. I can't afford a scene in public like that. I've got my future to think of. You've ruined everything."

"I haven't, Nigel. It wasn't my fault."

I don't care whose fault it was. We were crazy to think of it, anyway."

"Don't you love me at all?" she sobbed.

"Of course I do." With an effort he introduced a note of affection into his voice. "Look, darling. We've got to cut out this week-end. I'll go now. I'll get into touch with you later."

"You promise? Oh, Nigel, I can't bear it if you don't."

He was edging towards the door.

"Yes, yes, of course . . . Good-bye."

She heard his footsteps running down the stairs and the starting up of his car. She knew that she would never see him or hear from him again.

Half an hour later she entered the kitchen, where Tilly sat at the table skinning a bowl of almonds . . . Althea's rage and grief had spent themselves. Her face was grey and pinched, her eyes hard blue stones.

"Kindly pack your things and go at once," she said to Tilly. "If you aren't out of the house within half an hour, I shall send for the police."

"Yes, madam," said Tilly, deftly skinning the last almond and putting it into the bowl.

A few minutes later she was plodding down towards the bus stop, carrying the rush hold-all by its strap.

Chapter Twenty-Three

At Linden Rise the years seemed to slip by with almost terrifying speed.

"It *can't* be three years since we had those loose covers made," Mrs. Culverton would say.

"More like three weeks," Tilly would agree.

But Mrs. Culverton would consult her bill-file and it was three years. She felt vaguely affronted by the flight of time, resenting it as a sort of outrage, all the more exasperating because there was no one she could take to task for it. And, though the years passed quickly, the days themselves were monotonous broken chiefly by passages-at-arms with Tilly. Tilly refused to use the labour-saving appliances that Mrs. Culverton bought tor her, continuing to plod round with dust-pan and brush, scattering tea-leaves on the carpets, insisting on heating flat-irons in the kitchen fire, though a brand new gas iron stood resplendent on the dresser shelf. She regarded with deep distrust the hand-basin with running water that Mrs. Culverton had had installed in her bedroom and continued to carry up a can of hot water every morning.

"That there thing won't work one of these days, she would say, "and then you'll be glad of it."

Her greatest pride was the front doorstep, which she kept scoured to a dazzling whiteness. On the days when Mrs. Culverton felt in good fighting trim, she would step firmly on its surface, ignoring Tilly, who hovered grimly in the background with her jar of whiting, waiting to remove the footmarks. On the days when she felt unequal to Tilly she would go round to the back.

Tilly had intermittent toothache, during the bouts of which she would wear an expression of exaggerated agony, uttering strange harsh cries at intervals. She refused to go to a dentist. Mrs. Culverton would make appointments for her and even see her out of the cottage in time to keep them, but Tilly never turned up at the dentist's.

It was a source of deep and abiding satisfaction to Mrs. Culverton that Tilly had been summarily dismissed by Althea for impertinence.

"You see," she would say triumphantly, "no one but me would put up with you."

She was curious about the details of the dismissal.

"What did you say to her, Tilly?" she would ask.

Tilly's face would take on its most wooden look.

"I don't remember, madam," she would reply.

Mrs. Culverton paid short yearly visits to both Althea and Edmund. Of Edmund himself she stood greatly in awe. His perseverance and industry were reaping their reward and he was regarded by his superiors as a sound reliable man, even as a coming man". It was generally recognized that some small plum of office would fall to his lot when his party was returned to power. The art of public speaking, in which he had perfected himself, invaded his private conversation, so that his most casual utterances had something oracular about them. For several weeks after Mrs. Culverton returned from her visit, her remarks were prefaced by "Edmund says . . ." "Edmund thinks . . ."

Althea, too, was taking herself more seriously. She had emerged from an abyss of misery after Nigel's desertion with a cold hard determination to wrest all she could from life. Her shattered self-respect must be restored. Nigel had not wanted her, but others should want her . . . At a party given in London by Roddy's Wheatley cousins, she had come into contact with a small section of what was known as the Smart Set and by sheer hard work—learning its tricks, talking its jargon, entertaining lavishly—had firmly established herself in it. She was aware that this world existed on the fringe of another more important world and into this, too, she had determined to force an entry.

The chameleon-like streak in her nature served her well. She had learnt to gauge at once what character to assume to make the best impression. She was even learning to be intellectual— reading up the reviews, so that she could discourse knowledgeably on pictures she hadn't seen, books she hadn't read and music she hadn't heard.

Roddy, except on the rare occasions when she needed him, retreated more and more into the background of her life. He spent his time with boon companions and was beginning to wear a somewhat hang-dog air. The zest seemed to have gone even from his games, and, cheated of his hopes of home and children, he was indulging in a series of shoddy love affairs.

Althea now encouraged Mrs. Culverton's yearly visit. Background was important in the world she meant to conquer, and Mrs. Culverton, as a necessary part of her background, must take her place in the picture. Mrs. Culverton was gratified by the new position of importance accorded to her.

"Althea and I have always meant a lot to each other," she said. "I must be thankful that two of my children have turned out well."

"Which two?" said Tilly.

"Edmund and Althea," said Mrs. Culverton shortly, aware that Tilly knew quite well which two.

"What about Richard?" said Tilly.

"Oh, Richard!" said Mrs. Culverton with a shrug.

Richard and Polly were still living at Briar Cottage, and there was another little boy now called Martin, as sturdy and good-tempered as Nigger. Mrs. Culverton had offered to give both the boys a public school education, but Richard had refused the offer.

"Thank you very much," he had said with a twinkle in his eye, "but we don't want them brought up above their station. At present they think we're rather fine, but if they went to public schools they'd look down on us."

"But, Richard, what are they going to *do?*"

"Oh, there's always heaps to do," said Richard vaguely.

Miss Maple had taught Nigger to read and write before he went to the village school and was now busy on Martin. She took her office very seriously and had bought several books on child psychology, to the rules of which both Nigger and Martin refused to conform.

"And Miss Vere's not done so bad," said Tilly. "All them books and things."

"She's no right to go trapesing over the world like this. She ought to be at home looking after me."

In her frequent moods of self-pity Mrs. Culverton's thoughts were turning more and more to Vere. The mental vision that she had formed of herself, waited on and entertained by a devoted daughter—the vision that Althea had refused to transform into reality—was now centred in Vere. She would sit for hours brooding on her loneliness, recounting to herself example after example of unmarried daughters she had known who had devoted themselves to ageing mothers.

"It's her plain duty," she said to Tilly. "It's time she stopped all this nonsense. If she wants to paint she can paint at home. I'm old and ill and lonely and I need her."

"You're not ill," said Tilly.

"My rheumatism is more painful than you've any idea of," said Mrs. Culverton coldly, "and the doctor says my heart isn't strong. I don't suppose I shall live much longer."

"You'll last your time out like the rest of us," said Tilly.

"I need Vere, and her place is here at home with me. We could be very happy together, Vere and I." Her mind reached back uncertainly into the mists of the past. "She was my baby, you know. She always had a very special place in my heart."

Vere had spent a week at the cottage after her return from a journey through Arabia and had waited on Mrs. Culverton assiduously, listening with an air of gentle interest to the recital of her grievances and the latest local gossip. Since that week Mrs. Culverton had got the idea firmly fixed in her head that it was Vere's duty to come home and live with her. Vere, on her part, seemed to feel a certain responsibility.

"Does she really have a lot of pain, Tilly?" she had asked anxiously, as Tilly helped her pack her suitcase on the last morning of her visit.

"Not as much as she makes out," said Tilly.

"But she must be lonely. Richard's near her, but she's never forgiven him for marrying Polly, has she?"

"No, miss."

"And, of course, Polly's too busy with the children to have much time to spare . . . Tilly, you'll let me know at once if she really needs me, won't you? I hate to think of her ill and lonely without any of us here."

"Yes, I'll let you know, miss," said Tilly. "Where are you goin' a-travellin' next, miss?"

Vere stood, folding her nightdress, gazing absently in front of her.

"I don't know. I've been to all the places I really wanted to go to. Everything's a little unsettled. I shall stay at the flat for the rest of the year, anyway."

Tilly looked at her and suddenly, for no particular reason, remembered the day they had all set out for Bellminster and left her behind.

"If there's anything I can do for you, Miss Vere," she said impulsively, "you'll let me know, won't you?"

Vere threw her a quick glance, grateful and surprised.

"Thank you, Tilly." She was silent for a few moments then continued: "Actually there is something. I'm giving a party next week. There are heaps of people I ought to ask, so I've decided to ask them and get it over, but—right at the bottom—I'm scared of people. You wouldn't think so, would you?"

"Yes," said Tilly. "Give me that dressing-gown and I'll put it in this corner."

Vere smiled and handed her the dressing-gown.

"It's clever of you to know that," she said. "Not many people do . . .Well, if you'd come and give me a hand, Tilly, it would be a tremendous help. Just to have you there, I mean. I don't want you to do anything. Will you come?"

"Yes," said Tilly. "Now your bedroom slippers. They'll just tuck in here."

"I shall have to ask mother if she can spare you, of course."

251

"She'll have to spare me," said Tilly, ramming the bedroom slippers home with a determined gesture.

Mrs. Culverton was partly gratified, partly aggrieved by the request.

"You can't get on without us, after all, can you, dear?" she said. "Yes, I'll let you have Tilly, but I warn you she's quite impossible. Althea had to send her home the last time she went there. She found she simply couldn't put up with her."

"I'll put up with her," said Vere.

Tilly arrived, at Vere's flat on the afternoon of the cocktail party. The flat was large, airy and impeccably furnished, but there was something curiously impersonal about it. It was as if even here, even in her own stronghold, Vere shrank from revealing herself, as if she could not trust even these kindly household gods not to betray her. There were so few personal touches that the rooms might have come straight from an Ideal Homes Exhibition.

Together Vere and Tilly rearranged furniture and set out ash-trays and flowers.

"The caterers' men are bringing the drinks and food," said Vere, "and they'll do all the handing round."

"Food!" said Tilly scornfully. "I reckon there's nothin' I couldn't have made better if you'd told me what you wanted."

"I know, Tilly," said Vere, "and those cheese straws you've brought are lovely. People will like them much better than the stuff the caterers bring."

"Maybe," said Tilly, mollified.

"Tilly . . ." said Vere, pausing in her work of putting bronze chrysanthemums into a tall jar.

"Yes, miss?" said Tilly, who had seized a duster and was busily setting to work with it. "I don't s'pose they ever think of goin' behind this bookcase. Afraid they might come across a bit of dust if they did."

Vere smiled.

"I've been feeling worried ever since I went down to Linden Rise."

"Why, miss?"

"Mother's growing old. She's quite right. One of us ought to be with her."

"There's me," said Tilly.

"I know, Tilly dear, but I mean one of her own flesh and blood. She's not had an easy life, you know."

Tilly compressed her lips and made no comment.

"And I feel—I can't quite put it into words." Vere set the jar of chrysanthemums on a low table and sat down on an armchair, her face cupped in her hands. "I've been—running away from things all my life. All these years I've been—stalling, wasting my time."

"But them books you've wrote, Miss Vere, and them pictures you've painted!"

Vere shook her head.

"They were—drugs. I did them because I was afraid of real life. I've been living in a dream and—Tilly, I must stop. It's people that matter. It's wicked to cut yourself off from them, make yourself deaf and blind to them. I think I shall regret it all my life if I don't go to Mother now."

"Has she been at you again?" said Tilly.

"I had a letter from her the other day. You can read it if you like. It's there on the bureau."

Tilly took up the letter and read it.

. . . I do so wish you'd come, darling. With my weak heart it probably won't be for long. I'm a lonely, unhappy old woman and I need you. Couldn't you give up just a year or two of your life to make me happy? You could go on with your painting here, darling. After all, you were my baby, weren't you? I should so love to have you here with me, and we could look after each other . . .

Tilly replaced the letter on the bureau. Cunning old devil, she said to herself. Aloud she said:

"Don't you remember how things were when you were a child, Miss Vere?"

Vere considered.

"I remember that I was very—unlovable. I missed something in those days through my own fault, and I feel that if life's willing to give me a second chance I ought to take it. I feel somehow as if I'd come to the end of a chapter. I'm losing interest in the things I've been doing all these years. I don't quite know what's happening to me, but I know that I mustn't keep on running away. Do you understand?"

"No," said Tilly bluntly.

"I don't know that I do myself," said Vere, frowning thoughtfully. "It's all in such a muddle." She was silent, trying to disentangle the threads that were drawing her back to her mother. Was she still running away or was she at last facing life squarely? Was she influenced by an obscure wish to re-live her childhood, to find the lost, lonely child she had been and bring her back to a balanced, sane maturity? Or was it something deeper than that? "Perhaps I just want to go back into the past."

"That's dangerous, you know," said Tilly. "You might get stuck there so's you can't get out of it again. Don't make up your mind too quick."

"No, I won't," said Vere. "I'll sleep on it . . . And now let's put out the cigarettes."

The guests began to arrive soon after six. They were mostly literary acquaintances of Vere's, with a few artists, some neighbours from the flats, and people she had met at other parties. Edmund was speaking at a political meeting, but he had said that he would drop in later if he could. Althea had promised to look in on her way to a "first night."

Vere looked beautiful and stately in a dress of rust-coloured velvet with long barbaric earrings. She moved among the guests with the air of poise and sophistication that was her defence against the world, speaking in a voice that sounded confident, assured and just a little bored. But all the time it was as if she were fighting desperately and without success to get nearer them. The sense of isolation that had haunted her from childhood seemed to gather strength till it reached nightmare proportions. To herself she was saying: I'll go to Mother. That will be real. Or will it? Am I running away because I'm frightened, frightened of being hurt by something so badly that I'll never get back again to what I was before it happened?

Tilly, dressed in a black dress and white apron, was issuing curt orders to the caterers' men, who had intended to assume control but found, to their surprise, that they were merely doing what Tilly told them to do. Tilly had noticed the tall man with the deep-set grey eyes and brown imperial beard as soon as he entered the room. He stood against the wall, apart from the others, watching Vere. Wherever she moved his eyes followed her with a curious look of understanding and tenderness, as if they were stripping away the shell of hard sophistication and discovering the simplicity and integrity beneath, as if he saw the bewildered child who was imprisoned there. One quick glance had told Tilly all she needed to know. He's in love with her, she thought, as she filled a bowl with the cheese straws she had made the night before in the kitchen of Linden Rise. He's good, she thought, as she pushed a caterer's man out of her way to retrieve a cigarette end from the carpet. He'd better make haste before her mother gets her, she thought, as she removed a vase of roses that had several times been nearly overturned.

It was then that the telephone bell rang in the hall and she went to answer it.

Mrs. Culverton had evidently spent the afternoon in an orgy of self-pity.

"I want to speak to Vere," she said tearfully.

"Miss Vere's engaged, madam," said Tilly.

"You'd no right to go and leave me like this, Tilly," said the flat, complaining voice. "I'm not feeling at all well. I oughtn't to be left."

"I thought Miss Maple was coming to spend the night," said Tilly.

"She's not come yet and that's nothing to do with it," said Mrs. Culverton peevishly. "I oughtn't to be left in any case, with my heart and my rheumatism. I can't go on like this. I need companionship . . . I want to speak to Vere at once."

"I've told you Miss Vere's engaged, madam."

"Will you kindly tell Miss Vere that I wish to speak to her?" said Mrs. Culverton haughtily.

"Very good, madam," said Tilly.

She went into the kitchen, washed-up a few used glasses then returned to the telephone.

"Miss Vere says she'll ring you up later, madam," she said.

"Oh . . . well, tell her that if she hasn't rung by nine, I'll ring again."

"Very good, madam," said Tilly, replacing the receiver.

She returned to the drawing-room. More guests had arrived and were standing in a circle round Vere. The tall man with the beard was still watching her with that faint smile on his lips. Tilly threaded her way through the crowd and began to move a small table that stood just near him.

"Can I help you?" he said.

"Thank you, sir. It's only in the way here. I thought I'd take it to the dining-room."

He looked at her curiously.

"You're Tilly, aren't you?"

"Yes, sir."

"She told me about you."

"Yes, sir it's only cluttering up the room. There's enough tables without it. An' it's one of them old ones. It won't do it no good to have a lot of that drink spilt on it."

"Let me carry it for you."

"Thank you, sir . . . Here's the dining-room."

"Yes, I know the way."

They carried the table into the dining-room, and there Tilly closed the door and turned to him.

"Are you going to ask Miss Vere to marry you, sir?" she said. He shot her a startled glance.

"I hope to eventually," he said quietly.

The boot-button eyes bored into his.

"If you're goin' to ask her, you'd best ask her quick."

"What do you mean?"

"You'd best ask her before nine o'clock tonight."

"But"—he gave a puzzled smile—"I've only met her half a dozen times. She can't possibly care for me."

"I reckon she does," said Tilly. "Something's upset her and I reckon it's that. She's got in a muddle about running away. It's you she's running away from, but she don't know it."

"Why should she run away from me?"

"Afraid of getting fond of you, like as not," said Tilly wisely. "Doesn't know you've took to her an' is scared of takin' to you, case you haven't."

He was half-smiling, half-frowning.

"I can't possibly ask her to marry me with all these people here."

"They'll have gone by nine."

"I—Listen, Tilly. I'm an archaeologist and my job's at Haifa. How can I ask her to go out there?"

"Is it a long way?"

"Yes."

"The farther the better," said Tilly succinctly.

"And what's all this about nine o'clock?"

The sound of voices and laughter from the next room rose and fell like waves. Tilly put her hands on her hips and set her lips grimly.

"If you've not got her by nine her mother'll get her, and once her mother's got her you'll never get her back. You don't know her mother. I've known her since I was a child. She wears people down. She wore her husband down but he got away. She tried to wear Miss Althea down but Miss Althea's not the sort to be wore down and she got away. Miss Vere's not the sort to get away an' she'll wear Miss Vere down till there's nothing left of her. It'll be too late after nine o'clock. She'll have got her by then."

His eyes searched hers. There was something oddly impressive and compelling about the comical little figure.

"All right," he said shortly. "I'll take your word for it."

They returned to the drawing-room. The noise was still oppressive, but the party was beginning to thin. Edmund rang up, punctiliously courteous, to say that he and Lindsay would not be

257

able to come, after all. Althea made a meteor-like appearance, lovely in furs and diamonds, Roddy lurking sheepishly behind her, carrying her wraps. "Darling, it's lovely to see you," said Althea. A hard bright patina seemed to cover her whole personality. Her voice was high-pitched and penetrating and just a little shrill. "I can't *tell* you how I've been looking forward to it. How is everything? What outlandish place are you going to next? We must meet sometime and have a real talk. Seen mother lately? How is she? I meant to run down, but I haven't had a minute . . . No, I won't have another . . . So sorry I can't stay . . . We're going to the new play at St. James's . . . Lady Godstone has got a box and we're dining with them first . . . We really must fly. Come on, Roddy."

She passed Tilly in the passage, gave her a long, unsmiling stare, then swept out to the waiting car, followed by Roddy.

Soon all the guests had gone except the tall man with the beard. The caterers' men had been summarily dismissed by Tilly, who set to work in the kitchen—tidying, washing-up, putting away.

In the drawing-room Vere leant back on the settee, looking up with a faint question in her eyes at the man who stood on the hearthrug.

"Yes," he said, "I ought to have gone with the others, but I haven't done."

"Stay and have dinner," said Vere.

He sat down by her.

"I've only seen you half a dozen times, Vere," he said slowly, "but I think I've been in love with you from the moment I first saw you. Could you ever care for me enough to marry me? . . . Don't answer at once. Think it over."

She was silent while a rush of confused emotions surged through her. It was as if a curtain that she had thought concealed something dark and sinister had been withdrawn, letting in a flood of sunlight in which all her fear and hesitancy vanished like dew.

She turned to him.

"I don't need to think it over," she said.

Then the clock struck nine, and the telephone bell rang. She went into the hall to answer it.

"It's Mother, darling," wailed Mrs. Culverton. "I hope you aren't too busy to speak to me now."

Vere gave a soft tremulous laugh.

"I am rather busy," she said. "I'm just getting engaged."

"Why did no one tell me?" said Mrs. Culverton in a tone of peevish complaint.

"How could anyone?" laughed Vere. "It's only just happened. I'll run down at the week-end and tell you about it."

"Do I know him?"

"No."

Mrs. Culverton sighed heavily into the telephone.

"Congratulations, dear. Well, I mustn't keep you—"

"But—one minute, Mother. Did you ring up about anything special?"

"It doesn't matter now," said Mrs. Culverton.

Chapter Twenty-Four

The passage of time was marked for Tilly by domestic rather than by national events—by the new kitchen boiler (replacing the open range), the new roof to the coal-shed, the installation of electricity throughout the cottage (against which she fought strenuously).

Sir Godfrey died the year in which the mahogany-encased bath was replaced by one of white porcelain . . . Piers did not return to Priors Green. He continued to live, with his Italian wife, in a villa on the slopes of Fiesole, overlooking the Mugone valley, and Lady Lynneker, who now found the Hall too large and inconvenient, took a small house in a Wiltshire village near her childhood's home.

There was another new Vicar, too, with whose autocratic wife Miss Maple carried on a quiet but unremitting warfare. Miss Maple, having visited Paris, Brussels and Vienna, now considered that she had seen the world and contented herself with an occasional holiday at a Bournemouth boarding house. She took less care with her clothes and sometimes appeared amazingly like the Miss Maple who had come to Linden Rise as holiday governess more than thirty years ago. But the spirit of independence still blazed brightly in the insignificant-looking little figure, and, once Miss Maple had taken up a stand on any subject, few people cared to join issue with her. She still paid a daily visit to Richard's cottage . . . The boys were growing up—a sturdy couple with nothing of Richard in them but an equable temperament and a certain philosophical outlook on life. Neither was a scholar. They loved to work in Richard's plot or go over to Mallingford to help Polly's uncle on Hurst Farm. Their thick-set build and slow rather clumsy movements proclaimed the peasant stock that Polly had bequeathed to them.

It outraged Mrs. Culverton to see them pass the window in corduroy trousers and mud-stained hob-nailed boots. There was something in their pleasant healthy young faces that made her at times long to yield, but she conquered the weakness. Richard's marriage was one of her grievances, and she could not bear to surrender even the smallest of her grievances. She would sit by the fire every evening brooding over them. They were a sort of cloak covering her nakedness. She would have felt lost and forlorn without them. Richard . . . Vere (obscurely it increased her resentment to know that Vere was happy in her marriage) . . . Tilly . . . even Edmund and Althea. Edmund and Althea were fast becoming public figures—Edmund in the world of politics, Althea in the world of fashion—but they neglected her. They seldom wrote. They seldom came to see her, and she was too old and ill, she felt, to take the journey to see them.

Occasionally she invited Richard's boys to tea. They were well-mannered and at their ease, but their "farmyard talk" and their familiarity with Tilly always offended her.

"Tilly's only a maid," she would say. "There's no need to go into the kitchen and talk to her."

"She's my godmother," Dominic would reply, with a twinkle that reminded her uncomfortably of Richard.

Tilly had never again gone to Althea's, but Mrs. Culverton now "lent" her each year to Edmund and Lindsay for the weeks when their nurse was on holiday. Edmund had two children—a fairy-like little girl called Jessica, who reminded everyone of Althea, and a little boy called Jonathan, with Lindsay's dark eyes and air of shy remoteness. Tilly didn't enjoy the visit and never thought of it without a sinking of her heart. It occurred to her sometimes to refuse to go. She was tired of these Culvertons. They wore her out. I'm not a slave, she said to herself. They can't *make* me go . . . But, even as she said it, she was taking the rush hold-all from under her bed and getting her things ready to put into it. As she laid them neatly in place, she let her mind go back to the visit she had paid last year. It was then that Jonathan was just emerging from the nursery and beginning to take his place in the normal life of the house. He was slight and nervous and easily moved to tears—like Lindsay, knowing no mean between extremes—and Edmund had decided that his son must be "manly". "If we're going to make a man of him we must start now," he said. So he set about rigorously inculcating manliness into the child. One of the worst troubles was the "night fears" from which Jonathan had always suffered. He would awake sometimes in a state of uncontrollable terror and till last year had slept in the nurse's room. But last year Edmund had decreed that he must have a room of his own and had forbidden both Lindsay and the nurse to go into it during the night.

The edict, of course, had little effect. At the sound of the strangled cry of terror or stifled childish sobs, Lindsay or the nurse would be at hand, slipping noiselessly into the room to comfort him. Edmund had a vague idea that he was being disobeyed, but he was a heavy sleeper and could never catch the culprits in the act. Between him and Lindsay, however, a new secret struggle, was beginning. So diffident and self-distrustful was she, so lost and at sea in the world of practical, assured people among whom Edmund moved that she accepted his judgments blindly. Only in the matter of Jonathan was she beginning to defy him with a courage that was as fine-drawn as it was inflexible.

Mrs. Culverton was sitting by the fire when Tilly came into the sitting-room, wearing her hat and coat and carrying the hold-all.

"I'm off to Mr. Edmund's now, madam," she said. "Shall I give them any message from you?"

"Tell them my rheumatism's worse and my heart isn't any better," said Mrs. Culverton, adding as an afterthought, "and give them my love."

"Very good, madam," said Tilly, turning at the door to add: "And keep your eye on the baker. He charged a halfpenny too much last week."

Edmund came into the hall to greet her when she arrived at the house in Westminster. He had acquired an air of dignity and authority with the years. His good looks were marred only by two deep lines that ran from the corners of his nose to the ends of his lips, seeming to purse up his mouth.

"Well, Tilly," he said, "how are you? Did you have a good journey?"

"Yes, thank you, sir," said Tilly.

Edmund always went out of his way to be pleasant to Tilly during the time she spent in his house. He enjoyed parading his success before her and he liked to watch himself being kindly and patronizing to the little oddity who was his mother's maid.

"How's my mother?" he said.

"Fairly well, on the whole, sir," said Tilly. "She sent her love."

"Thank you," said Edmund. "Oh, here's Mrs. Culverton."

Lindsay came floating downstairs. She was still lovely, but she wore a vague, lost, half-frightened look.

"Oh, Tilly, darling," she said. "How nice to see you again!"

She bent down and kissed the smooth round cheek. Edmund watched, pursing his mouth. Lindsay was apt to be friendly with people with whom she ought to be distant, and distant with people with whom she ought to be friendly. He had tried in vain to cure her of the fault.

"Will you take Tilly upstairs, my dear, or shall I?" he said dryly.

Lindsay threw him a nervous glance.

"Come along, Tilly," she said. "Come and see the children first. They're in the schoolroom. It's the old nursery, but we call it the schoolroom now."

They went upstairs together, followed by Edmund.

"Here they are," said Lindsay, throwing open a door on the first floor.

It was a pleasant room, with a round table in the middle, toy cupboards and book-cases against the wall and a couple of easy-chairs by the fireplace. Jessica was sitting at the table, her paints and painting books spread around her; Jonathan sat in a corner of the room with his toys. Jessica threw down her paint-brush and ran across the room to Edmund, her arms outstretched.

"Daddy!" she cried eagerly.

He swung her up and set her down again. She clung to his arm.

"Here's Tilly come to look after you," he said, "though you're both getting too big to need anyone to look after you."

"How do you do, Tilly," said Jessica in the voice she kept for servants. Edmund smiled at her proudly. "Come and look at my painting, Daddy," she went on, drawing him to the table.

He sat down in her chair and, taking the paint-brush, continued the painting she had begun. She stood behind him, looking over his shoulder.

"You've gone over the line," she said with a peal of laughter, "You silly old Daddy! You've gone over the line."

"Oh, dear!" said Edmund in mock dismay, glancing at Tilly to make sure that she was appreciating the little scene. "I'm going to get into trouble."

Then he looked from Lindsay, who was sitting in the armchair, to Jonathan, who still sat crouched in his corner, watching warily.

"Have you no manners, my boy?" he said sharply. "Aren't you going to speak to Tilly?"

Jonathan gave Tilly a shy half-smile.

"Hello, Tilly," he said. "I'm glad you've come."

Though his eyes were Lindsay's, there was something of Richard in the long sensitive mouth, and Tilly's heart yearned over him.

"And what are you playing with?" said Edmund, going over to Jonathan's corner and speaking with a forced geniality that did not hide the underlying irritation.

"My Noah's Ark," said Jonathan.

He had the animals arranged in straight lines four abreast. They were not ordinary animals. They were magic animals. They were on their way to a small, footstool that was an enchanted castle inhabited by a dragon who was ravaging the countryside. They were going to attack it and free the victims.

"Noah's Ark!" said Edmund with a scornful laugh. "You surely don't still play with baby toys of that sort, do you?"

"Yes, he does," said Jessica. "He plays with his Noah's Ark every day."

Jonathan was putting his animals back into the cupboard to protect them from his father's scorn. His dark, silky lashes swept his pale cheeks. His mouth was tremulous. Edmund could never look at the girlish face without a feeling of exasperation.

"Why don't you play with the Meccano set I gave you at Christmas?"

"He can't," said Jessica with a superior laugh. "He's got stupid fingers."

"I asked you a question, Jonathan."

"I don't like it," said Jonathan simply.

"Are you so clumsy that you can't make the things?"

"I can make them," said Jonathan, "but I don't like them when they're made."

"You prefer a baby Noah's Ark?"

"Yes."

Lindsay was watching anxiously, Jessica with zestful interest, Tilly with her most wooden expression. Edmund shrugged.

"We shall have to do something to stop you being a baby," he said.

He returned to the table, bent down to look at the painting with a smile, then straightened himself.

"Well," he said, "I can't waste any more time. I have a lot of work to get through before dinner." He turned to Lindsay. "You called at the printer's, as I asked you, didn't you, about those leaflets?"

A blank look came into Lindsay's face, followed by a sudden flash of guilt.

"I'm so sorry, Edmund," she said nervously. "I can't think . . . I forgot . . . I did go that way, but it went clean out of my head. I suppose my mind was on something else."

"And because your mind was on something else," said Edmund, a note of schooled patience in his voice, "my entire day's work is thrown out of gear."

"I'm sorry," said Lindsay again.

"I thought it quite a small thing to ask of anyone who has the whole day at her disposal."

"I remembered to get those paper clips when you asked me, didn't I, Daddy?" said Jessica proudly.

Jonathan had got up and gone over to his mother, standing by her as if to protect her. They seemed to be ranged in two camps— Edmund and Jessica on one side of the room, Lindsay and Jonathan on the other. The muscles of Jonathan's small face were taut, his eyes fixed on his father with a curious intensity. Edmund tried silently to outstare the boy and failed.

"Dont lean against your mother like that, Jonathan," he said. "You aren't a baby, though you behave like one."

Lindsay dropped the arm that she had slipped round Jonathan, and Jonathan moved slowly and reluctantly aside.

"I'll go round to the printer's first thing tomorrow," said Lindsay with a note of propitiation in her voice.

"Don't trouble, my dear," said Edmund. "After all, we've no guarantee that your mind won't be on something else tomorrow morning as well, have we? Your mind appears to be as much in need of attention as the leaflets."

He spoke pleasantly, but the blood flamed into Lindsay's face. When annoyed with her, he would often make covert references to her mental breakdown, and the shafts never failed to strike home. He turned to the door.

"Well, I must get back to work, so I'll leave you now. I expect Jonathan's anxious to return to his Noah's Ark. You'll show Tilly to her room, won't you, my dear?"

He went downstairs and Tilly followed Lindsay to the small bedroom at the end of the passage. They entered and Lindsay closed the door.

"Jonathan's room is next door, you know, Tilly," she said. She had lowered her voice to a confidential whisper. "If—if he's frightened in the night, you'll go in to him, won't you?"

"Yes, of course, madam," said Tilly reassuringly.

"He's been better lately, but sometimes he still has those nightmares. I always wake, but—but I daren't always go in. If you go in, go very quietly. His father—doesn't understand. So, if you hear him——"

"I'll hear him, madam," said Tilly. "I'll know the minute he wakes."

The days passed with their surface amity and underlying tension. Edmund's fault-finding was sometimes pleasant, sometimes unpleasant, but it flowed from him incessantly. Jessica came in for little of it but Jonathan was constantly in trouble. The curious intensity of the gaze that Jonathan fixed on him in their encounters goaded Edmund into a severity of which he was sometimes secretly ashamed, but till the blue eyes faltered and fell before his as Lindsay's did the child was not thoroughly mastered, and Edmund considered it his duty thoroughly to master the child.

Tilly stood one morning at the dining-room window with Jonathan after breakfast watching Edmund go down the street. As he vanished round the corner, Jonathan drew a deep breath.

"Tilly," he said, "wouldn't it be lovely if he never came back, if we never saw him again!"

"Oh, hush!" said Tilly, drawing the small slight figure closer to her.

Chapter Twenty-Five

At the end of the first week of Tilly's stay Edmund had arranged to take the family to an Agricultural Show in Buckinghamshire. He always enjoyed playing the family man in public, and an important political personage, whose acquaintance Edmund hoped to cultivate, was to present the prizes. Jessica had been invited to a friend's birthday party on that day, but Edmund, seeing himself, Lindsay and Jonathan with Tilly, the quaint little family nurse, was quite satisfied by the picture.

Lindsay, who was accustomed to accompanying Edmund to functions of all kinds, took little interest in the affair till she happened to glance at the map, then excitement lit her like a flame.

"Oh, *look,* Edmund! The road goes just within a mile of Beechdene, the village just here"—she pointed it out with her finger—"on the edge of the beech-wood. It's where we used to live before we went to Priors Green, you know. Oh, Edmund, may we start early and go round by it? It won't take us far out of our way. I haven't been there since we left it, and I'd love to see it again."

Her eagerness vaguely irritated Edmund.

"Of course you may if you wish," he said, adding dryly, "I'd have taken you any time these ten years if you'd asked me."

"I know," she said. "It just didn't occur to me."

As she went about her usual duties, her thoughts dwelt on the visit more and more insistently and with a curious secret excitement. She saw the gracious Queen Anne house among the beeches as plainly as if she had left it only yesterday. And, as that memory became clearer, others leapt to life beside it . . . She had not thought of her childhood for years. The horror of her mental breakdown had stood like a barrier between her and the time before it happened. And now suddenly the barrier was down. She saw the dim glades of the wood, pillared by smooth grey trunks, beneath the green translucent tracery of branches. She was riding with Piers in the wood, walking with Piers through the shadowy lanes. Piers was the recurrent theme of ail her memories. It was Piers to whom she had turned in all her childish troubles, Piers who had protected and guarded her with never-failing devotion and understanding. The memory of his thin sensitive face, his tall, slightly stooping figure, his quick, uncertain smile became vividly clear. And, as the dream world grew more and more real, so the real world in which she moved grew more and more dream-like. Sometimes she looked at Edmund with a dull surprise, wondering how she had come to marry him. He was a stranger. He meant nothing to her . . .

On the afternoon before the expedition she set out to do some shopping and, coming home, sat down on a seat in the park. Formal beds of flowers made splashes of colour against the green grass. Lovers strolled along the path . . . children played beneath the trees . . . but Lindsay saw none of it. Pictures moved before her eyes—kaleidoscopic, merging one into another. Piers teaching her to skate . . . to ride . . . carrying her home the day she sprained her ankle. The first day of the school holidays had been a sort of ritual to them. Together they would visit the stables, the old apple tree that was their "castle", the beech-wood, the island in the lake. Roddy and the girls were there in the background—kindly friendly presences—but they had never been part of the alliance that united Piers and Lindsay. Then later had come holidays in Switzerland, where she and Piers had climbed together. Oddly, she had been a fearless climber, forgetting all her nervousness in the exhilaration of the heights and the clear crisp air.

She roused herself suddenly and looked at her watch. Half past five. She couldn't believe it was so late. She must have been sitting there for more than an hour. She got up and walked quickly home.

Edmund was in the drawing-room standing in front of the fireplace. He turned on her the look that always reminded her of Mr. Warwick's "authoritative stare" in *Diana of the Crossways*.

269

"May I ask where you have been?" he said frigidly.

"I went out shopping," said Lindsay. "Then I sat down in the park and forgot the time."

It was a statement of fact. There was no apology in her tone. Edmund didn't matter any more. His displeasure didn't concern her.

"You may remember," said Edmund, "that I rang up this morning to say that I should be bringing Sir Ralph Horseman home to tea, so I naturally expected to find you at home at tea-time." He paused for a moment, then continued, "As it happens, he was prevented from coming at the last minute, but that is no excuse for your behaviour."

"I'm sorry," said Lindsay.

He shot her a quick glance. Her tone was as casual as if she were apologizing to a stranger for some inadvert discourtesy. He felt at a loss and for that reason the more angry.

"I'll say no more about it this time," he said, "but please don't let it occur again."

Lindsay made no comment. She was gazing dreamily in front of her as if she had not heard. He went from the room, his mouth tightly pursed.

Lindsay slept little that night. She lay awake, wide-eyed, awaiting with tremulous excitement the day on which she would re-enter the world of her childhood and, as it seemed to her, find Piers again.

Her heart stopped beating when Edmund, with a careless glance at the window during breakfast, said: "Perhaps we'd better not go. It looks like rain," but she said nothing, aware that contradiction always roused his obstinacy. She even hid all signs of her relief, when, after breakfast, he went to the window and said: "I think we'll go. It'll be mostly under cover, and there'll be several people there it will be useful for me to meet."

It began to rain soon after they started, then the sun came out, turning the roads to streams of liquid gold. Lindsay, sitting next Edmund, was very silent. There was a look of exaltation on her pale face and her eyes, fixed on the distance, held a starry brilliance.

She saw nothing of the scenery they passed. She only saw Piers waiting for her . . . Jonathan sat behind with Tilly. He, too, was silent, sitting close to Tilly as if aware of something strange in the atmosphere. Only Edmund was unaware of it, discoursing in his resonant level tones on the Irish question and the iniquity of labour strikes.

"Beechdene's the next turning on the left, Edmund," said Lindsay suddenly. Her hand, holding the map, trembled.

"We're not going there," said Edmund.

"Not—?"

"There isn't time."

She stared at him.

"There *is* time, Edmund. We started early. There's heaps of time."

"There isn't time," said Edmund. There was a slow enjoyment in his voice and a triumphant little smile on his lips. "I've already told you that we aren't going there."

Then she understood. This was to be her punishment for yesterday's offence.

"Edmund, you can't," she pleaded wildly. "You can't . . . I must go . . . You promised." Her voice quivered, high-pitched with fear. "You can't be so cruel. You don't understand . . . I *must* go. . . ."

His brows shot together.

"Control yourself, Lindsay. You behave so insanely sometimes that one almost feels you should be put under restraint again."

She didn't even hear the words. She only knew that they had reached the little wooden signpost with "Beechdene" on it and that he didn't mean to turn into the lane. In a sudden access of panic she seized the steering-wheel. The car skidded across the greasy road and crashed into a telegraph post.

Lindsay died in hospital the next day without recovering consciousness. Edmund gave his account at the inquest with clarity and apparent sincerity. He had promised to take Lindsay a few miles out of their way to visit her old home. He had forgotten the promise till they actually reached the turning, then, reminded by Lindsay, he had taken the bend too quickly on the greasy road.

Standing there with his arm in a sling, he roused sympathy by his air of sorrowful dignity, and the thought of his two motherless young children enhanced the general impression of pathos. The coroner expressed condolence with him on his loss.

On the evening of the funeral he called the two children and Tilly to him in the library. There he took Jessica on his knee and made an attempt to encircle Jonathan with his arm, but Jonathan shrank away with a quick movement of recoil. Looking strangely unfamiliar to them in his black suit, his arm still in a sling, his face pallid and strained, he began what was obviously a prepared and rehearsed speech. God had taken Mummy to Himself, but they were not to grieve, because Mummy was happy. They would all miss her sorely but they would have each other. He would try to take her place and be mother as well as father to them. They must all be brave and cheerful and work hard at whatever work they had to do. Though Mummy was no longer with them, they must do that for her memory. He made frequent appeals during the speech, "You see, don't you?" . . . "You understand, don't you?" . . . and Jessica, dissolved into facile tears, sobbed, "Yes, Daddy" . . . "No, Daddy" . . . in docile response. Jonathan said nothing. He stood in front of Edmund, his eyes fixed on him with an intensity so great that the small pale face seemed to be consumed by it.

"Well, you'll remember what I've said, won't you?" said Edmund at last, withdrawing his arm from Jessica, relieved that the interview was over. "Now go back to the schoolroom with Tilly."

Jonathan spoke for the first time.

"It was your fault," he said in a toneless voice. "It wouldn't have happened if it hadn't been for you."

For a moment some emotion seemed to break up the composure of Edmund's face, then almost at once it regained its expression of heavy solemnity.

"Go back to the schoolroom with Tilly, both of you," he repeated as if he had not heard the words.

In the days that followed Jessica gave outlet to her feelings in frequent bursts of tears, especially among the servants or in her friends' homes. She enjoyed the process of being comforted and prolonged it as far as possible. Jonathan went about in the daytime with no sign of emotion except in the tight lines of his mouth. It was in the night that his repressed feelings found outlet and he would surrender himself to an abandonment of childish grief. He slept fitfully, his sleep broken by dreams more terrible than any he had had in his short life before. He saw Lindsay maimed and disfigured, Lindsay pursued and tortured by his father . . . He awoke from them in paroxysms of terror. Tilly was always at hand to comfort him, and he clung to her as the only consolation that life had now to offer. She would go into Jonathan's room as soon as she heard Edmund go to his and sleep as best she could on a chair by his bed so as to be there when he needed her. She never knew how Edmund discovered this, but the look he turned on her one day made her vaguely uneasy, and she was not surprised when, as she was silently opening Jonathan's door that night, Edmund's door shot open and he appeared on the landing in his dressing-gown.

"I thought I'd forbidden you to go into Jonathan's room at night, Tilly," he said.

He spoke pleasantly, but the lines from nose to mouth were tightly compressed.

"The boy gets upset, sir," said Tilly.

"Nonsense!" said Edmund. "He'll continue this form of exhibitionism as long as he gets encouragement. It's time that discipline was tightened up a little." He opened the door an inch or two, took the key from the lock, closed the door, locked it from outside and slipped the key into his pocket. "I shall do this every night in future. It's time the boy learnt self-control. I'm doing this for his own good." He continued in a pleasant, almost bantering tone: "It's a good thing that you're leaving us at the end of the week, and I think that the children are now old enough for your visits to be discontinued. Well, good night, Tilly."

He returned to his bedroom, closing the door.

Tilly went back to her room. Her heart was pounding in her chest and her whole short squat body trembled with anger. Standing with her ear pressed against the wall that separated her from Jonathan, she listened . . . Short sharp sobs, gasping and muffled. Jonathan had heard the turning of the key in the lock and was burying his head in his pillow, trying to hide his terror and despair. She went to the window and looked out. There was a small railed balcony outside her room and another outside Jonathan's. If she stood on the edge of the railing of her balcony, held the pipe that ran overhead, she could swing herself on to Jonathan's balcony. In cold blood she would never have attempted it, but, in her passion of love and indignation, she knew she could not fail. Hardly thinking what she was doing, with no realization of danger, she stood poised on the railing, stretched out her hands over the pipe and swung herself over, dropping heavily and clumsily on to the narrow balcony outside Jonathan's room. Then, in a flash, she was across the room, kneeling by his bed, gathering the terror-ridden childish form into her arms.

"There, my love, my little one!" she crooned. "Tilly's here . . . It's all right now. You're with Tilly now . . . There, there, my love! There, there, my little one!"

The thin arms strained round her so tightly that they seemed to drive the breath from her body, and gradually the strangling, choking sobs died down. She got into bed with him, and, still holding her tightly as if he dared not let her go, he fell asleep.

It was about half past seven in the morning that she heard the key turned softly in the lock.

Half an hour later Edmund came down into the hall. He had chosen the house chiefly on account of the hall. It had a spacious, imposing look and was in fact a miniature lounge hall such as few houses of this size possessed. Out of doors a dull persistent drizzle fell through a grey mist, but indoors a log fire burnt in the grate, and a bowl of roses on the window-sill made a pleasant contrast to the lowering skies. He took his letters from the oak chest and, standing by the fire, began to open them. They were all vaguely gratifying . . . letters of condolence on Lindsay's death . . . letters from less successful friends or acquaintances asking for help or advice . . . a letter of congratulation on one of his recent speeches

. . . letters asking him to address meetings, open local functions. He stood, holding the letters in his hand, looking into the fire, and a feeling of well-being swept over him. Lindsay's death had been a shock, but it was, he consoled himself, the natural lot of mortals. One must just put it behind one and take up the threads of life again. He still felt elated by his victory over Tilly last night. The boy must be mastered and, now that neither Lindsay nor Tilly would be here to interfere, he intended to master him. A sound made him turn round sharply. Tilly and Jonathan were coming downstairs. They wore their outdoor things and Tilly carried her rush hold-all.

"Good morning," said Edmund, a note of question in his voice.

Tilly ignored him, crossing the hall to the front door, holding Jonathan's hand.

"Where are you going?" he said, barring her path. Tilly turned her eyes to him in silence. They blazed with anger. As he looked at her the wooden expressionless face seemed to grow large and dark and menacing like the face of some monstrous avenging heathen god. A wave of fear swept over him. His assurance dropped from him suddenly.

"Get out of my way," said Tilly in a low, hoarse voice, keeping her eyes fixed on him.

His face was white and his mouth had gone slack. He shrank away from her, beaten and ashamed. The two walked past him. Tilly opened the front door and they went through it. He stood watching them as the mist swallowed them up, Tilly carrying her hold-all in one hand and clasping the child tightly with the other.

Neither looked back.

Chapter Twenty-Six

Tilly took Jonathan straight to Paddington and from there down to Lady Lynneker's house in Wiltshire.

Lady Lynneker stared incredulously from her window when she saw the two figures plodding up the drive, Tilly still clutching her hold-all in one hand and Jonathan in the other.

"Keep him, my lady," said Tilly succinctly. "Don't let his father have him back. And now I must go to catch my train I can't stop." That was all Lady Lynneker could get out of Tilly, for almost immediately she set off again through the rain, plodding down the path with her now sodden hold-all. Lady Lynneker's bewilderment was dispersed by the sight of Jonathan's white, pinched face, and she put him to bed at once, feeding him with bread and milk and staying with him till he fell into an exhausted sleep.

"Why did Tilly bring you here?" she asked as she tucked him up.

Jonathan considered.

"She was kind to me," was all the explanation he could give her—that and a sleepy, "I'm never going back, you know," as his silky lashes drooped over his pale cheeks. He looked unbearably pitiful in sleep, his dark hair falling over his fragile, blue-veined temples, the shadows lying like bruises beneath his eyes.

No word came from Edmund and, after sending a wire announcing Jonathan's safe arrival, Lady Lynneker sat down to compose a letter to him, deciding finally to appear to take for granted that Edmund had sent the child to her for a change of air, writing, "He's far from strong and it's very wise of you to send him out of London. I shall be glad to keep him for as long as possible."

She had seen enough of Edmund to have a shrewd idea of the circumstances. And Edmund's letter of thanks contained no mention of the boy's return. The matter was left indefinite and remained indefinite.

Edmund found himself glad to be rid of the boy. His presence was not only a constant exasperation but a reminder of something that Edmund was trying to forget. He had, he considered, taken on himself the blame for the accident that really belonged to Lindsay—and he felt a glow of complacency whenever he thought of it—but the child had probably misunderstood what had happened and might at any minute blurt something out that would have given a completely wrong impression. It was better for all concerned that he should stay out of London. And the household—himself and Jessica—was now a household completely to his liking. With the removal of Jonathan (he dared not let himself think, the removal of Lindsay, too) life seemed to become simple and pleasant and straightforward.

"London didn't suit him and he was fretting for his mother," he explained to friends, "so I sent him down to his grandmother in Wiltshire. She's lonely these days and likes to have him."

Mrs. Culverton had been surprised by Tilly's unheralded return.

"Why have you come back so soon, Tilly?" she said. "I didn't expect you till the end of the week."

"Ask no questions and you'll be told no lies," said Tilly. Immediately on her arrival she had summarily dismissed the girl from the village who had been looking after Mrs. Culverton and set to work on Mrs. Culverton's supper. "That slut's not touched the floor under the hall table since I went, by the look of it."

"I expect you were turned out for being impertinent just as you were from Althea's," said Mrs. Culverton with an air of satisfaction. "You see, no one but me would put up with you."

"Well, never mind that now," said Tilly. "Eat up your omelet. Been feeding you on kippers, I reckon, hasn't she?"

Mrs. Culverton raised a forkful to her lips.

277

"Good, isn't it?" said Tilly, watching her.

"Yes," agreed Mrs. Culverton and added with a certain reluctance, "I miss you, you know, when you aren't here, Tilly."

And then the years began to slip by again with treacherous speed. "It *can't* be five years since . . ." "It *can't* be as long ago as that when . . ."

Tilly's days fell into their ordered routine of housework, cooking, jam-making, spring cleaning. She bickered with Mrs. Culverton. She had toothache and sulked. She was so outrageous over the front doorstep that no one in the village dared approach it. She nursed Mrs. Culverton through bronchitis, pneumonia and a sharp attack of erysipelas, sitting up all night with her, waiting on her with clumsy tenderness, bearing with all her tantrums till she was well again, then starting to have tantrums of her own.

"She's quite impossible," said Mrs. Culverton and relied on her for everything every minute of the day.

They saw little of the rest of the family. Odds and ends of news filtered through to them. Roddy was behaving disgracefully, "going with another woman," and Althea was contemplating divorce. Jonathan was regaining health and stability with the gentle old lady in Wiltshire, who had first loved Lindsay in him and had then learnt to love him for his own sake. He went to a boarding school near Exeter and came home each week-end. Edmund had made no attempt to claim him and seemed almost to have forgotten his existence.

The highlight of Tilly's week was still her visits to Polly and Richard. The boys worked on Richard's plot and had bought a piece of land of their own, but they longed for something bigger and more satisfying. It was Dominic who first decided to emigrate to Canada and Martin quickly followed his example. Richard and Polly set about making preparations for their departure.

"It'll seem strange without the boys," said Richard, as Tilly sat with them one evening in the little garden under the apple tree.

Dominic, who was hoeing a bed of lettuces, swung round sharply.

"Come with us, Dad," he said. "It won't be any fun, anyway, without you and Mother."

Richard shut up the book he was reading with a snap and put it into his pocket as if in sign of a sudden decision.

"Why not?" he said. "What do you think, Polly?"

"Yes, I'd like it," said Polly in her slow sweet voice, not pausing in her work of drawing a strand of wool through a gaping hole in one of Richard's socks. "I'd like it fine."

Tilly's heart died in her as she faced the long empty years without Richard and his family.

"What do you think, Tilly?" said Richard.

"No reason why you shouldn't," said Tilly brusquely. Pass me them other socks, Polly."

Mrs. Culverton was outraged when she heard that Tilly was going to Liverpool to see them off.

"Most uncalled for!" she said and a little later: "Most officious! Who d'you think's going to look after me while you're away?"

"Nellie Durban can come in," said Tilly, "and you can have the cold meat for lunch with potatoes in their jackets and a milk pudding."

"Potatoes and milk pudding!" said Mrs. Culverton querulously. "Starch! Starch! Starch!"

"Well, starch never did anyone any harm," said Tilly, who had never heard that it did and wouldn't have believed it anyway, then relenting: "I'll make you a nice omelet when I get home in the evening."

When Richard and his family had gone, time suddenly began to drag. There seemed nothing to look forward to any longer. A few letters arrived announcing that they were happily settled. The boys both had work on a farm and Richard had taken a plot of land to work himself. They lived together and had, as far as possible, reconstituted their old life with the added zest of new friends and interests. A few postcards arrived for Tilly, but Tilly was no letter writer and did not answer them. Richard himself was little of a writer and the correspondence dwindled.

There were times when a heavy depression fell upon Tilly's spirits.

The village itself had changed. The Hall stood empty. So did Blenheim Villa, for Miss Maple had left Priors Green the same year that Richard went to Canada and made her permanent home in the Bournemouth boarding house, where the proprietor had come to rely on her so much that Miss Maple now ruled the establishment. Even The Red Lion had changed hands. Myrtle had married and Mr. Bailey had retired to spend his old age with his brother at Hurst Farm.

And now for the first time Tilly's sturdy health began to fail. She had rheumatism so badly that on some days she could hardly crawl about the cottage. She ignored the pain, refusing to see a doctor, refusing to answer Mrs. Culverton's enquiries about it, refusing even to have Nellie Durban in from the village to help her with the work. Mrs. Culverton herself seemed better than she had been for years and she regarded Tilly's incapacity with a feeling of kindly triumph.

Well, really, Tilly," she said one morning as Tilly crept painfully in with her glass of hot milk at eleven, "I seem to be the young woman these days and you the old one."

But that evening Mrs. Culverton collapsed as she was going upstairs to bed and died early the next morning.

Althea came down to the cottage. She was annoyed that everything should devolve upon her. Richard was in Canada. Vere in Haifa and Edmund on a political mission to Greece. The funeral was held in the little country church, and Tilly prepared tea at Linden Rise for the handful of neighbours who attended it. The rancour that Althea bore Tilly had not lessened with the years and she ignored her except to give her orders in a coldly dignified tone. She went back to London immediately after the last guest had departed.

"We're selling the house and furniture," she said to Tilly before she went, "so you'd better look out for another situation as soon as you can."

"Yes, madam," said Tilly woodenly.

But she did nothing about it. Her mind refused to look ahead. She couldn't make any arrangements beyond those immediately necessary. Alone in the cottage, she continued her dusting and scouring and sweeping. She did no cooking, but her rheumatism made her so slow that the housework occupied the whole day. She even intensified her efforts, dreading an unoccupied moment. She polished the furniture, the silver, the "surrounds", the windows over and over again. She embarked on an unseasonable spring cleaning, taking up the stairs carpet and scrubbing the Stairs, turning out all the rooms.

She didn't know why she did all this. She never even wondered. Blindly, doggedly, she was setting up against life the only defence she knew, seeing an added safeguard in each polished inch, each shining surface.

The boy who brought the telegram from Althea and planted a foot on her whitened doorstep was terrified by her anger. He fled aghast from the old woman who stood there muttering savagely, the telegram in her hand. She did not open the telegram till late that night.

House sold. Furniture being taken out next Wednesday.
Please be ready to go that day.

And still she continued stubbornly to scour and clean and polish, making no arrangements.

Althea arrived on the Wednesday morning to supervise the removal of the furniture, which she was sending to Bellminster Auction Rooms. When the last piece of furniture had been removed, she went to the dismantled kitchen, where Tilly stood at bay, still in her apron, holding a broom in one hand and a duster in the other. The rush hold-all stood in a corner of the room, where the meat safe used to be.

The two women looked at each other in silence for a few moments.

"You can get your things on and go now," said Althea at last. "Everything's been taken away."

Tilly continued to stare at her with boot-button eyes.

"You've got another situation, I suppose?" said Althea.

"No," said Tilly.

"Well, you've made some arrangement, I take it?" said Althea impatiently.

"No."

"Where are you going, then?"

"I don't know."

Althea's mouth tightened.

"Wait here," she said. "I'll be back soon."

She went to the Daimler that was waiting at the gate, gave some instructions to the chauffeur and drove off.

Tilly stood staring vacantly in front of her, then set to work sweeping out the hall and removing the traces of the removal men's presence—cigarette ends, bits of paper and string, fingermarks, muddy boot tracks. "Nasty, dirty creatures!" she muttered as she swept and dusted. Then, just as she was sweeping the kitchen floor, Althea returned.

"Get your things on," she said.

Tilly laid aside the broom, put on the shapeless coat and hat that hung behind the door and picked up the hold-all.

"I've found a situation for you in Bellminster," said Althea shortly, as she led the way down to the car. "Get in."

They drove in silence through the village and along the Bellminster Road.

"It's a boarding house," said Althea as they neared the outskirts of Bellminster, "and you're going there as a general servant. Your wages will be ten shillings a week. It's the best the agency could do for you. You're getting old and you're not very active."

Tilly stared out of the window of the car as if she had not heard.

Through the main street of Bellminster . . . then down one of the side turnings that led to the station . . . drab rows of houses . . . tenements . . . soiled lace curtains at the windows framing vases of dusty artificial flowers. The car stopped at a front door on whose cracked fanlight was painted the name "Mount Pleasant." A fly-blown card announcing "Board Residence" hung askew at one of the downstairs windows. The chauffeur got out and rang the bell. A stout blowsy woman in a dirty apron with her hair in curling pins opened the door and came to the car.

"This is Tilly Pound," said Althea, "and this is Mrs. Hexham, your new mistress, Tilly. I'm afraid I must hurry away now . . . I think that all the necessary arrangements were made through the agency. Good-bye, Mrs. Hexham . . . Good-bye, Tilly."

The car drove on down the street.

"Well, come on in," said Mrs. Hexham. She had a hoarse, throaty voice that somehow gave the impression of shrillness. "You'd better see the kitchen first."

Down a dark staircase, covered in broken linoleum, to a basement kitchen. Tilly looked round incredulously. Never had she seen such dust, such grime, such disorder.

"I've been without help for a week," said Mrs. Hexham. "There's plenty to do, so you'd best start right away and get down to it."

"Yes," said Tilly—her eyes went up and down the blowsy figure. Here was no "quality", but habit was strong—"madam," she ended.

Chapter Twenty-Seven

Tilly stayed on at Mount Pleasant because it never occurred to her to do anything else. With the disappearance of the Culvertons the mainspring of her existence seemed to have been broken. It wasn't that she had been deeply attached to the Culvertons. She had disliked Althea and she had disliked Edmund, but her very dislike of them had added a sort of zest to life, and with all their faults they had belonged to her. They had been her property. Without them life ceased to have any meaning. She was beaten. She gave up the struggle. She became a mere drudge, working doggedly from morning to night, driven by the loud scolding of Mrs. Hexham and constant cries of "Tilly!" from the lodgers. She never even took an afternoon off. She cleaned and scoured and set tables and washed dishes, raked ashes out of grates, made beds, emptied chamber-pots, cleaned boots and shoes and staggered up and downstairs beneath the burden of buckets of coal and trays of food. Up and down . . . up and down.

Mrs. Hexham found fault with her continually because she did not want Tilly to realize her usefulness but after the first week she dispensed with the charwoman, leaving Tilly to do everything but the cooking. Mrs. Hexham herself did the cooking. Tilly ignored the process, taking no interest in the soggy unappetizing messes that were served up as meals, eating her portion without taste or relish. She seemed to shrink and became smaller as she grew older. Her rheumatism settled down to good days and bad days, but she dragged herself about like something wound up that could not stop even on her bad days.

She could easily have gone out to Priors Green by bus, but it never occurred to her to do so. When she thought of Priors Green and the Culvertons it was like thinking of something belonging to another existence, something separated from her by an infinity of time. She read in the local paper of Polly's death in Canada, and for a moment it all became real again, bringing with it a pain that she had to dull by a ferocious cleaning of the flues and a resolute attack on the unsavoury recesses of the gas cooker, which was haunted by the ghosts of the soggy, greasy dishes that Mrs. Hexham produced from it.

Her toothache became so bad that she went to a dentist and had her teeth extracted, appearing, a few weeks later, in a gleaming denture much too large for her that clicked when she talked. Not that she talked much. She ignored the lodgers and Mrs. Hexham, seldom even replying when spoken to.

"She's a sulky, stubborn old bitch," said Mrs. Hexham, adding grudgingly, "but she gets through the work."

The lodgers were mostly very junior clerks, shop assistants and typists with, occasionally, a decayed gentleman or gentlewoman ekeing out a pension. To Tilly they had no separate individualities. They were so many voices shouting "Tilly!," so many beds to be made, so many boots and shoes to be cleaned. She never knew when one went and another came. She lost count of time altogether. The years flowed by and she seldom realized even what season of the year it was. Her life was bounded by the four walls of the dingy basement kitchen.

One afternoon in May, Mrs. Hexham sent her out to do some shopping. The air held the gentle warmth of spring, the sky a tender clarity of blue, but Tilly was concerned only with the details of her shopping list, trudging wearily with her weighted basket from shop to shop, muttering savagely at the crowds that barred her way.

She finished her shopping and boarded a bus to go home.

"Market Square," she said to the conductor.

"You've got on the wrong bus," he said. "This goes to Layland Cross."

Tilly made as if to take up her basket then sank back again into her seat. She was tired and hot and her feet hurt. She felt incapable of the effort of getting out of the bus.

"Layland Cross, then," she said indifferently.

The bus drove out into the country—past rosy clouds of apple blossom, between hawthorns starred with white rosettes of bloom. The opening leaves of the oak trees were like green fingers against the blue sky. Beneath the chestnut trees, fallen petals lay like pools of milk.

The bus stopped at Layland Cross. Tilly got out and stood irresolute, looking about her. A public-house, a church, a few cottages . . . She'd never been here before and, now that she was here, she didn't know what to do. But the indifference that had made her take her ticket to Layland Cross still held her spirit. She ought to go back to Bellminster by the next bus, but somehow she didn't want to. She couldn't just stand there, however . . . Already the driver and conductor were watching her suspiciously. Her body bent down by the weight of her basket, she trudged a few yards along the main road, then down a lane that ran by the side of a wood. Suddenly weariness overcame her and she sat down on the grass at the roadside, her basket by her side. For a time she felt nothing but relief at the silence and coolness, then she began to look around. On the banks of the lane grew clusters of primroses, and in the wood beyond a mist of bluebells stretched as far as she could see. She sat there, letting the sunlight seep into her, aware, not of happiness, but rather of a relaxing of something that had been taught in her since ever she left Linden Rise. She was like a spring, pulled to its utmost capacity, recoiling at last. The few people who passed along the lane threw her curious glances—a shabby old woman with broken boots, sitting on the grass, her basket beside her. Tilly did not even see them.

It wasn't till the shadows were gathering that she took up her basket and returned to the bus stop. She walked with a new briskness. Her basket didn't weigh her down any longer. She couldn't have told what her thoughts and emotions had been while she sat there on the grass by the roadside. She only knew that everything was changed. She knew that she couldn't stay at Mount Pleasant any longer. She didn't know what she would do or where she would go. She only knew that she couldn't stay at Mount Pleasant any longer.

She found Mrs. Hexham in the kitchen, clattering about noisily at the sink. She wheeled round as Tilly entered and faced her, arms akimbo. Her flat, flabby face was set in lines of anger.

"Where the hell have you been, you blasted old fool!" she said. "What did you think was going to happen to the dinner with the potatoes not peeled and the table not laid?"

Tilly put her basket on the table and began to take out the parcels without speaking.

"Have you gone clean out of your mind?" continued Mrs. Hexham. "If you think I'm going to keep a good-for-nothing slut who clears out and leaves me with the whole dinner on my hands, you can think again an' think pretty quick."

It occurred to Tilly that Mrs. Hexham was not raising her voice to its usual hoarsely strident note. It was tense and vibrant, but it was definitely lowered.

"And there's a gent come to see you," she went on. "Dunno who or why." She shot Tilly a suspicious glance. "Not been shoplifting, have you?" Tilly stared at her stupidly. "Oh, get on! Go and see him and come back here and give me a hand. He's in the smoking-room. You've wasted enough of my time today. I shan't forget this in a hurry, I can tell you."

Tilly went upstairs and opened a door at the end of the passage. A man who was standing at the window of the frowsty, smoke-fouled room turned as she entered. Her heart missed a beat as she recognized the Puck's face and quizzical half-smile. "Mr. Richard!" she gasped.

The room began to whirl round her and she sat down abruptly on the nearest chair.

"Take it easy, Tilly." He sat down by her, fixing kindly grey eyes on her and patting her hand. "There! There! . . . Better?"

"Yes." The room had stopped whirling round her.

"How on earth did you come to this grisly hole, Tilly?"

"Never mind me, Mr. Richard. Tell me about yourself. I didn't know you were in England."

"I've only just arrived. You heard about Polly?"

"Yes."

"Well, the boys both got married, so I thought I'd come home. I went to Priors Green to look at Linden Rise, then I dug you out. I had the devil of a job finding you . . . Now listen, Tilly . . ."

"Yes?"

"Linden Rise is up for sale. Let's take it and run it as a café, you and I. I think we could get no end of fun out of it, don't you?" She looked at him. Her black eyes shone, and her lips gave a sudden twitch.

"Yes," she said. "Yes, I do."

Chapter Twenty-Eight

The car drew up at the blacksmith's forge. In the east the daylight had faded, but westward the light still lingered and the trees stood out blackly against a primrose glow.

"It was down this lane," said the woman. "A little way beyond the bridge. It was called Linden Rise. I'd like just to look at it again."

The tall bearded man smiled at her.

"Shall I come with you?" he said.

"No . . . I think I'd rather go alone."

She got out of the car and went down the lane between neat hedges, freshly trimmed. Over the bridge and—yes, there it was, behind its row of pollarded lime trees. A board, somewhat erratically painted, announced "Linden Rise Café." She went up the path to the open front door. As she approached it a man appeared from inside the house. He was a kindly looking, grey haired man, dressed in shabby, well-cut tweeds. A battered book protruded from his pocket.

"Do come in," he said courteously, with the air of one welcoming an expected guest. "I'm afraid we've finished serving dinners, but we could manage something cold. Or an omelet, if you'd prefer it. Perhaps just a cup of coffee." He smiled. "We're rather famous for our coffee."

"Richard!" she said.

He looked at her, and the slender, handsome woman with the olive cheeks and dark brown eyes turned into a sallow child with black brows drawn together in a sulky scowl.

"Vere!" he said. "Come in, my dear. Do come in."

He led her into a small room full of tables. It had been the sitting-room in the old days and here and there were pieces of furniture that Vere recognized. The furniture—writing-desk, settee, chest-of-drawers, sideboard, a bookcase filled chiefly with classical texts, a rosewood piano—was ranged against the wall, hemming in the ranks of small tables and giving the room a curious makeshift appearance. The furniture was dusty and none too well kept.

"Sit down," he said. "Come and sit down on the settee."

He moved a pile of illustrated papers and they sat down on a ramshackle settee against the wall.

"I thought you were in Canada, Richard," she said a little unsteadily.

"I was," he said, "but Polly died and the boys started marrying, so I came home and routed up Tilly and we set ourselves up here. Tilly!" he called. "Vere's here."

Tilly came from the kitchen. She had regained her look of sturdiness and vigour. Except for her wrinkled face and greying hair, she might have been the Tilly of Vere's childhood.

"Oh, Tilly, I am glad to see you," said Vere.

"Come and sit down, Tilly," said Richard, making room for her on the settee.

"We've just come home on a short leave," said Vere. "We've already spent part of it in Paris and we're driving from Dover to London now . . . Richard, I can't get over it. This, I mean." Her eyes wandered round the room. "It's like a dream. The writing-table, the bookcase, the piano . . ."

"Oh, yes," said Richard. "You see, Althea sold all the stuff locally and I've hunted down as much as I could in junk shops in Bellminster through the years. Most of it the worse for wear, I'm afraid. Do you remember those vases on the chimney-piece? I expect they're hideous, but Tilly and I like them . . . The stone owl's still in the garden."

Vere laughed.

"Do you put daisy chains on it?"

"We did to celebrate the day the café opened, didn't we, Tilly?"

"Yes, rhubarb leaf an' all," said Tilly.

"And—the café's a success?"

"Yes, it seems to be," said Richard.

The café was a success. The fame of Tilly's cooking had spread through the neighbourhood and the gentle, unaffected courtesy with which Richard welcomed each customer as a guest (for to Richard each customer *was* a guest) gave the place a *cachet* that other places lacked. Even the higgledy-piggledy little room crowded with battered Victorian furniture added to the charm. It was "different". Richard was "different". The cooking was undoubtedly and deliciously "different". People from Bellminster and the neighbouring villages came to lunch and dinner. It was very seldom that all the tables were not booked. And the knowledge of the place was carefully guarded by the clientele. The undiscriminating passed it by—a ramshackle cottage with a badly painted sign.

"People come," added Richard vaguely.

"So you're making money at last, Richard?" said Vere with a smile.

"I wouldn't say that," said Richard. "You see, we spend rather a lot on the food. It's the cooking we enjoy, and it wouldn't be any fun if we cheese-pared."

"You have help, of course?"

"Oh, no. We wouldn't know what to do with 'help'. It would spoil it. It would make it a business. As long as it's just Tilly and me, it's an adventure. We just muddle along. Tilly's head cook and I'm assistant cook and housemaid. I do this room— dust it and keep it tidy, I mean."

"He don't do it too well," said Tilly indulgently, "but the cooking keeps me busy and I've got past mindin' a bit of dust. Don't see as well as I did, neither, an' what the eye don't see, the heart don't grieve at."

"I'm the waiter, too," said Richard proudly.

"He's a bit slow," said Tilly.

"Yes, but they don't seem to mind that," said Richard, "and they all seem to enjoy a little chat."

"And you still carry Sophocles about with you in your pocket?" said Vere, glancing at the book that protruded from his pocket.

"Pindar," he said, taking it out. "He's a little more difficult, but he's magnificent."

"Oh, Richard, it's nice to find you just the same. Tell me about the rest of the family. I've lost touch."

"We've all lost touch," said Richard.

"I heard of Piers' death. He was killed climbing, wasn't he?"

"Yes."

"And Althea's Lady Lynneker now, I suppose. She divorced Roddy, didn't she?"

"Yes," said Richard.

"Has she married again?"

"No," said Richard. "There's nothing of her left to marry. She died years ago, you know. She's just a corpse now. Quite a presentable corpse, as corpses go, but only a corpse. Where's that picture of her, Tilly?"

Tilly routed among the pile of tattered picture papers and drew out a copy of *The Tatler*. Richard took it and turned over the pages.

"Here it is. Lady Lynneker opening the Charity Fête at the Ritz. On the front page."

Vere examined the hard, smooth, beautiful face.

"I shouldn't have recognized her," she said.

"I suppose she was never quite real," said Richard. "She lived in a fairy tale and she was always the heroine of it. Edmund did that too. He lived in a fairy tale and was the hero of it."

"They've made a success of life," said Vere.

"Oh, yes," agreed Richard. "People in fairy tales do."

"Tell me about Edmund," said Vere. "I've been away so long. . . . I heard of Lindsay's death. Has he married again?"

"No. I believe his daughter rides him with a tight rein. He's something in the Government now—I can never remember what."

Vere smiled.

"I think I remember his voice best . . . clear and a little harsh."

"You can hear it if you like," said Richard. "Wasn't it this evening, Tilly? Where's the newspaper?"

Tilly unearthed a newspaper from the clutter of papers and glanced at the clock.

"It should be now," she said.

Richard went to the wireless that stood on the piano and turned the knob.

"The Right Honourable Edmund Culverton . . ." said the announcer's voice.

Then suddenly Edmund's voice filled the room—assured, incisive, clear, with the faint note of harshness that had always marred it:

"'The annual labour of every nation is the fund which supplies it with the necessities of life and which consists either in the produce of that labour or in what is purchased with that produce from other nations.' Adam Smith said that in 1776 and it is still true today . . ."

"Oh, turn it off," said Vere with a catch in her breath. "I can't bear it."

Richard turned the knob, and the voice faded.

"Is it funny or is it tragic, Richard?" said Vere. "I wish I knew."

"Both, I suppose," said Richard. "There isn't much difference really."

"Perhaps we've all got what we wanted."

"More than we deserve, probably," said Richard with his quiet smile.

"I wish I knew," said Vere again, gazing into space. "Perhaps we hadn't any chance. Perhaps we'd have ended up like this whatever we'd done." She turned her head to listen to the Greek words that Richard was saying. "Did Pindar say that and what does it mean?"

"No, Aristotle," said Richard, "and it means that, though we cannot alter ourselves now, there was a point at which we could have made ourselves other than we are."

"I wonder," said Vere.

Silence fell and with it a slight constraint. They had greeted each other, discussed the family and—nothing remained. The years they had spent apart had formed a barrier across which neither could pass.

"You're happy, Vere?" said Richard at last.

"Very very happy," said Vere. "My husband's in the car at the end of the lane. You wouldn't like me to fetch him in, would you, Richard?"

Richard hesitated.

"There doesn't seem much point in it, does there?" he said gently.

"No," she agreed. "Some families go through life together in a jolly crowd, but we've never been like that." She rose and drew on her gloves. "I've loved seeing you, Richard. I don't suppose we shall meet again. We're only over for a week or two and my husband's got a frantic lecturing programme fixed up."

Conventional insincerities rose to Richard's lips and died away. She was holding out her hand. He remembered that even as children they had never kissed each other. He took her hand in a firm clasp.

"Good-bye, Vere," he said. "Come along again if you've time."

"Thanks. I will," she said, but they both knew that she wouldn't.

She went down the lane and they stood at the. door, watching her till the clump of trees at the corner hid her from sight.

"Well, fancy that!" said Tilly.

"Yes, it didn't seem real, did it?" said Richard, following her into the kitchen.

For a moment the cottage had been full of ghosts, but the sight of the bowl in which Tilly had been mixing white of egg and lemon juice when Vere arrived dispersed them.

"What's the butcher sending for tomorrow?" he said.

"Veal," said Tilly. "Thought we'd make a *fricassée*. And I'm doin' lemon sponge for a sweet. If I get it done now it can stand overnight."

"Good! . . . I say, Tilly."

"Yes?"

"Do you remember that night when Mrs. Horseferry passed out? We made a *fricassée* then, didn't we?"

"So we did, Mr. Richard! I'd forgot."

"Well, don't put a laurel leaf in it this time, Mrs. Noah."

Tilly gave her hoarse cackle and set to work whisking the lemon sponge.

THE END